HELEN PHILLIPS

HERE Where the SUNBEAMS Are GREEN

DELACORTE PRESS

Text copyright © 2012 by Helen Phillips
Jacket art copyright © 2012 by Jen Bricking (front and back covers)
and szefei/Shutterstock (flaps)

All rights reserved. Published in the United States by Delacorte Press,
an imprint of Random House Children's Books, a division of
Random House, Inc., New York.

Delacorte Press is a registered trademark and the colophon is a trademark
of Random House, Inc.

Visit us on the Web! randomhouse.com/kids
Educators and librarians, for a variety of teaching tools,
visit us at RHTeachersLibrarians.com

Library of Congress Cataloging-in-Publication Data
Phillips, Helen.
  Here where the sunbeams are green / Helen Phillips. — 1st ed.
    p. cm.
  Summary: Sisters, Madeline and Ruby, travel to a Central American jungle to help find their missing father, a renowned bird watcher, only to discover a nefarious plot that puts their lives in danger.
  ISBN 978-0-385-74236-8 (hc) — ISBN 978-0-375-99056-4 (glb) — ISBN 978-0-307-97487-7 (ebook) [1. Missing persons—Fiction. 2. Jungles—Fiction. 3. Birds—Fiction. 4. Endangered species—Fiction. 5. Sisters—Fiction.] I. Title.
  PZ7.P5365He 2012
  [Fic]—dc23   2011051059

The text of this book is set in 11-point Baskerville MT.
Book design by Sarah Hoy

Printed in the United States of America
10 9 8 7 6 5 4 3 2 1
First Edition

For my sister, Alice,
brava and bold

CHAPTER 1

So here we are in this shaky little airplane high above the jungle, which is kind of (very) scary. On our first flight Roo got the window seat the whole five hours, so she insisted that I get it for the second flight, which is pretty thoughtful for someone who's only nine-almost-ten. But I really should've let her have the window seat this time too. Even though I'm three years older than my sister, she's the brave one who loves flying and other dangerous things. Plus I've been a bit more freaked out in general lately, ever since The Weirdness began. The amazing view is basically wasted on me—the only way I can get through the wobbly ride is by pressing my forehead hard against the window, trying to pretend the jungle below is a huge green trampoline and even if we fell out of the sky we'd be totally fine.

And then—right as I'm telling myself, *Listen, Madeline Flynn Wade, you need to calm down and get a grip*—I see it.

"There it *is*," I murmur.

"What? What!" Roo yelps. "Where's what?"

1

"There's the Lava Bird Volcano." I lean back in my seat so she can peek out the window. Dad taught us that not all volcanoes have the classic volcano shape, but this one sure does. It's big and blue and very, very perfect.

"Volcán Pájaro de Lava," Ken/Neth corrects me from across the aisle, where he's sitting next to Mom.

"Volcán Pájaro de Lava," Roo echoes with a perfect little accent, and I'm going, *How come she has that super-great accent when I've been studying Spanish for three years and she's only been studying it for one?*

Just as we pass the volcano, two rainbows jump up out of the jungle and crisscross each other. They truly crisscross each other! Roo unbuckles her seat belt so she can squeeze closer to me and see the rainbows better, and we go "Ooo, *rainbows!*" and start to feel really, really excited about what we're going to do this afternoon. Well, actually, Roo's been really, really excited all along. She always is. I'm the one who gets nervous about things.

Anyway, Roo and I are gasping and squealing and feeling hopeful until we look across the aisle to make sure Mom is watching the rainbows and instead see Ken/Neth whispering into her ear. It gives me an automatic stomachache. Dad never would have become friends with Ken/Neth if he'd known *this* was going to happen someday. Ken/Neth on an airplane with *Dad's* family, whispering things into Dad's *wife's* ear!

But I liked Ken/Neth too. Back in December when Dad brought him home for dinner and introduced him as Kenneth Candy (seriously, his last name is Candy), a longtime ecological developer and a newtime friend.

"Newtime?" Roo said, giggling, as Mom sighed and added another place mat to the table. "Is that really a word?"

"Ken's involved in that fascinating development in Central

America," Dad explained to Mom, pinching her waist in the way that makes her smile. "The one I've told you about, remember, that opened a couple years ago? It's won the World's Greenest Spa award for two years running. They're doing revolutionary work in the field of environmental development. It's the way of the future, Via. And the location is unbelievable—virtually untouched jungle on the flanks of a volcano. An ornithologist's dream!" Dad paused, and all the enthusiasm drained out of his voice. "Of course, it would've been more of an ornithologist's dream a few years back, before the Lava-Throated Volcano trogon was confirmed extinct."

Dad *hates* extinction. And he *loves* Central American birds.

"The most elusive bird in the world," Dad said dreamily as we sat down to eat, "long before it went extinct. Spectacular plumage but so shy—hardly ever let anyone get a good look at it. The females were especially reclusive. Even if you managed to spot a male, he'd never give you a hint about the location of his mate or their nest. They were monogamous, mated for life."

"Elusive, reclusive, elusive, reclusive," Roo rhymed merrily under her breath, twirling spaghetti on her fork.

Mom looked at Dad, shaking her head. "I still can't believe they'd build a spa right in the habitat of a rare trogon like that."

"Former habitat," Ken Candy corrected her, chomping down on a big mouthful of spinach salad. "Extinct"—chew—"is"—chew— "extinct," he said sadly (or at least as sadly as you can while chewing), almost as if someone from his own family had died. But really it was more like someone from Dad's family had died, because Dad's the one who's the world-class ornithologist, otherwise known as the Bird Guy.

"What's that place called again?" Mom asked. "The Magma?"

"La Lava," Ken Candy said with a spinach-toothed grin. "La Lava Resort and Spa."

"I love lava," Roo said. "It's like the planet's own hot caramel sauce."

"So," Mom said to Ken Candy, "what exactly do you do for La Lava?"

"Oh, mainly just some consultation about ecological development and that sorta thing." Ken Candy was smiling very brightly at Mom. "I'm based here in Denver but I travel there a few times a year."

"We need more people like you doing the kind of work you're doing," Dad said.

"Well. Who knows. But I sure do love what I do," Ken Candy said, pretending he wasn't proud of himself. "And not to talk business at the dinner table," he continued, "but . . . La Lava is seeking an expert ornithologist to help us track and catalog the native bird species, both for the benefit of our more curious guests and to further our green mission. What happened to the Lava-Throat should never happen again."

Ken Candy looked at Dad. Dad looked at Mom. Mom looked at Ken Candy.

"Interesting," Mom said. "Very interesting."

"It's quite a dazzling array of avian life out there, lemme tell ya," Ken Candy added.

"I'm sure it is," she said.

After dinner Ken Candy pulled some candy from his pockets and offered it to me and Roo. He just so happened to have a mini Snickers (my favorite) and a mini Butterfinger (Roo's favorite). "Since Candy is my last name," he explained with a wink. He was nice and also cute, even with spinach in his teeth, and I felt shy. Now I just wish Dad had never met him.

Because look where we are today, Ken/Neth pointing out the airplane window at the rainbows and leaning in too close to Mom to whisper, "Well, that's an omen if I've ever seen one, right, Sylvia?"

"Uh-huh," Mom says absentmindedly, because she's thinking about Dad. I can tell.

When Ken/Neth came over to our house back in February, after Mom called him to complain because Dad's trip had just gotten extended for the first time, he asked us to call him Ken rather than Mr. Candy.

"Like Ken and Barbie?" Roo said, staring down at him between the banisters of our wooden staircase. I was standing behind her, staring down at him too.

"Can I call you Neth instead?" I said. I knew I was being mean, but I was mad and sad about Dad, and he seemed like the best person to blame.

But instead of being offended, Ken/Neth was charmed. He thought I was being friendly.

"That would be great," he said, looking up at me and Roo. "That would be totally great if you called me Neth. No one's ever done that before." It made him feel special, like I was giving him a nickname. So I never call him Neth. Or Ken. Or anything. Except in my head, where he's Ken/Neth.

Roo can't sit still in her airplane seat. She reaches over across the little aisle and starts poking at Mom's arm, asking in a voice that's way too loud: "What's an omen? Hey, what's an omen?"

"¡Señorita! ¡Señorita!" a woman's voice crackles over the loudspeaker and says a bunch of words in Spanish. Then, again, "¡Señorita!"

"Hey, Roo-by, they're talking to you!" Ken/Neth says, pulling himself away from Mom's ear.

The third time Ken/Neth came over was back in March, when Dad had extended his trip for the second time. That day he called my sister Roo, and I had to teach him that only three people are allowed to call Ruby that—I nicknamed Roo when she was three and I was six, so I get to decide these kinds of things. Ever since then he's been careful. Every time he calls her Ruby I feel proud of myself. I like how he begins "Roo—" and then squirmingly adds the "by." I also make sure he never calls me Mad, because I only let people call me Mad once I've given them permission.

"Huh?" Roo says.

"They're talking to you, *señorita*," Ken/Neth tells her. He's the only one of us who really speaks any Spanish, and it was already bugging me in the airport hearing Mom going, Oh, Ken, what did he say? Oh, Ken, can you translate the menu for us?

The voice on the loudspeaker sounds more and more annoyed, and at the front of the short aisle the flight attendant is glaring at Roo. "They're telling you to buckle up!" Ken/Neth translates.

"Oh good lord, Roo, you're not buckled?" Mom shrieks. "Buckle up! Buckle up! Buckle up! Mad, help her! Quick, quick! Hurry!"

Mom's way more scared of small planes than I am. But Roo's not scared at all. Roo isn't scared of anything. She's not even scared of The Very Strange and Incredibly Creepy Letter, which she's pulling out of her little backpack now that I got her buckled. It's the last thing in the world I want to see because it's the thing I'm most scared of, the thing I've been most scared of ever since we got it in April. The Very Strange and Incredibly Creepy Letter is what I call the last letter Dad sent from La Lava before he stopped contacting us at all. That's when The Weirdness began. After that we didn't get any more letters or phone calls or emails from him. For a while Mom kept sending emails, kept leaving voice mails at

La Lava Resort and Spa. For a while I kept writing letters. Roo, of course, never stopped sending coded notes to Dad. But all we got in return were phone calls from some official person at La Lava, informing us that Dad was deep in the jungle and out of contact, and that he was doing very important work about which he felt very passionate, and that he sent us all the love in his heart and would be in touch soon, and was very sorry to keep extending his trip this way.

"All the love in his heart?" Mom repeated suspiciously.

"Indeed," said the extremely calm and beautiful voice on the other end of the line, which I know because Roo and I snuck upstairs to listen in from the phone in Mom and Dad's bedroom. We were dying to figure out more about The Weirdness. Roo said I had to start thinking like a detective. I said what about her, didn't she have to start thinking like a detective too? And Roo said she already did, obvi.

The voice on the phone was a woman's voice, and it had some kind of slight accent but I couldn't tell what kind. Actually, even though it was a calm and beautiful voice, it was also kind of a chilly voice. And what the voice from La Lava said *was* suspicious, because Dad would never say something like "All the love in my heart." He'd say, "I love you with all the bananas in my brain" or "I love you like a chair loves a table." But he would *never* say "All the love in my heart."

"I'm paraphrasing, of course," the voice said in its flat, elegant way, and then added, "Dr. Wade sends his regrets that his greetings to you can't be more personal."

We were used to it, sort of, because sometimes Dad went to look for rare birds out in The Middle of Nowhere so he could track them and count them and study their behavior and stuff. Then we'd have to wait a little while for him to get somewhere where he could call or email or even just mail letters. We missed him but it was okay because, as Mom always said, Being the Bird Guy is Part of What We Love Him For, Right, Girls?

But. It had never been like this before. It had never been seven months away from home and three months without contact. It had never been The Weirdness. It had always been a month at most. A month was no problem. A month we could do. When Dad headed off to La Lava and said it would just be a month, we didn't think it was such a big deal.

I feel stupid now, that we just said goodbye and let him go and didn't even worry.

And as Roo smoothes out The Very Strange and Incredibly Creepy Letter on the folding airplane tray table, I refuse to look at it. I don't want to see the way Dad decorated the page with badly drawn flowers and vines as though he's a little girl (Roo and I can both draw *way* better than that). I don't want to read the bizarro poem that makes absolutely no sense. I don't want to think about it at all, so that's what I'm doing. Not thinking about it.

Roo strokes the letter and bites her tongue in the corner of her mouth that way she does, then opens up her code notebook and writes a few things down. She's been trying to break the code ever since we got the letter.

The code, I've sometimes wanted to scream at her, is that there *is* no code! The code is that Dad has gone completely, 110 percent, totally, absolutely, *thoroughly* (Dad's word) CRAZY. Okay?

I used to be a tiny bit jealous of Roo and Dad's code thing. Pretty much as soon as she could read, Roo started to make codes. Dad got her the *Super Little Giant Book of Secret Codes*, and *Codes, Ciphers, and Secret Writing*, and the *Top-Secret Handbook of Codes*. I'm not really into that kind of thing. I'd rather just read, you know, books with stories. Like the ones Mom always brings home from her job at the library. But Dad and Roo had their code thing, just the way they had their bird-tracking thing, and whenever Dad was out of town he'd send us coded letters for Roo to crack. First it would be not too hard, like flipping the alphabet, so that you'd write Z when you meant A, and Y when you meant B, but then it got more and more complicated and I lost track of it, and I had a small feeling of, Hey, what about me?

Back in January, when Dad first went to La Lava, before The Weirdness, Roo didn't have too much trouble breaking Dad's codes. Those first few letters were exciting. He wrote that he was going to bring us lots of presents from the rain forest—rare extrasweet nuts and raw chocolate bars and pretty little animals carved from jungle wood. He wrote: *Madpie & KangaRoo & Mama Bear, I have some REALLY GOOD NEWS! But it's a big secret, so BE PATIENT!* Madpie—sort of like the bird—and Kanga-Roo. That's what Dad liked to call us. Another good thing to not think about. Anyway, nowadays I'm not at all jealous of Roo. I'm just glad I'm not the one who's obsessed with the freaky letter from Dad.

I pull out my poetry notebook, which I've been using a ton ever since I made the New Year's resolution to write a poem a day, but quickly I realize there's no hope of me writing a poem while I'm sitting this close to The Very Strange and Incredibly Creepy Letter. It's too much of a distraction in the corner of my eye. I put my notebook away and shut my eyes for a few minutes.

"Hey, Roo," Ken/Neth says from across the aisle. I open my eyes to glare at him. "—by. It's time to put your tray up. We're about to land! Hey, girls, listen to the flight attendant's announcements and see if you can hear any words you know from Spanish class. *Gracias,* you know that one, right?"

It bugs me a lot that anyone who overheard this would probably think Ken/Neth is our dad. Also, is there a single person in America who doesn't know the word *gracias?*

But Roo doesn't seem annoyed. She just carefully refolds The Very Strange and Incredibly Creepy Letter, slides it back into its envelope, kisses the flap, slips it into her backpack, and locks her tray.

The plane starts to descend, leaving my stomach behind with each jolt.

"Woo-*hoo*!" Roo goes every time the plane jerks downward.

Even though Mom has to grab Ken/Neth's arm (ugh) because she's so terrified, the little plane lands without anyone dying.

"Hey," Roo whispers to me as the plane brakes, her breath smelling like orange Tic Tacs, "do you think Dad is coming up with something special for when he sees us?"

Suddenly there's a huge hard lump in my throat. I can hardly wait to see him. I can't believe it's been seven whole months.

"Something special?" I say. "What kind of thing?"

"Well"—Roo pauses, thinking—"like, a song he made up just for us. Or a cake with our names on it."

Sometimes I feel so much older than Roo.

"I have no idea," I snap at her. "He's probably doing actual *work* right now."

I don't want Roo to know that my heart's swelling with excitement. It scares me to be this excited about seeing Dad. It makes me feel superstitious, like things might go extra wrong the more excited I am. I know if Dad were here, he'd tell me to take a deep breath. Slow and steady wins the race, Madpie. Slow and steady.

But slow and steady is really hard to do, because we're finally here, we're finally going to find out what's up with Dad. Roo and I have been begging Mom to take us to Dad in the jungle since March.

"I don't care if he's in the middle of the middle of the middle of the jungle!" Roo said back then, digging her fork into her mashed potatoes but not eating any. "I don't even care if he's in the middle of the middle of the middle of the *volcano*. I. Just. Want. To. See. Dad."

"I can't pull you out of school right now," Mom informed her. "You're learning about the solar system."

"Solar system schmolar system," Roo said.

"It's a work trip," Mom said quietly. "It's not like Dad's on vacation. He's very busy. He wouldn't be able to hang out with you. Besides, it's dangerous for kids."

I looked across the table at Roo to see if she realized that Mom wanted to visit Dad just as much as we did. But she was too young to notice.

"*What's* dangerous for kids?" Roo demanded.

"Roo," Mom said, looking suddenly exhausted, "please."

A few times, when Roo was out of earshot or over at a friend's house, Mom said to me, "Mad, what do you think? You think we should go and . . . ?" She always trailed off, not quite wanting to say *figure out what the heck is going on with Dad.*

"Yes, yes, yes," I told her, and once we even sat down and got online to look for plane tickets, but right then Ken/Neth called to ask if he could drop by with some ratatouille he'd just made. He'd accidentally doubled the recipe.

Things kept on happening. The lady with the beautiful voice would call again from La Lava to assure Mom that Dad was doing groundbreaking work in the inner jungle and his one regret was that he couldn't be in touch with us personally, but he knew we—more than any other people in the entire world—understood how much this work meant to him. Mom would hang up and say, "We've been overreacting, girls. Everything is fine."

Or Ken/Neth would stop by with a chocolate cake and three tickets for Cirque du Soleil. "It's the least we can do," he said, "given all that Dr. Wade is doing for us. You're very generous, ladies, to lend us your dad and"—with a wink at Mom—"husband for all this time." I don't know why I didn't say, Hel-*lo*, we didn't lend him to you; it's not like we had any choice, and besides, we had no idea it would take "all this time."

And then there was the night Mom opened the monthly bank statement and gave this enormous gasp, and I was like, "What's *wrong*?" After not being able to talk for a few seconds she said, "Well, Mad, La Lava is being exceedingly generous, that's all."

So weeks went by, and then months, and we never bought plane tickets. When Roo bugged her about it, Mom would say that as far as she knew, Dad might come home tomorrow, and business trips get extended all the time, and we just had to be patient and calm, and this is Part of What We Love Him For, Right, Girls?, and it really didn't make sense for us to leave school and for her to take time off from the library right in the middle of the semester, and Dad would be furious if we did.

It wasn't till May that Mom decided we really did have to go to the jungle. Ken/Neth had gotten in the habit of coming for dinner once a week or so, which was pretty much starting to get on my nerves. So he was there at the dinner table when Mom announced that the time had come—she was going to book the plane tickets.

But Ken/Neth insisted that she let *him* book the tickets.

"Are you sure?" she said, though I could tell it would be a relief for her if he'd take care of it. "I don't want to burden you."

"Sylvia," he said in that really sincere way of his, "it's not a burden, it's an honor."

I noticed Mom slightly rolling her eyes, but Ken/Neth didn't see.

"Not only that," he continued, "but it just so happens that today my contacts at La Lava informed me that they wish to invite you ladies to the Gold Circle Investors' Gala in early July."

"The what?" Mom said.

"It's La Lava's huge annual celebration for all of their investors, where they honor the 'Geniuses' who have contributed to the success of the organization in the past year. It's basically the party to end all parties. I know you girls will get a kick out of it."

"Oh!" Roo yelped with glittering eyes. "I love parties! When's July?"

"Roo," Mom said severely. "You know when July is."

"May, June, July," Roo recited. "Wait, that's not soon!"

"The time will fly," Ken/Neth said with a grin. "It's just a little over a month."

"July is good," Mom said. "We can all finish out the school year. And James very well may be back before then anyway."

"Maybe so," Ken/Neth agreed. "Maybe so."

And from then on it was all: Ken booked the tickets, Ken says we should head down the Sunday before the gala, Ken is going to notify La Lava that we're coming, Ken said we should be sure to bring some special dresses for the party, Ken this, Ken that.

And every day Mom's been telling us, "Look, girls, we'll see Dad soon and everything will be normal."

But I know the truth. The truth is that Mom is mad, and hurt, and confused, and lonely. She thought I'd left the kitchen when she

13

said to Aunt Sarah, "When I married James I never thought I'd be a single mother. And look at me now. Months now my kids haven't had a dad."

"Okay, okay, okay," Roo is saying as the plane glides to a stop on the runway. She shrugs and kicks gently at the seats in front of us, still offended that I snapped at her about Dad. "Jeez, I was just wondering if Dad's as excited to see us as we are to see him."

And the truth is: I've been wondering the exact same thing.

CHAPTER 2

The airport is by far the tiniest I've ever seen. We just walk right off the plane onto the ground—we don't go through one of those detachable hallway thingies. The second I step out onto the little staircase, I get slammed by hot, heavy air. I look over at Roo and see that her face is already shimmering with moisture.

"Man," Roo says, "what is *up* with this *air*?"

"Welcome to humidity, Roo," Mom says with a giddy laugh. Happy that we survived the tiny-plane ride. Happy that she's about to see Dad.

I feel like the air here is green. I mean, it's not *actually* green, but it has this thick, green smell as though the jungle leaves are breathing it out. Which I guess *is* what's happening, though it's been a while since Dad reminded me exactly how photosynthesis works.

We wait as the flight attendant and copilot pile everyone's luggage next to the plane, and before they're even finished Ken/Neth picks up his suitcase, and Mom's, and then grabs the rolly suitcase Roo and I are sharing.

"That's not necessary, Ken," Mom says. "Let us carry something."

But he just gives her his goofiest grin and starts walking toward the airport building, which looks sort of like a one-room schoolhouse. That's when I realize that, except for the runway and the building and the small parking lot, everything is jungle. All along the edges it's jungle, jungle, jungle, and there's a great noise rising from the jungle, or bunches of noises that add up to one.

"Hey," Roo says, "*what* is that growling sound?"

I'm impressed she can pick one sound out of everything.

"Howler monkeys." Ken/Neth grins. "Loud little buggers, aren't they?"

"Wow! Wow! Wow!" Roo says with each step. "I didn't know this is what it'd be like."

I definitely have to agree with her there. I didn't realize it would feel like we were on a different planet.

Ken/Neth moves quickly (his long legs are *so* long), and we rush to keep up. Inside the airport, a man dressed in white pajamas is holding a sign that says:

SEÑORA SYLVIA WADE

SEÑORITAS MADELINE Y RUBY WADE

"That's us!" Roo whispers loudly. "Fancy-pantsy!"

I'm waiting for Mom to mention the fact that she kept her maiden name, so she's actually Ms. Flynn, not Mrs. Wade, but she doesn't say anything. I look over at Ken/Neth to see if he'll say something, since he's sort of in charge, but he doesn't seem to notice—he's busy greeting the man in pajamas by holding up two fingers in a peace sign.

The man smiles quickly in our general direction without actually looking at us. He doesn't say a word as he leads us outside and loads our luggage into a van that's pure white, aside from a pair of elegant gray Ls on the side. He opens the side door and Roo clambers eagerly into the van, followed by me and then Mom. It has a sky-blue interior and is deeply air-conditioned.

"This," Roo announces, "is the most beautiful van in the entire universe."

Ken/Neth sits in front with the driver and they talk very softly, in English or Spanish—I can't even tell from the way backseat where Roo insisted we sit. Roo is in one of her wiggly moods. She grabs my hand and squeezes it, then drops it so she can put her nose up against the window to look out, then grabs it to squeeze it again as the van heads down a long, badly paved road lined with walls of jungle.

The cold air is giving me a headache, so I press the button to roll down my window and stick my head out into the humidity. I decide right then that I like humidity. It smells like flowers growing.

Roo is babbling to Mom, asking about how many different kinds of monkeys we're going to see, when I realize why this road is so bumpy—thick jungle vines sneak up between cracks in the asphalt, breaking the road apart. I get this creepy vision of the jungle as a gigantic monster with millions of octopus arms.

"Mad," Mom is saying, "Mad, the driver wants you to roll up your window, please."

I look up and see that the driver is staring at me in the rearview mirror.

"Okay," I say, embarrassed. I press the button. "Sorry."

But I don't like having glass between me and the outside, even though I'm already scared of the jungle. I stay quiet for the rest of the ride and let Roo shout the questions up to Ken/Neth.

"Hey, are those *pineapples* in the middle of those plants?"

"Yep, that's a pineapple plantation," Ken/Neth replies, grinning, as usual.

"I thought pineapples grew on trees!"

"Well, those are pineapples, Roo-by."

"Man, doesn't it look like Dr. Seuss invented that plant?"

And on and on. I tune it out, stare at the jungle. After half an hour or so, we turn onto a different road. Now we can see the silhouette of the volcano, as blue and perfect as before.

"Gettin' close," Ken/Neth announces.

The volcano seems bigger and bigger as we approach it on the very straight road. I close my eyes for a few seconds and then open them again, close, open, close, open, and I can create the illusion that the volcano is actually pushing its way out of the earth, growing with each passing second. Sometimes it's kind of fun to freak yourself out.

Then we turn right and suddenly we're too close to the volcano to really see it. Now we just have to imagine it. Which somehow feels even freakier, as though there's a monster standing right behind you.

"And here we are," Ken/Neth proclaims as the driver steers into a parking lot. "Welcome, ladies, to the Selva Lodge."

"The Selva Lodge?" I say, confused. No one ever mentioned a Selva Lodge. "I thought we were staying at La Lava." With our *actual* dad, I stop myself from adding.

"Oh shoot," Ken/Neth says apologetically. "I thought you knew. Kids can't stay at La Lava, so you'll be staying here. They have a pool!"

What? We seriously aren't staying with Dad? I turn to Mom, waiting for her to correct Ken/Neth, but she just shrugs at me.

"I'm sorry, honey," she says. "I thought I mentioned to you that kids aren't allowed to stay at La Lava."

First of all, Mom most definitely did not ever mention that to me, because I obviously would have remembered an annoying fact like that, and second of all, I hate places that don't allow kids. What's their problem?

Roo looks at me and I look at her. We're together in our rage, and that feels good.

"La Lava is *such a jerk*!" Roo says. "Why don't they want us?"

"Girls!" Mom says sharply. "Be grateful for where you are. The Selva Lodge is lovely too."

"Sure," Roo mutters, "whatever. But Dad isn't here."

"Ruby," Mom says in that threatening way of hers, and Roo has to shut her mouth.

From the van I can see that the pink 1950s-style sign for the Selva Lodge is missing some letters so it reads SELV L DGE, which is just real nice.

Then I hop out and get a better look at the Selva Lodge, which is pretty much like any old American motel except for all the weird animal sounds coming from the jungle.

Ken/Neth has already made it across the gravel parking lot. He opens the gate and I hurry over to follow him and Mom and Roo into a concrete courtyard. A few kids are splashing around in a pool, and the hotel forms a square around it, with three rows of orange numbered doors plus a little souvenir shop and café area on the fourth side. The café just has a half wall enclosing it, so the dining area is basically open to the jungle. I have to admit, it looks like a nice place to eat, sitting right there looking out at the layers of green.

"Ooo, pretty!" Roo says, and at first I think she means the big barrels of flowers placed throughout the courtyard, which are overflowing with red and orange and purple blossoms. But then I notice that she's pointing at the little neon-green lizards painted on the orange doors. So I guess it's not *quite* like any ugly old motel. But still.

Ken/Neth is yanking some papers out of his computer bag and flipping through them and making exasperated sounds. He's very talented at looking totally discombobulated (one of Dad's favorite words).

"Aha!" he says after a moment, holding up a piece of paper. "Here we are. Mad and Roo are in room number four, and Sylvia's in number five, and I'm in number eight. I'll just run and get us checked in."

"You're staying here, Ken?" Mom says, surprised. "You don't need to do that. You should stay at La Lava."

"Hey," Ken/Neth says, grinning, "anywhere that doesn't want kids doesn't want me!"

I can't help smiling—which bugs me, but hey, he's got a point there. I look over at Roo to exchange a giggle, but she's staring at the pool.

"Very cute," Mom says, "but I really don't want to inconvenience you. You should stay wherever you usually stay when you come here for work."

"My most important work is to keep you ladies company. The best job ever! La Lava wants you to have an excellent time while you're here, so I should be as close as possible."

"As you like," Mom says, gently shrugging. "Where's the front desk, then?"

"Pool, pool, pool?" Roo says hungrily.

As Mom and Ken/Neth go to check in and Roo runs over to dip her toe in the pool, I stroll toward room number four—and suddenly realize that the little neon-green lizards aren't painted onto the orange doors. They're actual, honest-to-goodness, living, breathing neon-green lizards that scatter as I approach. I'm pretty proud of myself for not screaming.

Roo and I are already pulling on our Speedos in our room (there's a bunk bed—weird for a hotel, but still cool, I guess) when Mom bursts through the door, half yelling *"Surprise!"* and holding up a pair of brand-new two-piece bathing suits—red polka dots for Roo and green stripes for me. She herself is wearing a maroon bikini I've never seen before. Actually, I've never seen Mom in *any* kind of bikini. She's always worn a navy-blue one-piece swimsuit. And she's always said that women who wear bikinis are silly, because bikinis fall off so easily that they're useless for swimming, and no daughter of hers was going to wear such absurd swimwear. When I remind her of all that, she just says, "Oh, lighten up, Mad! We need to have some fun finally. This is an exciting day." Meanwhile Roo's already pulled her Speedo off and is tugging her bathing suit bottom on and waggling her red-polka-dotted bum. I leave the new green-striped two-piece on the concrete floor beside our bunk bed and stay in my good old gray Speedo.

Before Mom and Roo and I are even settled into our lawn chairs at the pool, Ken/Neth brings Mom a pink drink with a pink umbrella in it. She looks like a lady on a postcard, lying there beside the pool at the Selva Lodge with her pretty drink and big sunglasses and straw hat (even though the lawn chair is sagging and some of the plastic strands have snapped).

"Isn't this great, Sylvia!" Ken/Neth says in his peppy way. "You look so happy. Relaxed. Madame Librarian, away from all those dang books. You've sure earned this."

I can agree with Ken/Neth on that one at least. Ever since The Weirdness began, Mom's lips have had this squeezed look to them, and right now they don't. Actually, it's a pretty big relief to look at Mom and not see squeezed lips.

Next Ken/Neth quizzes me and Roo about whether or not we know what *selva* means.

"It means *jungle,* Ken," Roo says as though she's never been so bored in her entire life.

"Well," Ken/Neth says cheerily, pretending Roo wasn't just rude to him, "I guess I'll head over to La Lava now!"

"Where's *Dad*?" Roo says, her tone still rude.

"Oh, you'll be seeing him very, very, very soon," Ken/Neth promises. Then adds, "*Adiós, amigos.* Or should I say *ami*gas."

Ken/Neth heads out of the pool area toward the parking lot, so at last it's just me and Mom and Roo. My Three Girls, as Dad called us. And boy, does it ever feel great being with my sister and my mom and no Ken/Neth, the three of us just lying here on lawn chairs relaxing in the sun, but then of course Roo jumps up and cannonballs into the pool. I don't feel like getting in. It's a hot, hot day and the pool water just feels warm and soggy. Mom reaches over to hold my hand. She smells like coconuts. It's comforting to feel her strong, familiar hand. Her palm is a bit wet with sweat, but so what. It's nice to know that Mom's hand is still Mom's hand, even after The Weirdness and everything. I'm glad we're at the Selva Lodge, where I don't have to worry about anyone I know seeing me hold my mom's hand even though I'm almost thirteen. Soon, though, Mom falls asleep and her hand slips limply out of mine, which makes me feel kind of lonely.

Roo's in the shallow end of the pool, playing some sort of underwater headstand game with these kids who don't speak English. Or Spanish. Or any language I know of. I can't tell where they're from. Mom smiled at the other parents in greeting, but we haven't heard anyone speaking English since we got to the Selva Lodge.

"Don't you wish this was our own private pool?" I said to Roo earlier.

"Kind of," Roo said, but I could tell she didn't. She likes other people. Wherever she goes, Roo always has oodles of friends. Sometimes I've been jealous of her, but mostly I just admire her for being that way.

"Rooooo!" I howl loud enough that she can hear me underwater. "Come here!" Because she loves me, she clambers up out of the pool. As she pitter-patters over to me, I tell her, "You're getting sunburned!" Which is not exactly true. She does look a tiny bit pink, but mainly I just want her to play with me and not with Random Kid #7.

"Okay," I order, holding up a towel. "Dry yourself off. Then I'll put some sunblock on your back."

"Mom put tons of stuff on me already," Roo protests, but at the same time she obediently turns her back to me.

It makes me feel right at home, to be hanging out with Roo and taking care of her. It's my favorite activity, being Roo's sister.

"Uh-oh," I say as I squirt the last globs of coconut sunblock into my hand. "It's all gone."

I knew all along that we were almost out of sunblock, and knew that this would mean we'd have to go to the souvenir shop to buy more, and knew that going to the souvenir shop with Roo would be fun.

So we prance across the courtyard, but as it turns out the Selva Shop is weird and not that nice. For one thing, there's no one in it. No customers, no employees. It's hot and dim. The floor is concrete, and there are lots of metal shelves with hardly anything on them. There's one shelf holding a single hot-pink shirt, XXL, with neon-green lettering, *Fui al Volcán Pájaro de Lava,* and on the back, *¿Y tú?*

"Found it! Found it!" Roo says from across the shop, waving in the air our exact favorite kind of sunblock. We always want to smell like coconuts. It seems like a miracle that they have it here. "How much is it?"

"How would *I* know?" I say, before realizing she's talking to someone else.

I squint into the dimness behind the counter, and can just make out a figure as it stands up.

It's a guy. A teenager. Suddenly I wish I were wearing my new two-piece and not this old bathing suit, and then I feel embarrassed for having that thought. Anyway, I pull the ugly hot-pink T-shirt down from the shelf and stroll to the counter with it.

"Excuse me, but what does *fui* mean?" I say. (I know what *Volcán Pájaro de Lava* means, obviously, and I can figure out that *¿Y tú?* means "And you?" So I guess I *have* learned a thing or two in Spanish class.)

The teenager shrugs and I discover that (a) he doesn't speak English and (b) his eyes are golden. I'm not kidding. Seriously. Golden.

Roo waves the sunscreen in front of him. She really can be kind of obnoxious sometimes.

"*Ho-la,*" she says. "*¿Cuánto?*"

He shrugs and says, "*¿Cuarto?*"

"*Cuarto?* What's that? Does that mean 'four'?" I blabber. This guy makes me nervous.

"It means 'room'. He wants the room number so he can charge it," Roo informs me. "*Cuatro* is 'four'."

How does she *know* all that?

"*¿Cuarto?*" the guy repeats.

Roo holds up four fingers. "*Cuarto cuatro,*" she rhymes with a grin.

He nods and marks something in a yellow lined notebook and then stares over our heads into space with his golden eyes.

So. I guess that's it.

"Um, *adiós*?" I try.

"Hasta luego," Roo yells before running back out into the courtyard.

"Hasta luego?"

I rush to catch up with her. "Where'd you get that?"

"Don't know," Roo says.

"What does it mean?"

"See ya later, alligator." She starts skipping. She skips all the way to the pool and then, without stopping, skips right into the water, the coconut sunblock still in her hand.

I'm about to follow Roo when I'm grabbed up in a hug from behind. For a weird half second I think it's the guy from the Selva Shop—until I notice the freckly arms of my mother.

"Where *were* you guys?" Mom whispers into my ear, her voice almost hysterical. "I woke up and you were gone! I've been looking for you. You can't just run off like that. It's *dangerous* here!"

"Dangerous?" I say, looking around the courtyard, its barrels full of flowers. "What's so dangerous here?"

"Oh, you know, the regular," Mom says, laughing with relief, but I can tell she's still upset. She leads me toward the pool. "Poisonous snakes, rabid monkeys, hungry jaguars." She sounds half teasing and half serious.

"JAGUARS? For real?" Roo yelps from the pool.

Ever since The Weirdness, Mom's been a little weird too. Or I guess *paranoid* is the word. At least, that's the word I heard her use with Aunt Sarah over the phone. "Sometimes I even wonder if the phone is being tapped," Mom had whispered. "But I know

I'm just paranoid. I miss James is all." Mom was the one who first started to notice strange sounds and movements around our house in Denver, back in March or so. Roo and I heard her complaining to Aunt Sarah about those too, and after that, we started to notice the strange sounds and movements. We called them The Creepies. Like, sometimes when you walked into a room it felt as though there had just been a shadowy face at the window. And yeah, was there maybe a soft clicking sound in the background when you put your ear up to the phone? Roo got excited about that, because all of her detective books have tapped phones in them. But me? I just got nervous. And paranoid. And extra lonely for Dad. Like Mom—who, ever since The Weirdness, sometimes grabs me and Roo up in a hug and squeezes way too hard.

"We were in the *Selva Shop*, Mom," I tell her. "Buying sunblock. Because we ran out, and you always say it's *dangerous* not to wear sunblock." I think this might be the sarcastic way teenagers supposedly talk to their parents. I immediately feel bad about talking to Mom that way.

"Okay, okay, you're right," Mom says, pulling me over toward our lawn chairs and smiling at me. "According to moms, everything is dangerous."

It's then that I notice an odd thing happening: Roo is clambering up out of the pool, and a short woman wearing a black dress and—get this!—a black lace veil is standing there with a towel in her wide-open arms. A creepy feeling flashes through me. I don't mean to be rude, but if someone told me to shut my eyes and picture a witch . . .

Roo runs straight into the witch's arms and squirms happily around inside them as the woman dries her off.

Oh great. So now Roo trusts witches too, the same way she trusts every single person she's ever met. I look to Mom for the Bad Girl frown she gives us when we do something stupid, but instead, she's just beaming at Roo.

"Señora Villalobos!" Mom says. "Do you ever have a way with children!"

What? How does Mom even know this lady?

"I love all children," the witch replies in a hoarse voice that comes out from behind the black lace veil. Heebie-jeebies for real. "But especially children like this."

And what's that supposed to mean?

"Apparently you've already met my Ruby," Mom says, "and here's my Madeline."

The witch sinks down into a lawn chair with Roo in her lap. Is Roo, like, a golden retriever or something, that just loves *anyone*? And why is Mom okay with a strange lady grabbing Roo?

"This one," the witch says in a very serious way, wrapping her arms around Roo. I notice her slight accent. "She has it."

Mom laughs, and I really can't tell if she's laughing awkwardly or excitedly.

"Both my girls have it," Mom shoots back, and the witch turns her head toward me for less than a second before returning her attention to Roo.

Boy, I wish she'd lift that veil up. It's really freaking me out. And I really wish she'd let go of my little sister.

"Madeline," Mom says, "meet Señora and Señor Villalobos, the owners of this lovely lodge. Ken and I were lucky enough to meet them when we checked in. They've had this place for over fifty years—can you imagine?"

Only then do I see the very skinny, very old man in the white linen suit perched at the other end of the lawn chair. It's almost as though he was invisible until the exact second when Mom said his name. He has a bright orange handkerchief in his left breast pocket. He nods kindly at me and for some reason I feel the sudden pressure of tears behind my eyes. Like, if I cried right now he wouldn't mind. He'd understand. I blink fast to make the tears go away.

But the tears disappear quickly enough seconds later, when Ken/Neth throws open the gate to the pool area and comes toward us with a humongous grin, balancing a bunch of paper plates and napkins in his arms. Mom waves at him across the pool.

"Hey there, *señoras* and *señoritas*," he says. I guess he doesn't notice Señor Villalobos, just the way I didn't. "A special treat for everyone!"

As usual nowadays, Ken/Neth's annoying cheerfulness gives me a stomachache, but at least he's not a creepy old witch.

"What is it! What is it!" Roo says, jumping out of the witch's lap and grabbing Ken/Neth's arm the way any kid would grab her dad's arm. My stomachache gets worse.

"*Jungle tacos!*" Ken/Neth announces in a fake-dramatic voice.

He arranges the tacos on a low plastic table beside Mom's lawn chair and Roo and Mom crowd around him.

"I'm very glad you're here, Señora Villalobos," he says to the witch as he lays out paper plates. "*Tengo una pregunta.*"

Even I know that means "I have a question." But Ken/Neth seems to get stumped after that, going "Uh . . . uh . . . ah . . . uh" and fumbling around with words until he just says, "I'm not positive how to say what I need to say in Spanish, so I'll just use English, okay?"

"Of course," the witch says, standing up to face him. Is it just me, or is she giving him the evil eye from behind that veil? I feel like I can hear the glare in her voice.

"My contacts at La Lava have invited Señora Sylvia to join them free of charge for a yoga retreat that's taking place this week. The theme is Relaxation and Rejuvenation," Ken/Neth says, talking very loudly and smiling overenthusiastically at Señora Villalobos, as though she's having trouble understanding him.

"Oh no!" Mom says. "Oh no. I could never accept such a gift!"

"This is the first she's heard of it," Ken/Neth explains. "It *is* a generous gift, and I want her to be able to take full advantage of it. Believe me, this woman has earned it!"

"No, really, I can't accept! James told me how much that place costs," Mom says firmly, "and besides, I'm down here to see *him*. We just want to spend the whole week with Dad, right, girls?"

"Yeah!" Roo yelps. I'm really glad I have Roo around to express everything I feel but am too shy to shout about.

"Wait, wait," Ken/Neth says. "You don't have to do it, of course. It's merely an invitation. You can sleep on it. But just in case, I'm wondering if Señora Villalobos knows of any local babysitters who might be able to keep an eye on the girls during the day?"

Outrageous!

"We don't need a babysitter," I mutter angrily. I'm twelve-almost-thirteen and perfectly capable of babysitting both Roo and myself. But everyone chooses to ignore me.

"*Sí, tengo a alguien muy bueno,*" the witch says.

Ken/Neth looks delighted with himself for understanding what she said. Big whoop.

"*Muy bien, muy bien, muy bien, muchas gracias, señora,*" he says. His bad accent hurts even my ears, and under her veil, the witch cringes from the sound of it—at least, that's what it looks like to me.

Then the witch says some words at Roo in Spanish. Roo nods, but it was really hard, fast Spanish, impossible to understand, and I know Roo is nodding just to be polite. And then, without another word, the witch heads toward the pool gate in a swirl of black lace.

Señor Villalobos follows her like a ray of light. I'm not sure Ken/ Neth ever even noticed him.

"Hey, so where's Dad?" Roo practically yells, jumping up into Ken/Neth's face. "I want to see Dad!"

"I've spoken to the folks at La Lava," Ken/Neth says, "and we've got a three p.m. appointment."

Um, *hello,* since when did we have to make an appointment to see our own dad?

"Huh?" Roo says. "An appointment? To see *Dad*?"

Have I ever mentioned that I love, love, love my sister?

"Three's right around the corner, girls," Mom says. "We'll just eat these tacos and then head over there."

Roo rolls her eyes but sits down by the table.

"He's very excited to see you," Ken/Neth adds. "Very, very excited."

At that my heart does a little jumping jack. Dad—very, very excited to see us!

"Well, here goes, girls," Ken/Neth says, saying *girls* in the exact same tone Mom uses. *Puh-lease.* He picks up the first taco and hands it to me, as though I'm the guest of honor. "You first, Madeline. Give it a try."

The taco smells rich and wonderful, like salsa and chocolate at the same time, and suddenly I'm very hungry. I take a bite and close my eyes, and there's this amazing crunchiness, followed by the crispness of lettuce and then an almost fruity taste, mango maybe— Mom's favorite fruit, and a treat we only get to have once in a while back in Denver. The taco is so good that I forget to be annoyed by Ken/Neth or anything else.

"You like it?" Ken/Neth says. "Come on, Roo-by. Your turn."

Roo goes up to him like an eager little animal and eats a bite of taco right out of his hand.

"Gross!" she yelps. "Gross! *Gross!*" She spits it out, into his other hand.

"Oh good lord," Mom says. She reaches her hand out for Roo's chewed food. "I'm sorry, Ken. No one but a parent should have to deal with such things."

Mom is one hundred percent right. No one but Mom or Dad should be doing what Ken/Neth's doing.

"No problemo," Ken/Neth says, smiling. Why is he never, ever in a bad mood? He pops up out of his seat before Mom can get to him and strolls over to the trash can, where he wipes Roo's chewed bite off his hand with a napkin.

"What the *heck* was that?" Roo says when he returns.

"Ask Madeline," he says in his most annoyingly jolly voice.

I shrug. "Don't know."

"But you liked it?" He smiles.

"She loved it!" Mom says.

"Okay, so what is it?" I say.

"You really want to know?" Now he's grinning *hard*.

"Sure," I say.

"Try to guess."

"I don't know. Celery." Although I'm pretty sure it wasn't celery.

"Guess again."

"Mango. I don't know."

"Yeah, partly, but guess again." Man, Ken/Neth's grin is really bugging me.

"Come on, tell us what's in the tacos," Roo begs.

"You don't want to guess anymore?" He grins.

"NO!" Roo says.

"Mad?"

I fake-yawn.

"Fried grasshopper," Ken/Neth announces.

31

"Ha," I say.

"I'm serious," Ken/Neth says. "They're a specialty here, savory jungle grasshoppers fried in coconut oil and served with this bitter chocolate sauce and mang—"

And I realize, oh my god, he's not joking.

I stand up and walk over to the pool and do a cannonball right in the middle of Ken/Neth's sentence. I let myself drift way down to the bottom in a little curled-up ball and stay there for a long time, coming up just once in a while to take a breath before sinking back down again. I swear to myself that I won't speak to Ken/Neth for the rest of the day. Making me eat *bugs*! Arranging an *appointment* with Dad! What*ever*! All I can say is that I am *dying* to see Dad and be done with stupid Ken/Neth forever.

When I finally come back up for good, the tacos are gone.

CHAPTER 3

"All aboard!" Ken/Neth hoots as Mom and Roo and I load into the gleaming white golf cart he brought over from La Lava. Mom is wearing a dress the color of an orange tulip and big, round blue earrings. She looks beautiful. Roo and I clustered around her earlier as she dusted silvery powder across her eyelids. Like a lot of other things at the Selva Lodge, the mirror was a bit crummy. It made us look like three blobs. Mom looked like a prettier blob, though. I'm glad Dad will get to see her looking this wonderful.

I've never ridden in a golf cart before. Dad gets mad whenever we pass golf courses in Colorado because you ruin tons of habitats when you plant all that grass. But I have to say I'm realizing that a golf cart is a pretty nice way to travel. You get to feel very close to the jungle, and there's just the right amount of wind blowing over you. Besides, Ken/Neth tells us there's no golf course at La Lava—it's just that golf carts are the best way to cover these not-too-huge distances—so we don't even have to feel guilty.

The golf cart bounces a ton on the potholed driveway of the Selva

Lodge. In a bad pirate accent, Ken/Neth keeps saying stuff like, "Aye, we'll make it yet, mateys, in our trusty craft!" Mom laughs. And because Mom laughs, Roo laughs, but I know they're not laughing at Ken/Neth's dumb jokes. They're laughing with happiness, because we're about to see Dad.

There's a breeze all around us, plus the big, loud, wacky noise of the jungle, so up front Mom and Ken/Neth can't hear me and Roo too well. And there's something I need to ask Roo about. Something private. Which for some reason suddenly seems really important.

"Hey, Roo," I whisper. "Remember that guy in the Selva Shop?"

Roo rolls her eyes. "Yeah, I remember him. That happened like an hour ago. Jeez, I couldn't forget him already. Maybe by tonight."

"I mean, did you notice anything in particular about him?"

"Well," Roo says, "his binoculars."

"His *binoculars*?"

"The ones around his neck," she says, and then adds, "duh."

"He was wearing binoculars?" How had I missed that? I'd been *staring* at him!

Roo yawns.

"Well, did you notice anything else?" I ask her.

"I don't know. He was kind of spacey, I guess."

"Did you notice his eyes?"

"Uh, yeah, he had eyes."

"What color?"

"Uh, I don't know, brown? Can we talk about something else? Like SEEING DAD!"

I guess Roo is just too young. I turn away from her and look out at the walls of jungle, the oversized leaves and thick vines and mossy tree trunks. I'm noticing the good smell of overripe mangoes when Roo lets out a little scream and points upward. Two red-yellow-blue parrot-type birds that look as though they flew right out of a cartoon are passing above us.

"Are you *serious*?" Roo says with awe.

"Hey, check that out!" Ken/Neth says. "Scarlet macaws."

"Breathtaking!" Mom whispers. "Unbelievable!"

It really *is* pretty unbelievable, like something that would only ever happen in a dream.

Right then Ken/Neth turns onto the main road, the one the van drove us down just a couple of hours ago. At the Selva Lodge, inside that concrete courtyard, I somehow managed to almost forget that we're in the jungle next to a volcano. But now I remember all about it. The volcano looks huge and flat against the sky. I'm imagining a bubbling pool of orange lava up there at the top, even though I know that's not what most volcanoes are really like.

Then I see something.

A thread of smoke rising from the volcano. It's white against the light-blue sky. But still. I can see it.

"Mom!" I yell.

"What?" she says happily.

"The volcano! Look!"

"Look at what? What is it?" Roo squeals. "I want to see!"

"It's gorgeous, isn't it, sweetie," Mom says.

"See the white smoke?" I panic. "We've got to get out of here!"

"Oh, yeah, I see it!" Roo yelps.

"I guess you're—right," Mom says slowly, gazing upward. Ken/Neth turns back to look at us with that annoying grin, enjoying his golf cart full of damsels in distress. "Relax, fair ladies." Which drives me crazy. Could he please stop being this way please? Who does he think he is—King Arthur? "The volcano is active."

"Active?" I practically scream.

"Hence the hot springs at La Lava. But it's totally safe," he promises.

"Safe?"

"The best experts have assured us there's little to no chance the volcano will blow in the next hundred and fifty years."

"Little to no chance?" I repeat.

"The scientists just have to cover their you-know-whats—pardon my French, girls."

I get that feeling again, that feeling of the volcano being a monster.

"Think about it," Ken/Neth says. "All sorts of movie stars and socialites and other rich and famous people stay at La Lava. Do you really think those kinds of people would allow themselves to be put in danger?"

I harrumph. Then Roo harrumphs, imitating me.

"I'm sure it's fine, girls," Mom says, although she doesn't sound so sure.

I try to stop staring at the smoking volcano. I guess Ken/Neth maybe does have a point about the movie stars. So I take ten deep breaths while beside me Roo chants "Dad! Daddy! Daddy-o! Dad! Daddy! Daddy-o!" under her breath.

Ken/Neth turns left onto a smooth—get this—*white* road! I've never seen white pavement before. It shines as though recently polished, and the golf cart glides down it. This is obviously the nicest road we've been on since we arrived. I can tell we're getting close, and my heart starts doing acrobatics.

"Um, why is this road white?" Roo asks.

"Better for reflecting the sun," Ken/Neth explains. "White roads, white roofs—they reflect the sun's rays more than black does. That's the kind of thing that could really help prevent global warming. Don't forget you're at the World's Greenest Spa!"

Thanks, La Lava brochure robot.

Soon the white road leads us to a pair of tall, gleaming metal doors in a huge stone wall. Ken/Neth raises two fingers in a peace sign to the guy in the booth, and the doors slowly swing open. Roo is the first to gasp once we're on the other side, but I'm quick to echo her.

Ahead of us lies a glowing white palace built into the side of the volcano. It reminds me of the palace on the cover of this book of Arabian fairy tales Mom and Dad used to read to us. I'm thinking big ballrooms and courtyards with rose gardens and marble bedrooms in towers.

But even more amazing than the palace itself are the pools. They seem to be everywhere! Down the hillside from the palace, there are twenty or more pools, all connected by waterfalls and streams. Some are made of white marble like the palace. Others are made of dark volcanic rock. Here and there among the pools are wooden patios holding elegant wooden lounge chairs (I can't help but think of Mom's lawn chair at the Selva Lodge, which suddenly seems extremely crummy) and piles of dark green towels in large bamboo baskets. The white road continues past the front gate, alongside the pools, and up toward the palace.

The water glitters in the sunlight, and I'm surprised to see that it's a different color in each pool. In some pools it looks almost turquoise, in others dark blue, and in others light yellow, pale purple, even pink.

And there are people. A good number of them. And they all seem to be moving in slow motion, getting into and out of the water, strolling down steps, lying on lounge chairs, sipping from glass goblets.

What's really strange is how quiet it is here. There's a hush over everything. Even the jungle doesn't make its usual ruckus. No noises rise over the quiet murmur of the waterfalls. All you can hear is the soft hiss of steaming water.

And then I notice another strange thing. As we coast toward the palace, I realize that the jungle surrounding the pools isn't *wild* jungle. I mean, it *looks* like wild jungle, but there's something different about it, different from the jungle around the Selva Lodge. It's . . . perfect. Like, there's no messiness between the trunks of the trees. Vines climb upward in even patterns. Tiger lilies and other poisonous-looking flowers peek out at just the right angles. Nothing looks wilted or chaotic. Or I guess what I mean is, the chaos looks sort of . . . controlled.

"Oh my goodness," Mom is whispering, and Roo keeps letting out these little *Oooo*s of amazement.

"Nice, right?" Ken/Neth says, delighted to see us all so shocked.

We pass a woman stepping out of a pool of bright pink water. She has long black curly hair.

Wait a second. Wait a *second*!

I have to do a double take, because no one else on the planet has hair that beautiful.

I grab Roo's hand, squeeze it tight, and, hiding my other hand in my lap so I won't embarrass anyone, point at the woman.

But Roo has already noticed, because she's squeezing my hand too, and pointing, but she's not being careful to hide her pointing.

"Oh. My. Gosh," Roo breathes. "Oh! My! Gosh!"

Vivi.

Our favorite actress.

The one who played Cleopatra in our Favorite Movie Ever, *The Secret Life of Cleopatra*. Plus she's been in a lot of other great movies too. Like *Rosa of the Flowers and Knives*, where she was a rebellious Guatemalan nun. And the whole Aphrodite superheroine series. And she was the voice of the brave, pretty wolf in *Wolf Story*, which we loved when we were little. And lots of other movies I can't think of right now.

Anyway: Wow. Double wow. *Triple* wow.

She's wrapping one of those thick green towels around herself. A young man in white pajamas approaches her with a green drink in a glass goblet. She takes it from him and then waves him away as she sips the drink and pulls her sunglasses down over her eyes.

I cry every single time I see the end of *The Secret Life of Cleopatra*, even though I've probably seen it about fifty times. She is so courageous. It is the best. The very, very best.

Mom is twisting around and looking back at me and Roo with huge, thrilled eyes. She knows how much we love Vivi. She loves Vivi too, because Vivi gives tons of her money away to libraries and children and environmental causes, especially in Latin America, since she grew up in Colombia and Mexico.

"Don't *stare*," she whispers, even though she's staring as much as we are.

Ken/Neth laughs at us as he steers the golf cart toward the front entrance of the palace. But rather than stopping at the wide golden doors—yes, *golden* doors—he keeps right on going and turns onto a pair of dirt tracks. He pulls the golf cart up alongside a row of thirty or so others.

"Resort rules," he explains. "Gotta hide the golf carts. The rich don't like to see the mechanics."

"What mechanics? Where?" Roo says merrily, hopping out.

"He doesn't mean mechanics like the guys who work on cars," I explain, very much the older sister. "Mechanics as in all the things that make a place like this nice."

But Roo's not paying attention to me anymore. Instead, she's leading us back toward the golden doors of the palace. The air is neither hot nor cold, and it smells like honey, and I kind of want to stay here forever. Roo grabs my right hand and Mom's left hand. Her hand is small and sweaty in mine. She skips and pulls us along

with her, and in her skip I can read her only thought: *Dad!*—skip—
Dad!—skip—*Dad!*

A tall man in white pajamas opens the golden doors for us. He
starts to bow low—then, recognizing Ken/Neth, he straightens up.
Ken/Neth makes a peace sign with his fingers, but the man doesn't
do the sign back to him. This doesn't seem to bother Ken/Neth,
though, because he just looks at us with his goofy grin and gestures
us inside as if it's his own house or something.

We step into a white marble lobby with an enormous golden block
in the middle. It takes me a second to realize that the golden block
is actually the front desk.

Behind the golden block stands the most beautiful woman in the
world (aside from Vivi, of course). And I'm not exaggerating. I'm
sorry to say it, but Mom looks a little bit old, tired, and shabby compared to this woman. Even Mom's pretty tulip dress somehow seems
silly now. The woman behind the front desk has green eyes and
bronze skin. Her skin looks as smooth as metal, as smooth as a mirror, as smooth as I don't know what. She's very tall, and she's wearing a red business suit, and she's tapping on the golden desk with
fingernails that are long and sharp and silver. So long and sharp
and silver that they make me think of miniature knives.

"Hey, Pat," Ken/Neth says. His tone seems far too casual for
speaking to a person like her in a lobby like this.

She must agree with me, because as she comes out from behind
the desk she responds very formally: *"Buenas tardes, Señor Candy."* Her
voice is perfect, like an extension of her face. Also: her voice reminds
me of something, but I can't think of what.

"Um, *buenas tardes,*" he says. "Girls, go ahead and say hello to
Señora Pat Chevalier, otherwise known as the manager of this
fine spa."

Why does he have to talk to us that way, as though he's our dad?

"*Señorita Patricia Chevalier,*" the woman corrects with a cool smile.

"Oh, my bad, sorry," says Ken/Neth. Which actually makes me feel the tiniest bit sorry for him. He can't help it that he's always saying the exact wrong thing.

Then Señorita Patricia Chevalier turns a very warm smile on me and Roo.

"*Hola,*" Roo says, grinning her most dazzling grin. She loves beautiful things.

"*Hola,*" I say.

"So you must be Madeline and Ruby," Patricia Chevalier says to us in that over-friendly way some women talk to kids. To be honest, I don't like it much, even though she *is* basically the most beautiful woman ever.

"Well, I'm Roo," Roo says, "and she's Mad." Roo loves grown-up women who are nice to her.

"But you can call us Ruby and Madeline," I say quickly.

"Well, Ruby and Madeline." Patricia Chevalier pauses for a fraction of a second, as though she can't think of another word to say to us. "What splendid names," she murmurs. I notice that her English is slightly accented. She turns to Mom. "And you must be Mrs. Wade?"

I can't believe it, but Mom is blushing. I worry that she's feeling shabby.

"Actually," Mom says, "I'm Sylvia Flynn. I kept my maiden name. Very nice to meet you, Patricia. We're so looking forward to the gala. Thanks so much for the invitation."

"I hear you will also be joining us for Relaxation and Rejuvenation this week," Patricia Chevalier says. "We are delighted. Our yoga program was recently ranked number one in the world."

"Oh goodness," Mom says graciously to Patricia while glaring over at Ken/Neth. "I actually haven't decided yet. I may want to spend the time with my family instead. But thank you so very much for the invitation."

Patricia Chevalier glances at Ken/Neth and raises one of her sculpted eyebrows.

"To be decided," Ken/Neth says awkwardly.

Then Patricia Chevalier looks at Mom in a strange way. She cocks her head and narrows her eyes and presses her lips together, as though she's trying to figure out something about Mom, like how much she weighs or how old she is or what makes her tick or something. Mom doesn't seem to notice, though—she's busy pulling a leaf or bug or crumb out of Roo's hair.

Anyway, Patricia Chevalier gives Mom a radiant smile before turning to Ken/Neth and saying a bunch of words at him in Spanish. He listens hard. At the end of it, he says, "Uh, Señorita Patricia, I'm afraid you lost me a ways back."

"Where exactly did I lose you?" she says politely, as though Ken/Neth isn't irritating her.

"Well," Ken/Neth says, chipper as ever, "frankly, I didn't catch much of it."

"I said that Dr. Wade will be ready to see you in ten minutes, as you arrived somewhat earlier than the arranged time; perhaps you would like to swing by the viewing balcony while you wait?"

She lifts one silver fingernail to point toward the balcony. The marble lobby is now blindingly white from the afternoon sun burning across the marble, pouring in from the open archways at the other end of the huge room.

"Thank you kindly," Ken/Neth says, not even a bit embarrassed that Patricia Chevalier had to repeat herself in English. "*Gracias.* We'll check out the balcony. The kids'll love it."

"I am sure they will," Patricia Chevalier says. "Our Gold Circle Investors' Gala dinner will take place in our outdoor dining area, which lies below the viewing balcony, so you can get a sense of what awaits you Saturday evening. I am sure you girls have beautiful new dresses to wear to the gala?"

Roo and I look at each other. The dresses we bought for the gala, which seemed so amazing back in Denver, probably won't seem very amazing here.

"Yes, thank you," Mom says to Patricia Chevalier. "Move along," she whispers to us, as though we're in a church. I try to remember the way Mom looked so glamorous this morning, there on the lawn chair by the pool with her big hat and umbrella drink, but now that I've been looking at Patricia Chevalier, it's very hard to picture.

Ken/Neth leads us out of the lobby and into a white marble hall-way that has numbered golden doors on the left-hand side and a bunch of open-air archways on the right-hand side, so you can see the grounds of La Lava. We follow him through an archway draped with honeysuckle onto the viewing balcony. The balcony is a large, white marble oval extending out from the side of the palace. Roo runs to the very tip of the oval and stands there sighing so loudly that I worry Patricia Chevalier will hear it and think we're all unso-phisticated and know that they're right not to allow kids to stay here.

"So pretty!" she says. "So so so so sooo pretty!"

Sometimes I wish I could express myself the way Roo does. It's true, seeing this place *does* make you want to go "So so so so sooo."

"Oh my gosh!" Roo says, pointing. "Look! Now Vivi's getting a *red* drink!"

I look down to see Vivi taking a drink off a tray held by the young man in white pajamas. She gestures him away with a rude flick of her hand, as though he's a mosquito or some other pesky thing, be-fore sinking onto a lounge chair to sip at her dark red drink.

Jeez. I really wish I hadn't seen that. I want to keep believing that Vivi is the kind of lady who's good to every single person she meets, no matter if it's a president or a waiter. She's always seemed that way to me. Plus all those charities she supports!

"Hey, Mad, see Vivi's red drink?" Roo says.

"Uh-huh," I reply flatly.

"Oh my gosh," Roo sighs, craning her neck over the banister. "I *love* her!"

"Who knows if she's even nice," I say, which comes out sounding meaner than I meant it, but Roo is already on to the next thing.

"Hey, check out the outdoor dining room! Oh wow. Look how all the chairs are *gold* and all the tables have *floating lily pads* in the middle!"

I crane my neck over the banister, like Roo, and gaze at the tables glimmering with crystal and silver—and yes, floating lily pads in glass bowls.

"Man, why aren't we staying here?" Roo whines. "I wanna stay here! I thought La Lava was paying for our whole trip."

Mom gives Roo her You're-Being-a-Brat face. "We've already discussed this, Ruby. You know kids can't stay here."

"Yeah, yeah, yeah," Roo says, "but what's their problem with kids?"

"You want to know what their problem with kids is?" Mom says.

"Yes," Roo says, putting her hands on her hips.

"You really want to know?"

"Uh-huh," Roo says, tossing her head.

"Kids are loud and lively and a tad bit crazy," Mom says, "and when people are paying thirty thousand dollars a week to stay somewhere, they're buying utter and complete freedom from loud and lively and a tad bit crazy, okay? In fact, you're lucky they even let your little tushie on these grounds in the first place."

"Thirty thousand dollars a week?" I echo.

"Well," Roo harrumphs, ignoring me, "can't we at least eat here tonight?"

Ken/Neth just stands there grinning, apparently finding all of this extremely amusing.

"Tonight we're going to get fried bananas at the Selva Café!" Mom says, trying to make the silly old Selva Café sound like something special.

"I want to stay here," Roo mutters sadly into the marble banister.

"This place is for *obnoxious rich people*," I inform her.

But the truth is I agree with her one hundred percent. More than one hundred percent. La Lava Resort and Spa is my favorite place. Of the places I've been. Which isn't that many. But still.

Right then Patricia Chevalier appears behind us, and I have a little freak-out inside myself, hoping she didn't hear what I just said.

"This way, please," she says in her gorgeous voice, leading us off the viewing balcony, through the honeysuckle archway, and down the long white marble hallway. Her stiletto heels make mini gunshot sounds on the marble. Once we get about halfway down the hallway, there are no more open-air archways—instead, there are numbered golden doors on both sides.

Two old ladies wearing sunglasses, lipstick, and silk robes come strolling toward us.

"Madame, Madame," Patricia Chevalier greets them, bowing slightly to each and saying a few words to them in what I think is French. But they look up at her in this weird, angry way, like they think she's a phony or something.

Suddenly I find my chin in the fingers of one of the *madame*s, who has a tight grip like an eagle claw, and she's saying something in (I'm pretty sure) French and showing me her big bloody teeth (I guess it's just the red lipstick). I'm stuck there for a moment with my face in her hand, and then she lets go and continues onward.

I'm going *Huh?* and looking back down the hallway after them, when Mom, who speaks French, says, "You should be honored, Mad. Those French women think you have great skin. She just said, '*This is the skin I want! This exact skin! And I can't wait another second!*' You know the French are the best judges of female beauty."

Patricia Chevalier glances over at me. Is it just me or are her eyes sort of cold? But her mouth is set in a brilliant smile.

"Youth," she says. "Right, Mrs. Flynn?"

"Sylvia, please," Mom says. "Just Sylvia."

Patricia Chevalier stops at the end of the white marble hallway. I wonder if Dad is behind the door to the left or the door to the right, and my heart starts doing jumping jacks.

My dad is So Great. It has been So Hard without him.

But rather than opening either door, Patricia Chevalier looks up at this little device thingy on the ceiling and the wall itself starts to slide away (!!!), making a gap just large enough for one person at a time to step through.

Roo squeals and yanks on my hand. A secret door! Secret doors are one of her top favorite things. Not that she's ever seen one in real life.

Ken/Neth steps through first, followed by Patricia Chevalier. I peek around them to see what's on the other side of the wall. It's a small, windowless white marble room. A man is sitting on a metal chair at a glass table, hunched over, holding his head in his hands. This man is much skinnier than Dad, and his hair is almost entirely gray, and he's wearing those white pajama-type things like all the employees here, and I wonder when the heck we're going to be able to see *Dad*.

Then the man looks up, and my heart trips over itself.

The man *is* Dad.

"KEN!" Dad cries out in this excited, desperate way, standing up from the chair and raising his arms, looking like he's about to leap across the room and hug Ken/Neth.

Before I can figure out why Dad is so excited to see Ken/Neth, Patricia Chevalier steps in front of Ken/Neth and the brightness drains from Dad's face, and his arms fall back down to his sides. He still hasn't seen us, since we're hidden behind Ken/Neth and Patricia Chevalier in the dim, narrow opening, and it's driving Roo crazy, so she pushes through them and bombs her way across the room toward Dad. I'm stuck just standing there watching Dad's face when he sees Roo.

Nothing has ever upset me as much as this:

When Dad sees Roo, his face fills with fury. I had no idea Dad could make a face like that. He's never in my entire life ever made that face.

He doesn't open his arms to the hot little cannonball of Roo the way he always used to. Instead, she just crashes into his legs and stands there looking up at him.

"Um, Dad, hello?" she says. Then, "Dad! Hi! We love you!"

He's staring at the doorway, where Mom and I are stepping out from behind the others.

"Sylvia," Dad says, and his voice gets a little funny, like he might cry, but when I look back at his face it's still furious. "Why are you here?"

It sounds more like an accusation than a question. Mom stares at him, shocked, her tulip dress hanging limply.

Excuse me, but didn't Ken/Neth say that Dad was "Very, very excited" to see us?

And now Dad is acting like we've done some big terrible thing by coming here?

Also, why did he call her *Sylvia*? Dad always calls Mom *Via*, as in short for Sylvia, "my road to good things," he liked to say, because *via* I guess means "road" in Italian.

"Hug your wife," Patricia Chevalier says, her voice smooth and sweet, and I'm grateful that at least someone around here is trying to make this go the way it should. "She came all this way to see you."

Dad glances at Patricia Chevalier, who nods at him, and then he takes five mechanical steps toward Mom. She grabs hold of his waist and pulls him toward her and nuzzles into his chest. This is the way my parents hug whenever they see each other at the end of the day, and I've always liked to watch them, because it makes everything seem safe and cozy and good, and for a second I feel all those lovely feelings, until I notice that this is just a weird version of that normal hug, because Dad isn't smiling down at Mom the way he usually would, and his face is still furious, and it starts to really freak me out.

Mom pulls back just a bit and looks up at Dad.

"Jimbo," she whispers, her oldest nickname for him. "What's going on?"

But Dad just shakes his head silently, maybe even sadly, as he gazes down at her.

Mom lets go of him and I can see that she's crying quietly. And it's awful.

Inside I'm going, *What the* heck? Maybe I didn't expect it to be perfect, but I sure didn't expect it to be this bad. This is So Much Worse than I ever could have imagined.

Roo is still standing where Dad left her, staring at his back and making little whimpering sounds. Noticing the noise, Dad turns around and walks over to her. He puts his hand on her head, the exact way he used to. But rather than smiling, Roo just looks worried. After a few seconds, she wriggles free from him and runs back across the room toward us.

"Madeline," Dad says, finally turning his attention to me. He never calls me Madeline. I wish he would call me Madpie. I wish a lot of things.

"Hi, Dad," I say. I feel weird.

"Hi," he says so softly I can barely hear it.

I feel like I need to do something, say something, to make this all seem less weird.

"It's really pretty here," I say, straining to sound normal. "We missed you a ton."

I guess those were the wrong things to say, because Dad just stares down at me (sadly? madly?).

Mom crosses the room to him. She puts her hands on his shoulders. "Jimbo," she says again. Her voice is very tender. "Can we talk, just the two of us, for a little while?"

Patricia Chevalier clears her throat.

Dad clears his throat.

"I'm sorry," Dad tells Mom. "But things are extremely busy right now. A lot of very urgent work to do. It's absolutely essential that I get back to it immediately."

Mom lets go of his shoulders. She's still crying. But now I can see that she's also angry.

"You are *not* this way," she practically hisses. "You need to tell me *what's going on.*"

"I'm sorry, Sylvia," Dad says, and he does sound sorry. But he ought to be calling her Via.

Right then the room is hit with a crazily loud sound, a huge whoosh of noise—a rockslide would sound like this, or an avalanche, or the end of the world—and I scream.

"What *is* that?" Mom shouts.

49

"The monsoon," Ken/Neth yells. "Every afternoon at 3:08! You could set your watch by it!"

And that makes me feel like we truly are on another planet, a planet where the weather tells the time.

After that no one says anything for a while; we just stand there in the white marble room in our three little clumps—me and Roo, Mom and Dad, Patricia Chevalier and Ken/Neth—listening to the pounding rain. *How* can it be so loud? There aren't even any windows here.

"I suppose we should be going, then?" Patricia Chevalier screeches over the noise with a bright smile. "Perhaps the Flynn-Wade family can have another visit later on."

Dad always used to call us the Flade family. It tickled our funny bone, to call ourselves the Flades. But right now Dad doesn't say a thing. He just sinks back down into the metal chair.

As I turn to leave I know I'll never forget this, the sight of our father sitting in that metal chair, elbows on the glass table, holding his head in his hands while the monsoon thunders all around him.

CHAPTER 4

We do order fried bananas—actually, fried plantains—at the Selva Café, but it's not as though we feel very happy about that, or about anything else. The four of us are just sitting here on the white plastic chairs at the white plastic table, not saying anything. It's a *very* quiet night at the Selva Café, a single waiter serving our table and one other. After trying a few times to get a conversation going, even Ken/Neth finally understands that we all just want him to Be Quiet. Mom's eyes are super bloodshot and the tendons in her neck are super tense. She looks kind of scary, to be honest. She's not even trying anymore to pretend for me and Roo that she's okay, the way she did during The Weirdness. Not that Roo's paying attention anyway—she's simply munching away on fried plantains. I'm pretty shocked she can eat so perkily, considering what's happened today, but as Dad liked to say, Roo has the appetite of a superheroine.

Since three sides of the Selva Café are open air and look right out into the jungle, I spend the whole meal staring into the trees and imagining Dad popping out from among the vines to tell us he was just playing a practical joke on us today: "I can't believe you thought I was serious! Don't you remember how much I love practical jokes? Hey, don't tell me you've already finished the plantains! Let's go to the pool after dinner."

It's still partly light outside, and it feels like this weirdo day is going on forever and ever, and all I want is for it to end, and I know I've never been as unhappy as I am right now.

It used to be that whenever I felt sad or angry or jealous, Dad would explain that just a few little chemicals were creating the feeling. He said: Just a few little chemicals, no big deal, easy to ignore.

He also said: Did you win the lottery?

And I said: No.

And he said: Yes you did! You won trillions of lotteries! First you won the lottery of the Big Bang, and then you won the lottery of evolution, and then you won the lottery of me and your mother being assigned to the same dorm in college, and then you won the lottery of our ex-girlfriends and ex-boyfriends being fools, and then you won the lottery of us falling in love and getting married. Not to mention the lottery of the United States of America and a loving middle-class family.

And I said: Oh.

And Dad said: So I don't want to ever, *ever* hear you say that you're unlucky or unfortunate or *anything*. Understand?

And now I'm sitting here in the Selva Café, wondering: Do I still have to feel lucky all the time, even after The Weirdness?

After the dinner plates are cleared, we sit in silence as Mom slurps the last drops from the mango daiquiri Ken/Neth ordered for her.

"Well," she says, the first word any of us has said in a long time,

"I guess I'll be doing that Relaxation and Restoration yoga retreat after all."

"Relaxation and *Rejuvenation,*" Ken/Neth corrects. "Why, that's great, Sylvia!"

"It sounds like just about what I need right now. Besides, it's not as though I have any other reason to be here," Mom says, her teeth clenched.

What about being with *us*? I want to yell.

"Except of course to spend time with the kids," Mom says, as though she's reading my mind, "but it's important for them to have Spanish lessons anyway."

"Spanish lessons?" I say. This is the first I've heard about any Spanish lessons.

"Wha?" Roo says.

"Oh," Ken/Neth says, "did I not mention that the Villaloboses can hook us up with a babysitter who also teaches Spanish? I'll go tell them after dessert that we'd like their babysitter starting tomorrow morning."

Um, *hello,* I'll be thirteen in September—I can take care of me and Roo, obviously! But I don't say anything out loud. We've already had this fight a bunch of times. I am *so* sick of babysitters. Mom sometimes tries to call them "companions," as though that'll trick me into not realizing what they are. We had two different babysitters in Denver this spring, sometimes a spacey college girl and sometimes a cranky old lady.

"Your minds are so malleable now, girls," Mom says, pushing her empty daiquiri glass away. "You need to take advantage of that. Now's the time to master a new language. It's too late for me to learn Spanish. I'm not even going to try."

"Malleable?" I say.

"So we can say things to each other in Spanish and you won't understand?" Roo says.

"Flexible, capable of learning easily," Mom says to me, and then "That's exactly right" to Roo.

Okay, well, this trip just got more awful, if that's even possible. Dad doesn't care about us anymore, Mom would rather do yoga than be with her daughters, Ken/Neth is annoying me more with each passing second, nobody seems to think I'm old enough to baby-sit Roo, and now we have to study Spanish?

"Hey, Roo," I say, "let's get outta here."

She looks at me. Mom let her order coconut ice cream, which hasn't come yet.

"First can I—" she starts, but I glare at her and she goes, "Okay, yeah, let's get outta here."

"Sure, whatever you want," Mom murmurs, not even noticing that I'm trying to be mean by abandoning her at the dinner table.

But even once Roo and I are back in our room, away from Mom and Ken/Neth, I don't feel much better, because now Roo is being annoying.

"Poor Dad," she says. "This is bad."

"Poor Dad?" I say. "More like poor jerk."

"Dad's not a jerk!" Roo protests. "He's just having problems is all."

"Yeah, *jerk* problems," I say.

"Please stop saying that word."

"You mean *jerk*? Jerk, jerk, jerk." I can't help myself. I know I'm being terrible—it's just that I'm so sad.

"We have to figure out what's going on," Roo says, ignoring me.

"He loves birds more than he loves us, that's what's going on," I inform her. "He didn't want to spend time with us today because he had to *work*! Not that it's been seven months or anything since he last saw us."

"It's got to be some kind of a code," Roo whispers, still ignoring me.

"I guess all this time he's cared more about birds than about us," I say, so filled with self-pity that it takes me a second to register what Roo said. "What's got to be some kind of a code?"

"When he put his hand on my head," Roo says, more to herself than to me, "it was a code."

"Ruby Flynn Wade," I say, borrowing the severe tone and use of the full name from Mom, "what the heck are you talking about?"

"At least, I'm pretty sure it was a code," she says.

"A *code*?"

"See, usually he'd just rest his hand there, but today he squeezed my head," she murmurs thoughtfully.

"He *squeezed* your head?" For some reason I don't seem to be able to do anything but echo what Roo says.

"Yeah, like a BE CAREFUL squeeze. Or like a I'M-STILL-THE-SAME-AS-EVER-BUT-I-HAVE-TO-PRETEND-I'M-NOT squeeze," Roo says, her eyes meeting mine.

I'm sorry, but I don't believe squeezes can contain that much information. I wish I did. Roo's eyes are so filled with hope, though, that I'm not about to say anything.

"We've just got to figure out *what exactly* Dad is doing in the jungle," Roo informs me.

Thankfully, Mom opens the door to our room just then, so I don't have to respond to Roo, don't have to disagree or argue with her.

"My daughters," she says. I can tell she's trying very hard to seem cheerful. "My precious, priceless daughters, are you ready for bed?"

As we brush our teeth and put on shorts and T-shirts for sleeping, I can't stop thinking about what Roo said. Is it possible that Dad *was* trying to communicate with her? That there *are* things he wants us to know but couldn't say in front of Patricia Chevalier and/or Ken/Neth? That we *do* need to find out what he's doing in the jungle? That maybe he *is* his same old self but has to pretend he's not? That by being so cold to us he's actually trying to *tell* us something?

But the problem is that I'm not nine years old anymore, and I know life doesn't work like a mystery novel. It's usually just what it looks like it is, and what it looks like now is that Dad has become a crazy workaholic who cares more about jungle birds than about his own family.

We get into bed and Mom tucks us in—well, maybe *tuck* isn't the right word, since it's so hot you don't even need a sheet, and also it's really Roo she's tucking in, not me, because I'm too old for that. I'm in the top bunk since heights are the one thing I'm not scared of that Roo is. Also she sometimes still wets the bed—at least, she's been wetting the bed since The Weirdness started—and I don't want to get caught sleeping beneath that whole situation. So Mom is curled up on the bottom bunk with Roo, and when I peek down I can see their two pairs of feet sticking out, Roo's little feet and Mom's pretty feet. I bet Patricia Chevalier's feet aren't half as pretty as Mom's.

I pull out my poetry notebook, because that's what I do every night since I made my New Year's resolution, and try to write a poem about arriving at the jungle today, but it just makes me really, really tired to think all the way back to my first sighting of the volcano, not to mention everything that came after. Ugh.

Down below, Roo is asking Mom what an omen is, because Ken/Neth said that thing about the crisscrossing rainbows we saw from the plane being an omen, and I'm going, *Wow, how can she still be thinking about that?*

Mom says: "An omen is a sign."

56

"Like a stop sign?"

"No, like a sign of something to come. Something that's going to happen."

"Something exciting?"

"Well, it could be something good or something bad. Just . . . *some*thing."

"So Ken thinks something bad is going to happen?"

It bugs me to hear Roo say the name Ken so easily, as if she's used to it.

"No, monkey, I'm sure he was talking about the *good* kind of omen."

"Can we visit Dad again tomorrow?" Roo asks.

Mom is quiet for a second. "Maybe later in the week," she says softly. Somehow Roo knows to keep quiet and not argue about that right now. "Good night, okay, girls? You'll have a fun day tomorrow with your new Spanish tutor."

Oh yeah. The Spanish tutor. I'd almost forgotten.

When Mom stands up after Roo falls asleep, the metal bunk bed creaks. The mattresses are thin and covered in plastic, and I can feel the bed swaying. I look down at Mom standing there barefoot in her tulip dress. She bought that dress for this trip. She said she thought Dad would like it. She seemed to have forgotten that Dad never notices what anyone is wearing. He'd let us wear our Halloween costumes to the pizza parlor in June. And he thought she was terrifically smashing no matter what she wore. Sometimes he would even say she looked smashing when she looked *awful*, like right after Roo was born. Even though I was only three I remember how scary-ugly Mom looked then. The tulip dress swirls around Mom's feet. It seems wonderful to me again, not shabby, the way it seemed this afternoon. It must be made of silk.

"Hey, Mom."

"Hey, Mad."

"Is that a silk dress?"

"Nope. It's rayon."

Even in the not-very-nice light of the single bulb hanging from the ceiling, Mom looks nice. Her reddish hair all wild from the humidity. The freckles on her face and her arms too. I wish we could sleep with her tonight like we used to when The Weirdness began. We'd curl up, me and Mom and Roo, like three squirrels. But Mom says she has a hard time sleeping with Roo kicking her every thirty seconds.

Mom stretches up to kiss my forehead and then my nose. Before The Weirdness, she smelled fresh, like grapefruit and grass, but lately she smells different to me, and older, like dust, or black pepper. At first this creeped me out, but now it's just the way Mom smells. She smiles at me innocently, as though she doesn't know what I've been thinking, which of course she doesn't. Then she gives me a final kiss, which is what Roo and I call The Bad Kiss. See, there's this one kind of kiss Mom gives that we can't stand: she gets high up on your cheek, really close to your ear, and makes this loud kissing sound that makes you go deaf for a few seconds. I *hate* The Bad Kiss, but I've never in my whole life said anything because it is very, very mean to criticize the way someone kisses you. I'm still recovering from The Bad Kiss when Mom reaches up to pull on the chain attached to the lightbulb, and then we're in darkness.

I hear all sorts of noises I didn't hear before, grumblings and hoots and groans. I think about asking Mom to turn the light back on and leave it on, but when I open my mouth, what comes out is, "Everything will be normal again someday, right?" Even though it's dark I can tell that Mom becomes very still, her bare feet no longer making the sticky sound of footsteps.

"Madpie," she says, her voice terribly gentle, "good night, little one. I love you."

She's silhouetted for a second by the blue light of the pool and the pink fluorescent light of the SELV L DGE sign before the metal door slams shut.

After just a few seconds I start to feel like the sounds of the jungle are inside my head. Shrieking, moaning, flapping, yipping. The darkness more scary than velvety, the jungle noises more freaky than friendly. And the faucet of the little sink in the bathroom. It drips. I try to calm myself down by picturing all the things in the room. The foggy mirror that makes our faces look like blobs with blobs of hair on top, mine brown like Dad's and Roo's reddish like Mom's. The metal closet. The bare lightbulb. The window with no curtain. Our red rolly suitcase on the floor. Roo asleep below me. The orange metal door through which Mom disappeared. Will those little neon-green lizards stay on the door all night? Am I scared of them or do they seem like cute sidekicks? Not to complain or anything, but the Selva Lodge is kind of a weird place. Outside, and inside, growlings and scrapings.

And that's when I realize it: The Creepies have followed us here. They aren't just in Denver, surrounding our house, making us feel like we're being spied on, forcing Mom to call Ken/Neth and invite him to dinner and ask if he's heard anything from Dad. They're also here. Scaring me in the night. As though there are eyes everywhere. Wouldn't you think that by coming all the way down here, to a whole other country, we might get away from The Creepies?

"Mom!" I yell. "MOM!" I'm sure she's already in her room, reading a book in bed, and even if she were right outside, the metal door is so thick she probably couldn't hear anyway.

I have to get out of here. I can't stand to be stuck alone in the dark with The Creepies. No way am I going to be able to fall asleep. I

59

climb down from the top bunk and glance at Roo. In the tiny bit of bluish light coming from outside, I can see her sucking her thumb. She never sucks her thumb anymore. I tug on her arm to pull her thumb out of her mouth but she's fast asleep and her muscles are surprisingly tense. I can't move her hand at all. Roo is the World's Best Sleeper. Even The Creepies never kept her from sleeping well. I wish she'd wake up to keep me company. But she doesn't, and I'm old enough to know I shouldn't wake her. I don't want her to have to be awake, thinking about everything the way I am. I'm jealous that she can sleep like that after a day like this, but I guess I'm glad for her too.

I don't even try to find my flip-flops before grabbing the key and stumbling out of the room, barefoot. It's nice to be outside. The air feels warm and humid and jungly inside my nose. I'm about to knock on Mom's door when I spot two figures sitting on lawn chairs by the pool.

It's Mom. And Ken/Neth. Talking quietly. My heart stutters. *Why* does he have to have such a big crush on her? If he could just see her with Dad for two seconds—with Dad the way he used to be, I mean—he'd understand that he'd never in a billion years have a chance with her.

Something stops me from calling out to Mom and Ken/Neth, from saying hi and waving and going over to sit with them and telling Mom about The Creepies. Instead, I walk very quietly into the flowering bushes alongside the pool fence behind them. At first they're talking about boring stuff. Ken/Neth is telling Mom about all the different awards La Lava's yoga program has won. Yawn. But anything beats being alone with The Creepies.

Then, out of the blue, Mom says, "I miss him so much." She turns to face Ken/Neth and I can see the tendons in her neck (her neck is so long and elegant but the tendons can be scary; they only come out sometimes but never used to come out at all, back before you-know-what).

Ken/Neth puts his hand on Mom's shoulder. Gross.

"I just keep wondering what's going on with him—what's going on?" Mom murmurs. "It doesn't make sense. Unless—is he in love with that woman? That gorgeous woman? It would explain so much. He kept looking over at her today, as though he was asking her permission for every single thing he did."

Ken/Neth strokes Mom's shoulder. Stomachache.

"But he's not like that!" Mom says. "He's never been like that!"

"He's not like that," Ken/Neth agrees. Ten points for Ken/Neth, finally saying the right thing for once in his life.

"He kept looking at her, though," Mom says. "She *is* stunning. I'm just an old lady in comparison."

"Oh, Sylvia, you're lovely," Ken/Neth sighs. Shut it, Ken/Neth.

"I miss him so much," Mom says again. "I miss him so much. I miss him so much." She's crying now. Ken/Neth keeps stroking her shoulder.

I've never seen Mom like this. Not even when The Weirdness started. She always stayed very, very, very calm.

I really can't handle hearing her say that over and over again. It's just . . . too true. So I have to go, back into the night, alone.

I curl up later with Roo and she wets the bed.

It figures, I guess.

CHAPTER 5

The next morning Roo and I are hanging out in Mom's room, watching her get ready for the yoga retreat. Here's the problem: She doesn't have any yoga pants.

"I don't even know what yoga pants are, really," she says. "But they told Ken/Neth to tell me I need them. Maybe I'll just wear my running shorts?"

Right then there's a soft knock at the door and my stomach falls. Ugh. Please don't let it be Ken/Neth, butting in again on the few little moments Mom and Roo and I get to be alone together.

"Did you hear a knock?" Mom says. "Go check, Mad."

I drag my feet the whole way to the door, and when I open it I almost faint. It's the guy from the Selva Shop. Golden as ever.

"Um, hello?" I say in an unfriendly way, but just because I'm nervous.

"Hola," Mom says to him in her bad Spanish accent. "Come on in."

I realize that I'm standing there blocking the doorway, my hands on my hips, so I move to the side and he steps into the room.

"Good morning, *señora*," he says to Mom. "Señor Candy says he's bringing the golf cart around for you."

His English is *perfect*—no accent at all!

"Hey," I say, shocked, "I thought you couldn't speak English!"

"I went," he says to me.

"What?"

"I went," he repeats.

"You went where?" For some reason my voice comes out sounding angry, and I'm blushing a ton.

"Fui," he says, "it means *I went. I went to Volcán Pájaro de Lava* on the front, and on the back, *And you?"*

Oh yeah. That ugly T-shirt in the Selva Shop.

"Okay," I say nastily. "I wonder why you couldn't have told me that yesterday." What is *wrong* with me? Why am I being this way?

He just smiles.

"I can't believe you speak *English*," I mutter.

"Mad!" Mom says. "Relax!" Then she turns to Mr. Perfect English, all smiles, and says, "So, I take it you've met?"

"Well, I'm from Ohio," he tells me, "so, yes, I speak English."

"Ohio?"

"Yeah, but we don't know each other's names," Roo says to Mom.

"Well then," Mom says, "let's do our formal introductions."

"Of course, *señora*," he says, nodding politely, though there's something in his nod that's not quite polite, as though he's rolling his eyes at us even though he's not rolling his eyes.

"Please, call me Sylvia." I can tell Mom already thinks he's wonderful. She thinks he's a *very intelligent young man.* "Girls, meet Kyle."

"Hi, Kyle!" Roo practically shouts.

Kyle is *not* the right name for Kyle. Kyle is a name for one of the Popular Boys at school: Kyle is blond hair, blue eyes, good at sports, and always throwing too hard during dodge ball in gym class. This Kyle should be called . . . Mars, or something like that.

"Kyle," Mom continues, "meet Ruby and Madeline."

"You can call me Mad," I say, astonishing myself. Roo and Mom turn to stare at me. In the past I've only ever let Mom, Dad, and Roo call me Mad.

"Mad as in *mad*?" Kyle smiles as though he's made a joke.

I hope I was right to say he could use my nickname.

"Well," Mom says cheerily, "looks like everything should be fine around here, then."

"What about the babysitter?" Roo asks. "And the Spanish tutor?"

Why did she have to mention the babysitter in front of Kyle?

Mom looks puzzled and gestures at Kyle.

And my legs turn to total Jell-O while Mom informs Kyle that we have notebooks for the Spanish lesson, that we can order lunch at the Selva Café and charge it to the room, that we should get in the pool if we want, et cetera.

"Okay, girls, now you be good students today, okay?" Mom says, opening the door.

"Okay, Mom, now you be a good student today, okay?" Roo says right back at her.

Mom just smiles. From outside the gate Ken/Neth honks the golf cart horn twice. "All aboard, Sylvia!" he yells.

And I stand there quietly freaking out, because I just can't believe this golden-eyed teenager is my babysitter.

Once Mom is gone, Kyle refuses to speak a word of English. He jibbers and jabbers in Spanish as he leads us toward the pool, and I can hardly believe he's the same super-silent guy we saw in the Selva Shop yesterday. All this Spanish makes me tired. I can't understand *anything.* Maybe he's saying, "You're two ugly little monkeys and you'll never learn a word of Spanish. You're so ugly and stupid I feel bad for you." Or maybe he's saying, "Mad, you are so amazing. I know you're only twelve-almost-thirteen but please will you be my girlfriend?" Or maybe he's saying, "This is the *pool*. This is the *table*. This is the *chair*. That is the *sky*." Whatever it is, there's no way for us to know.

"How do you say 'Can we please go to the jungle, please?' in Spanish?" Roo interrupts him.

"¿Por favor, podemos ir a la selva, por favor?" Kyle says.

Roo repeats the question with a perfect accent, and then adds, "I'm serious, Kyle, we really have to go there right away, it's very important," as though she's known Kyle forever.

Oh great. She's still stuck on this whole Poor-Dad-we-have-to-figure-out-what's-going-on-it-must-have-something-to-do-with-the-jungle-his-hand-on-my-head-was-a-code thing. Man, I really do wish I was still young enough to believe this crazy stuff, like that Dad needs our help, that he hasn't stopped caring about us, that the only thing standing between us and the way our life used to be is a march into the jungle.

Kyle looks at Roo with new respect and says something in Spanish.

"No," Roo replies, miraculously understanding whatever he said, "we *aren't* like other girls. We don't just want to hang out at the pool all day. We *love* the jungle."

Then Kyle stands and strides out of the pool area toward the Selva Shop. Roo jumps up to follow him, and I jump up after her.

"We gotta get to the bottom of this," Roo mutters at me as we cross the concrete courtyard. One of Dad's most used phrases. "It's really, really, *really* important."

She skips along after Kyle, and the only thing I can do is follow them both.

At the Selva Shop—which seems to be closed now that he's not on duty—he pulls out a key and unlocks the door, then heads to the back of the room.

"Um, what are we doing here?" I say.

Kyle replies in Spanish, so of course I have no idea what he says. Saying things to us that I can't understand seems to be his new hobby. He reaches deep into the freezer on the back wall and pulls out three Popsicles. Then he slams the freezer door, herds us back out of the Selva Shop, and leads the way across the concrete court-yard to a narrow chain-link gate I somehow haven't noticed until this exact second.

Kyle pushes the gate open, and Roo bursts past him.

"Oh," she breathes, "the *jungle*."

And I have to admit, it does kind of take your breath away. Actu-ally stepping into the jungle is very, very different from just looking at it from an airplane or a van or a golf cart or a café. To feel your-self surrounded by layers and layers and layers of green. To sense the ground and the trees and the vines crawling with all sorts of strange life. A thrilled-terrified shiver runs down my spine.

There's a path leading into the jungle, its dirt as dark and rich as Dad's French-press coffee grounds. Kyle heads up that path, and Roo rushes behind him.

A few steps in, though, she glances back at me, ready to convince me that I have to follow her and Kyle. She knows what a scaredy-cat I am. She *always* has to convince me to do things we shouldn't be doing. But this time here I am, right behind her, no convincing needed. She gives me a surprised grin. What she doesn't know is that I'd follow Kyle straight to the top of this volcano.

Speaking of Kyle: He's moving fast, and Roo's little pause gave him a ten-foot lead. He seems barely aware of us as he pounces up the trail. The jungle noises, which got loud the instant we opened the gate, seem to get louder with each passing step. Roo, now that she knows I'm not too scared, is having more fun the scarier it gets. She looks at me, her face glowing with humidity. "Cool!" she says.

Right then a big bright green iguana darts across the path in front of us, and I only scream a tiny bit.

"*Super*-cool," Roo whispers, watching the iguana vanish into the dimness.

We walk for a while, I don't know how long, it's hard to keep track. We climb up black volcanic rocks and step over slippery vines as thick as Roo's arms. Big, poisonous-looking jungle flowers give off heavy smells. Some of them have petals that look like black velvet. Others seem to be made out of pink plastic. I start to get sort of used to seeing tons of little neon lizards darting every which way. I even start to feel friendly toward the endless line of tiny red ants marching up the trail alongside us, each one carrying a leaf twice its size.

Sometimes, out of the corner of my eye, I think I spot a monkey tail or monkey arm or monkey face in the nearby trees, but the second I turn to look, there's nothing there anymore.

"Hey!" Roo yelps, pointing. "Check it *out*! The Froot Loops bird!"

I look up and see that Roo's right. The toucan from the Froot Loops box—not that Mom ever lets us have Froot Loops—is crossing from tree to tree above us, its enormous red and pink beak leading the way.

I have this sudden feeling like I'm about to cry, but not from sadness, more from amazement.

"No *way*!" Roo squeals a few minutes later. "A butterfly with *eyes* on its wings!"

She takes off running and shoves past Kyle, chasing some sort of moth-looking thing. Kyle stops and waits for me to catch up with him, which makes me grin, until I realize he was just pausing to examine some moss on a tree trunk.

Anyway, we head upward together. Turning the bend, we almost bump into Roo, who's standing frozen in the path.

"What's wrong?" I ask her.

"It *did* have eyes on its wings! *Owl* eyes!" Roo whispers. "And *here's* a secret path."

"Where?" I say, looking around, not seeing anything resembling a secret path.

"Here." She points to the super-thick underbrush on the right-hand side of the trail, and I start to wonder if now fifty percent of my family is insane, because there's no way in heck that's any kind of a path. But then next to me I hear Kyle making a weird sound, a sort of cough-sigh-gasp. When I glance over at him, his cool, calm face doesn't look so cool and calm anymore.

So I look again at the side of the trail. And when I stare hard, I *do* start to see a path—at least, I think I do. Hardly a path, more like the echo of a path, just the tiniest bit of interruption in the jungle underbrush. The path we're on is practically a highway in comparison. Roo's secret path is narrow, almost too narrow for feet, and it looks dangerous, heading off into deeper, dimmer jungle.

"Listen," Kyle says darkly. It's weird to hear him speaking English again. It makes what he says next sound even scarier. "You can't ever go down that path. Okay? Swear you'll never go down it."

He's being so melodramatic that I think he must be joking.

"Ha," I say. "Very funny."

Usually Roo would join in, saying something like *Ooo, scary, scary, scary!* and shaking her body in a silly way as though spooky chills were running up and down it. But when I glance over at her, her face is solemn.

That's when I realize that Kyle's not joking. He's not joking at all.

"Swear to me," Kyle says. I feel like his eyes are burning my face. "On your father's life. That you will never go down that path."

Our father's life.

Are we allowed to swear on that nowadays?

"I swear," Roo says quietly, looking at the ground.

"Mad?" he says. I can't believe he's staring at me this way, so intensely.

"Sure," I say. If he knew me better he'd know I'd never go down such a freaky path.

"I want you to swear," he says.

"Okay, okay, I swear," I say, blushing. His eyes, jeez. He stares hard for a couple more seconds before his eyes let go of me.

Then he continues walking up Normal Path, and we follow him. But Roo keeps glancing back at Invisible Path.

"Pay attention to the trail or you're going to trip!" I scold her, but mainly I just don't want her to be so fascinated by that path.

"I can't believe you spotted it," Kyle says to Roo after a few minutes. "No one ever does."

Does he really have to say that? Doesn't he know his praise will only encourage her?

Roo wriggles with the compliment. "You have to notice the tiniest things in the world. You have to think like a bird."

She's quoting Dad—it's something he says about bird-watching—even though she's acting like she came up with it herself. Well, good for her. Dad taught Roo a ton about tracking birds, because Roo is a *natural*. And me? I'm a bad bird-watcher. I have no patience for it, and I definitely don't know how to think like a bird. Neither does Mom.

"So, what's down that path anyway?" Roo says, her voice eager, secretive.

Kyle replies in lightning-fast, impossible-to-understand Spanish.

"Tell me what it is! In *English*!" Roo groans.

Wanting to distract her from thinking about the creepy path, I ask Kyle how old he is. Roo loves knowing how old people are.

"Fourteen," Kyle says.

Wow. I can't believe he's only fourteen. Just about a year older than me. He seems so grown-up and fearless.

Right then we burst out of the jungle onto a ledge of black volcanic rock. On the hillside below and above the ledge, the never-ending tangle of jungle. The air and sky are much lighter now, without the jungle surrounding us. From here you can stare up at the volcano, huge and perfect against the pale sky. Roo gives an admiring whistle, and I would too if I could whistle, which I can't.

"El Mirador," Kyle announces.

He plops down on the ledge and we plop down next to him. The volcanic rock with all its little holes is rough against our bare legs. Kyle says some long thing in Spanish and points at the jungle and the volcano.

"This is *not* a good classroom!" Roo says. "Everything around here is *way* more interesting than Spanish class!"

Kyle responds by asking us a question in Spanish.

"What'd he say?" I whisper to Roo.

"I think he wants us to guess what El Mirador means," Roo whispers back. "If we get it right, we get to have our Popsicles."

Kyle looks expectantly at us.

"Well," Roo tells him, "I bet it comes from the verb *mirar*. To look. Like, a lookout."

I seriously don't know how my sister got so brilliant. Kyle nods and hands each of us a melted Popsicle.

"Ooo, *gracias*!" Roo says, accepting the messy gift, and she's not being sarcastic.

When I finally get mine open, it explodes out of its plastic wrapping, sticky green syrup spraying all over me. But it's still delicious in a way, the sugar and the liquid.

Kyle looks at me—golden, yes! but whatever—and says something. Then he says the same thing again, and again. A short sentence. Obviously he wants me to repeat it. So, eventually, I try.

"Yo ab lo ven te i dio mas."

Kyle nods and repeats it several more times. I try again and again. Then it's Roo's turn. Kyle looks at her. She's perched behind us on the ledge, staring up at the volcano, her chin purple with Popsicle. *"Hola,"* he says. *"¡Hola!"* He has to say *hola* six times and tap her knee before she starts paying attention to him instead of the volcano.

"Yo hablo veinte idiomas," she says beautifully on her very first try.

So Kyle focuses on me again, making me repeat that stupid sentence like a hundred times. He keeps correcting my pronunciation, but I can't hear the difference between the way he says it and the way I say it.

Finally I get so annoyed I shout at the volcano: *"¡YO HABLO VEINTE IDIOMAS!"*

Kyle nods his approval. I seem to have gotten it right that time. I guess now he's satisfied with my Spanish, because—O wonder of wonders—he actually responds in English when I ask him, "What does that mean anyway, *Yo hablo veinte idiomas?*"

"I speak twenty languages," he says, lying down on the ledge.

"I speak twenty languages!" The least useful sentence he could have possibly taught us. "You are *so* mean!"

He just grins.

"You have to admit, it's funny," he says.

"Look, it's not my fault that I'm not fluent in two languages like some geniuses around here."

"I'm not a genius," he says with a shrug. "It's just that my dad is from here and my mom is from the States, so we use both languages. I was born in Ohio, but I spend every summer here working at the Lodge and bird-watching."

"You like bird-watching?" I say. "Our dad does too."

"Yeah," Kyle says, still lying down. "Your dad is my hero."

"Ken's not our dad," I say flatly.

Kyle rolls his eyes. "Not that goof," he says. "I mean your *dad*. The Bird Guy."

I get that hot, burny feeling of tears.

"You know our dad?" I whisper. If Kyle knows Dad, maybe he knows something about what *happened* to Dad.

"I didn't say I know him," Kyle says. "I said he's my hero."

Sometimes I forget that Dad is famous. At least to bird-watchers. Every bird-watcher in the world knows who James Wade is. I wait for Roo to chime in, to start bragging about Dad, but she doesn't. I turn around to see what the heck is stopping her, since telling people how awesome Dad is is her favorite hobby: *He's the best bird-tracker on the planet, and seriously, I'm not just saying that because he's my dad! The magazines say it too.*

But Roo isn't there.

"Roo!" I scream.

Kyle jolts up.

"Roo—she's gone, she's missing, where is she!" I panic.

He stands and grabs me by the wrist and pulls me running down the trail. If I weren't freaking out I might enjoy the feeling of his fingers, but right now I couldn't care less about Kyle.

"Roo, Roo, Roo, Roo, Roo, Roo!" I shout, pretending that somewhere out there in the jungle she's shouting back, Mad, Mad, Mad, it's okay, I'm okay, don't worry, relax. "Um, hello, shouldn't we be looking for her? Like, around *here*?" I yell at Kyle.

But he just keeps dragging me down the trail, and I keep slipping in the mud, and I keep calling for Roo.

Then he stops very suddenly, and I'm going, *Okay, why are we stopping now?* until I realize (of course, duh, here we are) this is the spot where the dim, secret path branches off from the nice, normal trail.

Of *course*. Where else would Roo have gone? If I'd stopped panicking for half a second I'd have figured it out too.

Kyle looks over at me.

"I really, really, really don't want to do this," he says. Then he tugs on my hand and together we plunge down Invisible Path.

We can't walk hand in hand on the narrow path, so Kyle lets go of me. I immediately start to feel more freaked out, if that's possible, more worried about Roo than I've ever been (and I've worried about Roo a *lot* in my lifetime). For some reason, though, I don't think I should keep calling her name. There's a hush over this part of the jungle, the animal sounds somehow muted here, a kind of quiet that seems as though it might have ears. I have this weird feeling that by saying Roo's name I might put her in extra danger. Instead, we just creep down the path, vines and leaves smacking our legs and faces.

"Faster," I hiss at Kyle. "Faster, please."

He tries to speed up but it's hard. The path is so vague, and slippery.

We've only been on Invisible Path a little while when there's this enormous whooshing sound above us, and for a second I'm positive the volcano is erupting, until I realize it's a sound I recognize.

We hear the rain for a moment before we feel it. It's up there, hitting the top leaves of the tallest trees, and now here it comes. I look up and see it rushing toward us like we're standing beneath a waterfall, and I think we're going to drown in it, so I shut my eyes and brace myself.

But the water doesn't hit.

I open my eyes and look up again. What I see is a huge blue . . . flower, I guess. Kyle is standing behind me, his chest almost touching my back, holding it over us like an umbrella. Its big, waxy blossom keeps us completely dry while the monsoon booms all around us.

I look back at him and can't help but smile in amazement. Amazed by the umbrella flower. Amazed that I'm standing in the jungle beneath an umbrella flower with this boy.

"How did you *do* that?" I ask, but it's way too loud to talk.

When the amazement wears off a few minutes later, though, I start to get really mad that the dumb old monsoon is slowing us down. We *have* to keep going. We can walk in the rain with the umbrella flower to protect us. I nudge Kyle and give him a come-on-wimp-let's-keep-walking face, but he's gazing off down the trail, looking shocked. Around the bend about twenty yards away, blurred by the heavy rain, comes a blue blob. It's some kind of crazy jungle creature, and I'm terrified, remembering all the things that could harm Roo—the jaguars and tarantulas and snakes and poisonous plants and sheer cliffs and things I can't even imagine. I inch closer to Kyle, because that creature is coming right at us, making my heart do acrobatics.

Then the little blob waves happily and practically dances down the trail toward us beneath her blue umbrella flower. She looks very small, walking between the walls of jungle in the rain, and I just want to squeeze her and cuddle her. But also I want to yell at her, and I bet Kyle does too, although no one can say anything over the sound of the water. The three of us stand there under the umbrella flowers, waiting.

When the monsoon ends, as quickly as it began, the first words out of Kyle's mouth are "How did you do that?"

"Do what?" Roo asks perkily.

"That!" Kyle says, pointing at her blue umbrella flower, which is already beginning to shrink. Ours too is shriveling.

"Well, you did it too, so I guess you know how I did it," Roo says. Kyle still looks shocked. "*No one* can do that," he says.

"I can do it," Roo says, "and you can do it."

"How did you know which one to pick?" Kyle demands. "How did you know where to squeeze it?"

"I don't know," Roo says. "I just . . . did it."

The umbrella flowers are deflating very, very quickly now. We watch as they turn into normal-sized blue flowers with waxy petals. I reach out for Roo's flower and she passes it to me. I squeeze it here, there, and everywhere. But nada. Go figure.

"Gee whiz," Roo says, "I can't believe it's already after 3:08. That day sure flew by."

"It's not after 3:08," Kyle says. "Why would it be after 3:08?"

"Ken says the monsoon comes at 3:08 every day. He says we can set our watches by it."

"That guy," Kyle says, shaking his head. "First of all, around here we don't call it the monsoon, we call it La Lluvia, with capital *L*s. And it does come every afternoon, but not always at the same time."

"*Lluvia,*" Roo repeats. "Even though it starts with an *L* you make a *Y* sound 'cause there are two *L*s in a row, right?"

She's doing that thing she does where she distracts you from her disobedience by bringing up other topics. It's just so Roo of her that I want to grab her up in a ginormous hug, but I think it'll be better for her in the long run if I yell at her now.

"Roo!" I freak out. "What were you doing? You swore you wouldn't go down here! I'm *so* mad at you!"

"Don't be mad, Mad," she says, grinning.

"How far did you get?" Kyle asks her.

"Well, La Lluvia started," she says, "so I had to turn back."

Kyle seems relieved for half a second before getting that dark look on his face.

"Ruby Wade," he says solemnly.

"Ruby Flynn Wade," I correct him.

"You have to believe me that what you just did was very dangerous," he says with a quiet fury. "Now do you swear for real that you'll never go down this path again?"

It's all pretty intense and I can't help wondering if Kyle is overreacting a bit. But he looks so very serious, and it's so obvious that he truly doesn't want us going down Invisible Path. Man, if I had Roo's personality rather than my own, I know I'd be *dying* to find out what it is that Kyle doesn't want us to see.

"I swear for real," Roo says with a smile.

Kyle glares at her. "Don't smile," he says.

"I swear for real," Roo says, this time with a huge, exaggerated frown.

He glares at her more and then turns and leads us back toward Normal Path.

CHAPTER 6

"Girls," Mom says that night at dinner in the Selva Café, smiling spacily into her piña colada, "I have a very special surprise for you."

She's been sort of weird ever since she got back from yoga this afternoon. I don't quite know how to explain it. Like, she's got this permanent smile on her face, which sounds like a good thing, but somehow it's just not. Maybe because her eyes are *so* calm, like robot eyes.

"Oh boy! What is it! Tell us, tell us!" Roo squeals. "Do we get to go see Dad now?"

Mom frowns for half a second before returning to her yoga smile. I frown too. I'm sorry to say it, but I don't really want to see Dad today, or tomorrow, or any time until he's normal again.

"No," Mom says, "it's something else entirely. Something you've never done before."

"A hot-air balloon ride?" Roo guesses. She loves hot-air balloons.

"No." Mom deepens her yoga smile. "It's a facial!" she says with a joyous sigh.

"A facial!" Roo echoes, imitating Mom's joyous sigh. Then, "What's a facial?"

"A massage for the face," Mom explains in her new, super-calm voice.

Ken/Neth butts in: "La Lava wants to treat you two girls to papaya-and-cilantro facials in its world-class massage facility!"

Hello, La Lava brochure. I hate it that all the other people in the Selva Café probably think he's our dad, and probably think we look like a Very Nice Family. It makes me want to glare at my rice and beans, so I do.

"Papaya and cilantro?" I say, as though I've never heard of anything more disgusting.

"Papaya and cilantro!" Roo exclaims.

"Good, I'm so glad you're excited," Mom says, giving Roo her deepest yoga smile yet. But I don't get a piece of that smile, not even a crumb. "It's an incredibly generous gift. Patricia Chevalier scheduled your facials for ten a.m. tomorrow. That's when Relaxation and Rejuvenation starts, so we can all head over together in the morning."

"What about Spanish lessons?" I blurt out.

Mom turns her smile on me, only now it's a surprised smile. "Mad, I didn't know you enjoyed Spanish so much! I'm sure Kyle can tutor you tomorrow afternoon."

"*¡Ay, que bueno!*" Roo says cutely. "Hey, we can visit Dad when we go there for our face massages, right?"

"Maybe," Mom says, looking at Ken/Neth and giving a tired little sigh. He—ugh—rubs her shoulder. As politely as possible, Mom scooches a few centimeters away from him.

Just then the fried plantains arrive and Ken/Neth moves his hand (phew!). I'm sitting there, simply trying to enjoy my plantains and not be grossed out by the insanely enormous moths flocking to the lights above us, when Mom starts acting all blissed-out again.

"So," she says, her normally energetic voice gone all soft and breathy, "today, during Relaxation and Rejuvenation, I was thinking about Lava-Throated Volcano trogons and how depressed your dad got when they were declared extinct."

Ken/Neth starts to look uncomfortable. What, does it really bother him that much when Mom mentions something having to do with Dad?

"I was just thinking how beautiful they were," Mom continues, "and how we're here in this beautiful place of theirs but they aren't anymore. And I've always loved birds that mate for life. James was furious to think that when he was a kid he could have seen a Lava-Throated Volcano trogon in the flesh but for his own kids that possibility no longer existed." Even though she's saying sad things, Mom's voice remains weirdly tranquil.

"Well, that's a real upper, Sylvia," Ken/Neth says in a joking tone, but it falls way flat.

"I'd do *anything*," Roo says, gazing dreamily out at the jungle, "to see a Lava-Throated Volcano trogon!"

And right then, at that exact second, the Selva Café plunges into darkness.

Startled yelps come from all over the restaurant, and you can hear kids calling out for their parents in different languages—Dad! ¡Mamá! ¡Papá! Mom! Da!

In the darkness, someone grabs my wrist. At first I think it's Roo until I realize it's an adult hand, a large adult hand, much larger than Mom's, and strangely cold. It must be Ken/Neth's, though I never noticed he had such thick fingers.

There's some shuffling to my right, I hear Roo muttering in Spanish, and my wrist gets yanked and then dropped.

Seconds later, a candle is lit in the far corner of the room, followed soon by another, a third, a fourth. Once there's enough light, I see that Ken/Neth is already back in his seat, across the table from me and Roo.

And the witch and Señor Villalobos are standing behind Roo's chair, gazing down at her in the candlelight. I can see the witch's frown through her black lace veil. Creepy! At least Señor Villalobos is smiling his gentle smile. Roo looks up at them and grins nervously.

The witch hisses something at Roo in Spanish, but of course I can't make out a single word. I'm glad it's not me she's hissing at. Roo loses her grin and lowers her eyes.

Now that there are so many candles the room feels bright again.

"Well, how 'bout that," Ken/Neth says cheerfully. "Never a dull moment in the jungle, right? Hey, another order of fried bananas, anyone? *Más plátanos, por favor, señora.*"

But without electricity, no fried plantains. Duh.

"His face looked so strange," Roo says from the bottom bunk. I'm in the top bunk, writing a haiku in my notebook, nice and easy because it's just three lines, five plus seven plus five syllables.

"Listen, Roo, I'm trying to write a *poem* here, okay?" I say, losing count of the syllables.

"His face looked *so* strange!" Roo repeats, annoyed.

"*Whose* face?" I ask, annoyed right back at her for interrupting my haiku, which I just started a few minutes ago when the electricity came back on and we could finally turn off our flashlights. I kind of go into my own world when I'm writing a poem. Roo is usually very respectful of my writing. I never show my poems to anyone besides her, and she's a big fan, so she's good at being quiet when I'm trying to concentrate.

But tonight she's not going to let me finish my haiku.

"*Dad's* face," she says as though I'm the biggest idiot on planet Earth.

"Dad's face?"

"You didn't see him? I thought you saw him too!" Roo says. "How could you not *see* him? Right before the electricity went out, he was there, coming out of the jungle. I saw his face, and it looked *strange*!"

What the *heck* are you talking about, you crazy little bean? I want to say, but I'm not mean enough to actually say it. "It was pretty dark out there," I say instead. "I'm sure it wasn't Dad. He's at La Lava."

"It was Dad," Roo says, so confident she doesn't even need to raise her voice. "It was Dad. He looked . . . weird, though."

I sigh and close my notebook. "Weird how?"

"Weird like . . . scared."

Dad scared? I couldn't even picture it. Dad just wasn't ever scared.

"Okay, Roo," I say. I don't believe her.

"You don't believe me," she says. Roo is very smart that way. "I can't believe you don't believe me!"

"Dad is never scared," I remind her.

"I know!" she says. "Exactly! *That's* why it's scary!"

The word *scary* reminds me of something important I forgot to ask Roo amid the chaos of lighting candles and finding flashlights.

"Hey, what did Señora Villalobos say to you when she was standing there behind your chair after the electricity went out?"

"I don't know," Roo says.

"You don't know?" I *know* she knows.

"I don't know," Roo says again, "but I think she said, 'Don't say that.'"

"'Don't say that'? Don't say what? What did you say?"

"I don't know. I said 'Dad' when I saw Dad."

"She doesn't want you to say 'Dad'?"

"She was speaking *Spanish*, okay? I don't know. Maybe I'm wrong."

We both get quiet. For some reason it feels like we're having a fight even though we're not. I don't want us to be annoyed with each other right now.

"Ken grabbed my wrist really hard when the lights went out," I tell her, trying to make it so that we're sharing our creepy secrets rather than just sitting there with them.

"That wasn't Ken," Roo informs me.

"What do you mean? How would you know?" Little Miss Know-It-All, I want to add.

"That guy grabbed me too. I had to bite his arm so he'd let go of us. And he had a hairy arm. Not like Ken/Neth's."

It's true. Ken/Neth has practically no arm hair.

"You *bit* his arm?"

"Yeah," Roo says. I can hear the shrug in her voice. "I'm a good biter."

It's true. She got kicked out of more than one preschool for biting.

"Well. Who was he?" I ask her.

Then below me I hear a familiar crinkle of paper and feel suddenly slammed with tiredness. That's the sound of Roo pulling out The Very Strange and Incredibly Creepy Letter.

"Roo," I say.

She doesn't respond.

"Roo," I say again.

She still doesn't respond.

"Please put that away," I order her. I don't want to lean over and glare at her because then I'd have to see The Very Strange and Incredibly Creepy Letter.

"It doesn't make sense, but I *know* it makes sense," Roo says. "We have to break the code. We *have* to. Then we'll know what's up."

"Roo, it's time for bed."

But Roo ignores me. Quietly she reads aloud the nonsense poem from Dad:

> *"There was a little girl*
> *Who had a little world*
> *Right in the middle of her pretend*
> *And when she was trill*
> *She was very, very trill*
> *And when she was smart*
> *She was silly."*

Just a messed-up version of the old nursery rhyme we always used to say to Roo when she was naughty (*There was a little girl / Who had a little curl / Right in the middle of her forehead / And when she was good / She was very, very good / And when she was bad / She was horrid*). But the really freaky part is the drawings, all the little-girly flowers and vines and butterflies around the border. As though Dad had been magically transformed into an eight-year-old girl. Never in our whole lives has Dad ever drawn anything for us. He is a Very Bad Drawer. Mom's the one who can draw.

"I LOVE YOU LEFT RIGHT UP DOWN LOL! XOXO, DADDY," Roo reads from the bottom of the page. Also freaky. Dad would

never say *LOL*. He probably doesn't even know what it stands for. And he's never signed a letter *XOXO*. And he's never called himself Daddy. He's always signed off with something like, "Love, Your Crazy Old Stinky Bird-Brained Dad."

I'm relieved to hear Roo putting The Very Strange and Incredibly Creepy Letter back in its envelope. I tug on the chain of the lightbulb and the room goes black.

"Mad," Roo says, her little voice floating up to me in the darkness, "there's something I have to show you tomorrow. When we get back here after the face massages."

But I pretend I'm already asleep.

CHAPTER 7

When I step into the Selva Shop the next morning, Kyle
doesn't even look up. He's sitting behind the counter, gazing down at the binoculars hung around his neck. I give the door an
extra rattle, hoping that'll get his attention, but he keeps ignoring
me. I was excited to come here, but now I just want to sneak away,
and I would, except that Mom told me to tell Kyle we'll be gone this
morning and would like to have our Spanish lesson this afternoon
instead.

"Um," I say.

Finally Kyle looks up.

"Hola," he says coolly. As though he's talking to any old tourist.
As though we didn't stand together in the rain yesterday beneath a
blue umbrella flower.

"We'regoingtoLaLavathismorningsonoSpanishlessonokay?" I say
super quick.

He gazes at me, his eyes dull, barely even golden right now.

"Okay," he says as though he couldn't care less.

Ouch.

"Well," I say, "bye." I turn and get out of there as quickly as possible.

I'm so bugged by him that I don't even realize until we're halfway to La Lava that I forgot to tell him we'd like to have Spanish class this afternoon instead. Oh *well*.

When Ken/Neth drops us off at the lobby of La Lava, Roo immediately asks Patricia Chevalier if we can see Dad. Patricia Chevalier gives her an exquisite smile.

"I apologize, sweetie," she says, "but your father is working in the jungle today."

Roo looks terrifically disappointed.

"Now, now, sweetie," Patricia Chevalier tells her. "You are going to love your facial. Please, follow me. I will show you our world-class spa facilities."

It's weird to hear such nice words spoken without niceness. I wonder if Mom and Roo notice the not-niceness too. But Mom just smiles yogically at all of us before vanishing down a hallway to wherever Relaxation and Dumbation takes place.

Patricia Chevalier leads me and Roo down a white marble staircase right off the lobby, each step as wide as three normal steps. La Lava seems even more spectacular now than it did the first time we came. Maybe because we've been spending so much time at the crazy old Selva Lodge, but everything here seems a hundred times more elegant than anything I've ever seen. And the air smells like honey! And it's the perfect temperature. And the sound of the waterfalls makes my heart feel smooth.

The marble staircase goes down and down. "Ooo, it is *so* pretty here," Roo coos. "I want to drink these stairs—they look like *milk*!"

At the bottom of the stairs, Patricia Chevalier veers to the right, around a curving white wall. Roo skips ahead a few feet and I hurry to keep up with her. I turn the bend just in time to see her crash head-on into a woman in a turquoise silk robe coming from the opposite direction.

Oh. My. God.

I can't breathe.

Roo just crashed into *Vivi*.

Vivi looks shocked and Patricia Chevalier looks enraged. Roo lets out a shaky giggle and I fall back a step to hide behind Patricia Chevalier.

But Vivi stares right at me, which makes my vision go all blurry with nervousness. I remember the way she glared at the Spaniards in *Rosa of the Flowers and Knives*.

"I didn't realize children were allowed down here," Vivi says. Her voice is low, sort of rich and sort of harsh, different than it sounds in the movies.

"Oh, well, it is, you know . . . ," Patricia Chevalier fumbles. It's *so* weird to see her acting this awkward. ". . . a . . . an . . . unusual . . . circumstance."

Vivi breezes past Patricia Chevalier, still staring at my face. Then—get this!—she touches my forehead with her thumb.

Vivi. Touching me. I have goose bumps.

"I wish," Vivi says, "I could just rip this skin right off you and put it on me."

Patricia Chevalier gives a long, high, fake laugh.

"Thank you," I whisper, though I'm not sure if it's the right thing to say.

But it makes Vivi smile, and her smile is partway gorgeous and partway fierce.

"Thank *me*?" she says, her thumb still on my forehead. "Don't, *chica*. I'm not joking. I've been waiting *three days* for my treatment"—

she shoots her glare at Patricia Chevalier, who blushes nervously—"and they've got me playing a twenty-one-year-old princess next, and I've got somewhere I have to be next Monday."

"It's only called a catfight if men are watching." The words suddenly burst out of me. "Otherwise it's a clash of goddesses." My favorite Vivi quote from *The Secret Life of Cleopatra*.

"Well, how about that," Vivi says, looking pleased. "Someone's been paying attention."

She half pats, half slaps my cheek and then drops her hand.

"*Adiós*, kiddos. Have fun," she says before vanishing up the stairway in a swirl of turquoise silk.

Roo and I stare at Vivi's back and then at each other. She's *just* like Cleopatra! Nice and mean at the exact same time.

Now Patricia Chevalier seems eager to get rid of us. She hurries down the hallway, her face pale and her hands trembling. "It could have been worse," she mutters to us, but then I realize she's muttering into a tiny microphone clipped to the inside of her blouse.

"Here," she says coldly, pausing at a beautiful wooden door carved with images of naked dancing women. "Ladies' changing room. Your temporary lockers are labeled with your names. Put on the robes and wait in the Silent Lounge."

Then she turns and marches away from us, her very high heels making those gunshot sounds on the marble.

It's wonderful once she's gone. Roo pushes open the naked-women door and we step into a room that leaves even Roo speechless for a moment. The floor is a whirling red and gold mosaic. There's a row of golden sinks, and between each sink is a red bowl shaped like a pair of hands, and each pair of hands cups a floating pink flower. Across from the golden sinks there's a row of showers carved from volcanic rock, the golden shower curtains pulled aside to reveal golden spigots gleaming against the black rock. The whole place is fragrant with a smell somewhere between cinnamon and roses. In the middle of the room, there's this enormous black cauldron filled with floating red flowers.

"The *walls*!" Roo exclaims, rushing toward the nearest one.

The walls, I notice then, are covered in a thin film of water, like a permanent waterfall, the soft swoosh running down black marble. When Roo touches the wall, the water parts around her hand. She looks back at me and squeals.

We have the place to ourselves. Even though there are two rows of wooden lockers, some labeled with names, no one else is around. We find our lockers easily, MADELINE and RUBY in red-ink cursive. Dark green terry-cloth robes hang inside them.

"Dang," says Roo. "I want a silk robe like Vivi had!"

I look over at her, about to tell her she's a spoiled brat.

"Just *kidding*!" she says. "Jeez!"

We take off our T-shirts and shorts and sneakers and put on the robes, then lock the lockers and hang the little golden keys around our wrists.

"So, what now?" Roo says, walking toward one of the water-walls and running her fingers along it. I follow her, hesitantly sticking my fingertips into the rushing water—who knows if we're even allowed to touch it. I'm surprised by how smooth and soothing the water feels.

"Okay, so is this the so-called Silent Lounge?" I ask Roo, gazing at the pink velvet couches and wondering which of them might qualify as the "Silent Lounge."

"Hmm," Roo says thoughtfully, looking all around the room. Then she lets out a soft yelp and rushes off toward a dark, narrow doorway beyond the showers—a doorway I didn't notice until this exact second.

I step behind Roo into a small room that feels *way* peaceful, no gold or red or pink here. It's a very quiet, very gray room, lit only by a few candles tucked into crevices in the volcanic rock walls. In the center there's a low table with a pitcher and glasses. The table is surrounded by many gray cubes, large enough to sit or lie on.

"Well," Roo says, "I guess this is it!"

"Shhh!" I say. Somehow it feels wrong to talk here. It feels like the kind of place where you shouldn't make any noise at all, where you should move in slow motion, but Roo skips over to the table and pours whatever's in the pitcher into two of the glasses.

We haven't even had time to discuss the drink—is it iced tea? juice? water? and what's that flavor? grapefruit? lavender? *basil?*— when we hear our names, very softly but coming from all around, as though the walls are talking.

"Madeline. Madeline."

"Ruby. Ruby."

It's too dim to see where they came from, but here they are, one touching my elbow and the other touching Roo's, two women in gray pajama outfits, separating us and leading us out of the Silent Lounge through two different narrow doorways. I know it's silly, but I start missing Roo the second she disappears through her doorway.

I had no idea that getting a facial meant being blindfolded. But that's the first thing this lady does after leading me down a short hallway and helping me onto a high bed and tucking the sheet in: She wraps something around my eyes so I can't see. I get only a glimpse of the small, shadowy room (a pot of orchids in the corner, a gleaming gray wall) before my eyes are sealed.

"What's your name?" I whisper, but I guess she doesn't speak English, because she just strokes my forehead and puts on some weird music that sounds like lots of gongs being hit one after the other.

Then she spreads all sorts of things on my face, hot things and cold things, and then she rubs my face and then there's all this steam blowing in my face, and then she starts picking at the one tiny little zit I happen to have high up on my forehead where it's covered by my bangs anyway.

"Ouch!" I say, but that doesn't slow her down.

Finally she's done with the stupid zit and I don't feel her hands for a while and I'm going, *Thank you, it's over, I'll never be doing that again, thank you very much,* when suddenly she lifts up my head and starts wrapping this too-hot towel around it, all the way down to my neck. I try to stay calm but really I can hardly breathe—the towel is so hot and I'm scared it's burning my face off, I'm scared I'm going to suffocate—and then she takes her hands and holds the base of my neck and starts massaging my throat, and then her fingers start tightening and I'm like, *Oh my god, she's going to strangle me.*

I pull my arms out from under the sheet and grab at her hands. I feel her resisting but somehow I yank the towel off and rip off the blindfold and here I am, alive, in the gray room with its pot of orchids and gleaming wall, but then I realize it's not a wall, it's a window, and standing there in the golden light on the other side of that window is my dad, and he's staring in at me with this horribly sad expression on his face. But before I can wave at him or move toward him or anything, the light flicks off and it's just a gleaming gray wall again, and it's like maybe I saw him, maybe I didn't, and the woman flings the blindfold back over my eyes and says, very softly, in English, so I guess she does speak English after all: *"Feel free to lie here as long as you wish to absorb the experience."*

"Wow, oh *wow*," Roo is going as we come up the marble staircase. "That was *way* wow! Oh my gosh. Did they put steam on you? Did they wrap a nice warm towel around your head? Didn't it smell *so good*?"

Roo doesn't notice that I'm not saying anything. I'm still all trembly after seeing Dad like that. Dad, on the other side of the glass, staring in, looking sadder than anything, while that lady pressed on my throat.

I want to tell Roo about it, but also I don't.

Roo's babbling fades into a happy sigh, and we're both quiet as we enter the lobby—so quiet that Patricia Chevalier and Ken/Neth, who are standing very close together behind the large golden rectangle of the reception desk, don't notice us. Patricia Chevalier is whispering and yelling at the same time—like she's screaming at Ken/Neth, but she's doing it under her breath. Ken/Neth nods slowly as he listens to her. I hear her say something, something "pressure!" And then something, something *"desperate."*

When Patricia Chevalier spots us, she stops talking midsentence. Ken/Neth looks up and his worried face turns into a smiley face.

"Heya, girls," he says, as though he wasn't getting screamed at two seconds ago.

"Hello, little ladies." Patricia Chevalier gives us her prettiest smile, not at all like the last time we saw her. "How were your facials?"

Rather than saying *Horrible/Scary/Awful, you freaky woman,* I let Roo respond: "It was SO COOL! I got this papaya stuff, and these hot towels, and now I feel *bea-u-tiful.*"

Patricia Chevalier giggles politely, but I can tell she's bored by Roo and is thinking about other things. "Mr. Candy will be taking you back to the Selva Lodge now, all right, *señoritas?*" she says before Roo even finishes the word *beautiful.*

CHAPTER 8

I'm exhausted by the time we get back to the Selva Lodge. It's tiring to be around someone who's always trying to be funny. Ken/Neth seriously needs to be reminded that we're nine and twelve, not three and six. We're too old for pirate accents.

"Go and tell Kyle you're ready for Spanish, okay, girls? Got to head back to my big-boy business at La Lava." Big-boy business—what's *wrong* with this guy? "Toodle-oo!" he hoots, creepy-friendly, as he steers out of the parking lot after dropping us off.

Roo was all droopy and yawny in the golf cart on the way over, and I'm sure she wants to take a nap, just like I do, so I head toward our room. It wore me out, seeing Dad like that.

"Let's not tell Kyle we're back yet," I say. "I forgot to tell him we wanted a Spanish lesson this afternoon anyway."

"Yeah!" Roo whispers excitedly, skipping ahead of me. I look over at her, surprised. A few seconds ago she looked like she was about to fall asleep.

But when we get back to our room, Roo doesn't flop down on her bunk. Instead, she starts grabbing things—water bottle, sunblock, bug spray—and shoving them into her backpack.

"Come on," she orders, "Hurry up!" She pulls my backpack from under the bed, which makes The Very Strange and Incredibly Creepy Letter slide out from where she hid it. I kick the letter back into the shadows. Roo reaches into the closet and throws my raincoat at me. "Quick! Pack this."

Excuse me, but who's the older sister here?

"This is our big chance," Roo says, talking fast. "NoKyleNoMom NoKen. Now we can go figure out what's going on."

"What's going on *where*?" I stand there, arms crossed, my backpack and raincoat relaxing on the floor while Roo freaks out.

"I *told* you I had to *show* you something, remember?" Roo yanks some Jolly Ranchers from the front pocket of her backpack. "Oh good," she says, examining the bright handful, "we have food."

"What's going on *where*?" I repeat, as if I don't already know. As if I'm not already filled with dread.

"In the *jungle* on the *volcano*," Roo says. "Duh," she adds, but not in a mean way.

"Roo. I am your babysitter."

"I think we're sort of babysitting each other now," Roo says. But she's not really paying attention to me. She's tugging at the zipper of her overstuffed backpack. It's a tiny backpack. It can barely hold anything.

"I forbid you to leave this room," I tell her.

With a huge final tug, she zips her backpack closed.

"Don't forget your raincoat," she says as she heads toward the door. "You're going to need it. I can just use a jungle flower."

What, she doesn't think I'm capable of turning those blue flowers into umbrellas? I'm offended. Even though she's right.

"Roo," I repeat, "I forbid you to leave this room."

"Mad. I forbid you to forbid me to leave this room." She pushes the heavy orange door open and as soon as she steps out it slams shut behind her.

I run to the door, open it, and yell after her, "I'm *not* coming. Mom will *kill* you!"

Ten feet away and counting. Roo shrugs her shoulders in that bratty way of hers. I close the door. For half a second I lie down on Roo's bunk and pretend to fall asleep, betting she'll be back any instant. But then I realize Roo won't come back. Of course she won't. She's way, way, way more stubborn than I am. So I shove my raincoat and a water bottle into my backpack. I run out the door and across the courtyard to the back gate.

She's only thirty or so feet up the trail, strolling slowly, knowing I'll be coming along.

"Hey," she says when I get to her.

"Hey," I say.

We walk along together as though this adventure is something we both agreed to.

"I have to protect you," I say, to prove I'm not here just because Roo bossed me.

"I have to protect you," she says.

"Hello, is there an echo here?"

"Hello, is there an echo here—here—here?"

Dad used to do that. Make echoing sounds at the end of sentences. He loves echoes. Once we went on a trip to the canyons in Utah. Echoes everywhere. Dad was so happy, yelling up at the canyons. It makes me sad to think of it, of that time when Dad was happy, when we were all happy, and for some reason thinking of it makes me feel extra worried about me and Roo, worried about what we're doing right now and what might happen in the jungle and what kind of dangerous things there are in the world that we don't even know about. So I try one last time.

"Roo. We're going back. Right now. This is too dangerous. If you don't come back right now, I'm going to tell Mom."

"If you don't stay with me, I'll bite you," Roo says, speeding up, forcing me to speed up alongside her.

Okay, I'll admit it—I'm scared of Roo. Her bites can draw blood. For some reason I don't even question her logic (if I don't stay with her, she'll bite me—but if I'm not with her, how can she bite me?). Instead, I give in.

"If we get in trouble . . . ," I say in a voice that I hope makes her at least a little bit nervous.

Then, suddenly, without even wanting or trying to, I get excited, just the way Roo is. I borrow the KangaRoo hop in her step. The jungle gets darker and darker, louder and louder, stranger and stranger, with each step. But for some reason it feels more magical than terrifying.

It's no surprise when Roo leads us off Normal Path onto Invisible Path. I gave up the fight a while back, but just to make sure, Roo turns to me and whispers "I'll *bite* you!" as she dives deeper into the jungle.

On Invisible Path, I start to imagine we're two sisters in a fairy tale, a haunted forest, a place where sprites battle monsters. This jungle feels older than history. The air smells of rotten eggs and flowers. Hanging above us, vines draped with moss like the hair of witches.

I feel shivery and dangerous and thrilled. It's fun, marching up the volcano with Roo, past flowers brighter than any cartoon. A few huge blue butterflies flutter slowly overhead, and neon lizards dart by our feet. A trio of turquoise parrots flaps among the branches. Roo bounces along in front of me. Even though it's practically impossible to see the path, she doesn't seem to have any trouble following it. A good companion for a tricky journey. Just me and Roo. On our own. Exactly the way it should be. We can handle anything. Maybe we can even handle things better than Mom, aka Ms. Yoga Brain. We don't need anyone. We just need each other. Slippery roots stretch out to trip us. Huge ferns try to tickle and poison us. But we keep on and on and on. It seems like fifty years might have passed. Maybe we'll go back to the Selva Lodge and Mom will be a very old lady, still waiting for us after all these decades. Or maybe the Selva Lodge will be gone, taken over by the jungle, the pool just an invisible rectangle under the dirt and leaves.

We hear the waterfall before we see it, a swift rushing sound up ahead, and then we turn the bend and there it is: a pure blue gush of water pouring out of the side of the volcano thirty feet above us. And I mean *pure blue*, blue like someone is standing up there dumping sky-colored paint off the ledge. When the water hits the stream below, it's still that crazy blue, and I can't even put into words how magical this whole scene is.

The impact of the waterfall on the stream creates a cool mist, and Roo and I just stand there feeling the mist on our faces, which is a very splendid feeling, except for the fact that the mist reeks like rotten eggs.

"Man, it *stinks*," I complain as soon as I stop being thunderstruck from the beauty.

"Whatever," Roo says, shrugging, "it's just a little bit of sulfur from the volcano. That's what makes it such an awesome color—so if you like the color, you gotta like the stink."

"Sulfur?" I repeat. "How do you even know that?"

"Hey, check it out!" Roo says, ignoring my question. "Isn't that the back of La Lava?"

I've been so distracted by the waterfall on our left-hand side that I haven't even glanced at the right-hand side. But now I follow Roo's gaze down from our little waterfall lookout, and sure enough, there's the unmistakable glowing white back of the palace at La Lava, a long ways down the hillside. The bright blue stream flows directly toward La Lava and then disappears beneath the palace—funneled out, I bet, to all those colorful pools on the other side.

"I'm confused," I confess. "How can we be all the way over here by La Lava?"

"Oh, Mad," Roo sighs wearily, "you're so bad with distances and directions."

"Please, stop with the compliments," I shoot back, but Roo is already launching herself across the stream, hopping from one mossy rock to another. And as I follow her over the dazzling blue water, I have to admit to myself that she was 110 percent right about coming up here—this is way more exciting than Spanish class or any other thing we might be doing.

Soon after we cross the stream, Invisible Path steepens. As we clamber up it, I notice lots of extra-bright lichen growing on the rocks, yellow and pink, purple and orange. Now we're going pretty much straight up the hillside (or, I guess, *volcano*side), and the path is just sort of clinging to it. On our right it's practically a cliff, all messy and jungly down below, and then on our left it's a black rock face stretching up and up. For the first time since we started, Roo's not marching. Instead, she's stepping very carefully, her legs shaking with her fear of heights. It's kind of miraculous that I'm not scared of heights, but I'm not, so I keep my eyes on her wobbly feet, ready to reach out for her if she slips.

Roo moves slower and slower, and when she turns back to look at me with this weird expression on her face, I bet she's going to say, *Hey, Mad, I'm bored. Let's go back.* She always pretends to be bored when she's nervous.

But that's not what she says. She just says "Mad," and lifts her finger, and points.

Ahead of us, the trail peters out into a patch of jungle that looks, if you can believe it, lusher and more brilliant than the whole rest of the jungle. Trees heavy with bunches of red bananas. Fat yellow mangoes dangling down. Flowers in a hundred different colors. It's as strange and shimmery as something from a myth, this glowing jungle grove crouched here between two cliffs, one falling away below and one stretching way up above.

"I *knew* it!" Roo whispers. I'm glad she at least knows to whisper. This definitely isn't the kind of place where you want to draw attention to yourself. "I *knew* there was something up here! Yesterday, when I came a little ways up the secret path, I *knew*, but then I had to turn around 'cause I thought you guys might be starting to worry, plus La Lluvia was coming."

"Well, cool," I whisper to Roo, relieved that we can go back down now that we've reached the end of Invisible Path and seen what there is to see. I guess Kyle made us swear not to come up here because he was worried about us on the steep cliff. Which is very cute of him. So, in honor of him, we'll be sure to take it extra slow on the way down. "Do you want to lead the way?"

But Roo starts walking *toward* the grove.

"Uh, Roo?" I say. "I meant the way *down*."

She ignores me.

"Uh, *Roo*?" I say again, trying to sound bossy without raising my voice.

As wonderful/beautiful/amazing/et cetera as this may be, it's simply not the kind of place you walk into. You just enjoy it from a distance for a few minutes and then head home.

Not Roo, though. Roo runs right up to where the path ends.

I notice a weird ringing sound in my ears. Maybe it's my own blood rushing around, but I have this feeling like it's the moan of the jungle, warning intruders to KEEP OUT.

I follow Roo to the end of the path. "Let's get out of this freaky place," I whisper.

But she's staring thoughtfully into the pathless muddle of leaves and vines and tree trunks. It looks like there's no way, absolutely no way, to go even a step farther.

From here I can see that the mangoes are actually more golden than yellow, and that the red bananas practically glitter among the shiny leaves. I spot a flower that's neon green, truly neon. I've never seen such a crazy flower before—it looks sort of like an iris but three times larger than normal. I'm wondering if that chocolatey smell is coming from the neon flower when Roo suddenly hurls herself forward into the grove and vanishes.

"Hey!" I croak. Roo! I can't lose Roo!

I whack forward through a patch of high ferns—probably rubbing up against tons of bugs and other poisonous things—just in time to see Roo's little bum waggling its way between a pair of moss-encrusted tree trunks.

Jeez. My sister really is brave sometimes. And idiotic.

There's barely enough of a gap between the trees to let a nine-year-old body squeeze through. I'm not at all optimistic about a twelve-year-old body. Besides, I have zero—let me repeat, *zero*—interest in bashing my way into a totally wild part of the jungle that's obviously abnormal or enchanted or haunted or *something*.

So I pause there, frozen, waiting for Roo to squeeze her way back to me so we can return to the Selva Lodge and, I don't know, go swimming or drink *licuados*.

But then Roo's face appears again, on the other side, staring back at me between the gap in the tree trunks. And for the first time ever, I spot a look of terror in her eyes. She quickly covers it.

"Hey," she whispers, "that was *fun*! Come on!"

If it weren't for how terrified Roo looked for that one instant, I might have said I'll just wait out here, thank you very much, Miss Fearless, because part of me has this paranoid feeling that once I go in I'll never come out.

But because of that expression I glimpsed on Roo's face, I find myself sighing and stepping forward and sucking in my breath and shoving myself between the trunks (skinning a knee, getting smeared with moss) to follow Roo into this weirdness.

When I emerge on the other side, Roo doesn't even thank me. She just gives a quick nod and forges ahead.

The mangoes seem to ripen before our eyes as we press our way through layers of leaves—leaves bigger than kites, than elephant ears, than sixth graders! Flowers bloom at our feet and at waist-level and face-level too, flowers tower above us and reach out to brush against us. These have nothing in common with the pretty little pastel flowers you might see in a florist shop in Denver. They're all strong colors, orange and mustard and maroon, purple and brown and black. They all look poisonous. And they all release rich, peculiar smells—chocolate and chile, dirt and honey, nutmeg and curry.

The magnetic force that pulled Roo between the trees—I start to feel it pulling me too as I follow her inward, slipping over roots and ducking beneath vines. From outside, the grove didn't look so large, hovering between the cliffs, but now that we're in here it feels endless. I'm still scared—terrified, really—but for some reason the terror starts to feel farther and farther away, as though it's floating ten feet above my head.

After who knows how long, we come to a big hunk of volcanic rock with a trickle of steaming red water running down it. I have this half-second thought—Wait, is that *blood*?—before I realize it's just that the rock is reddish, probably from rust or minerals. Roo is reaching out to touch the steaming water when my strange calmness vanishes, because suddenly I hear something coming, *something coming!*—a rustling on the other side of the rock, plus that water definitely looks hot enough to burn, so in super-bossy Roo-style I yank her away from the water and back into the underbrush, where I pull one of those ginormous leaves across to hide us.

I'm not just imagining things—there *is* something coming. Roo hears it too, and looks up at me, and for the second time I see terror in her eyes. I hug her with my free arm and feel her shaking, or maybe it's me shaking. Or probably both of us, trembling about whatever's going to happen next. What volcano monster is going to appear from behind the rock? What jungle witch is going to come claim Roo as her daughter?

It's hard to believe we're still on the same planet as the Selva Lodge, as Ken/Neth and his dumb jokes, as piña coladas and miniature decorative umbrellas and coconut sunblock and yoga retreats and Denver.

Here it comes, here it comes, whatever it is. I squeeze my eyes shut and cling to our leaf.

But then Roo pokes at me and I open my eyes and peek around our leaf and what do I see but two men in safari hats and those white jackets doctors and scientists wear, standing about eight feet away from us, on the other side of the steaming water.

Relief washes over me. It's just people. People I can handle—it's monsters I'm scared of. Still, we've got to stay hidden, because it's pretty obvious that we should *not* be here.

Their backs are to us. The taller one reaches upward, and it's only as he shoves his hands into what looks like pure jungle that I realize there's something there, camouflaged among the leaves. I can just make out its boxlike form amid the layers of green.

Taller pulls a metal cage-thing down.

"Zip, zero, zilch," he says to the shorter guy, shaking the box. "Big surprise. And that movie star wants someone's head, I hear."

"A trap is useless and irrelevant in this situation," Shorter says, so softly I can barely hear him.

"*You're* one to talk!" Taller retorts. "*We're* just trying to do everything we possibly can!"

Shorter doesn't reply.

"You've *gotta* find another," Taller continues. His voice is annoying. It pretends to be friendly. "Gotta, gotta, gotta. If you don't find a new one by the gala—"

Shorter nods sharply.

"Look," Taller says in this snobby way, as though he thinks Shorter is pretty darn stupid, "Chevalier's under some major pressure, clients on one side, investors on the other, the old rock-and-hard-place routine. The investors have no idea where it comes from, and we gotta keep it that way. And the sorts of clients we're getting around here these days! Who could've guessed. But nowadays, these last nine months or whatever it is, ever since that loudmouth rock star, everyone who's anyone wants what we got. And these people are not familiar with the word *no*. So she's got all kinds of super-rich folks from all over the world breathing down her neck. And when she feels the squeeze, *we* get quadruple-squeezed, okay?"

Shorter nods even more sharply.

"Hey," Taller says, "I'm not saying this isn't a bit of a slipshod operation. Yeah, people have gotten in over their heads. But this is just what you gotta do when this kind of opportunity comes along. We never planned to stumble into a gold mine, and sure, there's some scrambling going on now. But there's a heck of a lot of money at stake, so it's do what you gotta do, you know?"

Roo pokes me, hard. But I can't take my eyes off this scene.

"Sometime in the next four days," Taller says in his mean, friendly way, "you gotta. Or we're going to be dealing with a crowd of extremely angry extremely rich people. A royal PR disaster. It's all on you, buddy. We're just asking you for one right now. Just so that all the right people are happy at the big bash. Besides"—Taller pauses, seeming to relish the drama—"you know what'll happen if you don't find it."

Shorter stops nodding and just freezes. Roo keeps poking me. I keep ignoring her.

"Well. There you have it," Taller says, reaching up to put the trap back in the tree. "Before Saturday. It has to be. We can't shut down. Do you realize how much we stand to lose each week we're closed?"

But it's not really a question.

"Millions of dollars. *Millions* of dollars," Taller tells Shorter. "Mix your current failure with no progress at all on the synthesis or cloning, and we're getting close to being up a creek."

"It'll be months if not years on the synthesis and cloning," Shorter murmurs. "Lab wizardry like that requires patience. Time and patience." He has a wonderful, calm voice.

"Thanks, genius," Taller says nastily. He's the worst kind of person. "Soon you're going to be informing me that it's impossible to locate any eggs, and even more impossible to locate any females, and totally impossible to mate them in captivity."

Poke, poke, poke from Roo.

"We've gotta keep our eyes on the prize, buddy," Taller announces. "For now just find us another to tide us over. And keep imagining the day when you and I and a number of others will be rich as God."

I watch a shiver run down Shorter's spine.

"That could very well have been the last one," Shorter says quietly, intensely. "You know that as well as I do."

Such a wonderful voice.

A wonderful, *familiar* voice.

Dad?

Of course—Dad!

I look over at Roo—so *that's* what she was poking me about—and we grin at each other.

"We have our eyes all over them," Taller says in his awful way. "You know that as well as I do."

Dad's head droops forward.

"You gotta put in dawn-to-dusk days," Taller tells Dad.

"*Before* dawn tomorrow," Dad murmurs. "At the east trail, as usual."

"Whatever you say, boss," Taller says. But he smiles meanly when he calls Dad boss.

"Pip-pip-pip!" Roo chirps beside me.

What the *heck*? Roo!

Both men spin around to stare at the layers of underbrush where we're hiding. I freeze, clinging to our leaf, willing myself not to tremble. I hold my breath and beside me I can feel Roo doing the same. Yes, it's Dad for sure, Dad! But I've never seen him looking the way he does now, which is scary—his voice may sound more normal than it did when we saw him at La Lava, but his eyes look frightened. *Dad* is frightened. It seems impossible, but I can see that it's true.

I'm so worried about Dad that for half a second I forget to be worried about what will happen if Taller pushes through the vines and lifts up the big leaf and sees us there. But thankfully he turns back around.

"Unusual birdcall, eh?" Taller says.

Dad is still staring right at our leaf. I have to work really hard to stop my hand from waving at him. Roo squeezes my wrist and I squeeze hers. This doesn't seem like the best time to have a little reunion with Dad.

"Think that was one of 'em, Dr. Wade?" Taller jokes as he strolls around to the other side of the volcanic rock. "Mr. Bird Guy," he sneers, "Mr. Bird Guy!"

Dad turns away, tiredly following Taller, and I finally feel like I can breathe. I'm just releasing my held breath when suddenly there's a hand cupping my mouth. Beside me Roo starts to squirm—so whoever it is has grabbed both of us.

Panicking, I twist around to get a look. Our captor is wearing a mask, which seems to be made from a green T-shirt with eye-holes cut in it. He's also wearing a green T-shirt on his body, and a pair of jeans. He's strong, and drags/pulls both of us through the underbrush, still cupping our mouths so we can't make any noise. I'm sure Roo's slobbering all over his palm to annoy him, and extra sure she's trying to bite him, but he's really tough, and after a while both of us stop squirming. Strangely, the second we stop squirming he lets go of our mouths and grabs our wrists, still pulling us through the jungle.

"Wha—" Roo starts.

"SHHH!" he says sharply. Since we don't want him to grab our mouths again, we stay quiet.

The incredible thing is that he leads us right back to the gap in the trees where we entered the grove, and I almost want to be like, *Thanks!* because I seriously don't think Roo—and definitely not I— could have refound this spot.

He lets go of us so we can wiggle through the mossy gap, first Roo and then me, and as soon as I'm through Roo takes off running and I follow her while the guy in the mask works on squeezing his way between the trees. He's bigger than we are, and I really do think he might get stuck, not that I'm going to hang around to find out. We're free!

Until we get twenty feet down the path, to the super-steep part, where Roo has to stop running because her legs are shaking, and I hear the masked man rushing up behind me, and I know he's going to grab us again or maybe he'll just push us off the cliff (we should have listened to Kyle!) or who knows what. I'm ready to slap his hands away from me and try to bite him or whatever (though I've never bitten or fought anyone—that's Roo's thing). But he doesn't touch me.

Instead, he says, very calmly, "Focus, Ruby. Pretend you're just walking across your bedroom. Go as fast as possible."

I turn back to stare at Kyle. His hair is sticking up all crazy from being under the T-shirt mask, which he's now crumpling into a ball and trying to shove into his pocket.

Roo looks back at him and gives a huge grin.

"Oh," she says to Kyle, "*you're* not evil."

"Keep *moving,*" Kyle says without cracking a smile.

Kyle doesn't speak again—except to occasionally command "Faster! *Faster!*"—until we've turned off Invisible Path onto Normal Path.

"You swore on your father's life you wouldn't go down that path," he says. I have this strange sensation like I can actually feel his fury making the air around me heavier.

107

"I swore I'd never go *down* it," Roo replies. "I never swore I wouldn't go *up* it!"

"Faster," he says, ignoring her obnoxiousness. He's not breathing hard, even though we've been running practically the whole way. We barely even slowed down to cross the sky-blue stream. I'm out of breath from the pace, and from being terrified, and from worrying about everything, but mainly I'm just grateful for each footstep separating us from that grove, from that man who was talking at Dad in that awful way and saying those things that made just enough sense to fill me with a deep uneasiness.

"Man, I was really, really *scared* back there," Roo gasps happily.

"Yeah," I whisper, almost nauseous with the memory of Dad's frightened face.

"This is *exciting*," Roo breathes.

"More *scary* than exciting," I tell her.

"More *exciting* than scary," she corrects me.

I glance back at Kyle, who's glaring at Roo.

"Roo—" I beg.

But she just grins and changes the subject. "Hey, does anyone know why Dad was wearing that flashing green light around his ankle?"

"It's going to rain soon," Kyle says, ignoring the question.

"What flashing green light?" I say.

"That thing," Roo says impatiently, "around his ankle. It blinked green every other second."

What's wrong with me? Do I not have *eyes*? Why is Roo always seeing things I don't?

"Oh" is all I say.

"Kyle," Roo says, *"dígame."*

Dígame. Dígame. What does that mean again? I know I learned it in Spanish at school.

"I don't know," Kyle says quietly. But the way he says "I don't know" makes me pretty sure he does know.

"Tell me what's up with that green light!" Roo insists. *"¡Dígame!"*

Oh yeah. *Dígame. Tell me.* How does Roo know a million times more Spanish than I do?

Kyle doesn't say anything.

"Fine, then," Roo says, "don't tell me. I don't need you to tell me. I already know."

Kyle still doesn't say anything.

"I bet you anything it's a tracking device, like they use on birds and other animals!" Roo announces. *"Someone* is keeping *track* of *Dad."*

Right then there's the enormous whooshing sound that I now recognize as the start of La Lluvia, La huge, crazy, gigantic Lluvia, which is about to make all these trees sway like flowers.

I think Kyle yells "RUN," or maybe it's Roo, or maybe it's even me, but it's impossible to hear anything, and we all start running like crazy.

CHAPTER 9

The second we slide into the concrete courtyard of the Selva Lodge on our muddy sneakers in rain that's like taking thirty showers all at once, the door to the kitchen of the Selva Café pops open, as though someone has been waiting for us.

And who should be standing there but the witch. In her black lace veil. Gesturing us inside. I'd really rather just go back to our room and rest and try to not freak out and try to figure out exactly what we saw up there and what it means and what we can do about it. But Roo grabs my hand and pulls me toward the kitchen.

"¡Abuela!" Kyle calls out across the courtyard, jogging over to the doorway and disappearing inside.

Abuela . . . abuela . . . I *know* I know that word! I search my memory, and, wait a sec—doesn't that mean "grandmother"?

"The *witch* is Kyle's grandmother?"

I don't realize I said that aloud until Roo corrects me: "The *fairy godmother* is Kyle's grandmother, duh. You didn't know that?"

Of course! It makes sense. . . . Kyle comes here every summer. . . .

He's related to the spooky old lady and the sweet old man! But somehow I had totally missed that fact until now.

"Why do you think his name is Kyle Nelson *Villalobos*?" Roo asks.

I just look at her. The fact is, I *didn't* know his name was Kyle Nelson Villalobos, and I wonder how Roo did. I guess she just knows that the same way she knew Dad was wearing a tracking device. Man, there's simply no competing with Roo.

"Come *on*," she says, tugging me with her across the courtyard and into the kitchen.

It's a big white kitchen with oversized appliances and a gray linoleum floor. But somehow it still feels kind of cozy. There are bright striped dishrags hanging on a bar above the enormous stove, and red plastic chairs at the metal table in the middle of the room, and one of those neat spiral stairways in the far corner—I wonder where it leads. Spiral staircases always seem to me like they must lead somewhere special.

Kyle is already seated in one of the red plastic chairs. The witch is pouring a thick red liquid into the glass in front of him. The word *poison* jumps into my mind.

"Uh, hi," I say, staying near the doorway as Roo hops over to the table, pulls out a chair, and plops herself down.

"*Un licuado de papaya y hibisco,*" the witch says.

"A papaya and hibiscus smoothie!" Roo exclaims as the witch pours another glass. "*¡Dámelo!*"

"Oh," I say awkwardly, wondering how Roo always makes herself at home wherever she goes, never the least bit anxious or untrusting. "I didn't notice that one on the menu."

"*Abuela* is testing it out on us," Kyle explains. "And it's great."

"It tastes funny!" Roo says around the straw in her mouth.

It tastes funny. Oh my god.

111

"It tastes funny," Roo says again, "but I *like* it."

Beneath the black lace, the witch's smile grows. She turns toward me, and I can't help it, I get nervous.

"You would like to try it," she says in English, and I don't know if she's asking me or telling me.

I look around the kitchen, at the white countertops and the gleaming white fridge. There's a way-outdated calendar on the wall, from the year Roo was born, with a picture of a lady saint in a purple robe. I mean, it really *does* feel pretty good and safe and clean and nonpoisonous in here. Plus, haven't I been eating every meal in the Selva Café anyway? Besides, whatever's in that red liquid can't be worse than grasshoppers. I'm about to say, "Okay, sure, papaya and hibiscus, whatever," when I notice the bowl of fruit on the counter. Flies laze through the air above it, bouncing around among papayas and mangoes.

"I'm not . . . hungry," I whisper, staring at the flies.

"It's a drink!" Roo insists. "You don't have to be hungry."

"I'm not thirsty either."

The witch goes over to the bowl of fruit and flicks at the flies.

"If you are not thirsty, *querida,* then it must be story time," the witch says, pointing at one of the red plastic chairs.

Story time? I have no idea what she means by that. But I cross my arms and plunk down into the chair, because I bet she's going to keep staring at me from behind that veil until I do as she wishes. Slowly, she lowers herself into the seat across from me.

"Once upon a time," she begins, and even with just those four words my mind starts to calm down and listen, "a brave young man from the village had a habit of walking up the volcano where nobody else went. He always wore a cloak as blue as dusk, and everyone in the village was scared of him. One day he walked all the way to the rim of the volcano, and there he saw a young woman. She lived inside the volcano. She was a goddess. Of course they fell in love, because they were both so strong and so brave. He wished to marry her, and she wished to marry him too, but she pretended she did not. He got very sad. For months he asked her why she would not marry him. Finally he forced it out of her: If he wanted to be her husband, he would have to jump into the volcano. That was the only way she could be married. She came up to the surface for just a couple of hours a day, the hours she spent with—"

"Oh *man*, Señora V, you speak *such* perfect English!" Roo butts in. "I want to speak Spanish the way you speak English!"

I shoot Roo a *shush!* look, because I hate it when a good story gets interrupted, and she shushes. And then I wonder what's up with Roo calling Señora Villalobos "Señora V." I guess that's just Roo doing her thing, giving nicknames to anyone she likes.

But Señora V doesn't seem to mind either the interruption or the name. "I have to be able to speak English to the mother of my grandson," she explains. "And you will speak perfect Spanish some-day, *querida*."

"Keep *going*, please!" I say. Hello, you can't just stop at the climax of a story.

Señora V looks over at me—I'm surprised to see the pleased grin on her veiled lips—before continuing: "The young man said that was fine. He would jump into the volcano. She explained that he would die, that their marriage would be that of a ghost and a god-dess. Again, he said he did not mind. That is how much he loved her. He was so strong, so young and full of life, that it made the volcano goddess very sad to think of him dying. But he was deter-mined. He stood on the rim of the volcano and jumped. At the last second, though, she could not stand to see him drown in lava. She raised her finger and gave him wings. He pulled up away from the lava just in time. Before he flew away from the mouth of the volcano, a single drop splashed on his throat and left a fiery streak. He had been transformed into a bird with feathers as blue as dusk and, on the throat, as golden as lava. But the magic of the volcano goddess was very powerful and could not be undone, even by her. She could not transform him from a bird back into a man. For the rest of time, the volcano bird would dwell in the jungle near the top of the volcano, soaring over the pool of lava, forever seeking union with the volcano goddess."

Roo gasps: "The Lava-Throated Volcano tr—"

"*Sssss,*" Señora V hisses at Roo, turning very witchlike again. "You know you must not say that name here! Remember what happened last time?"

Last time? Huh?

"The electricity cannot go out now," the witch growls. "I have flan in the oven."

"Oh," Roo says, blushing.

"Supposedly it upsets the volcano goddess to hear her beloved's name spoken by a child," Kyle explains. "Reminds her of the children they can't have."

Oh yeah. Kyle. I'd gotten so caught up in the story that I'd forgotten about him being right there next to me. Wow. It gives my heart a little jump start, the way he says *beloved.* What boys I know would ever use the word *beloved?* And then I feel my cheeks getting all flushed, because into my head pops this image of Kyle marching up the volcano in a blue cloak, his face serious and solemn and full of love.

"*Muy poderoso,*" comes a voice from the doorway, and we all turn.

"Señor V!" Roo exclaims, her nickname for Señora Villalobos extending to the old man as well.

And there he is, in his bright white linen suit with its bright orange handkerchief. I can't believe I didn't realize he was Kyle's grandfather—how could I not have noticed that he has the exact same thoughtful look in his bright brown eyes?

"*Muy peligroso,*" he says.

"Okay, okay," Roo says, rolling her eyes, "I'm sorry, I get it, I know, I know, it's dangerous to say the bird's name, it's powerful, got it!"

"This is not a joke," the witch says severely.

Señor V steps across the room and murmurs something into the witch's ear. She sighs, and gazes at me and Roo through black lace.

"There are four truths about the volcano," she finally says. "I learned them when I was a girl, and my husband learned them when he was a boy."

Beside me, Kyle clears his throat and stares angrily at his grandmother.

"The time has come to tell them," the witch informs him.

"They're just kids," Kyle says.

Just kids? Ouch. Ouch to the max. Why does Kyle have to group me with Roo, as though I'm not closer to his age than to hers? Do I really just seem like a kid to him?

"They are his daughters," the witch replies.

"I'm not sure it'll even help," Kyle mutters.

Help *what*? I want to ask. But that's probably the kind of thing a kid would say.

"Time is running out," she says. "And if we do not tell them, they may stumble upon it in a most dangerous fashion. They already almost did. You know how this one is." She points at Roo. Then she turns back to face us. "You already know the first truth of the volcano: Children must not utter the name of the volcano bird aloud."

"Got it," Roo says. I'm glad she doesn't roll her eyes. I'm starting

115

to feel very nervous. I'm not superstitious, because Dad has zero patience for that, and I don't think words can be magic spells, and I know it's just a coincidence that the electricity happened to go out when Roo said you-know-what. But I *am* scared of the witch. And she doesn't want us to say *Lava-Throated Volcano trogon*. So I sure as heck won't.

And you know what else? I don't really want to know the three other truths. I think I'd rather just go and take a nap, or a shower. I don't like sitting here wondering, What difference does it make that we're Dad's daughters? What is time running out for?

"The second truth," the witch announces. "Anyone who tries to capture the volcano bird will be driven insane."

"Well, considering the bird is extinct, I guess we don't have to worry about that one," I say brightly.

"Because the volcano goddess still wants to protect her bird, right?" Roo says, gazing at the witch.

The witch ignores me and smiles at Roo. To counterbalance the witch, I frown at Roo. The thrilled, fascinated expression on my little sister's face is only adding to the melodrama. I can tell she's hanging on the witch's every word when she should be taking all this with a grain of salt. Dad always taught us to take everything with a grain of salt.

"Third," the witch continues, her face reflecting Roo's glow, "the volcano can restore lost youth."

"So he'll always be as young as he was when she fell in love with him!" Roo says. Jeez, I wish she weren't quite so into this. I wish she weren't so full of belief about an old myth—a cool old myth, sure, but a *myth*. A made-up story.

"And fourth: Once the last bird dies, the volcano will blow."

"Because they'll finally be reunited!" Roo exclaims. Then she adds doubtfully, "Or because she'll be so angry that the bird is dead?"

"Well, who knows!" I say, my voice high and peppy to cover the unpleasant feeling in my stomach. "Too bad the volcano didn't blow when the species went extinct. Then we'd know myths are true. That would be pretty cool."

Kyle is staring at me. The witch is staring at me. Señor V is staring at me.

"You're right," Kyle says slowly. "The volcano hasn't blown yet."

They're all still staring at me, and Roo is smiling like she knows a secret.

"Well," Roo says after a moment, "maybe it hasn't blown yet because the last bird isn't dead yet."

Dad told us all about Lazarus species. Lazarus species are probably his Number One Favorite Thing in the World. That's when a species believed to be extinct turns out not to be extinct (which is why it's named after Lazarus, the guy who Jesus supposedly raised from the dead). Dad said the idea that an extinct bird might not be extinct helps him get out of bed in the morning.

So, here we are, in the kitchen of the Selva Café, sitting in the silence following Roo's suggestion, and Roo is squirming in her chair and bobbing her head and holding her breath, and then she releases her breath and reaches deep into the pocket of her shorts and digs something out and puts it on the table.

A golden feather.

A small, delicate, blindingly golden feather.

"Where the hel—heck did you get that?" For the first time ever, Kyle sounds surprised.

"Up there," Roo says with a shrug. "It was just on the ground."

How did she sneak that into her pocket without me noticing?

"I've never found one of these," Kyle murmurs, "not that I haven't tried." There's a strange radiance in his eyes as he reaches for the feather and places it in his palm.

We all stare at it. It glimmers softly under the fluorescent lights, looking more precious than actual gold. Lying there in his hand, the feather almost seems to whisper, *Life, life, life!*

The witch and the old man glance at each other. And I hear Taller's voice echoing through my head: *Think that was one of 'em, Dr. Wade?*

Then it hits me in the stomach, and in the heart.

"The bird," I whisper, shocked. "It's not extinct?"

"It is virtually impossible to find the male bird," the witch says. "And it *is* impossible to find the female bird, much less her eggs. That is why everyone—most everyone—believes the species is extinct."

"*This* is why Dad was so happy when he first came down here!" Roo explodes. "The Really Good News. The Big Secret. It's that Dad saw a Lazarus species!"

Okay, fine, maybe. But Roo is forgetting something huge—The Weirdness. If Dad had succeeded in tracking a Lazarus species, why The Weirdness?

And then it dawns on me in a dark and horrible way: ANYONE WHO TRIES TO CAPTURE THE VOLCANO BIRD WILL BE DRIVEN INSANE.

I look over at Roo and watch her grin droop into a frown as she realizes it too.

"Madeline," the witch says. "Ruby. Your father has been—"

"We know," I say, pretending I'm not close to crying. "He tried to capture the bird. Probably so he could gather information about it. And now, if your volcano truths are true, he must be crazy. And he *has* been acting crazy. Okay, great, what next."

"That is not all." The witch's voice couldn't sound sadder. "He has not only been trying to capture the bird. He has been trying to kill it."

I laugh when she says that. A short, miserable laugh, but a laugh. How to explain this to a witch: Dad would never, ever, ever, ever, ever try to kill a bird, much less a member of a Lazarus species.

"You're wrong," Roo informs the witch.

"We have observed your father in the jungle on the volcano," the witch murmurs. "Tracking the last of them. He has been successful at least twice. In January, and again in May. We saw him capture the birds."

"He did not *kill* any birds!" Roo insists. "He may have captured them, but he did not kill them. Be*lieve* me."

I'm grateful that Roo is saying all the exact right things, because I'm having trouble finding my voice right now.

"The flesh was found," the witch says very softly. "All the bones removed. Rotting up there deep in the heart of the jungle."

And I get this image in my head of a pile of bloody flesh and twisted tendons. A dark feeling moves down my spine, and suddenly my fingers get shaky.

"Up there in that grove," Kyle adds, "where you were this afternoon. Where you saw your father. The place I told you not to go. Because bad things happen there."

"Dad would *never* kill a bird! And he would never, *ever* kill *that* bird!" Roo's voice is rising by the second.

"You do not know him anymore," the witch says. "He has changed. He is not a bad man, but he is not himself right now."

And the truth is there's not much we can say to that.

Roo turns to look at me. "But why," she says softly, asking just me, "why would Dad kill a Lazarus bird?"

I don't even have it in me to shrug. And no one else replies either.

"It's La Lava!" Roo exclaims. "La Lava is making him do it! We saw him with this scientist guy who—"

"Dad wouldn't kill a bird just because some people were *telling* him to," I scold Roo. How can she have so little faith in Dad? She knows better than anyone else how brave he is. He'd stand up to anyone who wanted him to do something idiotic like that!

"Who knows why they want the volcano birds dead," Kyle says, ignoring me, "but they do. We can't waste time wondering about their reasons."

Señor V says something to Kyle and the witch in Spanish, and I guess Roo understands too, because she says, "*We* have to stop him?"

"He will listen to his daughters," the witch hisses.

"You think he'll listen to *us*?" I say, remembering the way he was when we visited him in the white marble room. Acting like we were the last people on the planet he wanted to see.

"You and only you can stop him before he kills the last of the volcano birds," the witch chants at me and Roo, almost as though she's saying a spell. "You and only you can stop him before the volcano blows."

The golden feather seems to glow with its own light, there in Kyle's palm.

"Will you do it? Will you do it? *Will you do it?*" the witch whispers from behind black lace. The rhythm of her questions starts to match the rhythm of my heart. "Will you *stop* him?"

CHAPTER 10

In the morning, I wake up to the sound of Roo squealing. A soft, amazed squeal. I lean over the side of the bunk and look down. Roo is sitting on the edge of her bed, legs extended, staring at her toes.

Sprouting from each of her toes: miniature yellow flowers.

No kidding.

I lean even farther to get a better look, almost tumbling out of bed. Then I scramble down the ladder and grab Roo's heels and stare at the flowers. They're simple flowers, three petals each, and smaller than Roo's pinky fingernail.

"Pret-ty," Roo breathes, the first word of the day.

"CREEPY!" I say. "You. Have. Flowers. Growing. From. Your. Toes!" I shake her heels with each word. One of the flowers falls off.

"He-ey," Roo moans, and slaps my face.

"Ow!" I shriek.

"You made my flower fall!"

"Jeez, sorry, jeez." I press my hand against my cheek, hot from the slap.

Roo steps out of bed, walks carefully across the room on her heels, and opens the door.

"Hey, where are you going?" I say. "You're still wearing your pj's."

"Kyle will know why I have flowers on my toes," she says prissily, and I just roll my eyes. Since when is Kyle *God*?

But underneath the eye-rolling I'm going, *Hey, why don't I get to have flowers growing on my toes?*

I follow Roo as she toddles across the concrete courtyard to the Selva Shop. Even though she moves as gently as possible, still she leaves a little trail of fallen flowers that I have to step around.

"Darn!" she yelps as each flower falls.

By the time we reach the Selva Shop, there's only one flower left.

Inside, Kyle is arranging bottles of sunblock. Roo marches up to him, or marches as much as someone trying to make sure a delicate flower doesn't fall off her right big toe can, and lifts her leg to show him her foot. I stay in the doorway, watching, grateful that my pj's don't look too much like pj's.

"Huh," he says, looking at it for a millisecond before continuing to stock the shelves.

"Hel-*loo*?" Roo insists.

"Hello," Kyle replies, as though he doesn't hear her tone.

"I have a *flower* growing out of my *toe*," Roo says.

"I see that," Kyle says.

"Well, isn't that kind of *weird*?" she demands.

"Not really."

"Not really?"

"It happens sometimes. Here in the jungle near the volcano. It's a kind of fungus."

"A kind of *fungus*?" Roo echoes.

I can't help but laugh—Little Miss Special I-Have-Flowers-on-My-Toes Roo shoots me a mean look.

"Yeah. It only happens to little kids. Before they get, you know, older." Kyle gestures toward the doorway where I stand. My belly does a little flip. Kyle, pointing at me. Kyle, referring to me as *older*. "I got it when I was younger too. *Abuela* says it's either a sign of being close to the goddess of the volcano or a sign of having dirty feet. Probably the latter, in your case."

"Ha!" I say from the doorway. Roo frowns and pulls the final flower off her toe. She throws it at me as she runs past me out the door.

"MomMomMom!" I hear her yelling out in the courtyard, "I woke up with flowers on my toes! I'm special! I'm special!"

"That's interesting," Kyle says, though it seems like he's talking to himself and not to me.

"What's interesting?" I say, blushing for no reason.

"She's going to be good at this," Kyle murmurs, still more to himself than to me. "The jungle is extending an invitation to her."

"A *fungus* invitation?" I say doubtfully, jealous of Roo all over again. Who knows exactly what that means, *the jungle is extending an invitation to her,* but whatever it is, it does sound pretty special. Then again, I'd be the first to admit that Roo is special. More special than I am. Obviously. I've always known that.

"It's just been said, it's an old . . . superstition," Kyle says darkly, "that people who get the flowers are somehow . . ."

"Unsanitary?" I offer.

"Chosen . . . ," he murmurs, and then pauses. "The more flowers, the higher the level of insight. Or, magic. But let's not make too much of it." Why doesn't he *look* at me? "It'll work best if she's not self-conscious about it."

"Um, okay," I say. And I realize that if it were anyone else saying this stuff to me, I'd probably think they were wacko. But there's something about Kyle that makes me believe every word he says.

"You can help too," Kyle adds. "Not as much as your sister, but you can definitely help."

I have to wonder if it will always be this way, Roo being the amazing one and me sucking.

"So," I say, pretending I'm not annoyed, "I guess we'll head up once Mom and Ken go to La Lava?"

"Of course," Kyle says, as though I'm being silly to even ask. As though it's a given that Roo and I will charge into the jungle with him and make sure our crazy father doesn't kill an extinct bird. Our father, who we don't know anymore. Our father, who doesn't care about us anymore. Our father, who won't listen to a word we say. Our father, who pays more attention to Patricia Chevalier than to his own wife.

Now that we've been in the jungle and talking to the witch and seeing a whole other world, it feels strange to be around Mom and Ken/Neth. Since Weird Life has become normal, Normal Life seems weird. It's odd to be having cornflakes for breakfast at the Selva Café, talking to Mom and Ken/Neth about boring things— like how Mom simply *loves* Relaxation and Rejuvenation, and how La Lava is just the most *uplifting* place, and how transformative her "flow" yoga class was yesterday, and what are we learning in our Spanish lessons, and do we think we'll go to the pool—when what we're really going to do today is try to prevent Dad from murdering the last of the Lava-Throated Volcano trogons. The Villaloboses never said we shouldn't talk to Mom about all this, but it's pretty obvious. Every day she seems more blissed-out from yoga, if that's even possible. Mom is just *not* the kind of person who describes things as

124

"uplifting" and "inspirational," but now those seem to be her two favorite words, and she says them all the time in her new, smooth voice.

"Hello, what planet are *you* on?" Roo says to Mom after one particularly silly comment about how inspiring she finds the fragrance of the hand soap in the bathrooms at La Lava. "Are you dehydrated or something?"

The weather is gray and heavy and different from before. It's nothing like the other mornings here, which have been as bright and vivid as a commercial. The air smells more like rotten eggs than flowers—"The smell of the volcano," Ken/Neth informs us over his coffee mug. Roo and I are sitting across from Mom and Ken/Neth, facing the volcano, in the perfect position to notice that it's spewing extra stuff.

"The volcano is spewing extra stuff," I tell Mom and Ken/Neth.

"Really?" Mom says, twisting to look. "Gosh, you're right. Look at that, Ken."

Ken/Neth twists too. A steady wisp of white smoke rising from the volcano stands out against the grayish sky, and then there are all these extra puffs of steam or smoke or something.

"Cute," he says as a puff puffs out. "The volcano is saying good morning to us."

I stare disapprovingly at him. For one thing, why does he keep forgetting that we're not two years old? Plus I think it's bad luck to make jokes about semiactive volcanoes. Maybe I used to be less serious, back before The Weirdness, but not anymore. "Hey, don't tempt fate," I scold Ken/Neth, borrowing one of Dad's phrases.

"Gosh," Mom says breathlessly, "*nature.* Isn't it so inspiring?"

Somehow I manage to stop myself from saying something nasty to her.

"Listen, girls, I understand your concern," Ken/Neth says with a grin, "but as I told you, La Lava has brought in the greatest volcano experts in the world, and they all agree that this volcano will not blow for at least another century and a half. Now, that may not be so long in volcano years, but it's plenty of time for us. I promise you we'll all be long gone by the time anything dangerous happens around here. Look, I've said it before and I'll say it again: Do you think all those movie stars would come to La Lava if they weren't positive it was safe?"

I have to admit, I do find it pretty comforting that Vivi thinks it's safe to stay at La Lava when she could vacation anywhere she wanted on the entire planet. That makes me feel better for a few seconds, until the witch's words pop into my head: *ONCE THE LAST BIRD DIES, THE VOLCANO WILL BLOW.*

Mom and Ken/Neth leave straight from breakfast for La Lava, and Roo and I head back to our room to get our things together. The first thing Roo does is to put the golden feather in the envelope with The Very Strange and Incredibly Creepy Letter, along with a tiny handful of her wilting yellow toe-flowers. The sight of this little collection sends a chill through me. It looks like craziness. It looks like witchcraft. And I can't stop myself from yanking the envelope away from her.

"Hey!" she shrieks. "That's mine, give it back!"

I watch as the rage passes through Roo and stiffens her spine. Her anger is so familiar that it makes me smile. Good old angry Roo, back in business. She lunges at me, locking her teeth on my wrist. I scream and throw the envelope. Roo howls amid the whirlwind of falling letter and flowers and feather.

"If you hadn't bitten me, I wouldn't have dropped it," I say.

"If you hadn't taken it, I wouldn't have bitten you," she says, scowling at me before spinning away and moving slowly around the room with her envelope, picking up the pieces and placing them inside. She looks so dejected that I hate myself for upsetting her.

"I'm sorry," I say. "It's just . . . all this kind of creeps me out."

"It's okay," she says softly, even though it's not okay.

I feel bad, but still I can't handle watching Roo cling to her small pile of hope, so I head out to the parking lot to check if Mom and Ken/Neth have really left for the day.

And who should I see there but Kyle, crouching on the gravel. He doesn't notice me. I get closer and closer. He keeps not noticing me. I feel funny, like my feet are too big and I'm breathing too loud. It doesn't seem right to just say *Hey* or *Hi* or *What's up?* to someone who's crouched down this way in the middle of a parking lot.

But before I get the chance to say anything, Kyle whispers, "Come here."

So he *did* know I was nearby! I crouch beside him.

And what's there is really, really disgusting.

It's a beautiful little blue frog with black spots. But the right side of the frog has been totally crushed and clear pus is oozing from it. There's a pattern of smeared tire tracks leading away from the frog. Its left side is twitching and wriggling in the most awful, pathetic way.

But you know the craziest thing?

Kyle is crying.

I don't want to embarrass him, so I pretend I don't notice. Instead, I say, "It's a beautiful little frog."

"It *was*," he corrects me. "Stupid golf cart."

"Golf cart?"

"Yeah," Kyle says.

I get an automatic stomachache.

"Ken/Neth?" I whisper.

Kyle doesn't need to respond.

We crouch there for a long time and then we keep crouching. The left side only twitches sometimes now. It's too sad. Suddenly I have this weird urge to stroke the gross little oozing frog as it dies. I've never seen anything die except wasps and houseflies and spiders, that kind of thing. I reach out to stroke the frog, but Kyle slaps my hand, hard. His skin leaves a burn on my skin. Jeez! My second slap of the day.

"Why are you so *mean*?" I yelp, rubbing my hand.

"Its skin is super poisonous," Kyle says.

So, I have to forgive him, but my face is hot with awkwardness as I stand there and watch the frog die.

"It's too bad," Kyle says quietly.

"I know," I say. I feel terrible.

"I don't mean the frog," Kyle says. "I mean, that's too bad too, but what I meant was your dad."

My blood starts to buzz. "What about my dad?" I say.

"Too bad he hasn't stood up to La Lava. I always assumed the Bird Guy was brave."

I get hot all over, like my stomach and my brain are boiling, and my heart is boiling too, and I stand up, and my eyes get really huge and my voice gets really low, and I say to him in a loud, slow, mean way, *"MY DAD IS BRAVE."* Then I stomp once on his fingers, which are resting on the gravel, but I don't know if Kyle does anything when I stomp on him, because through my blurry eyes I can't see anything except my stomping foot.

Right after that the area around my heart starts to hurt, like I've pulled a muscle or something, and I'm crying when I go, and I'm crying as I stumble across the concrete courtyard. Because you know what? I don't know if it's true. I don't know if Dad is brave, or if he's evil.

"Do you really think Dad is trying to kill the bird?" I ask Roo as we zip up our backpacks. I have this shaky, nervous feeling and my fingers are trembling.

Roo heaves a long, tired sigh, the sigh of a much older person, as she shoves the envelope containing the flowers and the feather and The Very Strange and Incredibly Creepy Letter into the front pocket of her backpack.

"No," she says, but it's not a confident no.

We've gotten so used to the tiny neon lizards hanging out on the other side of our door that we don't even react when they scatter as we open it.

"Man," Roo says, leading the way across the courtyard, "why does Mom have to be all bizarro now?"

"Yeah, what's up with that?" I say, relieved not to be alone in noticing Mom's freaky new yoga personality.

"Sheesh!" Roo says. "It practically seems like she's under some kind of magic spell!"

Magic spell. I wish she wouldn't use that term. I don't believe in magic spells, but for some reason it sends a shiver through me. Dad killing birds, Mom falling into yoga—it's all upside down. I reach for Roo's hand and give it a squeeze. At least *she* hasn't changed one bit.

Kyle is waiting for us by the back gate, leaning against the concrete wall of the Selva Lodge, binoculars around his neck. I immediately start blushing, but I guess he's decided to pretend I didn't stomp on his fingers less than ten minutes ago. He just gives us a quick nod and opens the gate. We head up Normal Path in silence, and I'm struck all over again by how dark and rich-looking the mud is, and how many different sounds are made by the birds and monkeys and whatever else.

When we reach Invisible Path, Kyle turns off Normal Path without saying a word and leads us right down the secret trail. I guess that since we've already gone all the way into danger, he's not going to try to keep us away from it anymore.

As we wade deeper into the layers, it strikes me how impossible it'll be to find Dad. There's a lot of jungle out here.

"Um, so," I say. The first words any of us has said since we entered the jungle. I'm behind Roo who's behind Kyle. "How exactly are we going to find Dad?"

"You just have to listen to the jungle," Kyle says casually.

Oh. Okay. Well then.

"Also," Roo adds, "he said the east trail."

Kyle looks back, surprised. And I'm impressed that Roo remembers that little detail about the east trail. I'd pretty much forgotten it, but she's totally right.

"What? When?" he demands.

"Yesterday," Roo replies. "At that place. When we saw him. He said it to that scientist guy. The east trail. As usual. Before dawn."

Kyle glares at her. "And you didn't tell me?"

"Gee whiz, mister," Roo shoots back. "Relax. I *did* just tell you. Besides, I thought you were spying on them the whole time we were."

Kyle turns sharply off Invisible Path, leading us straight into the jungle, no trail at all.

"Um, hello, where are we going?" I ask, staying on Invisible Path.

But Kyle has become Mr. I-Don't-Answer-Questions.

"Um, hello, to the east trail, probably," Roo mocks me as she barges behind Kyle into the thick layers of leaves, her mean tone payback for my grabbing her envelope this morning.

I sigh, groan, and plunge after them. This—the pure, pathless jungle into which I'm now being forced to follow Kyle and my little sister—is way, way, *way* worse than Invisible Path. You can't take a single step without all these vines reaching out to grab your ankles and all these branches whacking your face and the disturbing feeling that all sorts of poisonous critters are crawling down your neck or up your leg.

And then suddenly some huge gray insect thing is flying into my face and I'm blinking and swatting at it with my hands and shrieking.

"Relax!" Roo mutters back at me. "It's just a bug."

"JUST a bug!" I half scream. Excuse me, I don't think there's anything "just" about it when it's as big as a hand. But at least I seem to have scared it away, whatever it was.

I trudge on behind Kyle and Roo as they sneak between vines and branches. They seem to be having an easier time of it than I am, but even so it's Roo who, after about twenty minutes of this, says, "Jeez, if only I could break that darn code! Then we wouldn't have to fight the jungle just to try to figure out what's really going on with Dad!"

When Kyle stops in his tracks, Roo almost crashes into him, and I almost crash into Roo.

"Code," he says, spinning around to face her. "What code?"

"Well, Dad sent us this letter and—"

"WHY DID YOU NOT MENTION THIS BEFORE?" Kyle thunders, for once not being respectfully quiet in the jungle.

Roo's already pulling The Very Strange and Incredibly Creepy

Letter out of her backpack. She hands it to Kyle, who examines it for a minute, his eyes widening.

"Oh man," he says with a low whistle. "This is going to take a while."

He pushes past us, rushing back the way we came, back toward Invisible Path and Normal Path and the Selva Lodge.

CHAPTER 11

"Is this *your* room?" I whisper as Kyle opens the wooden door at the top of the spiral staircase that starts in the kitchen of the Selva Lodge. It's a very small room with a green-blanketed bed that looks even narrower than a twin, but it has a big window facing the volcano. I never knew teenage boys could actually keep their rooms tidy.

Kyle doesn't reply to my question. Before we're even through the doorway, he's holding The Very Strange and Incredibly Creepy Letter up, staring at it.

"A code!" he says, his eyes gleaming as he gazes at the dumb poem and childish drawings. He reads aloud, very slowly:

> *"There was a little girl*
> *Who had a little world*
> *Right in the middle of her pretend*
> *And when she was trill*
> *She was very, very trill*

And when she was smart
She was silly.
I LOVE YOU LEFT RIGHT UP DOWN LOL!
XOXO, DADDY."

A weird hot feeling comes over me, a feeling that seems like it could lead to either laughing or crying, and I hear myself saying, "*Maybe* it's a code. Or *maybe* Dad's just crazy."

Roo and Kyle ignore me. Together they flop down on the round red rug next to Kyle's bed and stare at Dad's letter. "Have you tried the first letter of each word?" Kyle asks Roo.

"Uh, *yeah,*" Roo says, offended.

"How about every other word?"

Roo rolls her eyes.

"How about the last letter of each word?"

"*Puh*-lease," she says.

"Are you sure it's a code?"

"As I said—" I butt in.

"YES," Roo says. "Every single letter Dad ever wrote me was a code."

"Okay," Kyle says excitedly, "it's such nonsense that there's got to be something more to it. Let's try some complicated patterns. How about, every second vowel and every third consonant."

"Humph," Roo harrumphs. "I actually haven't tried that one yet."

I give a theatrical yawn and sink down onto the bed. I'm pretty sure The Very Strange and Incredibly Creepy Letter is just that— very strange and incredibly creepy, and nothing more. Dad sent it in April, which we now know was *after* he had captured at least one Lava-Throat, so he was already insane, right?

Anyway, while Kyle and Roo do their little back and forth, I sprawl across the bed and try to put my face at its nicest angle for Kyle and let my hair fall down across my cheek in a way that I hope is kind of glamorous. But Kyle isn't the one who notices these gestures. Instead, Roo interrupts her code-breaking to ask, "What are you doing? Do you need a barrette? Why are you putting your hair there? That's weird." Meanwhile, Kyle just keeps talking to Roo, as though he has a special blind spot for me.

"What if the code is based in Spanish rather than English?" he proposes. "We should think about that too."

I stop trying to get Kyle's attention and just zone out and stare up at the volcano. Which is now spewing some bluish smoke. It's probably fine, I tell myself. And even if it isn't, what can I do about it?

I rest my head on my arms and time passes. It's boring, lying there while the others work on their impossible task, and I can't stop feeling sad about Dad being crazy. Next thing I know I must've fallen asleep, because the sound of La Lluvia starting with a slam jerks me awake.

As soon as I realize it's just the rain, I relax and sink back down. I'm lying there, groggy, listening to the rain, when the thought crosses my mind: Right where I'm lying right now, right where I just took a nap, this is where Kyle sleeps every night! I can't help it, the thought makes me blush, and I get up off the bed before the blush turns into a giggle, and I flop down alongside Kyle and Roo, who are making all sorts of complicated charts on pieces of scrap paper. I prop my chin in my hands and do one of my least favorite things, in hopes that it will make me stop blushing about Kyle's bed: I look at The Very Strange and Incredibly

Creepy Letter. I've never really stared at it before, and now that I am, it hits me what a totally, seriously, *unbelievably* terrible drawer Dad is.

"Jeez, his flowers don't even look like flowers," I say. "That one just looks like a *W*."

Roo and Kyle keep scribbling away.

Then, suddenly, Kyle stops.

"Wait a sec," he says, snatching Dad's letter up off the floor. "*W . . .*"

"*W . . . ,*" Roo repeats, tracing it with her finger.

"Hey!" Kyle exclaims, pointing. "An *M*!"

"THEY'RE LETTERS!" Roo shrieks, dropping her pencil. "THE *FLOWERS* ARE *LETTERS*!"

We work our way around Dad's flowery border, finding letters disguised as flowers and vines and leaves, and writing them down. Once you know they're there, it's not so hard to see them—the bars of an *F* stretching up into a leaf, and *B*s and *D*s forming blossoms, and *S* as part of the main vine, and *L* a vine that curlicues off the main vine, and *M* and *N* and *H* composing the bases of flowers, et cetera.

"Oh my *gosh*," Roo mutters, "I am so stupid. Why did I not figure this out forever ago?" She groans. "And there's even *huge* hints in the letter! I love you left right up down! Plus that being smart is being silly. The goofy flowers are the silly part! He was basically *shouting* at me to look at the border!"

Sometimes we wonder, wait, is that supposed to be a *K*? Is that a *V*? But every time we wonder, we assume it *is*, because Dad's careful that way. This is what we end up with, going around the four sides:

```
L   L   W   L   L   H   R   M   M   M   R
S                                       F
T                                       D
Y                                       D
H                                       S
M                                       N
S                                       T
T                                       K
Y                                       L
H                                       L
M                                       L
S                                       T
T                                       V
Y                                       T
H                                       S
M                                       
L   T   V   T   B   N   K   P   S   P   P   L   Y   N   G
```

It's thrilling to find letter after letter when all I saw before was scary craziness and bad drawing.

This is obviously what Dad wanted us to figure out.

Happiness gushes through me, because now I know he's not insane! No insane person could be this clever.

But as I gaze at the letters my heart gets heavy all over again. They still don't mean anything. There are no vowels to help us along.

"The left-hand side . . . ," Kyle murmurs.

"Something repeated three times!" Roo says. "An abbreviation, like LOL!"

"Something important, I guess," I add. "Maybe—stop him, stop him, stop him?"

"It's a *Y*," Roo tells me quietly. "Not a *P*."

Embarrassed, I shut up.

"Stay!" Kyle says. "Stay, stay, stay! It's got to be S-T-A-Y! Stay him?"

"Isn't that an old-fashioned way of saying *Stop him*?" I ask.

"STAY HOME!" Roo yelps.

Oh yeah. Duh. Stay home. Stay home. Stay home. Of course. Dad didn't want us to come. That's been obvious from the first day, when he was so cold to us. When he said to Mom, *Why are you here?*

Stay home, stay home, stay home. Well, it's a little late for that, isn't it.

But why did Dad want us to stay home? If he were having problems, wouldn't he have wanted us to come help? Wouldn't it have made him happy to see us again?

Anyway, okay. Stay home. But what about the rest? We're all staring so hard at the letters that we jump when the door creaks open.

It's the witch, standing there at the top of the spiral staircase with a plateful of black muffins and three glasses of emerald-colored liquid on a tray.

"*Black* muffins?" I say suspiciously. Boy, you don't get much witchier than that.

"From black corn, *querida*," the witch replies. "A local specialty."

"What's that green stuff?" Roo says. "It looks too healthy. Does it have seaweed in it?"

But still she grabs and chugs from the glass the witch hands her, and Kyle swoops out to seize two muffins. Then the witch shoves the tray toward me, insistent.

I look at Kyle and Roo, devouring the muffins and gulping the drink, not keeling over from being poisoned or anything. And I don't want to be paranoid the way Mom got during The Weirdness. And it's not as though I actually, truly, one hundred percent believe the witch is a witch or the green stuff a potion.

So I reach out for a muffin and a glass.

Only after Roo and Kyle have thanked the witch about a hundred times for the incredible snack, only after she's smiled secretively behind her veil and trundled off down the spiral stairs, only then do I take a sip of the liquid and eat a crumb of the muffin.

And I have to admit: The emerald substance is amazing, as rich and sweet as jungle flowers. And the black corn muffin melts like butter on my tongue.

When I look back at our rectangle of letters, the top line suddenly flashes into words before me, as though I'm seeing it through a whole new set of eyes.

"*L-L*," I say, "La Lava! La Lava *W-I-L-L H-A-R-M M-M-R*."

Roo and Kyle stare at me, surprised. And impressed. We all crouch over the paper.

"*M-M-R*," Roo whispers. "Mom-Mad-Roo. Or Mad-Mom-Roo."

"*F-D* doesn't kill—" Kyle says, moving his finger very slowly down the right-hand side.

"*L-T-V-T*s!" we all say at the same time.

"Okay," Kyle says, "but *F-D*?"

"If Dad . . . ," I murmur with a strange certainty.

"Yeah!" Roo says. "Left, right, up, down. Stay home, stay home, stay home. If Dad doesn't kill LTVTs, La Lava will harm Mom, Mad, Roo. But what about the bottom? *L-T-V-T,* easy-peasy, but what about *B-N-K*?"

"Bank?" I suggest, feeling like I'm on a roll.

"Bank," Roo mutters. "That doesn't make sense."

"P-P-L," Kyle says. "That's easy too."

"People!" Roo yelps.

"People," I echo. "But . . . *B-N-K-P-S*?"

"Let's try for *Y-N-G* first," Kyle suggests.

"B-N-K-P-S . . . ," I say, ignoring him, totally stumped.

"Young!" Roo cries out. "LTVT blank people young!"

"B-N-K-P-S," I repeat. *B-N-K-P-S. B-N-K P-S? B-N K-P-S? B N-K-P-S?*

"K-P-S—" Roo says. "Keeps! Keeps, keeps, keeps!"

"But what's the *B-N*?" I wonder. *"LTVT* blank keeps people young . . . ban? Bin?"

"Bone!" Roo says victoriously. "Bone, right? It's got to be! *That's* why the Villaloboses saw those carcasses up there without any bones!"

"LTVT bone keeps people young," I whisper.

"Wait," Roo is muttering, "wait, wait, wait, oh my gosh, it's like that thing about the volcano! About how it makes you young!"

"THE VOLCANO CAN RESTORE LOST YOUTH," Kyle quotes.

It's so miraculous to see the words taking shape before our eyes that I've forgotten to be upset about what we're learning. But now my crouching legs give out and I fall back against the bed.

LTVT bone keeps people young.

So. That's it. There you have it.

That's why Taller was putting pressure on Dad yesterday. That's why La Lava is holding the best bird-tracker in the world hostage.

And La Lava will harm us. If Dad doesn't provide LTVTs. Which they need for Vivi and everyone else's crazy-expensive miracle youth treatments. Which he's having trouble finding. Which he better find by the time of the gala or else. Which is in four days. Or, now, three days.

Roo and I were wrong when we said the Bird Guy would never kill a member of a Lazarus species. Of course he would, if that was the only way he could protect us.

"Well," Roo says matter-of-factly, "we have to help him find a bird so La Lava won't hurt us."

"Yeah," Kyle agrees. "We'll go into the jungle early tomorrow morning and tell him we'll help." Then he adds, sounding almost happy, "I *knew* he had a reason."

Excuse me, but how can they be discussing this in such a calm way?

"Um, what if La Lava hurts us while we're wandering around the jungle?" I ask. *We have our eyes all over them.* The sentence flashes back to me out of nowhere. I didn't even realize I remembered it. Taller's sneering voice, talking down to Dad yesterday. So *we're* the "them."

Kyle and Roo barely look at me. "They won't," Roo says flatly. "If they hurt us before the gala, Dad will stop having a reason to find a bird."

"Okay, well, shouldn't we tell someone about this? Like, an adult?" I say.

"Who?" Kyle says, almost mockingly. "Ken? Your mom?"

I shiver, thinking of Ken/Neth's ridiculousness and Mom's yogafication.

"Great idea!" Roo says sarcastically. "Let's talk to Ken, who works for La Lava!"

"I—I don't know who," I stammer. I hate it when Roo is sarcastic. But she's right—it *is* pretty creepy that Ken/Neth works for La Lava. I wonder how much he knows about everything. All that aside, though, I really do think we need to get a grown-up involved. "Like . . . the police or something."

"The only police out here are on La Lava's payroll," Kyle says with a short laugh.

"I guess it's up to us, then," Roo says perkily.

Up to us? *Up to us to do what, exactly?* I wonder silently, not wanting to ask the question aloud because I don't want to hear Roo's answer.

"So he *has* been trying to kill a bird all this time," Kyle says, more to himself than to us. "My *abuelos* knew it. But then why . . . ," he says, trailing off.

"Why what?" Roo demands.

"A few weeks back, I was in the jungle, tracking your dad, and he released one."

I can picture it like a movie in my head, Dad spreading his arms, freeing a bird.

"You *saw* Dad release a Lava—" Roo stops herself before saying the name.

"He caught it in a net," Kyle says, "and looked at it for a few minutes, and then opened the net and let it fly away."

"Why didn't you tell us this before?" I say, happy that Dad isn't a total bird murderer but also freaked out that he let a bird go when he should've turned it in.

"It never came up," Kyle says coolly.

I feel betrayed. Kyle, who's practically our best friend now—correction: who *is* our best friend now—never mentioned that he'd seen Dad, in the jungle, releasing a bird! Instead, all we heard was the horrible thing the witch said about how they'd seen Dad capturing birds to kill. I hope Kyle at least told his grandparents this one redeeming thing about Dad, but if he did, it clearly didn't make as much of an impression on them as Dad's bird-capturing.

"*Why* would he have let it go, though?" I ask irritably. As much as Dad would want to release a Lazarus bird, it's hard for me to imagine him doing so if it would put us in danger.

"Well, he knew what was going to happen to the poor thing if he kept it, duh!" Roo says.

"Yeah, and he also knew what was going to happen to *us* if he *didn't* keep it!" I retort.

"So probably he had plenty of time," she says. "Probably they had enough bird bone back then, so he didn't have, have, have, *have* to give them another bird right that second, and he thought he'd just wait until it was *really* necessary, because killing a bird is the worst for him!"

"That's pretty darn *risky*," I say, my voice going all high and out of control.

"Dad *is* risky," Roo replies.

"That's being risky with *us*, though," I tell her.

"Maybe he was seeing enough LTVTs around," Roo says. "Maybe he was sure that when the time came he could find one. Or maybe he thought he'd be able to make a plan to get out of all this before he had to kill another. Maybe he was trying to do both—save the birds *and* us."

"Okay, fine," I say angrily. "Fine. Maybe Dad was gambling with our safety. So, what now? He can't find a bird so La Lava is just going to . . . ?" But it's too scary to finish that thought.

Roo sighs impatiently. "Well, he's obviously having a bit of trouble finding a bird right now, so *we're* going to help him find one. As I said."

"Three kids? Are going to help the best bird-tracker in the world? Find the rarest bird in the world? Before Saturday?" My voice rises even higher with panic.

"I've seen two of them this month," Kyle says casually.

We both turn to stare at him.

"You what?" Roo says.

"I've seen two of the birds this month. The one I saw your dad release, plus another."

"Or maybe it was the same one twice," Roo points out.

"You think you're a better bird-tracker than Dad?" I ask Kyle with a mean grin.

"No," Kyle says, "but I'm as good as he is. And so is Roo."

I harrumph.

"We have it," Kyle says. "Your dad and Roo and I, we all have it."

I'm not going to give him the pleasure of hearing me ask what "it" is. Instead, I sit there feeling like chopped liver (Dad's phrase), since I obviously don't have "it."

Then I feel Kyle looking at me, and I meet his gaze, and it's as though we're looking at each other for the first time ever. I mean, sure, we've *seen* each other before, but we've never really *looked* at each other. At least, *Kyle* has never really looked at *me*. His eyes *are* golden, truly golden, no question about it, golden and golden and golden. He looks at me in this silent, serious, solemn way. The way adults must look at each other. You can't wiggle out of this gaze by acting cute or girly. I try to look back at him with the same even stare but it makes me want to giggle. Not a pleasant, funny giggle. A stupid, terrified giggle.

"We have to do this, Mad," he murmurs.

"I know," I murmur back. Because I do know. They have to do it. Roo and Kyle. They're the ones who can do great things. They're the ones with powers. It's not like I haven't known all along that they can do things I can't. That they know things I don't. "You do."

"*We* do," Kyle corrects me. "We need you too."

It's a very nice thing for him to say, even though it's not true at all.

144

It's pretty much impossible to act normal that night at dinner, but thankfully Mom is so yogafied that she just grins absentmindedly at us when we say we had "a very fun day," and her grin only widens when we tell her that Kyle is going to take us into the jungle super early tomorrow morning to watch the sunrise over the volcano. If things were different, I'd rush to tell Mom everything. I'd want her to know that Dad is a prisoner of La Lava, that they're forcing him to kill Lava-Throated Volcano trogons, that they're using us to hold him hostage, that La Lava grinds up the bones of an almost-extinct bird to make people look young. I'd want her to help us figure out what to do. I'd want her to say we're imagining things. But somehow I don't think it would help to talk to her about any of this, and somehow I can't shake the feeling that La Lava is *doing* something to Mom, because she's sitting there seeming not at all like herself, looking totally spacey in her tulip dress as she laughs at Ken/Neth's stupid jokes.

And Ken/Neth. Now I'm not only annoyed by him, I'm scared of him (the guy who put Dad in touch with La Lava! the guy who encouraged Mom to bring us down here!). He's been so foolish and friendly all the way along I've never really believed he could be anything more than a silly, pesky guy with an unusual job and a crush on Mom. But who knows—maybe he's known this whole time what's going on with Dad. Maybe he's well aware that Mom and Roo and I are in danger. Maybe he's *spying* on us.

Looking across the table at him, though, I decide it's impossible that he's in on La Lava's plot. The way he tries so hard to entertain Mom and me and Roo. The way he accidentally knocks over his piña colada. The way he fails to speak Spanish. He *is* just a goofy guy with a huge crush. He's annoying as heck, but he's not *evil.* There's no way anyone with all the resources of La Lava would choose to give a guy like Ken/Neth any real power. Besides, everyone I've seen Ken/Neth interact with at La Lava always seems irritated by everything he says. As much as I dislike him, I know that when it comes to what's really going on with Dad, Ken/Neth is as innocent as Mom. A pawn of La Lava, just like the rest of us.

"Dessert?" Ken/Neth proposes when the plates are cleared.

The thought of dessert on top of everything we've learned today makes me feel extra ill, but Roo says, "Yes, please!" as though she's not in the least bit of danger.

CHAPTER 12

The next morning, when Kyle wakes us up before dawn with three quick knocks at our door, Roo discovers an even larger batch of the little yellow flowers on her toes. "She's got roses on her toeses, roses on her toeses, roses on her toeses," she sings to herself as she pulls on her shorts and sneakers. I'm too tired to remind her that what she's got on her toeses is fungus.

Outside, it's absolutely dark except for the pinkish light of the fluorescent SELV L DGE sign. Kyle leads us toward the blackness of the jungle and opens the gate.

"Do you have a flashlight?" I whisper.

But Kyle just steps onto the dark path.

Who does he think he is? The guy who doesn't have to answer questions? The guy who doesn't need a flashlight?

"It's *sooo* dark!" Roo says.

"No it's not," he says.

And, in a way, he's right. Once my eyes adjust to the jungle, there's a sort of grayness to the blackness. *Almost* enough light to see by. So I keep my mouth shut and we stumble along for a while.

We've been walking for about ten minutes when Roo trips right in front of me. I hear the hard thud of her body on the jungle floor.

"Roo!" I yelp, leaning down and reaching out for her in the darkness, my hands failing to find her. "Are you okay?"

Roo cries out, "I'm bleeding! I'm bleeding!" but she hops right back up, her back brushing my fingertips as she stands.

"Isn't it too dark to tell whether you're bleeding or not?" Kyle says.

Jeez, what a jerk! Now it's Roo's turn to ignore the question.

"Wait here," Kyle says. I hear him stepping off the path into the jungle—to pee?

Then a moment later, he's back, cupping something in his hands—something that gives off a greenish glow. He blows into his palms and the light inside his hands strengthens until it's illuminating the path, showing us that, though Roo is covered in mud, there's no blood.

"I'd rather not use this," Kyle says. "The dark is better. But I guess we need it for now. Safer, I guess."

Roo's no longer thinking about her injuries, though.

"What—*is*—that?" she says slowly, breathlessly.

Unlike Roo, I'm not so shocked by Kyle's little light bauble. It's probably some kind of plastic glow-in-the-dark thingy. I'm just surprised he hasn't turned it on till now.

But then Kyle bends over to show Roo what's in his hands and I catch a glimpse. It's a small, pale mushroom. A *glowing* mushroom. As I watch, the mushroom's greenish light seems to seep away. Kyle cups his hands and blows on it, and the light of the mushroom intensifies again.

"What. Is. That?" Roo repeats.

"Oh, nothing," Kyle says. "Just a volcanic mushroom."

"I want one!" Roo insists.

"They're all over the place," he says. "Come on, let's keep moving."

As we walk, I stare into the jungle and realize that there *are* mushrooms growing on almost every tree trunk, so many that I'm shocked I didn't notice them before.

I pluck a mushroom and blow on it but nothing happens. When Roo blows on one, it gives off a tiny little gasp of light, which is better than nothing, but it's just a dim glint compared to the steady, cool light of Kyle's mushroom leading us through the jungle.

"You'll get the hang of it," he tells Roo, ignoring me, which I'm getting pretty used to.

We continue onward, eventually ducking off Normal Path onto Invisible Path. The jungle seems more mysterious to me now than ever before. The animal sounds are louder than usual and getting louder with every step. I hear the whoops of monkeys high above us. Maybe I can listen to everything better now that my eyes aren't distracted by all the bright colors of daytime. As we walk along, I have that feeling again where I wonder if we're still on the planet Earth, or if maybe we're a million miles from anywhere.

As we continue up the volcano, Kyle and Roo murmur back and forth to each other in their own language. That language is partly Spanish, so of course I can't understand much of it, and partly tracking, which I understand even less. Dad and Roo used to talk tracking all the time, but it's just not my thing so I got used to tuning it out. Anyway, Kyle will point to a bent vine and say to Roo, *"¿Aquí?"* and Roo will say, *"Tal vez."* Then he'll point to a snapped branch a little farther along, again asking her *"¿Aquí?"* and she'll say, "Yeah, because of the angle," and he'll "Hmm" thoughtfully in agreement.

Very quickly their tracking leads us off Invisible Path and into pure uninterrupted jungle, the old vine-tripped, branch-slapped, probably-poisonous-snake routine.

"He came through recently, yeah?" Roo whispers.

"That footprint looks at least two days old."

"But look here! This one doesn't seem as old."

"Hmm. *No sé. Tal vez.*"

"That could be a hide, couldn't it?"

"Could be," Kyle says, turning his binoculars upward, "but not sure how it would be for high-fliers."

I keep wanting to say, "*Hola,* is anyone wondering *my* opinion?" but in my heart of hearts I know this is too important for that kind of sensitivity, so I just follow behind and notice the colors of the jungle appearing as the day lightens until we don't need Kyle's mushroom anymore. It's funny in a way, or weird, that all those years Dad taught Roo all these techniques for tracking birds and now she's using them to track him.

"He came through here," Roo says after a long silence. "Right through here, earlier today, this morning! See that?"

I peek over her shoulder and follow her pointing finger to a patch of mud. I don't even see a footprint there. But, "You're right!" Kyle says, gazing at the mud. "You're totally right!" *Man,* I think, even though I know it's an inappropriate thought, *I hope someday he's that excited by something* I *say.*

I still can't tell what it is they're seeing, but whatever it is, I guess it means DAD, which makes my heart do acrobatics.

But not much has changed by midmorning. We're still just bush-whacking through the jungle, no Dad in sight. It's the second gray day in a row, which feels strange after the cartoon-perfect weather of the first mornings here. The humid air creates a soggy feeling in my brain. The weather seems to be affecting the birds too—the air above us is still, almost no movement anywhere. The only birdcalls we hear are distant and muted.

I'm starting to get frustrated and impatient, sweaty and hungry. How in the world are we ever going to find Dad in this crazy jungle? It makes me want to scream. If only we could rewind back to a year ago, when everything was fine.

Roo and Kyle, though, don't seem discouraged at all. They just keep talking quietly to each other, staring deep into the jungle, looking closely at everything, acting as though we're about to find Dad any minute now.

I look down and step carefully over a moss-encrusted log, and that's when they vanish. Because when I look back up, they've disappeared. One second they were up there ahead of me, and now they're gone, absolutely gone.

But I can hear them, shouting and screaming. I run up to where they were a second ago, and when I see them there in the bottom of a pit I'm partly thinking I'd better stick with them, partly not thinking at all, and partly tripping over the same vine that must have tripped them, and then I'm sliding down the muddy wall of the pit, slamming into them as I land.

"Umph," we all go from the impact.

Kyle looks at me with desperate, disappointed eyes. "Mad!" he says. "Why didn't you *stay up there*? Then you might have actually been able to help us!"

Roo, who can tell I feel so terrible I'm about to cry, glares at him. "Shut up!" she says. We're not allowed to say *shut up*. That's the one thing Dad is strict about. He doesn't care about bad words. But *shut up*—that's bad, because it means you aren't willing to listen. "She didn't so she didn't," Roo informs him, "so that's that." I'm too ashamed to make eye contact with either of them.

Kyle backs up as much as he can in the tiny space and takes a running jump at the muddy walls, grabbing for the vines and roots dangling over the top. But the pit is just deep enough that he can't reach. He slams himself against the mud wall. "Stupid sinkhole!" he yells. Then, after a few minutes, he shrugs. He slides down to sit with his back against the wall and looks mad. Mad and sad. His silence is actually way worse than his yelling and jumping.

"I'm sorry," I offer up shakily. I can't tell if I'm more nervous about Kyle being mad at me or about the fact that we're stuck in a pit in the middle of the jungle.

"It's okay," he says with an exhausted sigh, putting his face in his hands.

Right then Roo's stomach growls so loudly that we all can hear it. It makes a ferocious sound, like an angry rodent.

"Jeez, Roo!" I can't help but giggle.

"I'm hungry!" she defends herself.

"Poor Roo," I say. "I'm hungry too."

"Poor Mad," she says, patting my stomach.

Have I mentioned that my little sister is my best friend in the whole wide universe and I love her so much that even when we're stuck at the bottom of a pit just being near her makes me way less scared than I would be otherwise? Roo digs around in her backpack and comes up with a handful of grape Jolly Ranchers, which is a bummer.

"Ugh, I hate the grape ones," I say.

"Me too," Roo says. "That's why they're the only ones left."

But she unwraps three of the Jolly Ranchers and hands one to me.

Kyle's face is still in his hands. Roo shoves a Jolly Rancher between his thumb and finger.

"I guess we'd better save the other four," Roo says gloomily, gazing with longing at the hated grape Jolly Ranchers. "We might be here awhile."

It's not till Roo says that—*We might be here awhile*—that I begin to feel deeply scared.

"Please be quiet," Kyle whispers, his first words in many minutes. His voice is dead calm, nothing like the cold angriness of before. "Something's coming."

My heart starts going quadruple time. Panicking, I grab Roo's hand on one side and Kyle's on the other. Roo's is hot and sticky and friendly and squeezes back. Kyle's is cold and wet and limp.

I strain my ears, try hard to hear whatever it is that Kyle hears, but all I hear are the sounds of the jungle, and they seem to grow louder every second. Or wait. I think I *do* hear something moving through the underbrush—a nightmare come to life—something approaching, approaching. *What is it?* My mind whirls—what's coming, animal or monster or witch, or, worst of all, someone from La Lava? Yes, I can hear it, can make out footsteps coming toward us, can separate that noise from the jungle noise, and my fear deepens, knotting up my gut.

Then a figure appears above us and stops at the edge of the pit. It's wearing a black hooded jacket, and its face is hidden by the shadow of the hood. It lifts its right hand as though to wave but then freezes there with its palm facing us. I can feel it staring at us. Its eyes and teeth glow white in the green light of the jungle. It's like a robot, or an alien, the way it stands there so still and silent as it prepares to do whatever it's going to do to us. I shut my eyes and hope as hard as I can that whatever it is will leave us alone.

It's not till Roo says, "Hi, Dad!" that I open my eyes and notice the blinking green light around the figure's right ankle.

"I thought this pit might slow you down," Dad says, sitting on the rim, dangling his legs over the side. He pushes his hood back to reveal newly gray hair. "I barely avoided it myself when I came through here earlier."

All I can think is, *Oh my* gosh*! He's being* normal*!* I mean, he seems just like his regular old self, stepping into our kitchen after a trip to the grocery store, getting ready to tell us about the Risky Item. (Dad had this rule that each time he went grocery shopping he had to buy one thing he'd never bought before—an unusual spice, a weird vegetable, a Russian jam, et cetera.)

"You've done a fantastic job tracking me today, kids," Dad continues. "I'm impressed, no doubt about it."

I glance over at Roo and Kyle, who are the ones Dad should be impressed with. They're both grinning up at him like fools, and I realize I've been grinning up at him like a fool too. Dad's just that way. There's just something about him that makes you want to smile. And it feels like now that he's here, everything's going to be totally fine.

"Dad!" I find myself calling up to him. "We missed you so much!"

"Well, if you almost fell in it yourself, why didn't you wait here to warn us about it?" Roo says, half angry and half giggling.

"Don't even get me started about missing, Madpie," Dad says to me, and his voice has such a great big huge sadness in it, such a ton of worry, that I'm relieved when he moves on to answer Roo's question. "I have very important and pressing business to attend to today, Miss KangaRoo. I couldn't just stand here waiting for three ragamuffins who shouldn't be in this jungle anyway. But I did plan to circle back here, just in case. And it's a good thing I did, right?"

Oh man, it is *so* great to hear Dad saying our nicknames!

"I guess so," Roo says sheepishly. "But mainly what's cool is that this whole time we've been looking for you and now we found you! Or, I guess, you found us. Anyway, here we are!"

"Dr. Wade," Kyle says, his voice high and nervous, and I realize that this entire time he's been silent, "my name is Kyle Nelson Villalobos. I am a great admirer of your work."

Dad smiles down at Kyle. I can tell he already likes him, which makes me happy.

"I know all about you, Kyle Nelson Villalobos. You're talented, but you need to move through the rain forest more gently. No rushing, you know?"

Beside me, Kyle blushes. Kyle shy and embarrassed—imagine that!

"But you *do* have what it takes," Dad goes on. "If you didn't, I never would've been able to catch that bird with you less than twenty feet away."

Kyle breathes in sharply, surprised, and Dad laughs. It puts a ginormous grin on my face, the sound of Dad laughing. His laugh is one of my favorite sounds in the world, and I didn't realize until this second how horribly much I've missed it.

"Of course I knew you were there, my friend," Dad says. "You know as well as I do it's not only birds we birders can sense."

Kyle swallows hard and then says in the tiniest little voice: "Why did you let it go?"

Dad stretches his arms up over his head and gives a big, bored yawn. "That's a story for another day." But I know he doesn't really feel bored by Kyle's question. It's just that he doesn't want to answer it.

"Dr. Wade," Kyle says.

"James," Dad corrects him.

"We know what's going on," Kyle continues.

I stare up at Dad, dying to know what he'll say, what he'll explain about everything. He peers down at us. He's acting casual and jolly and normal, which fills me with good feelings, but when I truly look at him I see that his eyes are bloodshot and dart anxiously among our three upturned faces. I glance over at Roo to see if she's noticing how Dad's really feeling, but she's just gazing up at him in her adoring away.

"You do, eh?" Dad says, his warm voice mismatched with his worried face. I keep staring at him, at the stress on his wrinkled forehead and in the tense corners of his mouth.

"We do," Kyle says solemnly, "and we are here to help."

"We broke the code in your letter yesterday!" Roo says.

Dad raises his big eyebrows. "Did you," he says. "Only yesterday?"

"I'm sorry, Dad," Roo says, practically in tears. "I know I should have figured it out sooner, but I couldn't!"

"No," Dad says softly, "it's my fault. I'm sorry. I was trying to hide it well, but not that well. I should've known—I was so shocked when you showed up here with Mom. I know I must have acted awfully strange, but I wanted to scare you away from this place. I was desperate for you to turn right around and head back home to safety. I'm sorry, girls. I'm so sorry. I haven't been at my best. I should have done a better job with that and with the code and with all of it." The fun, familiar version of Dad is quickly fading, and I'm already missing him again.

"You could never scare us away, Dad!" Roo announces.

"Roo and I," Kyle says, ignoring Dad's apologies, "we're here to help. You know we can help. You know we have it too, Dr. Wade."

This time Dad doesn't correct him. I can tell by his expression that he's busy thinking about other things. And I'm so concerned about Dad that I barely care that Kyle didn't mention my name.

"You want to help me?" Dad says thoughtfully, after a long moment.

"Yes!" Roo yelps.

"You promise you'll do whatever I ask?"

"Yes, yes, yes!" says Roo.

"You're brave, and willing to do what's right?"

"Of course," Kyle says, offended by the question.

"Okay, good," Dad says. "Now, are you ready for your instructions?"

"Yes," Roo and Kyle say breathlessly. But I know Dad, and I know he's got something up his sleeve.

"First off," Dad says, "I'm going to give you guys a hand getting out of this pit. Second, you're going to march on down this volcano and find Mom. Third, you girls are going to throw a huge, earth-shattering fit and convince your mother that you have to go home to Denver right away. Make an excuse, be sick or homesick or whatever, but get her and yourselves out of here."

My first thought is: *Yes, great idea, we should go home, back to somewhere safe and normal!* My second thought is: *Good luck getting Ms. Yoga Brain to pay attention to any fit we throw.* My third thought is: *Wait, is home really any safer than here—remember The Creepies?*

"What!" Roo says, her good old Roo rage kicking in. "That's not *helping* you! That's just running *away*! And how in God's name do you expect us to abandon our own *father*?"

How in God's name do you expect. One of Dad's most used phrases.

"If you really do know what's going on," Dad says quietly, "then you know what's at stake. I've already made a few mistakes and I can't afford to make any more. You girls and your mother have got to get out of here."

Right then something clicks for me, something I didn't realize until this exact instant that suddenly seems miraculously, positively obvious.

"La Lava is spying on our house in Denver!" I cry out.

Of course! What else would have caused The Creepies, Mom's suspicion that the phone was being tapped, the feeling of eyes at the windows?

Dad's face falls, and for the first time ever in my entire life he seems old to me. "So it's true," he whispers. He gazes upward, takes a deep breath, and then looks back down at us. "Be that as it may," he says, "you're safer in the U.S. It's much harder for them to arrange a convenient accident there."

For some reason, the calm, logical way Dad is talking about this makes the danger feel far more real. And now I am *scared*, scared in a whole new way, scared as I've never been scared.

"I won't help you out of there until you promise to do as I say," Dad says.

I don't even stop to think, *Jeez, would our own father really leave us in this pit?* before the words rush out of my mouth: "Okay, okay, yes, totally, of course, we promise! We'll be out of the country by tonight at the latest, I swear!" I even start to imagine it all: running down to the Selva Lodge, faking a mysterious headache or an intense pain where my appendix is, calling Mom to come back early from Relaxation and Dumbation, begging her to take me to our pediatrician, lots of tears and gagging, two planes and three airports later arriving home. . . .

"Do you promise?" Dad says firmly to Roo and Kyle, who nod

at him, wide-eyed and serious. "You all promise, one hundred per-cent?"

"We *promise*!" I say with great emotion.

"Don't cry," Dad instructs me, noticing that I'm close.

He throws a thick vine down to us. Roo shimmies up it first, then me, then Kyle. As soon as Dad gets all of us over the edge, Roo bumps up against him for a hug. Dad gives her the world's shortest hug before letting go.

"Go now!" he yells under his breath. "Fast! Go! *Now!*"

I want to hug Dad too. I want to say goodbye. Who knows when we'll see him again.

But he wants us to go. So we go. Kyle leads the way, and next comes Roo, and then me. When I turn to get one last look at Dad, he's already disappeared. And since he's not around to see me do it, I decide I'm allowed to cry.

For a while we bushwhack in silence, moving as quickly as possible given all of the jungle's hurdles. Once we're back on Invisible Path, Kyle slows the pace and I start to catch my breath. Then he turns around to look at me and gives me the biggest, brightest smile ever. I had no idea he could smile like that. Wow.

"Great work back there, Mad," he says. "You did a killer job."

I have no idea what he's talking about.

"Yeah," Roo agrees. "You were awesome. Totally convincing. You almost convinced me!"

"Totally convincing?" I echo, confused.

"Your dad *definitely* believed you," Kyle assures me.

"I didn't know you could lie that well!" Roo says. She gives an impressed whistle.

Before I can say, "Um, hello, I wasn't *lying*," Kyle steps around

Roo and reaches back to grab my hand. His hand may have felt cold and wet and limp before, but now it feels warm and energetic and gives me this strong, thrilling squeeze that leaves me speechless.

"You're the best, Mad, you know that?" he says.

"Yeah!" Roo pipes in. "The very, very best!"

And for a second it almost makes me forget that I really did want to go back to Denver and leave my dad at La Lava. Almost.

CHAPTER 13

When we step into the concrete courtyard of the Selva Lodge, it seems absolutely amazing to me that there are normal people here in the normal world, kids splashing in the pool and adults drinking colorful drinks with miniature umbrellas. But we don't stick around to enjoy the vacationy feeling. We scoot across the courtyard to our room, rushing to get there before anyone notices that we're covered in jungle slime. Roo has green and black smears of mud up and down her legs and a smudge across her forehead, and Kyle and I aren't much better.

"Do we just call over to La Lava and ask for Mom?" I say to Roo and Kyle once I've locked the door behind us. No matter what those two think, I'm going to take Dad's instructions seriously. "I know she wrote the number down somewhere."

Roo giggles and plunks down on her bed. Kyle stares at me.

"Is she serious?" he asks Roo, leaning back against the wall.

"Yeah," Roo says.

"We promised Dad we'd find Mom right away!" I say. "I promised we'd be out of the country by tonight!" I don't even care if Kyle hates me; I just want to do what Dad told us to do.

"Yeah," Roo says, "but you were just saying that so he'd help us get out of the pit."

"I was *not*!" I protest, furious. Roo knows I'm never dishonest like that.

"Yes you were," Roo replies.

"No I *wasn't*," I say, realizing with a sinking feeling that there's no way Roo and Kyle are going to follow my lead.

"Madeline," Kyle says. It feels strange and somehow special to hear Kyle using my full name. "Sit down," he orders, and, suddenly exhausted, I join Roo on the lower bunk. "Of course what your dad asked you to do makes sense. He's worried about protecting you. But there are other lives to worry about too."

"Oh yeah?" I say. "Last I checked you hadn't received any freaky threats from anyone."

"Not me," Kyle says. "At least, probably not. But a species is in danger. And your dad is in danger."

"See?" Roo yells in my ear. "We! Have! To! Do! Something!" She raises her hands high above her head and shakes them with every word.

Well, I'm sorry, I can't really worry about birds—even almost-extinct birds—over my sister and my mom and myself.

But Dad. If Dad is in danger . . .

"How do you know Dad's in danger?" I ask, though the second the words leave my mouth I realize it's a dumb question.

Kyle doesn't reply and Roo rolls her eyes.

"Okay," I say. "Okay, so, La Lava is dangerous and Dad's in danger. And we have no idea how long they'll keep him or what they might do to him. Okay. So we can't abandon him. But what *can* we do?"

162

Roo and Kyle look at each other.

"There is only one way to get the attention of an evil corporation," Kyle says, and I think he's trying to sound like a voice-over in a movie preview. "We must publicly out La Lava. We have to prove that while La Lava has been claiming to be the World's Greenest Spa, it has in fact been hunting the World's Rarest Bird." Roo nods along, her eyes glowing.

"O-kay," I say very slowly. "And we'll do this *how*?"

"At the Gold Circle Investors' Gala, of course!" Roo announces. The gala—man, I've been so distracted by everything else that I'd sort of forgotten about the gala. "We just have to capture *it* and bring *it* to the gala and prove to everyone that *it's* not extinct and explain that they've been using *its* bones for their make-your-face-young creams!"

"Thus revealing to the world that La Lava has been keeping the Bird Guy hostage for his tracking skills by threatening his family," Kyle says, his usually calm, cool face now intense with urgency. (*Wow,* I think, *he's even using the word* thus.) "At which point La Lava will be forced by the international community to release your father and stop hunting the birds!"

"The international community?" I parrot, somewhat rudely, but I can't help it—I'm nervous. I mean, *sure,* it all sounds great, but it also sounds impossible.

"Yep!" Roo answers for him.

"And we're going to get this bird *where*?" I ask, annoyed by her perkiness. She acts like it's the easiest thing in the world to locate a bird that's practically extinct.

"No prob," Roo chirps.

I really want to tell Roo to shut up, but in honor of Dad, instead I go: "So, Ruby Flynn Wade, you're telling me you want to capture a pretty-much-impossible-to-find-bird and smuggle it into La Lava's gala, thus"—take that, Kyle!—"saving not only ourselves and our parents but the entire species as well?"

"That's right!" Roo beams at me, reclining on her pillow.

"Actually," I inform her, "that's impossible. And insane."

Kyle crouches down in front of us and puts his hand on my knee, maybe as a comforting gesture or maybe just for balance. But before he can say whatever it is he's about to say, La Lluvia begins with its enormous whoosh and thump, as though responding to me.

Agreeing or disagreeing? Who knows.

"IT'S *NOT* IMPOSSIBLE," Kyle shouts over the racket of the rain. "HARD, YES, BUT NOT IMPOSSIBLE. TOGETHER ROO AND I CAN TRACK BETTER THAN THE BIRD GUY."

Okay, thanks so much, good for you, Mr. Egotistical, I think.

Kyle reaches into his back pocket and pulls something out. A beat-up Polaroid. He holds it up in front of us.

"OOOO!" Roo gasps loudly, and I gasp too.

The bird gleams, shimmers, there on its vine. Bright golden feathers on its neck and chest, a glowing blue coat, a long black tail feather with a bluish glint, a short red beak. It looks like it could spread its wings and take flight straight out of the photograph. *Spectacular* is the word Mom would use. Or, maybe, nowadays, *inspirational*.

"WHERE DID YOU GET THIS?" I yell at Kyle.

"I TOOK IT IN JUNE," he shouts back. "ALL WE HAVE TO DO IS FIND ONE JUST LIKE THIS. LOOK HOW CLOSE IT LET ME GET!"

"*All* we have to do," I mutter cynically under my breath, but of course no one can hear me with the sound of La Lluvia filling our ears.

I keep staring at Kyle's photograph. *Feathers as blue as dusk, throat as golden as lava.* Somehow I'd forgotten it until this very second, but now it comes rushing back up at me: ANYONE WHO TRIES TO CAPTURE THE VOLCANO BIRD WILL BE DRIVEN IN-SANE. Probably—maybe—just an old witch's tale, but still I have this urge to ask Kyle, what about the curse? On top of every other problem with this whole plan, *what about the curse?*

"Anyone who tries to capture the volcano bird will be driven in-sane," I say out loud, though neither of them is paying attention to me, because now Roo is screeching at the top of her lungs, over the noise of La Lluvia, "LET THE MISSION BEGIN! LET THE MISSION BEGIN!"

Then again, maybe Roo's already insane.

"The *mission?*" I repeat weakly, to myself.

"But only if you're trying to harm the bird. That's the other part, the part my *abuela* didn't mention," Kyle says, coming close to my ear so he doesn't have to scream. "Anyone who tries to capture the volcano bird will be driven insane, *but only if they're trying to harm the bird.*" So he *was* paying attention to me! And his breath smells like the jungle!

"Really?" I say. Surprised, and relieved, and wondering if this is why Dad didn't actually go crazy—because he didn't want to harm the bird, only La Lava did.

Kyle hands me the photograph.

"WE HAVE TO DO THIS!" Roo shrieks at me. "IT'S IN OUR BLOOD!"

In our blood? I get an image of a flock of miniature birds flying through my veins.

"IN OUR BLOOD?" I echo, gazing at the Lava Throat.

And right then, before I've even finished saying *blood*, some-thing happens inside me. Something changes, something clicks, and suddenly I'm not doubtful anymore. I don't know exactly what's going on, but I know it's somehow coming from seeing the photo of the bird. I feel strong. Like Kyle. Like Roo. The strength rushes through me, pounding in my head and feet. Yes. We have our Mission. Dad always said everyone needs a mission in life. And he's right. It's good to know what you need to do and then to go and do it. And yes, I'll admit it: I've always dreamed of being the heroine of a story like this one.

It's me who opens the door of our room, me who runs out into La Lluvia while Roo and Kyle hang back, watching. Doesn't this seem like the kind of thing Roo would love to do that I'd never be wild enough to do? But here I am, letting La Lluvia wash over me. I gesture to them, try to get them to join me, and after pointing at me and laughing for a moment they do, they come join me, my two best friends in the whole wide world—yes, I'm not embarrassed to say it—and we're all three prancing around getting blasted by the rain, feeling very clean and very hopeful, enjoying it like a ride at an amusement park, when it stops.

Just like that.

La Lluvia has transformed the concrete courtyard into a shallow pool, and the swimming pool itself is overflowing with water. We wade around the courtyard while the sun comes out brilliant again, making the jungle sparkle and wink.

Then I notice lots of little rainbows popping up from the tops of the palm trees, and all these orange flowers by the gate open their petals and blossom right before our eyes. Everything looks totally magical, and I wonder why I never noticed until now how amazing the moments after La Lluvia are. Even Kyle gets this silly smile on his face. Roo skips around, splashing through the courtyard to pick one of the big orange flowers and shove it behind her ear.

"Oh pretty!" Roo yells. Then, *"¡Hola, señora!"* she cries across the courtyard, and I turn to see the witch standing in the kitchen doorway, staring at us from behind her black lace veil. I'm so filled with excitement that the veil doesn't even creep me out right now. *"Es muy bonito después de La Lluvia, ¿verdad?"* Roo calls to Señora V, and I'm going, *Seriously, where the* heck *did she learn all that Spanish?*

I look over at Kyle to ask him what Roo said and when he taught her that and why he didn't teach me, but he's standing there looking at me and I forget what I was going to say.

"You believe we can do this," he says. I'm not sure whether it's a question or a statement.

"I do," I say, believing it completely at this particular radiant moment, the image of the Lava Throat still vivid in my mind. And then I get this funny little feeling, remembering that *I do* is exactly what people say at weddings.

By the time I look back over to where Roo is prancing around in front of the witch, the orange flower already looks wilty, like a dirty dishrag flopping over her head.

That night at dinner, Mom tells us that Kyle and Señor and Señora Villalobos will be sharing our table at the Gold Circle Investors' Gala on Saturday. Patricia Chevalier asked Mom where we'd like to be seated and Mom thought it would be more fun to be with people we know, even though otherwise we might have lucked out and been seated with actual famous people. I shoot Roo an Oh-My-Gosh-Are-We-Really-Going-to-Try-to-Mess-Up-the-Gold-Circle-Investors'-Gala glance but she's so good at keeping secrets that she doesn't react at all, not even to sneak a look back at me.

"Oh yay!" Roo says. "Everyone together! I can't wait to have a fancy dinner with Dad plus all of us!"

"Daddy," Mom says with a gigantic smile, "will not be sitting with us. He has other obligations at the gala."

"What?" Roo pouts. "That's dumb."

Mom just shrugs gently. And I have to say I'm pretty freaked out by that gigantic smile on her face. It's a huge, blank smile. A Yoga Smile. Her eyes seem focused inward, like she's radiating all that empty bliss outward with her mouth but not with her mind. Plus: It's weird to hear her refer to Dad as *Daddy*. She never does that. She'll say *Dad*, or *your father*, or *James*, or *Jimbo*, or *my beloved birdbrain*. But never *Daddy*, which is too babyish, she always said. And why does she have to smile like that when delivering the bummer news that we don't get to sit with Dad? A cold, clamping sensation seizes my stomach. Am I just paranoid from all the crazy stuff that's been going on lately, or is Mom truly under some kind of yoga enchantment that's totally draining her brain?

Anyway, I do a little experiment: I inform Mom that Roo and I are going back into the jungle before dawn tomorrow because we had such a great time watching the sunrise with Kyle this morning. If Mom were her normal self, she'd ask a bunch of questions about that—what was it like, and what animals did we see, and do we really have to wake up before dawn again, and aren't we tired. But instead, she just nods and says, "Lovely, lovely."

Surprisingly enough, it's Ken/Neth who distracts me from Mom's freakiness, by asking how our Spanish is coming and clapping when Roo, and then even I, say a few little things in Spanish. The truth is: Ken/Neth is nice. I never said Ken/Neth wasn't nice! Maybe he's an amazing actor and it's a big show he's putting on. I try once again to be scared of him, really I do. I try to imagine that he's dangerous. I remind myself that he could very well be a spy from La Lava. I make an effort to feel creeped out by his stupid, innocent-seeming jokes. But it's just so obvious to me that he's a genuine goofball who doesn't know anything about anything. And frankly, right now it's kind of comforting to have an adult around who's actually paying attention to us and asking us questions and at least trying to make us laugh, while Mom on the other hand just keeps making occasional meaningless comments about Relaxation and Dumbation, saying things like, "I did Downward Dog for five minutes today—do you understand how hard that is?" And inside I'm going, *No, I have no idea how hard that is, nor do I ever want to know.*

As we're strolling across the concrete courtyard back to our rooms after dinner, the night all velvety except for the fluorescent-pink SELV L DGE sign, Ken/Neth stops us.

"Ruby. Madeline. Sylvia," he says, turning to face us.

"Yeah?" Roo says.

"I just want you to know that you are three of the strongest, most amazing women I've ever come across." He says it in this super-sincere, intense way. "You've been through so much this year, and you are all so . . . strong and amazing. You amaze me."

"Thanks," we all sort of whisper. I feel myself blushing in the darkness, and at the same time I wonder why he can't seem to think of any words besides *strong* and *amazing*.

Then he starts walking again and we start walking again.

"Sorry if that was weird," he says, more to Mom than to us, "but I really mean it. You guys are just amazing."

"Thanks," Mom says, "for those uplifting words, Ken. We appreciate it."

He did mean it, I know he did, and you know what? He's totally right. It's about time someone came out and said that to us.

"What's that?" Mom says a little later, when she comes to tuck in Roo.

"Nothing," Roo says, shoving the glowing golden feather under her pillow. She's been lying on her bunk, holding the feather up

169

to the light and squinting at it in preparation for The Big Search tomorrow.

"Seriously, what is it?" Mom says. She walks over and reaches under the pillow.

"No, no, no!" Roo practically screeches. But the feather is already in Mom's hand.

"Re-*lax*!" Mom says. She suddenly sounds like her old self. Smart and determined and concerned about us. And I'm flooded with relief. "Where'd you get this?"

"I don't know. In the jungle," Roo says.

"Where did she get it, Mad?" Mom says. Her voice is very stern.

I shrug indifferently, as though I don't know a thing about it. "In the jungle, I guess." Mom stares at me for a few more seconds, but I keep my eyes flat and secret. Man, I'm doing such a good job. Usually I can't hide anything from Mom. Usually I'd just start telling her everything. I guess I've been learning from Kyle and Roo.

Mom gazes at the soft shimmering feather for a moment, and then the enormous Yoga Smile spreads across her face again.

"Well," she says, "okay." And I'm immediately disappointed that she gave up so easily. If she weren't all spacey now, she'd never let this kind of thing go. She *has* to know, or at least part of her has to know, that she's holding a Lava Throat feather! She loves Dad, and Dad loves birds, and Dad taught her a *lot* about birds over the years. If only she hadn't been yogafied. Then she'd keep asking us questions until we'd have to tell her what's been going on. Part of me wishes she would ask and ask and ask, and then once she knew everything she could tell us exactly what to do.

She bends down and crawls into bed beside Roo, handing the feather back to her.

"It's a very beautiful feather, Roo," she says brightly.

"I know," Roo says, clutching the feather. "Hey, bedtime story, please?"

But Mom's bedtime stories just make me miss Dad's bedtime stories. Dad's are always long and complicated and wonderful. In comparison, Mom's are pretty much disappointing. Dad can make up wild adventures and fairy tales, while Mom can only tell stories from real life.

I tune out the story Mom tells Roo about her first trip to Latin America when she was seventeen and instead try to write a poem. But I'm having trouble writing anything tonight. It's almost like there's too much to put into a single poem. The color of the mud in the jungle, the way it felt to be walking there in the early-morning dark, the glowing mushrooms. Seeing Dad. I keep having trouble so what I end up doing is drawing the volcano in my journal, the perfect shape with a wisp of smoke coming out the top.

Finally Mom leaves, and for maybe the first time ever since The Weirdness, I don't feel a ping of sadness as she closes the door behind her.

CHAPTER 14

"You know the drill," Roo says in the morning after Kyle's knock wakes us.

Yet another phrase from Dad. He loved to say that. *You know the drill.*

We're so focused (and, in my case, stressed out) this morning that neither of us comments on the crop of yellow flowers growing from Roo's toes. But Kyle's words about the fungus flowers keep playing through my head—*a sign of being close to the goddess of the volcano, close to the goddess of the volcano, close to the goddess of the volcano*—as Roo hops around the room, getting dressed, sticking the golden feather into her pocket.

"You better be good today," she warns me as we exit our room and step into the predawn darkness, where Kyle awaits us with his transparent bird net in hand. Man, why does Roo have to talk to me that way, as though I'm the little sister?

Then again, it *is* true that I'm way more likely to get freaked out when we're out there in the jungle trying to do something that's probably impossible.

By the time day breaks, we've veered off Invisible Path and have been walking for what feels like weeks. It's even grayer and heavier than yesterday morning. Roo, a few feet ahead of me, keeps putting little skips of excitement into her step. I couldn't skip right now if someone paid me. The thrilled feeling that struck me yesterday during La Lluvia has faded. The heaviness of the day makes it especially ominous to be heading into the depths of the jungle. I try to distract myself by paying attention to the flowers we pass—weird spiky-looking pink flowers I've never seen before (maybe the extra-humid weather is making them blossom?), and also those big orange flowers that appeared after La Lluvia yesterday, all wilted and dead now, faded carcasses on the jungle floor. I spot poisonous-looking flashes of bright red and yellow as bugs and frogs, and probably snakes too, move amid the trees. The jungle seems ferocious to me today, and with each step my sense of threat increases, until my heart feels like a continual whir of motion, no beats at all. Meanwhile, Roo keeps rushing perkily through the jungle behind Kyle as though she's done this a million times before.

Was it really only two days ago that we set out into the jungle to beg Dad not to capture and kill any LTVTs? Was it really only *yesterday* that we set out to offer him our help in capturing LTVTs? And here we are, and the gala is tomorrow, and we fly home on Sunday, and it feels like our entire future depends on us finding an LTVT, like, *now*. . . .

"So," I say, the first word any of us has said in a long time, "I know we need to capture *it* today"—Roo and Kyle have taken to calling the bird *it*, so I guess I better too—"but how exactly are we going to do that? Are we just going to, sort of, wander around the jungle?" I don't mean to sound quite as negative as I do, but I can't think of a more positive way to say it.

Roo sighs with irritation at my questions. I can tell her exasperation is only a show, though. In truth she's buzzing with so much energy that nothing could bother her.

"Weren't you *listening?*" she says. "We're going to find *it*, easy-peasy."

Okay, sure, easy-peasy, finding a basically extinct bird in a crazy jungle, whatever, but what I want to discuss is *methodology*, as Dad would say. No matter how brilliant a bird-tracker you may be, it's not as though this is a straightforward task. I wish I felt calm, logical, smart. I wish the day weren't so gosh darn *humid*, filling my brain with fog. I wish I weren't just gazing out into layers upon layers upon layers of jungle where hundreds of Lava Throats could hide without anyone having any idea. I think back to Kyle's Polaroid, the bird ready to spring into life and fly out of the photograph. How will we ever find, much less catch, a pigeon-sized creature like that in all this chaos and vegetation?

"Easy-peasy?" I repeat sarcastically. "Yeah, the way a Herculean labor is *easy-peasy*." Herculean labor: another of Dad's favorite phrases, and pretty impressive for a twelve-year-old to use if I do say so myself, though Kyle doesn't seem to notice.

"Remember what Dad always says about tracking!" Roo scolds me. *"You have to notice the tiniest things in the world. You have to think like a bird."*

"Oh," I say, even more sarcastic. "Okay, great, perfect, that's helpful, I'll get right on that. Hello, I'm a bird, I need to eat, fly, poop, sleep."

I know I sound really dumb, and also rude, but hey, I'm kind of dehydrated. I wait for Roo and Kyle to respond to my little outburst, but they don't say a word. They just keep pressing on, deeper into the jungle. And, blushing a bit, I follow.

Once in a while one of them looks back sharply when I snap a twig or stumble over a log, but other than that, they pretty much ignore me. For some reason none of us has brought up the fact that they'd be way better off without me tagging along behind. But I guess they don't want to be mean, and there's sure as heck no way I'd ever be able to find my way back to the Selva Lodge alone.

So I try to forget about Dad and LTVTs and all the things I'm worried about and instead just think about the jungle, the amazing colors of it, the hundreds of shades of green as you look deep into it. Also I think about Kyle, a few yards ahead of me, holding his transparent bird net out in front of him. Kyle and Roo keep their necks craned upward, and whenever a bird darts overhead they freeze and stare. I try to catch a glimpse too, but can I just say this is *so* hard? I mean, the bird is here and gone in less than half a second!

"Was it an *it*?" Roo mouths to Kyle, or he mouths to her, and every time the answer is NO. No, no, no, no.

So this is it, the search for the Lava-Throated Volcano trogon? Three kids wandering around the jungle in the general area where it might possibly be possible to spot the last living members of a species about to go extinct? Three kids playing make-believe? I'd laugh at us if I didn't want to cry with hopelessness.

Still, we keep on keeping on, same old same old, Roo and Kyle doing their thing while I bumble along behind. Finally, sometime in the middle of the day, after I've been starving for a long time but have bravely not complained, Kyle stops and pulls some food out of his backpack: black-corn tortillas, pineapple chunks, strangely shaped nuts that make me sad for a second because these are probably the unusual jungle nuts Dad wrote us about in one of his early, normal letters back in January.

"*¿Comida de tu abuela?*" Roo asks.

"Claro," Kyle says.

The witch's food is the most satisfying food in the world. Even though there isn't a lot, after eating it I feel very full and very strong. It's actually kind of eerie how much that little bit of food does for me. My senses are more alert, my ears perked to the screeches and hoots and howls and trills of the jungle. Now that I'm truly listening, the jungle seems to overflow with the noise of demon creatures. But I'm with Roo and Kyle, and Roo and Kyle are with me, so I try to stay calm.

By late afternoon, though, Kyle is in one of his don't-you-dare-talk-to-me moods and Roo looks like she wants to kick somebody. Even though I was right all along about this being impossible, it's not as though I'm enjoying my rightness. The jungle keeps getting darker and darker, La Lluvia's warning sign. Kyle says something to Roo in Spanish and she turns around and starts leading us back downhill, back toward the Selva Lodge. So even Roo and Kyle are finally giving up after this stupid exhausting useless march. I can feel Kyle storming along behind me. I wonder if he's thinking that my hair looks nice and dark and shiny, or that it looks dull and dark and dirty, even though I pretty much know he's not thinking about my hair at all. I glance back at him, hoping that maybe he'll be looking at me, but he's staring at the high branches of the trees, his eyebrows wrinkled with Big Thoughts, and somehow I bet his Big Thoughts are also very dark thoughts, and a fresh layer of worry spreads over all the worry I've already got.

As usual, everything is normal back at the Selva Lodge, parents standing up from lawn chairs and wiping sweat off their foreheads and yelling at their wrestling, squealing kids to get out of the pool because the rain is going to start any second now and besides, it's siesta time. I'm surprised all over again to see people actually vacationing.

The concrete courtyard quickly empties of tourists, and Kyle and Roo head straight for the kitchen of the Selva Café, so I follow.

"*Tengo sed,*" Roo mumbles as she staggers in the door.

"*Yo también,*" Kyle says.

It's a little lonely being the only one who doesn't know what *sed* means. And I feel extra lonely when we discover that the witch isn't in the kitchen, which is like something out of an impossible nightmare, because she's *always* in the kitchen at this time of day. And it strikes me that I'm not so very scared of Señora V anymore. When I call her a witch I'm doing it out of habit, or even as a compliment. I mean, yes, I still think she's powerful, I still bet she's capable of doing some scary things, but I'm just not that scared of her. And I really wish she were here right now.

Roo and Kyle and I plunk down into the red plastic chairs at the metal table and just sit there staring blankly and not talking. Kyle puts his elbows on the table and his face in his hands. My head feels fuzzy and heavy, and I bet theirs do too. Tired and mad and sad and tired. Hot, thirsty, hopeless. We've become so limp, so *lame,* and I realize that this must be us giving up for good. The gala is tomorrow and we've got nothing, nothing, nothing.

I stare out the kitchen window and notice that the volcano is steaming and smoking even more than usual.

"Can we get *outta* here?" Roo says to me, her voice rising with frustration. "If she's not around I'd rather just take a nap or something."

"Sure." I leap on Roo's suggestion. I want to get out too. I never thought I'd feel this way, but I'm finding that the kitchen seems absolutely horrible without the witch, dull and doomed.

Kyle doesn't pay attention to us, his face still buried in his hands. Roo and I stand up to leave, but the *exact* second we reach the door, La Lluvia comes crashing down.

And when we turn around, who should be there but the witch in her beautiful black lace veil, pouring something hot and red into three mugs on the metal table. I swear, it's like she appeared out of *nowhere*!

Kyle heaves a huge relieved sigh as he gazes up at his grand-mother. It only takes me an instant to get up the courage to flop down into the chair right beside his, my ankle thumping against his ankle and then staying there, touching. I guess that's the kind of friends we are. The kind of friends who let their ankles touch under the table while La Lluvia does its thing outside. I have to bite down on the grin that pops onto my lips.

The witch pushes one of the mugs toward me. Frankly, the liquid in the mug looks more like blood than anything else. But here's the strange thing, which hits me right then as I stare at that steaming, poisonous-looking liquid: Now I'm excited, not scared, to drink the witch's drinks.

I take a sip. And much to my surprise, it tastes like honey and chocolate, two of my favorite flavors.

"Ooo!" Roo gasps. "Vanilla! And pink Skittles!" Vanilla and pink Skittles—two of Roo's favorites. But it's most definitely *not* vanilla and pink Skittles. It's honey and chocolate!

"No," Kyle corrects, "it's Dr Pepper but without the fizz, plus candy canes."

Well, okay, whatever. The witch smiles on us from behind her veil with a warmth that feels almost physical, like the way the sun feels on your arms, and suddenly I'm calmer than I've been all day.

A few sips in, I notice what a pleasant smooth sound the rain is making all around us, so loud we can't talk, but such a lovely sound that it softens my thoughts, and I'm really enjoying the warmth of Kyle's ankle against my ankle. We're just touching the tiniest of bits (like, he probably doesn't even notice) but there's this *heat* coming off his skin. And suddenly I'm thinking: *Maybe it's all going to be okay, maybe it's all going to be fine, maybe it's all going to work out very, very well.* For a while I stare deep down into the red heart of my drink, and then when I finally look up, my vision feels somehow different—warmer, more glowing. Maybe someone flicked on a light, I'm not sure, I was kind of spaced out there, but anyway, when I look over at Roo and Kyle and the witch, they seem extraordinarily wonderful to me. Bright little fireball Roo, perking up to listen to whatever Spanish words the glorious good witch Señora Villalobos is murmuring into her ear while smart, solemn, radiant Kyle looks on. They all just look *exceptionally* beautiful! But not only beautiful. They look . . . larger than life. Like ancient gods or something. Kyle's golden eyes seem to be creating their own light. My head and fingers and belly feel very airy. Sort of like they don't weigh anything anymore. Almost as though I'm drifting toward the ceiling. It's a splendid, splendid feeling. A floating, joyful feeling that erases my frustration. I can't wait to try again, to go back into the jungle tomorrow and look for that bird. I stare at Kyle and Roo, wondering if they're feeling the same thing I am. I want to ask them, but my vocal cords are as drippy as honey and I can't speak. So instead, I just smile, huge and loving, the way Señora V smiles behind her veil, and Kyle is looking back at me with an expression that I think might be awe. Kyle looking at me with awe! Just the way I'm looking at him! I feel my heart straining inside me and hold out my mug for another serving of the hot red liquid, whatever it is.

At that exact second, La Lluvia ends.

"*¿Qué pasa, abuelo?*" Kyle says, turning to look at the side of the room, his concerned voice cutting through my dreaminess.

It's only then that I notice Señor V sitting on a stool in the corner of the kitchen. Wait, has he been here all along? How could I have missed that? But what's really odd is that his face doesn't look serene. Señor V's worried face is one of the most frightening things I've ever seen, because I've never seen his face *not* looking serene, and I can't shake the feeling that if he's worried, the rest of us better be *really* worried. Then it strikes me that, for all her veiled smiles and generous pouring, Señora V is distracted today too. She picks up her broom and paces around the kitchen, not sweeping but just wandering back and forth. As I watch her, the happy, hopeful feeling starts to drain away from me, and I feel sad, so sad.

"El volcán," Señor V says simply.

We all turn to stare at it, and as we do, it releases a large burst of sickly greenish steam.

Roo whispers what we're all thinking: *"Once the last bird dies, the volcano will blow."*

The witch sits down with us at the table. Broom in one hand and pitcher in the other, she pours more red liquid into my mug, and then into Kyle's, and then Roo's.

"Tomorrow," she says, almost growling, no longer the gentle witch of a few minutes ago, "you must do what you set out to do."

"The day of the gala?" Kyle says. "There's no way."

The witch slams her broom down on the metal table, making a tremendous noise, and I cringe. Maybe I was wrong not to be scared of her.

"Drink!" she commands.

It's hard to tell who she's talking to, so we all gulp from our mugs.

"We would do it if we could," she says, "but only you three can do it." I get a little flutter in my stomach when she puts me in the same category as Roo and Kyle, even though I know she's just being polite. "It requires youth," the witch explains, "the pure conviction of youth."

She gazes up at the ceiling with shiny wet eyes like those of the lady saint on the wall calendar behind her. Then she stands, mutters *"Arriba,"* and shuffles toward the winding staircase in the back corner of the kitchen. Kyle and Roo and I get up and follow in silence.

When the witch opens Kyle's door, I'm puzzled to see three pairs of loose-fitting green pants and three long-sleeved green shirts laid out on his bed. One small, one medium, one large.

"Uniforms!" Roo gasps, clapping her hands.

"Put them on," Señora V orders.

We pull them on over our shorts and T-shirts, and all the garments fit perfectly. Weirdly perfectly. The witch smiles, pleased.

"We'll blend in so well!" Roo whispers excitedly. "We'll be *invisible.*"

Man. Sometimes I wish I were nine and could still believe in invisibility and that kind of thing. I'm about to tell Roo she needs to have a reality check when Kyle grabs our hands and leads us over to the small circular mirror on his wall. Only then do I notice that the garments are made from cloth that's green like the green of the jungle—a green that contains many different shades of green, a green that changes with every movement I make.

We stand there, shimmering. The feeling I got from the red potion returns. I'm suddenly flooded with belief, belief in impossibility and invisibility and magic. I squeeze Roo's hand. I squeeze Kyle's hand. Here we come.

CHAPTER 15

*J*t takes until the next day—around the time I tell Roo and Kyle to please stop marching onward because I really, really have to pee—for all the magic to wear off. The magic of pulling on our amazing camouflage clothes before dawn. The magic of Roo having an extra-large batch of yellow toe-flowers this morning—*oodles* of toe-flowers, such an incredible crop that even I had to compliment her on it. The magic of believing that today the toe-flowers are a good omen rather than a bad one. The magic of believing that ANYONE WHO TRIES TO CAPTURE THE VOLCANO BIRD WILL BE DRIVEN INSANE doesn't apply to us, because we are a force of good. The magic of Kyle looking happy, truly happy, to see us when we met him at the back gate. The magic left over from the potion—that red, thrilled feeling—carrying us lightly upward into the jungle, up Invisible Path and beyond, convincing me there's a Lava Throat around the next bend. The magic of Roo glancing back to nod and wink at me, except that she can't wink, so her version of winking is to blink in a very friendly way. The magic of the three of us, out in the jungle, alone.

But now it's past noon, and the gala starts in a matter of hours, and there are no more skips in Roo's steps. Instead, she scowls up at the trees and gives an occasional fear-of-heights shiver as our route steepens. Kyle looks as exhausted as I feel, his skin almost grayish, his golden eyes bloodshot. The jungle seems extra weird, extra claustrophobic. With every passing second I get more and more worried, more and more scared. I try not to think about what will happen to Dad, what will happen to Roo and Mom and me, if we don't find an LTVT, but the thought hovers there like a dark fog, making it hard for me to breathe and sometimes even to see.

Anyway: My bladder is about to explode. I've been holding it for a *long* time, first because I didn't want to distract anyone from The Mission, and then because we got going up this super-steep part with practically a cliff on the right-hand side and it was clearly not a good place for that kind of thing. I was planning on dealing with the situation as soon as we got to a less-steep place, but there doesn't seem to *be* a less-steep place, and I seriously don't think I can make it another step without using the so-called bathroom first, even though I hate asking Roo to stop in a place that's making her fear of heights come out.

"Okay," Roo says generously. "I have to pee too." I flash her a weak smile of thanks. Whenever I've had to pee in the jungle over the last few days, Roo's always stayed beside me, because I'm basically a wimp, and not all that happy about having to crouch down where any sort of exotic scorpion could bite my bum at any second, and it makes me feel better if Roo's there, because she's most certainly not a wimp.

"Fine, I'll go on ahead a bit," Kyle says impatiently. "Be fast."

I take a look around for a possible place to go, but since there's a steep slope stretching down to our right and up to our left, Roo and I have to squat exactly where we are.

"Darn!" I say, trying to crouch enough to pee but not enough that my bum touches any of the underbrush, which, let me just say, is a truly tricky balancing act.

For the first time ever, Roo seems to be finding it more upsetting to pee in the jungle than I am. She keeps glancing over her shoulder at the drop-off on the right side.

"Darn, darn, darn, darn, darn, darn, darn!" I say the whole time I'm peeing, because that's the kind of thing that would usually amuse Roo. But she doesn't even crack a smile. She just looks petrified. And it makes me realize how lucky I am that I'm always the one who gets to be scared while she's always the one who has to be brave and try to buck me up. It's hard being the brave one.

It's right then, as we're retying the drawstrings on our jungle pants, that it happens. Maybe because of the warm liquid seeping into the loose dirt, maybe because of something going on deep inside the volcano, who knows, but suddenly a chunk of the slope breaks away beneath Roo's foot. She shrieks a colossal shriek, and I give her a solid push up onto safe ground before I go slipping, sliding, catapulting downward.

First I hear voices, faraway echoes, someone screaming my name in a dream.

Then I open my eyes to find myself surrounded by hazy green darkness. I blink a couple times but it's still dim. I feel vines—vines beneath my back, vines in my fists, vines at my ankles. I'm half lying, half sitting in the half darkness, my legs sinking slightly into thick black mud. I can actually *hear* the mud, a soggy sucking sound. I turn my head, look up and around to try to figure out where I came from, but all I see are layers upon layers of identical hazy dim green jungle rising all around me. Then I hear something else. It's a bubbling sound, and it's not coming from the mud. About a yard

184

beyond my feet, there's a narrow little stream running over the black mud.

But—*wow*—my eyes suddenly attach themselves to something across the stream, something terribly bright in all this haziness, something dazzling.

It's a pile of glimmering round objects as red as blood lying just inside a rotted-out tree trunk. I'm squinting at it, trying to see what it is—a crop of rare mushrooms? the guts of an animal? the world's hugest rubies?—when I get slammed from behind in this totally backbreaking way, the wind so knocked out of me that I can't even scream in pain before I get slammed *again*!

Behind me, Roo moans and Kyle grunts.

"Ow!" I yell. Although I'm so happy they're here that the pain fades pretty quickly. "You came after me?" I say, twisting around to look at them.

"Of course!" Roo says merrily, though her face is bleached white with fear. Jumping down that drop-off is probably the scariest thing she's ever done. I can't even describe how much I love my sister right this second.

I wait for Kyle to say something too, such as "No problem, Mad. I'd follow you to the ends of the earth," but when I look over at him I see he's not thinking about me at all. Instead, he's staring at that bright red pile across the stream.

"Dios mío," Kyle murmurs.

Even I know that one. *My god.*

A weird expression spreads across his face—excitement or terror, I can't quite tell. Roo follows his gaze and her eyes widen until I can see the whiteness all around her irises.

"No *way*!" Roo breathes, staring hard at the thing across the stream.

As usual, they're in on something I'm not in on.

"Uh, excuse me," I say, "do you guys know what that is?" And why does Roo always understand everything while I'm always left in the dark? And why do I always have to be confused at the wrong times?

"Shhh!" Roo hisses. "It's probably nearby."

"*What's* nearby?" I whisper.

"Do you understand," Kyle says, his voice even softer than mine, "that no one *ever* sees this? Like, *no one*? *Ever?* Not even your *dad*?"

"Sees what? What *is* it?" I try to speak as softly as Kyle but it's impossible.

"Eggs," Kyle mouths, his face brilliant with delight.

Eggs?

I squint, trying to see the red blobs better. I had no idea eggs could be that color, or look so moist and shiny. Or that they could glow.

"The sacred red eggs Señora V told me about!" Roo whispers in awe. *"Eggs as red as blood!"*

Well, no one ever told *me* anything about any sacred eggs. When the witch mentioned them she must've been speaking Spanish, murmuring under her breath to Roo, because I've never heard a word about any bloodred eggs.

"Wait a sec," I whisper back. "You mean the eggs of—"

"Yes, yes, yes!" Roo mouths silently.

LTVT eggs! *LTVT eggs!* Maybe even the last LTVT eggs in the entire universe . . .

Very slowly, on all fours, Kyle crawls through the stream toward the nest. Roo follows, also crawling, and I do too, pretending it's not at all annoying to crawl through this thick black clinging mud.

"Four eggs!" Kyle says, stopping to crouch a yard away from the rotted-out trunk. The nest emits a strange, slightly metallic smell.

We all stare at the eggs. Somehow they just make you want to stare at them. "*Four* eggs!"

"Shhh!" Roo scolds him, grabbing a handful of mud and spreading it across her face. "Hide yourself. Lie down. Be silent. Think like a bird."

Much to my surprise, Kyle nods obediently. He smears mud across his face and lies down near the nest, imitating Roo, the bird net in his hands. When they lie there like that in their green uniforms, they practically vanish into the jungle, becoming part of the dimness, only the whites of their eyes giving them away.

"You!" Roo mouths at me. "Hurry!"

Yet again I let myself be bossed by my little sister, and soon enough I too look like part of the jungle floor. I even start to *feel* like part of the jungle floor, lying there frozen with mud on my face, gazing upward into all those leaves and branches and vines, the cool green light, the layers turning every last sunbeam green. Whenever a bird swoops by overhead, I look for a flash of gold, a rush of blue, staring and hoping, my eyes dizzy with greenness. But: No gold, no blue, and frankly, even though it's pretty cool we found these eggs, I'm not sure how much good they're going to do us. What we need is a real, live LTVT by six o'clock tonight. After a while I notice that both my legs have fallen asleep. But when I start to wiggle them to wake them up, Roo looks bullets at me, so I just have to stay here, unmoving.

I'm still on the lookout for gold and blue when I notice a brown bird circling down amid the layers of jungle. It's definitely the dullest, most boring bird we've seen since we left the United States. It looks like any old bird you'd see in Denver, about the same size and color as a pigeon, and I think, *Poor bird, it must feel so unpretty compared to all the splendid birds around here. Especially the LTVT.*

The bird keeps descending toward us, toward the nest, and

then—get this! get *this*!—lands on Roo's camouflaged stomach, and stretches its neck out toward the tree trunk as though it's checking on the eggs.

If I didn't know better, I'd assume the nest belongs to this bird. Or maybe, just maybe, Roo and Kyle are sadly mistaken, and those *aren't* LTVT eggs?

Roo lies there, as still as dirt beneath the bird, barely breathing, and I slide my eyes over to Kyle's eyes, and his eyes are gleaming with shock and amazement, and I'm wondering why he's so excited about a bird that's not the bird we're looking for, when suddenly the bird realizes something fishy's going on. It turns to look at Roo's mud-covered face and spreads its wings up high and threatening, preparing to attack Roo—like it's going to peck her eyes out—and I realize with horror that this bird wants to *kill* my sister! And I'm trying to move my fallen-asleep body so I can save Roo from getting blinded, and Roo is blinking very fast, and the bird rises up ferociously and rushes at Roo's face (and right then I see that it *does* have a golden throat—there's kind of a slight golden tint to the feathers there) and then the bird lands on Roo's neck, and nuzzles up against her ear.

"Wait, is that a—?" I ask Kyle, my voice at normal volume, because it really doesn't seem like there's anything that could scare this bird away right now, considering the way it's winding itself into Roo's hair and smiling, at least as much as a bird can smile.

Kyle sits up and nods slowly, stunned, the bird net limp in his hands. "A female," he says. "Impossible to find. One of the rarest things on the planet. Even my grandparents haven't ever seen one. I'm sure your dad hasn't either." He shakes his head and wipes a smear of mud off his forehead, leaving an even larger smear.

"But that's not what's weird. I mean, yeah, that's weird, but this is *weird*."

He gestures at the bird, which is now cooing into Roo's ear. Roo giggles as though she's being tickled.

"Mad, that's a *wild animal*. A famously *elusive* wild animal."

"I know," I say.

"You realize this is a miracle, right?" he asks me.

"Roo's a miracle. Always has been." Man, for all my wanting to be a heroine like the girls in my fantasy novels, Roo is so clearly the special one with magical powers. "She's the special one," I tell him.

"Yeah," Kyle says, "but you're the one who found the eggs."

His voice is full of admiration, and I'm going, *Are you* serious? Kyle is going to give me credit for finding the eggs just because I lost my balance and rolled down the side of the volcano like an idiot? I would love to take credit, really I would, but I can't. I just can't.

"That was an accident, Kyle," I say.

"No," he says, "the volcano doesn't allow for accidents of that sort."

Oh great. Now he's starting to sound like his grandmother. But hey, I should probably take whatever compliments I can get from Kyle.

"Okay," I say awkwardly. Then I change the subject: "The males are a lot flashier and prettier, aren't they?"

Roo and the bird are clucking and cooing at each other. Roo looks utterly, insanely happy.

Kyle shrugs. "Flashier, yeah. Prettier? I guess it's a matter of opinion."

I like Kyle extra much in that instant—he truly thinks the boring brown female plumage with just a bit of gold hidden away is prettier than the super-spectacular male plumage!

The bird hops up to Roo's head and prances around. "Ooo, head massage!" Roo sighs.

"This," Kyle says, shaking his head, "is by far the craziest thing I've ever seen."

"Yeah," I say, staring at my sister. "So . . . what next?"

"Well," he says with a dazzling grin, "I guess we have our bird."

Roo, who I thought had been completely tuning us out, jumps right in: "We'll go to the gala tonight and show them what's what, isn't that right, Miss Perfect?"

And I'm like, *Wow, that's really cute that Roo's new nickname for me is Miss Perfect, plus I guess I* am *the one who found the eggs and all,* until I realize she's talking to the bird.

When Roo stands up with Miss Perfect on her head, getting ready to follow Kyle downward, Miss Perfect lets out a long, loud cry, a sound so human it makes goose bumps pop up on my arms. The bird cranes her neck back toward her nest, her radiant blood-red eggs, and her body curves with longing.

"I'm sorry, Miss Perfect," Roo says, close to crying herself. "I'm so, so sorry. But you understand. This is all for their sake."

And I know it seems impossible, but Miss Perfect bobs her head as though she's nodding in agreement with Roo—a nod of solemn understanding. The bird turns away from the nest and buries her head under her wing for a moment. Then she releases her head and holds her neck up stiffly, proudly. I think about La Lava taking Dad away from us, and get that hot feeling of tears behind my eyes.

"Will the eggs . . . be okay on their own?" I stop myself from saying *Will the eggs survive?*

"I don't know," Kyle murmurs. "They can go half a day at most, I'd guess, before there's permanent damage."

"Half a day!" I repeat. "The gala won't even be over by then! Mom says bands have been hired to play till dawn."

Kyle shrugs nervously.

"Oh, la di da," Roo says, "we'll get you back here in no time, right, Miss Perfect?"

And Miss Perfect faces bravely forward as we rush down through the jungle, which somehow seems to part more easily for us than it ever has before—the big leaves bowing back out of our way, the vines shrinking to the sides, the screams of the monkeys encouraging us along—although perhaps it's just the new exhilarated lightness in my feet.

CHAPTER 16

It's only once we're safely in Kyle's room, with the door locked and La Lluvia raging outside and Miss Perfect perched calmly on Roo's shoulder, that we truly celebrate. Today we don't need Señora V's red potion to make us giddy. Roo keeps jumping this way and that, putting her face up in our faces and smiling and laughing, squeezing and stroking Miss Perfect, calling out bunches of questions: *How should we sneak Miss Perfect into the gala?* and *Won't Dad be so proud of us?* and *Wait, could I maybe hide Miss Perfect, like, on my body?* and *Miss Perfect, how would you feel about that?* Roo's joy is super contagious, and in the middle of it I somehow forget to worry about everything else, such as the fact that right this very second La Lava may be preparing to punish Dad for not providing another LTVT before the gala—preparing to do whatever they've threatened to do to his family.

It's pretty obvious that Roo is the one who will have to carry Miss Perfect into the gala. The bird tolerates Kyle and will even let him touch her a little, but for some reason she really hates me. Every time I coo at her or reach out to stroke her, she hisses and raises her wings and backs away. I pretend I'm not offended.

"Miss Perfect!" Roo scolds, unlacing her sneakers. "She's my *sister*."

"Don't worry," Kyle murmurs apologetically. "That's how she'd act toward any normal person."

Oh. Great. So now I'm just any normal person.

Roo yanks her socks off and what should fall out but oodles of the yellow toe-flowers. Jeez, I'd almost forgotten what a huge batch she had this morning.

But get this: As soon as the flowers hit the floor, Miss Perfect dives off Roo's shoulder and pecks them all up in a matter of seconds, swallowing them with a sound that can only be described as *Mmm!* I never would've guessed a bird could make a sound like that. I have to say, it's a little gross. So now Roo's fungus flowers are the preferred food of the world's rarest bird? What are the chances? And is it just me, or do Miss Perfect's golden feathers suddenly glint a little brighter?

We're all transfixed, gazing at Miss Perfect, when Kyle clears his throat.

"Now," he announces, "the time has come to clarify our plot. I'll give a speech once we get up onstage. And toward the end of my speech, we'll need to show the bird to prove that everything I'm saying is true. So let's begin with the plan for the smuggling of the proof."

It strikes me then that we have little to no idea what we're doing, that our plan is pretty darn vague. Just as I have that thought, Miss Perfect shoots me a nasty glare. Boy, what's that bird's *problem*?

I don't usually have good ideas about smuggling and that kind of thing anyway, so I decide to hole myself up on Kyle's bed, as far away from Miss Perfect as possible, leaving it to Kyle and Roo to create a little sack for Miss Perfect out of Kyle's bird net.

The sack will dangle from a string tied around Roo's waist, and the bird will be hidden beneath the poufy skirt of Roo's dress. When Roo asks Miss Perfect if she's okay with being tied to her that way, Miss Perfect nestles adoringly against Roo's shoulder, just as she did up in the jungle. Kyle and Roo work on it for a while, folding the net and rigging up the sack and then winding the string through it. By the end it's basically a pouch, which Roo can open easily enough with just two fingers. Roo is mainly concerned about Miss Perfect's comfort. Kyle is mainly concerned about Roo being able to release Miss Perfect quickly when the time comes in his speech. He explains this moment to us as though he's seeing it right before his eyes: The bird will swoop dramatically over the crowd, a swoop that will stun the world and save her eggs as well as her species.

I'm mainly concerned that no one will recognize Miss Perfect as an LTVT anyway, considering she looks *way* less dramatic than a male bird. And I'm extra concerned that by trying to save Miss Perfect and her eggs we're giving up on our own safety.

"How do you know she'll even make this so-called dramatic swoop?" I say, a little nastily. "I mean, she's a wild animal. She might just fly away."

Roo looks at me like I have palm trees growing out of my ears, and, from inside her pouch, Miss Perfect hisses in my direction.

"Mad," Roo says as though she's sad I'm so dumb, "Miss Perfect *knows what's up.*"

Aggravation blurs my vision but no good retort jumps to my lips.

Kyle wrinkles his forehead and says, "There's still a problem, though."

"What?" I say irritably from my post on the far corner of the bed, ever more annoyed by Miss Perfect's obvious dislike of me.

194

"What a good wonderful bird you are, Miss Perfect!" Roo whispers as she opens Miss Perfect's pouch and lifts her out. Then she adds, "What a wacky funky chicken you are, Señorita Perfecta!" Miss Perfect doesn't seem to mind.

"The security will be very high," Kyle says. "All those rich and famous people. There's no way we'll be able to just hop up onto the stage. They'll probably have us in handcuffs before I'm three words into my speech. If I'm even able to get to a microphone in the first place."

I hadn't thought that far ahead. My imagination had stopped at finding an LTVT. In fact, it hadn't even gone as far as *actually* finding an LTVT. But Kyle's totally right. Just as I always suspected. This isn't going to work at all. Not even a little. Disappointment and relief merge inside me, and I take a deep breath.

"Well," Roo says, cocking her head at Miss Perfect, "we need help."

"Help!" Kyle almost laughs. "Help from whom?"

And I'm going, *Yeah, help from whom?* Into my mind pop the Villaloboses, Señora V and Señor V—who, to be frank, are probably the most responsible adults in my life right now. But they have no help to offer when it comes to the La Lava corporation. Mom, Lady Yoga Brain? I don't think so. Dad? Considering *we're* the ones trying to save *him* . . . No. Ken/Neth? I can't believe that name even crossed my mind.

"From the most powerful person at the gala," Roo says simply. "Whoever that is."

Now it's Kyle's turn to look at her like she has palm trees growing out of her ears.

But right then it hits me.

The most powerful person at the gala.

"Vivi!" I practically scream. All of them—including Miss Perfect—turn to stare at me.

An enormous, thrilled grin spreads across Roo's face. "Vivi!" she echoes. "Of *course*."

"You're right, you're right, you're right," Kyle says. "You're right, Mad."

"I know her! I mean, I've seen her!" I babble. "She's . . . she . . . she thinks I have good skin! I've seen her, like, a bunch. Well, at least, like, twice. And we talked! Sort of. She wants to take my skin!"

"Okay," Kyle says, ignoring that last bit, his eyes brighter than bright. "Okay. This is good. This is perfect. Vivi can get us up on that stage. She could get anyone anywhere."

But listening to Kyle's confident proclamations, I tumble out of my excitement into doubt. I remember how Vivi seemed half nice and half mean. Maybe even more than half mean. I think of how I saw her flick her hand rudely at that waiter who brought her a drink, and how scared Patricia Chevalier was of her. And Vivi *is* scary. Or at least very intimidating.

"I don't know, though," I mutter. "I don't know if she'd really help us. I mean, isn't she at La Lava because she's dying to get the miracle treatment?" I pause, disappointed, and then admit, "I have no good reason to believe she'd help us."

"Sure you do!" Roo says as Miss Perfect flaps up to sit on her head.

"I do?" I say uncertainly. I try to imagine how Vivi will *actually* get us up on the stage, how we'll *actually* convince her that three kids have something worth saying to a crowd of important grown-ups, and it all comes crashing down.

"Think about it, Mad," Kyle says. "What matters to Vivi more than anything else?"

"Um," I say, thinking. "Her skin?"

"No!" Kyle and Roo scold at the same time.

"Being a philosopist!" Roo cries out.

"A what?" I say.

"I think you mean *philanthropist*," Kyle whispers.

"Yeah, that," Roo says.

"She's famous for caring about green causes, and kids' causes too," Kyle reminds me. "She's at La Lava because she thinks it's the greenest place to be. Imagine how she'll feel when she learns that that's not true at all."

I guess they have a point. Although I'm still not convinced Vivi cares more about her causes than about her skin. But, say she would help—how are we even going to get in touch with her?

"How exactly will we get her to help us, though?" I ask them. "How will we *find* her? How can we possibly explain all this craziness to her?"

"Easy-peasy!" Roo exclaims, in that way only she can. "You, Mad. Obviously."

"Me?" I say. The one who can't speak Spanish or track birds? The one who's never had a single yellow flower growing from her toes?

"You're the poet, you know it!" Roo chants, pulling my notebook out of her backpack.

"Hey, what're you doing with that?" I yelp, annoyed. Roo knows better than anyone—in fact, she's probably the only one who's ever noticed—that I wrote *PRIVATE* all over the front, back, and inside of my poetry notebook. Not that it's so private from Roo. I mean, I *am* always reading my poems to her. But still.

"You're just going to write her The Most Awesome Letter Ever," Roo says, "telling her all about everything that's been going on with Dad and La Lava and the birds and Miss Perfect, and explaining how she can help us, and then we're going to sneak it to her tonight when she goes to the bathroom. Even movie stars have to go to the bathroom, right?"

Roo shoves the notebook toward me, and Kyle pulls a pen out of his pocket, and they both stand there by the bed, waiting for me to accept what they're offering. Even Miss Perfect gazes solemnly down at me from her perch on Roo's head. I look at the three pairs of eyes—Roo's hopeful, Kyle's expectant, Miss Perfect's demanding—all certain that I can do what needs to be done. I guess it's probably true that writing is the closest thing I have to a magical power. And considering the way my companions have been calling on their powers this whole time, I guess it's probably my turn.

Slowly, reluctantly, I reach out for the notebook and the pen.

"Yippee!" Roo shouts. "Yippity-doo-da!"

I sink down onto Kyle's bed and suddenly forget how you're even supposed to start a letter. Should I put the date at the top? Should I write *Dear Vivi* or *Dearest Vivi* or *Hi, Vivi* or *Hey, Vivi*? For a couple of minutes I sit there, pen hovering above paper, quietly panicking, trying not to let on to the others, who continue to stare at me. Then it occurs to me, simply, clearly, that I will begin the letter with just *Vivi*. And off I go.

Time stands still as I work on the letter that will make Vivi feel as though she absolutely must help us. I sprawl on Kyle's bed and focus all my brainpower on the words, barely even noticing when Kyle gives my ankle an encouraging pat or when Roo interrupts the cooing game she's playing with Miss Perfect to mutter "Mad the Mad Scribbler" in a silly voice or when Señora V drops off a plate of steaming coconut cookies and freaks out with joy about Miss Perfect being there.

"Okay," I say eventually, folding the eight-notebook-page letter into thirds and shaking out my tired wrist. "I'm done."

"Is it good? Is it great?" Roo says.

"Let me see," Kyle says, reaching for it.

But I tuck it into my pocket.

"No!" I say. I don't want him to look at it and think it's bad. And I don't want him to look at it and tell me it's good. I don't want to have my hopes dashed, and I don't want to get them up either. I've written the best letter I'm able to write, with the most honest telling of this whole story, and that's that. It's for Vivi's eyes alone.

"Okay, okay," Kyle says, raising his hands and backing off. "Want a cookie?"

It feels good, *really* good, to be sitting on Kyle's floor, eating Señora V's coconut cookies and rubbing the jungle mud off our faces with napkins dipped in water and being totally flabbergasted that we're here with an actual LTVT. Miss Perfect flutters above us, often landing on Roo's head and sometimes on Kyle's. I ignore Roo's constant flow of chatter to Miss Perfect and instead keep sneaking glances at Kyle's feet, which (as I've just noticed for the first time) are surprisingly small, which seems super charming to me, a grown-up teenager like Kyle with feet that still look like a kid's.

Right as I'm having that thought, I hear Mom's voice snaking up to us through the open window. She's down in the concrete courtyard, which is odd. Why is she back from Relaxation and Dumbation so early? Then she yells, *"Ru-by! Mad-e-line!"* which is bad, because when she calls us by our full names it pretty much means we're in trouble. *Sometimes* it means she has something exciting to tell us, but not usually.

Kyle's already on his feet. "You guys have to go," he says, concern deepening his voice. "Right now."

"Why?" Roo says, reaching up to stroke the bird on her head.

"We can't have her getting suspicious. She can't start wondering

199

if you two are up to something. And she *cannot* see the bird," Kyle says. "Go now! Go to your mom. Just . . . lie low and do whatever it is she wants you to do. Pretend everything's normal."

Normal. Ha.

"But what about Miss Perfect?" Roo whines. "I can't leave Miss Perfect."

Kyle shakes his head. "Miss Perfect has to stay with me," he says firmly.

"Madeline! Ruby!" Mom keeps yelling, louder and louder.

"Please, tell her she needs to stay with me," he says to Roo. "This is important. Come back here after you're dressed for the party and we'll tie her on, okay?"

Frowning, Roo clucks and whistles up at Miss Perfect, who gloomily leaves Roo's head and lands gracelessly on Kyle's shoulder. I've never seen a bird look peeved before. And, hello, my sister now speaks not only Spanish and tracking but also bird language?

"Go!" Kyle commands.

As I run, half tripping, down the spiral staircase with Roo following close behind, I seriously start to feel like we're kids in a book, kids who have adventures and secrets and powers that their parents don't know a thing about.

Downstairs, Mom runs across the courtyard toward us in her tulip dress, smiling, her cheeks very pink and her eyes very shiny. I can't help being creeped out yet again by how happy she seems. How can she look so radiant when her husband is a prisoner of La Lava? It's like she doesn't even remember Dad, doesn't think or wonder or worry about him. She grabs both of us up in a huge squeeze of a hug, which I wish she wouldn't do when Kyle might see. I twist around in her arms and look up at Kyle's bedroom window. I try to shrug at the window and roll my eyes, just in case he's watching.

"Ohgirlsgirlsgirls! Hello, my girls!" Mom says. "Yoga was positively dreamy today, but I skipped out a bit early so we could have a little fun before heading over to the gala!"

Yoga was positively dreamy today. My mom is *not* the kind of person who says that kind of thing. It sends a shiver through me.

"My *goodness,*" Mom says, "where did you get those beautiful green outfits?"

I look down at myself and over at Roo and realize that we're still wearing our jungle uniforms. I'd totally forgotten about that in the excitement of everything.

"From Kyle's grandma," Roo explains.

"Well, I hope you're planning on writing her world-class thank-you notes," Mom replies.

Mom. She's just so clueless. As if Señora V doesn't already know how insanely grateful we are.

"Let's order some *licuados,*" Mom says brightly, "and head to the pool, girlios!"

Girlios? Seriously, Mom is not Mom right now, and it's freaking me out all over again.

"I want us to have a nice, relaxing time before the gala," Mom continues. "I want us to feel our hearts opening up so we're really able to enjoy this special event."

"Uh-huh, okay," Roo says doubtfully, and I understand her tone, because I'm thinking the exact same thing—*Who* is *this lady?*

But we let Mom lead us into the Selva Café to order *licuados,* and we pretend to be two jolly kids on vacation. We act as though everything is perfectly ordinary, not giving Mom even the least cause for suspicion.

"Boy, you girls are full of beans," Mom says as we're looking over the menu at the Selva Café and imagining new combinations of *licuado* we might order.

"Pineapple-mango-papaya-passionfruit-plus-piña-colada-and-bubble-gum-with-a-cherry-and-an-MandM-and-a-red-umbrella-on-top!" Roo announces. "And pink Skittles!" she adds.

"I'm glad you girls can still be silly like this," Mom says. Little does she know we're not being silly. We're just trying to seem normal.

"So, yoga was inspiring today?" I ask Mom, to change the subject.

She looks pleased—pleased that her own daughter has asked such a thoughtful, adult question. "Mad, how sweet of you to ask." Then she starts going on and on about Sun Mutation, and now I'm absolutely positive that all this yoga *has* done something to her, has put some kind of creepy spell on her. It suddenly occurs to me that Dad's not the only parent who needs saving tonight. We need to get Mom away from La Lava and their world-class yoga as soon as possible. I glance over at Roo to see if she's thinking the same thing, but she's yawning and sighing with boredom, and I know she just wants to be upstairs with Miss Perfect rather than down here having to watch Mom act like not-Mom.

Anyway, we order simple mango *licuados,* which seems like the most normal thing to get, and then Mom sends us off to our room to put on our bathing suits. I stand there for a second, my trusty gray Speedo in one hand and the green-striped two-piece Mom got me in the other. But as it turns out it's not such a difficult decision. For some reason I'm no longer scared about showing up at the pool in a two-piece. Maybe because I have much bigger things to be scared about at this particular moment.

A few minutes after we get ourselves settled at the pool with our *licuados,* sunbathing like the other tourists and pretending we're just kids on vacation, Ken/Neth pulls into the parking lot in the golf cart, talking on his smart phone. I'm actually enjoying fake-relaxing with Mom and Roo, and I'd really rather have the two of them to myself, but what can you do. When Ken/Neth spots us he lifts his arm to give a huge wave. He parks the golf cart and strides over to us on his skinny legs. He's wearing a khaki safari hat and a mud-colored T-shirt and sunglasses on a thick teal band around his neck. He looks so dorky that I almost feel sorry for him. And he's even perkier than usual, if you can believe it.

"Good afternoon, ladies!" he booms. "Let me just say, ladies, everything is coming together BEA-U-tifully for the Gold Circle Investors' Gala! Now we just need you three to get all dressed up and impress everyone with your gorgeous selves."

Two things: (1) The Gold Circle Investors' Gala! Jeez. Are we seriously going to do what we're planning to do? and (2) I don't like it when he refers to us as "your gorgeous selves." Ugh.

Roo slurps up the last of her *licuado*. "Hey, can we get in the pool, dudes? I am *done*," she says, burping at Ken/Neth. I have to bite down on my grin.

"Gosh, she sure is a firecracker, isn't she?" Ken/Neth says as Roo cannonballs into the pool, scaring all the other kids.

At least I can agree with him there—within five minutes, Roo has every kid in the pool involved in a huge round of Vol-Cano, a game she's made up that's exactly like Marco Polo except that instead of saying *Marco Polo* you say *Vol-Cano*. It's easy to play no matter what language you speak. All I see of her now is a flash of wet arm or leg here and there as she somersaults and doggy paddles across the pool with her seven-minute best friends. The kids bounce around, screaming and laughing, Roo screaming and laughing the loudest. Everyone looks like they're having such a great time that I decide to jump in and join the game, even though I'm way too old for this kind of thing. The water feels nicely cool and it's fun to be weightless and to not be worrying about anything except Vol-Cano. I'm screaming and laughing just like the little kids when I happen to glance at the fence and see Kyle standing there staring at me in this very serious, calm, adult way, mouthing my name and gesturing for me to come over, and my heart does a jumping jack. Man, why did he have to catch me acting like a baby?

I climb out of the pool, straighten my spine—thank goodness I'm wearing the new two-piece—and walk toward Kyle with beautiful adult posture, preparing to say something like, *Whew, it's so tiring to keep little kids entertained, you know?* But when I get closer I realize Kyle couldn't care less about my posture and my two-piece, about the pool and whatever it is I'm doing in it. He's got something else on his mind, his eyes glistening strangely, looking over and through me but not at me. And you know what I realize right at that instant? Kyle thinks of me as a sidekick, nothing less but also nothing more, and my heart does this painful little twist inside me.

"What's up?" I say, trying and failing to sound casual.

Before he can reply, Roo paddles over and pushes a huge spray of water onto me and Kyle. It's *amazing* that such a small person can create such a big splash.

"¿Dónde está mi pájaro?" Roo demands, lifting herself out of the pool on her strong, skinny arms and scurrying up to us, dripping water everywhere. Her little friends immediately start to look lost and bored without her. "Did you leave her alone?" She sounds outraged.

"No te preocupes," Kyle says, wiping pool water off his forehead. *"Está con mi abuela."*

Oh my gosh. I understood that! I understood that *whole thing*! It just somehow clicked in my brain. Roo said "Where's my bird?" and Kyle said "Don't worry, she's with my grandmother."

"Hey!" I tell them. "I understood that!"

But Kyle has already moved on: "If your mom asks why I asked you to come over here, tell her I finally figured out how to explain the difference between the verbs *ser* and *estar*."

"Huh?" I say. I'm proud of myself for knowing those two verbs *exist*—it's never even crossed my mind to wonder about the difference between them.

"But," he continues, glancing nervously at me, and in the pause between his words I get terrified that he's about to tell us La Lava is coming for us and we need to run for it right this second, "the real reason is because I can't find Mad's letter anywhere."

I laugh with relief. Kyle! More nervous than I've ever seen him, all because he thinks he lost my letter! Boy, he must think my letter is super-fantastic.

"It's in my pocket, back in our room," I tell him, blushing.

"Oh," he says, "okay, great."

But he still doesn't sound right. Is it just me, or does he sound almost disappointed, as though he *wanted* me to have to follow him back up to his room and write the letter all over again?

Maybe, maybe not. I'll never know, because before I can say anything, Kyle turns sharply away and marches across the concrete courtyard toward the kitchen.

I'm feeling a bit breathless and strange from our little chat with Kyle as Roo and I stroll back over to Mom. Ken/Neth has vanished. I notice a couple of sunbathing girls around my age looking at us with envy. I guess it does make us seem pretty cool to know an older guy like that. An older guy with golden eyes.

"Gosh," Mom says, "what was that all about?"

"Verbs," I say quickly. Hey, maybe I'm not so bad at lying when I have a little help.

"*Verbs?*" Mom echoes nosily.

205

"Kyle finally figured out how to explain the difference between the verbs *ser* and *estar*," Roo says. It's a good thing I have Roo around to remember the specifics.

"My goodness!" Mom says. "I'm impressed. What *is* the difference?"

After a half second of silence, I start with, "It's hard to explai—"

"Feminine/masculine," Roo, brilliantly, jumps in.

"My *good*ness," Mom repeats, eyebrows raised. "Boy, you three sure are good friends. Aren't we lucky that you get along so well with Kyle?"

Roo and I nod dutifully. I resist the urge to wink at Roo, who dives backward into the pool and within seconds has started another screeching round of Vol-Cano.

Mom is telling me that Ken/Neth will take us to La Lava in the golf cart and it's probably time to start thinking about showers when she's interrupted by the appearance of Kyle, who's walking straight toward me across the concrete courtyard and through the pool gate. My eyes are stuck on him as he comes, right at me, me, *me*! Mom watches me watching Kyle.

"Hey again," Kyle says when he reaches us.

"Hello there, Kyle," Mom says.

I don't say anything. I feel all warm and splendid. Kyle just used his muscles to walk toward me! He wasn't walking toward anyone else . . . only me. I stand up.

"Something to show you," Kyle explains.

"Okay," Mom says with an amused grin, "you can borrow my daughter for a moment, but she better be in the shower fifteen minutes from now."

Kyle nods solemnly.

"Bye," I whisper to Mom as Kyle grabs my hand (!) and leads me back across the pool area. Holding my hand! In public! My heart is beating so fast that it feels like it's tripping over itself.

We pass through the concrete courtyard and out the back gate, onto the jungle path. If it were anyone else I'd probably say, "Hey, can we maybe not go on a *hike* right now, considering all I'm wearing is a two-piece bathing suit and flip-flops?" But because it's Kyle I don't say anything. Kyle must have a plan—he always does.

About twenty yards up the trail, he stops in front of a tree trunk.

"What?" I say.

"Just look," he whispers.

So I stare at the tree trunk. I squint and stare and look and gaze and stare some more. And I don't see anything except just a regular old dark brown tree trunk.

"What?" I repeat.

"Use your eyes," he commands softly.

I look and look and *look*.

Then! I see it. A creature so perfectly matched to the tree that it doesn't look like a creature. I squeeze Kyle's hand which, miraculously, is still holding mine.

"A good omen," Kyle murmurs. "It's rare to see this. My grandparents will be glad."

We stand there together staring at the chameleon.

"Don't be scared," he says.

"I'm not," I lie.

"If we're brave the plan will work."

"I know," I whisper, even though I don't know.

I take a really deep breath and for a second stop feeling nervous about everything. Kyle tugs my hand and we turn back. At the gate he lets go of me.

"Roo already believes. She doesn't need good omens," he says. "I had to show you."

"Thanks," I whisper. But there's something else I want to add, something I can't find the words for. Instead, I just say "Thanks" again.

Kyle flashes me a brief smile, then turns and heads for the kitchen. I watch him as he goes, his straight posture and thin arms, and I have this weird little feeling like there's something I know about him that no one else knows. I'm wondering what exactly it is, this thing I know about him, when suddenly Roo comes pelting across the concrete courtyard toward me, a trail of wet footprints behind her, her body slamming hard against mine. "I missed you I missed you I missed you where were you?"

"Jeez, Roo, relax," I tell her, opening my arms to hug her. "I was just checking to see if they sell hair bands in the Selva Shop." I can't remember the last time I lied to Roo. Maybe never.

"They don't," Roo says cheerfully. "You shoulda just asked me. I looked for hair bands there *days* ago."

"Oh yeah, Miss Know-It-All?" I give her a squeeze and together we hurry to our room, where I send her into the shower first. Roo may boss me when it comes to the jungle, but I boss her when it comes to hygiene.

"Did you wash between your toes?" I ask her as we swap places, me in the shower and her out.

"I can't wash my toes too well right now!" she exclaims, as though I'm being ridiculous. "My *toes* are serving a *purpose*."

I spend my whole shower grinning about that sentence. My *toes* are serving a *purpose*.

"Roo," I say when I step out of the shower, "are you scared?"

"Scared of what?" she says.

"Things not working out tonight." I stop myself from adding *obviously*.

"No," she says matter-of-factly.

"Why not?"

"We have Miss Perfect," she says.

"But what about Vivi? What if we can't find her to give her the letter? What if she doesn't want to help? What about La Lava and the way they've told Dad they'll, you know . . . ?"

Roo shrugs. Jeez. I will never understand her. She's so much braver than I'll ever be.

"The volcano goddess is on our side," she says simply.

I roll my eyes at her, but she's drying her hair beneath a towel and doesn't see.

"Besides, Kyle's the one who has to give the speech," Roo continues. "If I had to give a speech then I might be scared. I hate giving speeches."

I'm so focused on Roo that I startle when Mom bursts through the door of our room carrying the dresses we got for the gala back in Denver.

"An official delivery for my beautiful girls! Beautiful dresses for beautiful girls. Beautiful, beautiful, beautiful girls!" I've never heard Mom say *beautiful* so many times in a row.

Roo goes first. Mom unzips the red taffeta dress and slips it over Roo's shoulders, and I zip it up and tie the sash. With her messy hair and bare feet and cherry-red dress, she looks like a naughty little princess. There'll be more than enough room for Miss Perfect under all that pouf.

"I *love* my red *dress*!" Roo chants, hopping around the room, so cute I want to grab her. I'm amazed that she can act this light-hearted right now—but I guess she's not acting. She doesn't feel the same heavy weight of fear that I do. She starts jumping around on her bed and then bangs her head on the bottom of my bunk, but she gets over it after moaning for just a few seconds.

"Your turn, Mad," Mom says, holding my dress open. I step into it and she zips it. It's a grassy-green color, with slender shoulder straps and a green satin sash. A grown-up dress, no poufs or frills.

"Wow," Roo says breathlessly, "you look like a tree!" Which I know is a compliment, coming from her.

"*Very* Audrey Hepburn," Mom says to me as she gathers Roo's hair into a high ponytail.

"*Way* pretty!" Roo adds, grinning at me.

And I can't stop myself from grinning back at both of them like a fool.

After we put on our patent leather shoes, mine white slip-ons and Roo's black with straps and buckles, Mom whips out a tube of light-pink lipstick (we *never* get to wear lipstick) and instructs us to pout our mouths. It sends a pleasant quiver down my spine, the feeling of Mom applying the pinkness to my lips. Then she cups our shoulders and steers us over to the somewhat foggy bathroom mirror. The phrase "a lovely young maiden" pops into my head as my eyes meet my mirror-eyes. Embarrassing, I know, but those are the words that come to me.

"*Wow!*" Roo gasps, gazing at our reflections.

If it weren't for everything else, I'd be wildly excited about wearing the most beautiful dress I've ever owned, plus lipstick. Once upon a time, putting these dresses on would have been the highlight of our day. But now I have so much on my mind that the second Mom leaves I forget all about the dress and instead start worrying about the gala as I fold the letter for Vivi again, into ninths, and tuck it into what I guess you would call the bodice of my dress. Then

I look at Roo, and Roo looks at me, and Roo nods at me, and I nod back at her, because I guess we're pretty much as ready as we'll ever be.

Roo flings the door open, scattering neon lizards. Glancing over at the pool area as we rush across to Kyle's room, I think, *Gosh, wouldn't it be nice if we could just play at the pool, drink* licuados, *read fantasy novels, and then put on our party dresses and go to the gala and dance and stroll among the pools and eat lots of dessert?* What if we were just regular girls, not girls on a Mission? What if we still didn't know anything about La Lava being evil and Dad being a prisoner and the LTVT not being extinct? What if I didn't have to be worried? That would be great, wouldn't it?

But then my heart of hearts responds: No. That wouldn't be great. That wouldn't be great at all. And I realize that something's changed far inside me, that I'm not exactly the same girl I was when we first showed up here.

"By the way," I say to Roo as we head up the spiral staircase to Kyle's room, "I'm not scared anymore." And at that moment it's one hundred percent true.

"Big whoop, Mad," she says. "I've never been scared."

CHAPTER 17

The late afternoon is at its most golden when Roo and I approach the golf cart. Roo's red taffeta shines in the gushing sunlight, Miss Perfect silent and invisible beneath the puff of her skirt. My dress casts a delicate shadow across the gravel of the parking lot. I gaze down at myself, at the sheer green fabric of the first layer of my skirt, and feel light and lovely, as though I might rise up off the ground. We look like we should be getting into a horse-drawn carriage rather than a golf cart. But that's life.

Ken/Neth is there with his camera, waiting, and as we walk across the parking lot he pretends we're famous, taking pictures and calling out things like "Can I get a smile over here?" and "One, two, three, GLAMOUR!" For some reason he seems more charming than irritating to me right now. He's wearing a black tuxedo with a bright orange tie. It's a little dramatic, but no more dramatic I guess than the moments after La Lluvia, when all those plants release those crazily orange blossoms.

"Boy, is your mom ever going to love this shot!" he calls out as Roo twirls around me.

Speak of the devil, just then Mom comes rushing across the parking lot toward us. She's wearing the most gorgeous dress. How is it possibly possible that Roo and I didn't know about this dress of hers? It's white, or I guess *champagne*, satin, long and slim, and Mom looks like a billion dollars, her hair swept up in a bun and her neck so long. Her skin like the moon, if I were writing a poem. Like she ate the moon and now it's glowing inside her.

"Gosh, I guess we're all set to go, right, kiddos?" she exclaims. Her words contrast so much with her goddesslike appearance that part of me wishes she wouldn't say anything.

Wow, I'm so mean sometimes.

Ken/Neth seems as shocked by Mom's appearance as I am. He stares at her in this stunned way, as though he doesn't believe she's actually there. As though she's a woman stepping out of his dreams. I groan inside. We need Dad back, fast.

"Get a grip, Ken," Roo commands under her breath.

But luckily Ken/Neth doesn't hear. He just murmurs, "All set to go except for Kyle."

"Wait, what?" I say, my stomach fluttering. "I thought he was going with his grandparents." That's what Kyle told us less than fifteen minutes ago, crouching still unshowered in his room, sliding Miss Perfect into the pouch hanging from Roo's waist.

"I promised them we'd give him a ride. They headed over already," Ken/Neth explains. "Kyle was taking too long to get ready."

I'm trying to control the wild little moths playing around in my stomach when Roo yelps, "I'll go get him!" Then she's dashing off across the parking lot, her shiny black shoes sending pebbles flying. I hope Miss Perfect isn't getting motion sickness.

Soon enough, Roo returns, leading Kyle into the parking lot.

And here's what's really crazy: For the first time ever, Kyle looks ridiculous.

"I don't own a tuxedo," he says to us before they're halfway across the parking lot, "so I had to wear this." I can't believe it, but Kyle actually seems to be blushing about his appearance!

"Hey, man," Ken/Neth says, "you look groovy."

"It's my grandfather's wedding tuxedo," Kyle mutters, avoiding eye contact.

It's a three-piece thing, very old-fashioned, and baggy on Kyle (Señor V must've been a lot bigger and stronger back when he married Señora V), so he just sort of looks like a pile of brownish tuxedo. I've *never* seen Kyle not looking amazing. Even in the silly outfit, though, his eyes are as golden as ever and his face is sharp and smart.

Annoyed, he fiddles with the bow tie, his quick fingers turned sloppy on the silky maroon fabric. Ken/Neth comes over and works on it like an expert, and soon there's a solid bow under Kyle's chin. I look at Kyle, wanting him to look back at me, because he hasn't yet gotten the chance to really *see* me in my dress. First he was busy with Miss Perfect, then with being embarrassed, then with the bow tie. But his eyes refuse to meet mine, and the moths in my stomach heave a little sigh of disappointment.

"Milady?" Ken/Neth says to Mom, gesturing to the front of the golf cart. It's unpleasant to watch the way he helps her get settled into her seat before going around to take his place behind the wheel.

Meanwhile, Kyle and Roo hop up onto the backseat. It's pretty tight, but there's nothing for me to do but squeeze myself between them, so I do. Roo sits with her right leg extended to try to make it more comfortable for Miss Perfect.

"Funtastic!" Roo yells as Ken/Neth steers out of the parking lot.

"Isn't this just fabulous?" Mom's in a great mood. A creepily great mood, otherwise known as her yoga mood, which is the mood she's always in nowadays. She simply *adores* going to La Lava, she tells us.

The golf cart picks up speed until we're sailing along in the warm golden wind. I'm shocked by the sudden flash of excitement that jolts through me—excitement at the thought of being at La Lava again . . . the way it smells of flowers and minerals . . . such a perfect place . . . paradise. I'm ashamed about feeling this way—I know it's crazy, I know La Lava is evil—yet somehow I can't help but look forward to every last detail that awaits us. I'm imagining candles and lilies and bubbly drinks and moonlight on marble.

I'm so far gone in picturing it all that when Kyle leans over to whisper something to me I don't catch it.

"What?"

He repeats it, and I realize he's speaking Spanish. Whatever he may be saying, it makes Roo giggle. My earlier magical moment of understanding Spanish has definitely passed.

"No," I beg. "Say it in *English*. Please. I don't understand you."

"*Sólo español.*" He grins at me, looking devilish, his tuxedo-inspired awkwardness already vanished.

"*¡Por favor!*" I insist. I wonder why he's playing this old game right now.

He refuses. Roo does her friendly wink/blink thing at him. The little brat! Then she giggles again and I realize he must be making fun of me.

"Tell me what he said, Roo! Tell me, please!"

But Kyle and Roo just grin at each other and I know nobody's going to tell me anything. So I sit back and try to enjoy the golden afternoon and pretend that whatever Kyle said to me was exactly what I'd want to hear.

La Lava seems more magnificent than before, and also less magnificent. The silken white pavement of the private drive and the gleaming doors by the guard station still make me feel as though we're entering a magical world—but compared to the magical world of the jungle, La Lava seems like just the weak imitation of magic.

Even so, passing through that shining gate and entering the heart of La Lava just as the sky is turning from gold to red, I can't help but catch my breath at the gorgeousness of it. Scary-gorgeous. The interlocking pools are ablaze with pink light, reflecting the sky above. The slight mist in the air gives shape to the sunbeams passing through the trees. Already people are beginning to gather, men in tuxedos and women in glimmering evening gowns strolling among pools and leaning over marble balconies. It looks like a scene from a very long time ago, like ancient Greece or something, when there were gods and goddesses roaming around, or maybe not even from a long time ago but instead from a time and place that never existed on this planet, from some kind of parallel universe where everything is always absolutely lovely.

"Look at the orchids! See? See?" Roo shouts, pointing at the enormous golden vases placed here and there on the balconies and paths, palm fronds stretching high and elegant out of them, orchids spilling over the sides. "Hey! Didja see? I've never seen *black* orchids before!"

"Awesome, right?" Ken/Neth sounds almost as excited as Roo. He steers the golf cart past the golden doors of the lobby and pulls into the hidden golf-cart parking lot.

As the others stroll toward the lobby, I hang back, suddenly overwhelmed by a bad thought.

The thought is: We're walking into a trap.

It's not what I want to think, but it's what I think.

We're walking into a trap.

These people want to harm us, and here we are, on their turf, in this creepily beautiful place, exactly where they want us to be.

Secretly, in my heart of hearts—I'm scared to even put it into words—I know that our plan isn't going to work, that we won't find Vivi, that if we do find her she won't want to help us anyway, that we are headed into true danger.

Right then Kyle looks back at me and smiles. Just like that, out of the blue. The sunset pink across his face. And something inside me calms down at the sight of his golden eyes.

"Why so slow, *mi chica*?" He says it in a casual way. He could just as easily have been talking to Roo or to anyone. But he said *mi chica*—my girl—and he said it to me!

Roo (wiggling uncomfortably to adjust Miss Perfect) turns back to look at me too. After checking to make sure that Mom and Ken/Neth are up ahead a ways and out of earshot, she whispers, "Wow, guys, we are *so brave*!"

Okay, okay, okay. At this point, I guess I don't have much choice but to just hope our plot might maybe possibly work out. I jog up to join them, Kyle and Roo, and there's something about the way it feels here now, so brilliant yet so quiet, that makes us all naturally move in a graceful, courageous way as we approach the golden doorway.

Patricia Chevalier is standing in the middle of the lobby in a wine-red dress, looking like the beautiful devil sister to Mom's beautiful angel sister, and her perfect beauty suddenly seems terrifying to me. It's the kind of beauty that could mask a lot of evil. The kind of beauty that could inspire people to do things they wouldn't do otherwise. She's not the sort of woman you want as your enemy, and fear chokes me all over again.

"Hola, bien, gracias," Mom is saying to Patricia Chevalier, her three words of Spanish. The way she speaks Spanish the syllables sound just as flat as English. It's embarrassing, and I'm relieved when she switches back to English. "Yes, thank you, I'm sure they'd love to check it out," she says. "Ah, there you are, kids! Señorita Chevalier has just suggested we go to the balcony to get a good view of the whole scene."

"Don't you look splendid," Patricia Chevalier says, smiling radiantly at me and Roo, as though she was never the least bit angry with us for embarrassing her in front of Vivi. As though she thinks we're the most delightful young ladies in the world. It's very, very hard not to smile back at her, but I don't. Roo, on the other hand, does—she just can't help it.

Then it occurs to me: Maybe Roo thinks we're better off if Patricia Chevalier believes we adore her. I decide I should probably smile at Patricia Chevalier too, but by the time I get my smile going, she's already spun away from us and is vanishing down a marble staircase.

"To the balcony then, milady?" Ken/Neth says (what's up with this whole *milady* thing?), showily putting his arm out for Mom. Mom hesitates (and I'm going, *Yay! Ten points for remembering your beloved husband!*), but then she giggles softly and places her hand in the crook of Ken/Neth's elbow. Gag plus automatic stomachache. The slight warm feeling I had toward Ken/Neth back in the parking lot of the Selva Lodge dissolves *completely*.

Still, we have to follow behind as Ken/Neth swoops Mom a few steps down the hallway and then through the honeysuckle-draped archway and out onto the white marble balcony. We all stroll to the end of the balcony and look out over La Lava. I can't believe we stood at this exact same spot less than a week ago—it feels like decades if not centuries have passed.

I thought this view was perfect when we saw it the first time, but it's far more perfect now. I guess this is what they mean by breath-taking: something so enchanting that it's *actually* hard to breathe when you see it. Even Kyle is speechless. The tables set with golden plates, the ginormous bouquets, the shiny dance floor reflecting the sunset, the stage where men in white tuxedos are just now pick-ing up their brass instruments, the linking pools, the manicured jungle—and high above it all, Volcán Pájaro de Lava releasing an elegant, twisting strand of yellowish smoke, as though La Lava has made sure that even the volcano will be on its best behavior tonight. The volcano looks calmer than it's been in a while, aside from the odd, intense color of that smoke.

"Whoa, mad styles!" Roo gasps, pointing at a man in a bright yellow sequined tuxedo strolling alongside a woman in a matching bright yellow sequined ball gown.

"Don't point!" I mutter, pulling her hand down.

"Banana split," Roo jokes to herself under her breath.

"Stunning!" Mom sighs. "Absolutely *stunning*! Girls, what do you *think* of this?"

"I have to pee," Roo says, hopping back and forth, imitating so well a little girl who can't hold it anymore that it takes me a second to realize what she's doing. Of course! We need to get to the ladies' room ASAP to wait for Vivi. How did I manage to get distracted from that?

"Well . . . ," Mom says, still wanting to talk about how *stunning* it all is rather than about Roo having to pee, "first things first, I sup-pose. Your hair could use a comb too."

It's true—Roo's ponytail is already slipping and her hair is starting to frizz. I don't mind her frizz, not at all. Roo's hair has always been just as disobedient as she is.

"Where's the main ladies' room?" Roo says.

"Mad, you'll go with her, yes? On the right-hand side of the lobby, down the hallway."

"Okay, but is that the *main* ladies' room?" Roo asks.

Mom looks at her strangely, pulling a comb out of her beaded purse and handing it to me. I try to give Roo a don't-ask-weird-suspicious-questions glare, but she doesn't notice.

"It's a ladies' room, Roo," Mom says. "There will be toilets, I promise."

Ken/Neth giggles. I didn't realize grown men could giggle.

"Okay," Roo grumbles, playing the spoiled brat, "I just really want to use the *main* one that all the *fancy* ladies will be using."

Mom rolls her eyes. "I'm sure plenty of fancy ladies will be using it," she says. "Why don't you go and establish the precedent?"

I'm not positive what *establish the precedent* means, but anyway, Roo takes off running, slightly lopsided from the weight of Miss Perfect.

Before following her I whisper "Bye" to Kyle, who's still leaning against the balcony, gazing out over La Lava, speechless. Or maybe not speechless—knowing Kyle, he very well may be refining our plan in his head based on the layout below.

"See you by the pools," Kyle murmurs back at me with careful casualness, as though he's not giving me an instruction. I give a quick nod and rush off after Roo.

"Don't *run*!" Mom calls out to Roo, but Roo's far enough away that she can ignore her.

I catch up with Roo just as she passes beneath the honeysuckle archway. We hurry through the white marble lobby, past the golden block of the front desk, and down the hallway to the right, as Mom instructed.

On the other side of the frosted glass door where golden letters spell out LADIES' LOUNGE, there are golden toilets and the sink is a long, shallow rectangle filled with black stones and more orchids. The floor is glass, and beneath the glass there's this collage of pressed jungle leaves and flowers, and there are silky red cloths for drying your hands.

In other words, it's the most wonderful bathroom I've ever been in. And at least for now, we have it to ourselves.

"Um, hello, can we live in this bathroom, please?" Roo says, leaning against the golden wall and lifting her skirt way up high.

"Roo, what are you *doing*?" I scold her before I realize that of course she's checking on Miss Perfect, who's there in her pouch, limp, eyes closed.

My heart actually skips a beat when I see her. Is she—? I panic for a half a second before the bird slowly opens her eyes and gazes at me.

"How's she doing?" Roo asks, pawing at the fabric of her skirt and trying to crane her neck around it. It's hard for her to get a good look at the bird, what with all the layers of taffeta.

"Hey, Roo, why don't you at least go in a stall. People could be—"

"How are you doing, Mademoiselle Perfect?" Roo interrupts, ignoring me.

The bird doesn't even have the energy to hiss at me right now. Instead, she stares up from her hiding place with this exhausted yet calm look. I wonder why she seems so weak. Is she thirsty? Or hungry? Or scared? Or stressing about her eggs? Or all of the above?

"She needs water," I tell Roo confidently, as though I know what's what.

But right then the frosted glass door of the bathroom starts to swing open. Roo swiftly drops her skirt, and by the time the newcomers see us, the taffeta has fallen back into place.

"Why, hello," the rich ladies say to us. They're wearing so many diamonds it's hard to look at them—it almost burns your eyes.

For an instant I think one of them is Vivi, but that's just because I'm hoping for her. They're definitely not Vivi. They're all blond, for one thing. Or, at least, dyed blond. I feel suddenly nervous, standing there in the bathroom. What if the rich ladies get suspicious of me and Roo, hanging out in the ladies' lounge for no apparent reason?

But: "If you two aren't ever adorable!" the ladies say on their way out. "Imagine! That *skin*!" "Youth, youth, youth!"

"Thanks," Roo and I say awkwardly.

The second they're gone we work fast. Roo pulls her skirt up again and I fill my hands with water from one of the automatic golden sink spigots, squeezing my fingers tightly together so only a bit of water leaks through. Then I kneel down and hold the water up to Miss Perfect. She sticks her beak through the netting of the pouch and sips from my hands. It feels surprisingly great to have a bird (a bird that can hardly stand me, no less) drinking from my palms. The light touch of her beak reminds me of that pleasant sensation when Mom put lipstick on me.

The water revives Miss Perfect somewhat, but she still seems fragile.

"Oh, Miss Perfect!" Roo murmurs worriedly, gazing over the bunched layers of her skirt.

"Better drop your skirt before anyone else comes in," I warn her, as much as I too wish we could keep an eye on Miss Perfect. If Miss Perfect is too weak to do what we need her to do . . . well, let's not even go there.

Grudgingly, Roo lets her dress fall back into place.

"So, what's next?" I say.

Roo, who I can tell is still fretting about Miss Perfect, doesn't respond.

"Listen," I say, "we can't both hang out here this whole time. Two girls in the bathroom are a lot more noticeable than one. And if Mom and Ken catch a glimpse of at least one of us out there, they won't get suspicious. So let's trade off, okay? Every fifteen minutes or so, okay? Kyle told me to meet him by the pools, so how about I head out there now?" I pull the letter for Vivi out of my bodice and pass it to Roo. "I'll come back to trade spots with you really soon. Just . . . wait here and act normal and be ready to give this to Vivi."

I'm shocked, absolutely shocked, that I can talk this way right now, that I can make a plan and give orders and boss Roo. I'm even more astounded that she nods obediently and sinks down onto the golden bench.

"Sounds good," she says softly. "I'll just sit here with Miss Perfect. The peace and quiet will be nice for her anyway."

I feel lonely, leaving the ladies' lounge without Roo. I wish we could stick together through everything. But I think this is the best way to do it. Now we've just got to trust that Vivi will have to use the bathroom at some point before everyone gets seated for dinner.

It's the cocktail part of the evening, which means people are sipping from crystal goblets as they stroll among pools and balconies, up and down marble steps, laughing and talking in carefree voices, everyone as beautiful as movie stars.

But instead of noticing the gorgeousness, I focus my energy on finding Kyle. It seems like it shouldn't be so hard to spot a teenage boy among all these grown men—the one guy whose tuxedo isn't tailored to him. I resist the urge to run as I look for Kyle in the crowd. I hurry down staircases, past tuxedoed waiters swirling by with bright drinks on silver trays, past a woman almost falling backward into a pool as she snaps at her tall-dark-and-handsome date, through clusters of ladies and gentlemen clinking champagne glasses, all of them blurring into nothing more than hurdles to navigate in my search for Kyle. I'm desperate to touch base with him about the plan. But I'm even more desperate just to see him, to gain confidence from his confidence that we can do this.

Floating candles appear in the pools. The air smells more fragrant by the second, honeysuckle and minerals. There's some new beautiful thing—a vase of yellow calla lilies, a miniature waterfall—everywhere my eyes land. Enchanting, almost like it's casting a spell over my brain. I shake my head, clear my mind, and think about Kyle.

By the time I finally find him, standing alone in the shadows on one of the smaller balconies and holding a tall glass of pink liquid, it's almost time for me to head back to the ladies' lounge to swap spots with Roo.

"Whatcha drinking?" I ask, trying to sound one hundred percent more casual than I feel.

"Don't know," Kyle says, gazing upward, once again not noticing my dress. "Some kind of virgin grapefruit something or other."

I'm surprised by how calm he sounds. I realize I had this idea that when I found him he'd fling his arms open and thank me for tracking him down and tell me that just the sight of me makes him feel brave. Which is, yes, probably what I would do if our positions were reversed.

Plus, am I the only one who's terrified about this gala and what we have to do here?

"Where is everyone?" I demand irritably.

"Your mom and Ken are chatting with La Lava yoga people

somewhere around here," Kyle says, knowing exactly who I meant when I said *everyone*. "And my grandparents wanted to get settled into their seats at the dinner table early."

Meanwhile, he's still gazing upward like it's his job. Annoyed, I follow his gaze.

And who should I see there but Vivi, several balconies above us! So *that* explains Kyle's staring. My heart speeds up. Of course we knew she'd be here, but somehow actually *seeing* her makes it all feel a little more real. Also, get this: Her dress is pretty much the exact same grassy-green color as mine! There are about fifteen people crowding around her as she throws her head back to let out a low, kind of growling laugh.

"Look!" I whisper to Kyle. "Vivi and I are wearing the same color! That seems like a good sign, right?" This comment is partly meant to be relevant to The Mission and partly meant to see if I can get Kyle to notice what I'm wearing. But he just nods and tips his glass back.

The instant Kyle drains the glass, a silver tray containing two new pink drinks appears practically out of thin air. Man, this place is *unbelievable*. Before we can even thank that waiter, along comes another waiter with a tray of appetizers, some lovely thing I don't even recognize—yellow and green and white piled on a cracker. We each take a couple. It's then, when I notice Kyle's hand shaking as he lifts a cracker to his mouth, that I realize he's nervous too, no matter how cool he may seem. And frankly, that makes my own hand shake.

"I've got to go back and trade spots with Roo," I inform him. "We decided it's less suspicious that way. Hopefully *she'll* come along soon." I poke my chin upward, at Vivi.

Kyle nods again, barely acknowledging my existence as he stares at Vivi with that familiar Big Thoughts look on his face.

"Hey, *Kyle*," I say, wanting some kind of reassurance from him before I go, "do you really think this whole bathroom plan is going to work?"

"Absolutely!" Kyle says, *finally* looking at me but still not seeing my dress.

Kyle's bold *Absolutely!* echoes in my mind for a while, but by my third shift waiting for Vivi, I think he's very, very wrong. Tons of ladies have come and gone and come and gone while I've been waiting in here, but not Vivi. Never Vivi. Meanwhile, whenever Roo's in the ladies' lounge and I'm on the outside, I see Vivi on this or that balcony, frowning and drinking and laughing and pronouncing, always surrounded by people. It's maddening! I'm really starting to wonder how we convinced ourselves we'd definitely cross paths with her in the bathroom. It makes me feel like we're just three dumb kids in way over our heads.

Suddenly a gong sounds out over all of La Lava—a long, deep, rich note that hovers in your ears for a moment afterward.

"Good lord, what's that?" a lady washing her hands asks her friend. She's swaying in a funny way, as though she can't remember how to stand up straight.

Like most of the women who've passed through the lounge while I've been waiting, these two don't actually seem to realize I'm here. Once in a while a lady—usually an older one—will give me a quick smile and compliment my skin. But mainly they just ignore me while I sit at my post on the golden bench. It almost makes me feel as though I have the superpower of invisibility. Or maybe a normal-looking American girl is just no big deal to anybody.

"The dinnertime gong," the friend says. "At least, that's what that sexy bartender told me."

"Dinnertime!" she gulps, clinging to the edge of the sink. "But I am *so* smashed!"

Dinnertime. The word makes me go cold all over. Already? My heart deflates. What do we do now? I *knew* this wasn't going to work. Didn't I say this wasn't going to work?

For the next ten minutes there's a big rush of women to the ladies' lounge, everybody emptying their bladders before going to their tables, and I sit there invisible as ever while the dinner gong sounds a second time, then a third, wondering what I should do—give up, leave the lounge, find our table, make a face at Roo and Kyle to tell them I didn't manage to get the letter to Vivi, acknowledge that I've failed Dad, failed Miss Perfect, failed everyone?

The frosted glass door swings shut on an extra-noisy group of women, leaving the bathroom quiet and empty, and I'm slowly, despairingly standing up from the golden bench, when who should come in but Patricia Chevalier in her wine-red dress . . . followed by Vivi in her grass-green dress. Vivi! *At last!* But then I freeze. I can't do or say anything with Patricia Chevalier watching! I panic and dart into the third stall before they notice me.

"Twenty-one," Vivi is saying in her low voice. "*Twenty-one*, Patricia." She pronounces *Patricia* the right way, with a Spanish accent, and I decide that Patricia is actually a very beautiful name. "Thirty-eight years old playing a twenty-one-year-old. It's a fabulous role. But this could be extremely embarrassing."

"You look exceptionally young for your age." It must be Patricia Chevalier who's speaking, but she sounds so timid that I barely recognize her voice.

"Not *twenty-one* young," Vivi says, "and please, I don't want your flattery; I just want your treatment."

"I am very, very sorry," the nervous version of Patricia Chevalier says. "There has been a bit of a delay but it will be ready tomorrow by noon. I absolutely promise."

And I'm going: Wow, how can she be making that promise? As far as Patricia Chevalier knows, there's not another LTVT on the entire planet!

"I've been waiting a *week*," Vivi says, the growl swelling up in her voice. *"Esperado, y esperado, y esperado,"* she adds, whatever that means. If only Roo were here to translate!

Patricia Chevalier murmurs something I can't make out, maybe because it's Spanish or maybe because of her fearful voice or maybe both.

"I don't wait, okay," Vivi says, her voice getting deeper. "I don't wait, Patricia."

Patricia Chevalier's response is lost in the sound of them locking the doors of their stalls.

A strange, paralyzed feeling comes over me as I realize that this is my moment. I wish more than anything it were Roo on duty right now. She'd be totally fine. She wouldn't be standing here suddenly unable to move.

But then I think of Dad. Of that time we talked to him up there in the jungle, when we were in the pit, and I knew how worried he was, even though he was pretending not to be. I just have to pretend I'm not scared. I gather myself up and tell myself, *Here goes!*, exclamation point and all, forcing my legs into motion.

I open my stall and pull the letter out from where I stuck it when Roo and I last swapped. Stepping toe-heel, toe-heel—the quietest way to walk, as Dad taught us when we were little—I go stand across from their stalls and look down at their feet.

And I freeze.

Whose shoes are whose?

One set of feet is in a pair of black stiletto heels. The other set of feet is in a pair of simpler, lower, tan-colored heels. Both sets of ankles are slender and tanned. Both dresses are pulled up too high for me to see their color.

I have to get this right. It is so insanely important that I get this right.

Okay, okay, stay calm, I tell myself. Let's think this through. Vivi is a movie star, so wouldn't she wear super-high, super-fancy stilettos? Isn't that what movie stars *do*? But then again, Vivi is so famous she can do whatever she wants, and maybe she doesn't *want* to wear uncomfortable shoes, even if they *are* glamorous. And the tan shoes are pretty, in their own way. Patricia Chevalier, though, seems like the kind of woman who wouldn't mind being uncomfortable if it meant she got to appear extra glamorous, plus I've only seen her in stilettos. But she *is* also more of a normal person who might own more normal tan-colored heels. And she has to do lots of running around and hostessing tonight, so maybe she wouldn't choose to wear those impractical stilettos.

I don't know. And I don't have much time.

My heart is banging, my fingers shaking. My whole body feels terrified and thrilled. I try to ignore the feeling that this isn't going to work as I reach my hand under the stall with the tan shoes and hold out the letter.

"Ah!" The woman releases a brief, startled gasp. I can't tell whose voice it is just from that gasp. And I've already made my decision anyway—I have to stick with it.

I wiggle the letter, begging Tan Shoes to take it from me.

A hand reaches out to snatch it.

Then, before anyone gets the chance to see me, I dash out the frosted glass door and head down the marble steps toward the dining area, breathing hard, my blood buzzing through me.

CHAPTER 18

*t takes some searching but eventually I find the table in the outside dining area where Roo, Kyle, Mom, Ken/Neth, Señora V, and Señor V are seated. There's an empty chair for me between Kyle and Roo. And boy, can I just say that after being stuck alone among all those bizarro rich ladies it is *really* nice to see some familiar faces, even Ken/Neth's. They're all looking at me and smiling, and I feel lots of love enveloping me as I sit down. I glance at Kyle and Roo, who are staring at me with these expectant, forced grins, like they're dying to know if I succeeded but they'll try to not be totally devastated if I failed. I give them a small victorious nod, a nod so small no one else would notice, and then their smiles relax and become genuine, and in my mind I pretend I *did* hand the letter to Vivi, ignoring the fact that it's possible I've failed big-time, that I've done *worse* than the opposite of succeeding—that Patricia Chevalier is reading my letter right this second and learning every single detail of our plan for tonight. I just swallow that thought and smile back at them as if everything is perfect.

"Mad! I didn't know where you were!" Mom exclaims with a vast Yoga Smile.

"In the bathroom," I mumble.

"Oh, doesn't their hand soap have the most *uplifting* fragrance?" Mom says. If she weren't yogafied, she'd be asking me what took so long and if I'm feeling okay. But I guess it's just as well, because I don't know what I'd say to that.

Anyway, the gong saves me from having to respond to Mom's silly question, and a bunch of waiters deliver avocado and papaya salads all at once. As we unfold our napkins and begin eating, we fall into awkward silence. How can it be this awkward to sit at a dinner table with my sister, my mom, and my best friend (because now it really feels 110 percent true that Kyle is obviously my best friend aside from Roo—who knows if I'm his best friend, but he definitely is mine), not to mention Ken/Neth "I'm Friendly" Candy, plus the most interesting old people I've ever met?

I try to just sit there enjoying the sight of all these people I love (well, in one case, only sort of sometimes *like*). They look so radiant in the candlelight, lifting their forks and buttering their rolls and sipping their drinks, and I tell myself I was right about the tan shoes and everything is going to work out and we aren't in danger.

And I try not to be mad and sad that Dad isn't here at this table with us. I wonder where he is right now. Up on the volcano, still searching for a bird? Trapped in that white marble room?

The awkward silence continues, everybody thinking private thoughts, I guess. Señora V and Señor V look wonderful—Señora V in a dark purple dress and an extra-lacy black veil, a golden handkerchief replacing the typical orange one in the pocket of Señor V's white suit—but they seem distracted, even more anxious than they were yesterday, glancing apprehensively at each other and then gazing off into the distance. I twist around to see what it is they're looking at and am struck by what's there. The volcano. Of course.

A dark feeling seizes me and I wonder if I've been directing my fear toward the wrong threat. There may be bigger things to be scared of tonight than La Lava. The volcano is starting to seriously smoke. It's coming out in huge swelling yellow clumps, which is by *far* the most dramatic it's been since we arrived.

ONCE THE LAST BIRD DIES, THE VOLCANO WILL BLOW. The words push their way into my head as yet another billow of smoke rushes upward. And I think of Miss Perfect, limp and weak in Roo's pouch. Is she the last bird? Are the volcano stories true? Does the volcano have reason to believe the last bird is about to die?

I twist back around, hoping to meet Kyle's eyes to see if he's noticed the volcano, but he's staring solemnly at a piece of papaya on his fork. So I look over at Roo to see if *she's* noticed, but she's looking off in the opposite direction, up toward one of the tables closest to the stage—a table with a bouquet larger than any of the others. A woman in a grass-green dress and a woman in a wine-red dress sit at that table, their backs to us.

I stare at Vivi's back, trying to figure out if it's the back of someone who's just read a life-changing—well, if not life-changing, at least very important—letter. But it's impossible to tell. Her back is strong and hard. And when Vivi turns to say something to Patricia Chevalier, I see the profile of her face. She looks like her normal ice-queen self, and my stomach sinks.

Suddenly I feel absolutely positive that I gave the letter to Patricia Chevalier.

Meanwhile, our table continues to be stuck in silence, and man, would I ever like to have some normal chatter to hide beneath. It's Ken/Neth who finally rescues us by asking Kyle a question about

Spanish grammar, something about how to use articles. I never thought I'd be this grateful for Señor All-Friendliness-All-the-Time. Kyle—who looks even more like he's drowning in his tuxedo when he's sitting down—has an excellent answer, I'm sure, but I wouldn't know because I tune it out and instead focus all my energy on Vivi, willing her to turn around, look at me, and blink three times, as instructed in my letter.

Beside me Roo wiggles restlessly in her seat, and I turn my attention to her.

"You okay?" I mutter under Kyle's little Spanish-grammar speech.

Roo looks at me, wide-eyed and—I realize—scared, then gives a tiny shrug, staring meaningfully down at the place under her skirt where Miss Perfect is attached, and lets her neck go limp for a second.

Oh *no*! Miss Perfect, fading fast beneath Roo's dress! But I can't waste another second on Roo and Miss Perfect—I know Roo can take care of Miss Perfect (far better than I can, at least), plus I *have* to keep my eyes on Vivi and hope for a sign from her.

The gong sounds and the salad plates are cleared. Then it sounds again, and the entrées are served. If I weren't totally focused on Vivi, I'd fall in love with tilapia in mango sauce, something I've (obviously) never had before. But I can't really enjoy the food, because I'm so super nervous, and because I'm so busy staring at her with all my might.

I notice that yet another awkward silence has fallen over our table. I wish I could say something casual to break the silence, but the weight of all the secrets I have to keep hangs too heavily over me.

Then Ken/Neth saves the day yet again by asking Kyle about the life span of jungle frogs. After Kyle gives a very detailed response, Ken/Neth launches into some funny stories about the problems the

La Lava management has encountered in trying to keep the resort pristine (in the mornings they have to chase monkeys away from the pools, because the monkeys like to sit there staring at their reflections, and if the monkeys are feeling aggressive they'll try to pee on whoever's shooing them away). I pretty much tune it all out—except for that funny thing about the monkeys—because I'm still looking at Vivi like there's no tomorrow. It's nice to have a bit of chatter going on at the table. It makes me feel more hidden as I stare at Vivi.

I'm getting very, very close to giving up on Vivi when Mom says with a sigh, "Oh, girls, my beautiful, beautiful girls, I wish your father could see you right now." She almost chokes on those words, *your father*—I hear them getting snagged in her throat—and for a second I wonder why I find that statement so incredibly creepy, until I realize it's because Mom sounded like she was talking about someone who was dead.

Somehow that feeling of creepiness makes me want to believe even more that Vivi got my letter, and I stare at her twice as hard as before, if that's even possible.

I stare as the waiters move among the tables, clearing dinner plates. And I stare as the gong sounds again and the waiters wheel out golden carts piled high with desserts.

"Coconut flan with lime foam?" Roo repeats after a waiter announces the dessert, first in Spanish and then in English. "YAY, YAY, YAY!" I honestly can't tell if Roo is playing the role of Excited Innocent Little Girl At Big Party or if she's truly able to get excited about dessert even with everything that's going on.

Ken/Neth asks Kyle another question—this one about poisonous snakes. Amazingly, Ken/Neth seems fascinated by all the million things Kyle has to say on the topic, and Kyle responds energetically to Ken/Neth's in-depth inquiries. As with Roo, I'm not sure if Kyle is pretending to be the passionate teenage naturalist or if he's genuinely getting swept up in his conversation with Ken/Neth. Either Roo and Kyle are phenomenal actors or they know how to compartmentalize their fear big-time. Jeez, I have a lot to learn from those two. But now's not the time to learn it, because I'm keeping most of my focus on Vivi, whose back still looks just as perfect and serene as it has this whole time.

The band is winding down, the last notes of a slow, romantic song washing away into the violet evening. The band members in their white tuxedos leave the stage and the only music now is the sound of forks clinking against golden dessert plates. The gleaming dance floor stretches out from the raised stage, reflecting the rising moon.

The gong sounds yet again and now there's new activity on the stage: Patricia Chevalier is walking up the stairs that lead to the elevated platform, followed by five men in dark tuxedos. I strain to catch a glimpse of her shoes as she steps upward, but her dress is too long. She marches over to the microphone while the men sit in five chairs that have been placed in a row behind her.

But as they all take their seats, it strikes me that one of the tuxedoed men is very familiar. And then I realize that it's Dad! He was paraded out right in the middle of those other guys. I look around and notice a table on the opposite side of the dining area with five now-empty seats. And my stomach goes all funny from the strangeness of it. He's been there all along, sitting at that table, while we've been over here missing him? And why is La Lava putting their prisoner on the stage, in a tuxedo no less? It's really, really, really weird to see Dad in a tuxedo. He's not even wearing a tuxedo in his wedding photos! I glance at Roo and Kyle, who are grinning at the sight of the Bird Guy.

It takes me a second to realize what's actually weird, way weirder than seeing Dad in a tuxedo: What *really* makes him unrecognizable is that he looks happy and peaceful and calm. I haven't seen him so happy and peaceful and calm since he left Denver. Happy and peaceful and calm even though he's sitting on the stage that belongs to the people who are holding him hostage and threatening his wife and daughters. Happy and peaceful and calm even though Volcán Pájaro de Lava is billowing smoke on the horizon.

The sight of Dad up there alongside those other tuxedos, looking completely unworried, is seriously the scariest thing I've seen since our plane landed, and there's been a lot of competition for that distinction. What I suddenly understand, seeing Dad now, is that he *is* crazy. He's gone off the deep end. La Lava has driven him insane, or maybe it's the curse of the volcano, but anyway, I can tell he's crazy because he doesn't look the least bit concerned. He looks as if everything's fine. As if no one's in danger. Kind of the way Mom always looks nowadays. If Dad were himself right now, he'd be up there looking furious, plotting an attack on whoever was trying to harm us.

Right then, Roo kicks me hard under the table. I mean, *hard*. I'm about to yelp when I realize she was just helping Kyle get my attention. They're both looking at me, eyebrows raised with the silent question: *So, is Vivi on board?*

I'm sorry, but I can't do anything except shrug at them. *I . . . don't know.* I glance over at Vivi's strong back.

Okay then.

Plan B, right?

But we have no Plan B. Why didn't we assume that Vivi wouldn't help us (or, that I might fail to give her the letter)? We are *such* idiots.

Desperate, I try to think. Maybe, if we moved fast enough, the three of us could stampede up onto the stage. I look over at the staircases on either side and notice what I could have *sworn* weren't there a minute ago—pairs of large, looming men guarding the steps. So. I guess Kyle was right about the whole high-security thing.

We have no way, absolutely no way, of getting up on that stage.

The realization sinks through me, from the top of my head down to the soles of my feet, making me crumple into myself, unable to look at Kyle or Roo.

"Ladies and gentlemen," Patricia Chevalier says into the microphone, her sophisticated voice booming out over everyone. I squint, once again trying and failing to catch a glimpse of her shoes. "Welcome to the annual Gold Circle Investors' Gala at La Lava Resort and Spa. Please help me welcome this year's Geniuses!"

After a huge round of applause fades out, Patricia Chevalier begins going down the line, introducing the men one by one. All of them look exactly the same to me, with big, round, rich-guy faces, except for Dad. Patricia Chevalier speaks in English, and her words are translated into Spanish and French and what looks like Japanese or maybe Chinese (I'm embarrassed to admit I can't tell the difference) on these digital red translator screens running along the bottom of the stage. The introductions blur together—president of this, president of that, CEO, CFO, chairperson, architect, all the way here from London, New York City, Tokyo, Paris, instrumental in development, marketing, advising, blah, blah, blah.

And then Dr. James Wade, hailing from Denver, Colorado—MPhil Cambridge, PhD Yale, a list of all the universities where he's taught, all the research grants he's won, all the awards, all the articles by and about him. And to be honest it gets a little boring, but then at the end she finally mentions that among his fans he's known as the Bird Guy, which, if you ask me and Roo, is one of the coolest things about Dad's work.

After lots more clapping and me shrinking further into myself and refusing to look at Kyle and Roo and trying to think if there's any way we can maybe sneak up onto the balcony to get everyone's attention from there or climb up on our table or something, Patricia Chevalier starts talking about "all the environmental awards La Lava Resort and Spa has received in the last twelve months alone" and "how very proud we are to have been ranked the World's Greenest Spa each of the past two years since the spa was founded." She goes on and on about "the emphasis we place on being in harmony with the volcano and the rain forest ecosystem," maintaining La Lava as an "environmentally sound, low-impact place, even imitating the exact foliage of the rain forest on our grounds" and "using the volcano's natural energy to power the spa, which is essential to making this an entirely organic institution." She talks about the yoga classes that "channel the ancient energy of the volcano." It all culminates in "the capstone of the La Lava experience," "our supreme achievement"—the "miraculous and priceless skin treatment" developed "by our brilliant resident biochemists over the course of the last nine months, and recently trademarked." This substance "restores our clients to their most perfect natural state" due to the "incredible antiaging properties of our intricate formula, created entirely from all-natural and locally-sourced ingredients," which has been "proven to not only reduce the signs of aging but to in fact *reverse* the aging process" in a way that has been "described as groundbreaking by experts and mind-blowing by our clients." She mentions all the ecologists brought in for "multiple, in-depth consultations." She thanks "in particular Dr. Wade, for contributing so much to the ornithological mission of the spa." She tells us "it is both an honor and a responsibility to be the best on the planet, setting the golden standard for ethics in rain forest development."

Then! She mentions the Lava-Throated Volcano trogon, which,

"having been confirmed extinct four years ago," is "one of the great tragedies of this region." She informs us that "La Lava is committed to making sure such an extinction never again occurs in the area. What happened to the Lava-Throated Volcano trogon must not be repeated. Even as we expand and flourish, we vow to treasure and protect delicate habitats."

I'm still not totally clear on the exact definition of *irony*—we just started to learn about that in English class at the end of the school year—but I'm pretty positive this is it.

And then it hits me: Patricia Chevalier definitely knows. She knows everything about our plan. She has the letter. She's wearing tan shoes (I try yet again to spot them beneath her dress). Because why else would she be going on so much about LTVTs? We failed—*I* failed.

My head feels painfully heavy. I put my elbows on the table and let my forehead droop down into my hands. After a long moment, I gather my courage to look up at Kyle and Roo.

But they aren't paying the least bit of attention to me. Their faces are bright as they gaze hard at the side of the stage, where there's some kind of shuffle going on, some kind of fight or heated conversation—a regal woman in green speaking sharply to the bodyguards protecting the steps. From up on the stage, Patricia Chevalier shoots the men a let-her-through-you-stupid-fools glare, and the bodyguards part to let the movie star pass between them.

As Vivi strides onto the stage, radiant and green like a jungle goddess, murmurs of delighted surprise pass through the crowd, followed by applause way, way louder than any Patricia Chevalier received—applause plus screams of excitement, whistles, and hoots and howls. Who knew such an elegant crowd could make such a ruckus?

But that ruckus doesn't even come *close* to the ruckus inside my own body as Vivi grabs the microphone, as she steps forward and I spot a flash of tan (Oh my god! I was right! I was *right*! I *knew* Vivi wouldn't wear those silly stilettos!), as Patricia Chevalier (after looking out uneasily toward the back of the dining area, almost as though seeking instructions from someone) wilts aside and fades back into the shadows behind the line of seated men.

"*Hola y* hello, *damas y caballeros,* ladies and gentlemen," Vivi says in her low, rich voice, the words ringing out loud and forceful through the microphone.

"*¡Hola!* Hello!" the audience shouts back. They all love her so much! They're all hanging on her every word—but no one's hanging on her every word as much as I am. I'm dying to know what she's going to say, what she's going to do, if she's on our side or if she's not. I can hardly breathe in the long seconds while she gazes powerfully out over the crowd, waiting for the applause to fade.

"I would like to invite some very special guests up—" Before she can finish her sentence, her words are overwhelmed by applause. Vivi spreads her gazillion-dollar smile over all of us and puts one hand up to quiet the crowd. "Some very special guests up to the stage. Please help me warmly welcome Madeline Flynn Wade!"

From the stage, Vivi's gaze is fixed on me, so now the entire audience is staring at our table. In a matter of seconds, I notice that (a) Mom's Yoga Smile is stretched to the point of breaking as she looks back and forth between me and Vivi, shocked, (b) Ken/Neth is grinning the world's goofiest grin right at me, (c) Señor V is winking gently at me, (d) Señora V is giving me a thumbs-up, a gesture that looks kind of bizarre coming from her veiled form, (e) Kyle is glancing at me with a sharp, confident nod, as though he knew all along I would get Vivi on board, and (f) Roo is already standing up. I feel dizzy.

When the applause quiets a tad, Vivi continues: "Madeline Flynn Wade, along with her sister, Ruby Flynn Wade . . . the daughters, I might add, of Dr. James Wade."

More applause, more eyes boring into us. Amid the massive clapping, I'm struck by two thoughts: (1) The time has come. Now's the exact moment when we have to leave our table and rush up to the stage before anything else happens. Before we miss our chance. (2) I can't do it. I'm too scared. Filled with dread. I don't want to go up there. I don't want to stand in front of all these people, exposed. And who knows, who knows, what La Lava will do to us. It's all happening too quickly. I'm too terrified, too self-conscious, too unbrave.

"And, finally," Vivi announces, "Kyle Nelson Villalobos!"

I grab Roo's hand and mouth at her *"I CAN'T!"* but she's already stepping away from our table, heading toward the stage, her fingers slipping out of mine. She looks back at me and mutters, "Whatever, dude, *relax*." I'm sitting there frozen, watching Roo go, when suddenly I feel something: the warm, solid sensation of Kyle's hand in mine, squeezing, pulling me up. My terror loosens its grip a little. My heart is still doing acrobatics, mainly panic-related but now also partly Kyle-related. And I can't believe my mind is actually able to have the thought, *Gosh, I hope my hand doesn't feel clammy to him,* and also the thought, *His hand is super clammy, but I really don't mind.*

And then here we are, walking through applause so deafening it seems like an actual substance, like walking through water or something, and all those eyes too, hundreds and hundreds of eyes—you can practically *feel* them touching you.

Pressing on toward the stage, toward Vivi (smiling her gorgeous, ferocious smile at us), toward Dad (the happy-peaceful-calm expression quickly draining from his face), I take a deep breath and try to get brave. I think about Miss Perfect, about her bloodred eggs out there alone in the jungle, about me and Mom and Dad and Roo sitting around the table together at home, in Denver, laughing about something. I think about the jungle, how green and amazing it is, all its weird flowers and animals, and the chameleon Kyle showed me (was that really *today*? because it feels like ages ago).

Roo is the first one to reach the stage, the first one to prance between the bodyguards and up the steps, followed by Kyle, who turns back to smile at me as he goes—is it just me, or was that a nervous quiver I spotted on his lip before he dashed up the steps?

And I—I follow.

Roo skips over to Vivi and tugs on the movie star's hand. Vivi bows as though Roo is the Queen of England, and the audience laughs. The three of us line up like a row of ducklings beside Vivi. It seems the applause is getting louder by the second, making my ears ring.

"It is with great excitement," Vivi says, "that I turn the stage over to my young friend Madeline Flynn Wade and her *amigos,* who have something very important to tell you."

And I'm going: *Wow. I can't believe Vivi just called me her friend. Wow. I can't believe we're really on the stage at La Lava and the crowd is going wild and Vivi is smiling at me.* So many impossible things all at once.

Vivi steps backward and hands the microphone to me.

"You," she whispers, very close to my ear, "are an extremely odd child. But," she adds, "I like you."

Then she strides away and I'm left there with the hot-potato microphone, which I quickly pass off to Kyle.

And now. It's just us. Me and my little sister and a barely teenage boy, looking out over the vast expectant crowd, the clapping finally quieting down as everyone awaits whatever it is that Vivi's baby-faced friends have to tell them. I glance back at Dad, hoping for something—I don't know, a thumbs-up or *some*thing, anything to make this stage feel less terrifying. But he's staring at us with a furious, stunned look on his face, slowly shaking his head in this way that makes me feel extra terrified.

Kyle takes a step forward. Raises the microphone to his mouth. And doesn't speak.

My stomach plummets as I remember his quivering lip. Kyle with stage fright! Who could have guessed? And—*what now?*

An awkward silence falls, everyone waiting for Kyle to say something. As the seconds pass I begin to hear the buzz of the audience's impatience.

I stand there blushing and blinking in the stage lights, unsure what to do with my hands, unsure how to help Kyle, and meanwhile Roo bends over and starts fussing with the strap of her patent leather shoe, and I tap her back in a way that means *Seriously? You're worrying about your* shoe *right now? Get a grip!*

"THE LAVA-THROATED VOLCANO TROGON," Kyle suddenly booms, his voice way too loud in the microphone, "IS *NOT* EXTINCT."

The hum of the expectant crowd drops and suddenly it's dead silent. My relief that Kyle has finally spoken is followed immediately by a shiver passing down my spine: He said the bird's name aloud! And doesn't a fourteen-year-old still count as a child? Won't the volcano goddess react? I look out at the volcano. It's glowing bright red against the purple evening sky. Right then an orange flare swells upward. My stomach clutches, flips.

"FOR GENERATIONS," Kyle continues, "THE BIRD HAS BEEN RUMORED TO POSSESS THE POWER TO RE-STORE LOST YOUTH."

Part of me is freaking out about the volcano, wondering if it's acting up because Kyle uttered the name, or because the last LTVT is approaching death, or both. And the other part of me is gazing at Kyle, feeling amazed that he can stand there looking so strong and certain even in his absurd suit, and I'm thinking the audience must be feeling amazed by him too, when I notice that Roo is still fussing with her feet, wedging her right foot to remove her left shoe.

"Stop drawing attention to yourself!" I hiss almost silently at her.

She rolls her eyes at me like I'm stupid and continues to wiggle her foot out of its shoe.

"THIS IS WHY LA LAVA HAS BEEN PRETENDING THE BIRD IS EXTINCT, AS IT WAS OFFICIALLY DECLARED FOUR YEARS AGO, WHEN IN FACT THE SPA HAS BEEN MURDERING THE LAST REMAINING MEMBERS OF THIS LAZARUS SPECIES IN ORDER TO MAKE ITS TRE-MENDOUSLY LUCRATIVE SKIN PRODUCT."

I wait for it, the gasp of horror from the audience, the noise of outrage, but the crowd remains dead silent. Roo's left shoe pops off her foot and a small spray of yellow toe-flowers lands on the stage. She bends down to work on removing her right shoe.

"Roo, *what* are you doing?" I mutter under my breath. Does she really want the whole world to see her personal fungus?

"IN ADDITION, LA LAVA HAS CO-OPTED" (*co-opted—* what exactly does that mean again?) "THE SKILL, EXPERTISE, AND TALENT OF THE BIRD GUY, OTHERWISE KNOWN AS DR. JAMES WADE, IMPRISONING HIM AND FORCING HIM TO ENTRAP THESE EXTRAORDINARILY RARE CREATURES, THREATENING TO HARM HIS WIFE AND HIS DAUGHTERS, THESE TWO YOUNG CHILDREN YOU SEE BEFORE YOU" (I pretend Kyle didn't just call me a *young child*) "IF HE DOES NOT COMPLY."

I glance back to check on Dad's reaction to this . . . and discover that Dad is no longer on the stage! The five chairs are empty, and Patricia Chevalier is nowhere to be seen. How could all that have happened without me noticing?

Roo kicks off her right shoe and a second bunch of toe-flowers showers the stage. Then she starts pulling her dress up.

"I KNOW THIS ALL SOUNDS IMPROBABLE, VIRTUALLY IMPOSSIBLE TO BELIEVE," Kyle continues, and right then the thought hits me: Hey, wait a sec, why isn't anyone from La Lava trying to stop Kyle? Isn't it sort of *impossible* that La Lava isn't doing anything about this situation? I start counting the seconds until someone comes to grab the mike away from him.

Roo's fighting against her layers of taffeta in an attempt to get at Miss Perfect. She glances over at me like *Hello, want to help?* and I feel bad I wasn't already on it, so I kneel down beside Roo and reach for Miss Perfect's pouch and work to tug it open.

"SURELY ALL OF YOU ARE SITTING OUT THERE DEMANDING PROOF FOR THESE OUTRAGEOUS CLAIMS. SURELY YOU NEED TO BE CONVINCED THAT THE LAVA-THROATED VOLCANO TROGON IS NOT YET EXTINCT. WELL . . ."

Kyle's *Well* . . . is hanging in the air above us when Miss Perfect's body drops out of the pouch and falls onto the stage with a flat thud.

She lies there, shrunken, limp, dull, like any old brown bird. Like any old *dead* brown bird. And Roo crouches over her.

Horror swells inside me, along with that saliva-rush feeling that comes right before you throw up. I look up at the volcano, which continues to radiate red and orange. What revenge will the volcano goddess take now that her bird is dead?

"WE HAVE JUST SUCH PROOF!" Kyle announces victoriously. Since he's facing the crowd, he doesn't yet know that Miss Perfect is dead.

This is the moment, the exact moment, when she should be soaring over the tables.

"JUST SUCH PROOF!" Kyle repeats the cue before turning around to see what's causing the delay. And his face falls.

So. This is it.

Roo gathers up her yellow toe-flowers and starts sprinkling them over Miss Perfect. I'm stunned, extremely stunned, that Roo can move this quickly onto the funeral stage of things.

The silence of the crowd takes on its own weight. I can feel it pressing down on us, on me and Kyle and Roo and Miss Perfect, or rather on Miss Perfect's body, as Roo runs a toe-flower along the bird's beak. I look up at the fiery tip of the volcano and wonder what the heck we should do now and how many seconds we have before the crowd starts booing and before La Lava separates Kyle from the microphone and before the volcano does whatever it's going to do.

But then—get *this!*—Miss Perfect's beak opens, just the *tiniest* bit, like at first I wonder if maybe I'm imagining it, and Roo drops the toe-flower into Miss Perfect's mouth. And then she drops in a second, a third, and Miss Perfect blinks and rolls over and stands and pecks up all the other toe-flowers lightning-quick, and then she steps onto Roo's outstretched hand, and Roo stands up with Miss Perfect on her palm, whispering something into the bird's ear, and I'm thinking, *Dang, that is one sick-looking bird,* but at least she's alive, she's definitely alive!

Miss Perfect spreads her wings and pushes off from Roo's hand. With just a few flaps, she rises high above the stage, hovering there for a moment before swooping dramatically toward the crowd. As she passes, I see her chest glinting, her feathers gleaming, her body expanding. In the candlelight her throat looks truly golden, glimmering as though her feathers are creating their own radiance. She glides over the audience, proud and potent and alone, looking exactly like the last member of a magical species.

For once in my life something is actually happening the way I imagined it, or even better than I imagined. Miss Perfect *is* perfect, soaring over La Lava, bright! breathtaking! larger-than-life!, silhouetted by the red light of the volcano. I have this feeling almost like my heart is attached to her tail feathers, like with each beat of her wings my heart is being lifted up above everything until I'm no longer scared, until I can finally believe that the good things in the world will overcome the bad, that we're going to bring La Lava down and get Dad back and be happy again. *We did it!* I shout inside myself, looking at Kyle and Roo with my best smile. But their thrilled eyes are fixed on Miss Perfect as she approaches the end of the dining area, magnificent.

It suddenly strikes me, though, that something is off about this whole scene, and a cold anxiety cuts through my exhilaration. The crowd remains strangely, uncomfortably silent—not the silence of awe, none of the oohs and aahs you'd expect at a time like this. Maybe they don't realize Miss Perfect is an LTVT because of the female plumage . . . but even so! Isn't it wildly obvious that the bird soaring above them is something special?

A loud shout from the back of the audience breaks the silence—an outburst of Spanish in a man's voice. Kyle raises his eyebrows in surprise, and Roo glances over at him, similarly surprised. (I hate it how everyone knows Spanish except me!)

"What is it?" I whisper at Kyle. "What did he say?"

Kyle just mutters.

"*What?*" I say.

"He said, 'You guys are cute,'" Roo tells me.

I'm sure she misheard, but then another cry comes from another part of the crowd, a woman's voice, in English: "*Too* adorable!"

The audience avalanches us with supportive words, in English and Spanish and other languages too but of course I only understand the English ones.

"Great performance, kids!" "You were awesome!" "Bravo, budding actors!" "Thanks for the show!" "*Very* convincing!" "You've sure earned your dessert!"

At first I think they're being really nasty—nasty and sarcastic—but then I realize they mean every word. They love us—they truly do think we're fantastic, charming, entertaining, talented. They think this whole thing is some kind of cute skit.

Rage rises hotly in my chest. Don't they realize they've just seen something that's basically a *miracle*?

They're clapping, grinning at us, showering us with approval. And now they're standing. A standing ovation. For the three of us, clustered on the stage, feeling smaller than ever.

As the clapping roars around us, Kyle looks over at me with the most awful expression on his face, anger and bewilderment and, more than anything, sadness. The disappointment of it all hits me hard in the stomach. We're not going to be taken seriously.

I can't stand to look at Kyle so I turn toward Roo. But Roo is completely spaced out, ignoring the standing ovation, gazing entranced at Miss Perfect, who's swooping way out there in the dimness beyond the dining area, swerving now to fly back to her beloved Roo.

Even though I'm following Miss Perfect with my eyes, I still don't see exactly what happens—one second she's flying and the next she's falling, tumbling downward as if she's been shot, yet there was no gunshot, no sound, no flash—

Roo screams a spine-chilling scream, but that noise is covered by the noise of the volcano, which lets out a tremendous roar just then, a sound to go along with the huge burst of redness up there, a growl like the earth itself has awoken in anger.

CHAPTER 19

I'm so distracted by the sight of the growing redness at the top of the volcano that I don't notice the three men in black tuxedos until they're centimeters behind us on the stage. Before I can say anything to Kyle or Roo, the men take hold of us. They grab our shoulders in what might, to the crowd, look like congratulatory hugs, but the grip is tight enough that I can hardly move.

Patricia Chevalier steps between the tuxedos and puts her red lips up to the microphone.

"Thank you!" she screeches into it, her voice tearing across the night. "Thank you, thank you very much, to our talented young performers—*muchas gracias, jóvenes. Muy bien. Muy interesante.* What great imaginations! It never ceases to amaze me how *creative* kids are! Thanks to our honored guest Vivi for paving the way for that delightful performance. Now, ladies and gentlemen, *damas y caballeros,* let the dancing begin *ahora*!"

The instant Patricia Chevalier says *ahora,* a drumbeat booms right behind us. I twist around as much as I can with this guy holding on to me, and I'm shocked. An entire band has taken its place on the stage—men in gold-sequined tuxedos and a lady in a black ball gown, brass and bass and all, the drum set coming to life.

I'm not tough enough to put up a fight against my tuxedoed guard, and whatever fight Roo and Kyle put up against their tuxedos is hidden by the three of them surrounding us as they remove us from the stage. No scuffle, or so it seems. They herd us away with nice smiles on their faces and tight grips on our shoulders. As they press us down the stage stairs, I look over at our table, desperate to make eye contact with Señora V or Señor V or Mom or Ken/Neth, desperate to show them that we need help, that these grinning guys are not actually grinning—but our table is empty, which creates a whole other bad feeling in my chest.

The tuxedos "escort" us across the dance floor toward the marble steps amid the sound of hundreds of bottles of champagne being uncorked. I wonder why Roo isn't squirming to get out of their grasp. I thought I could always count on her to behave like a wild animal, defending herself (and me) from anybody who tries to mess with us. Isn't she the one who got kicked out of preschool for biting? But she just floats alongside the tuxedos, gazing at the place where Miss Perfect fell, a single quiet tear on her cheek. Roo hardly ever cries, and it's upsetting to see. Her mouth crumpling in on itself, becoming very tiny.

I glance back at the stage, where the lady in the black ball gown is singing very fast and furious in Spanish, where the brass is going *ta-da, ta-da, ta-da,* where one of the digital red translator screens scrolls a series of English words: "PLEASE SHOW YOUR SUPPORT FOR OUR YOUNG PERFORMERS WITH A STANDING OVATION! PLEASE WELCOME SERAPHINA AND THE BRASS BOYS!"

And I'm going: *What?* The audience was getting instructions that whole time? They were being told to clap, to stand, to tell us we're cute? And I realize: These people, these La Lava people, they've thought of everything. They're cleverer and mightier than we could ever hope to be. We never, *ever* should have tried to outsmart them.

Before I can figure out a way to get Roo and Kyle's attention so I can point out the digital banner, the tuxedos sweep us up the marble steps and into the lobby. And there, in the lobby, is Dad, a bodyguard on either side of him.

"I *brought* you a *bird*!" he's saying to them, his voice harsh with fury. "It may've been last-minute, but *I* brought *you* a *bird*! That was the *deal*! *You can't do this to them!*"

Then he turns to look at us with an expression somewhere between tenderness and horror.

"Kids!" he says. *"How* did you find her?" And when I hear his voice I understand four things all at once: (1) Dad is himself, his total normal noncrazy self, and always has been, (2) he captured an LTVT, so Miss Perfect isn't the only one! (3) he's flabbergasted that we found a female bird, and (4) he thinks we're in a ton of danger.

Before I can say anything to Dad, before I can even get a grip on how petrified I am, there's a commotion beside us, a pair of guards shoving Señor V and Señora V into the lobby, and behind that comes Mom—*"VIA!"* Dad exclaims—in the grip of another tuxedoed guard, her gown slipping off one shoulder, the Yoga Smile completely vanished from her face, and behind all that is Ken/Neth with another pair of guards. So many strong, silent guards with emotionless faces, standing around us like a wall, making us look extra helpless in our party clothes.

Thank *goodness* for Ken/Neth! Gosh, I never thought I'd feel this way about seeing Ken/Neth, but boy is it nice to spot his bright orange tie amid all these guards, and boy are we lucky that he knows the La Lava people and can reason with them. He's our best hope for getting out of this mess. I'm waiting for him to greet us with a *Whoa, hey there, kiddos, what's up here?* or something along those lines. But, strangely enough, he doesn't have his regular old goofy grin on his face. In fact, he's not smiling at all. His face has gone absolutely flat. He jerks his neck slightly to the left and the ten tuxedoed guards immediately line up and start marching us off down the long, white marble hallway with the numbered golden doors on the left side and the open-air arches on the right.

And then it's a very, very dark feeling that fills me.

Because I knew all along, didn't I? *I knew all along,* but I let myself forget. A bright rage—rage at Ken/Neth, yes, but mainly rage at myself—flashes through me, making me nauseous. How could I have been so stupid, to ignore what was one hundred percent obvious, just because he put on a silly smile and told dumb jokes and dressed like a dork?

"Ken!" Mom cries out, the yoga softness fallen away from her voice. "KEN!" I look over at her, twisting this way and that in her guard's grip, her face fierce, her features rich with emotion and intelligence and fury. Mom is back! Normal, smart, great, brave Mom! Being manhandled by La Lava guards seems to have broken La Lava's spell. This is no time to celebrate that, though. *"Ken!"* Mom shouts again. But he turns away like he can't hear her.

"Via," Dad calls out to her as his guards yank him violently forward, "it's no use. I'm sorry, I didn't realize—he's on the inside, always has been, he—"

But Dad's words are drowned out by the great groan released by the volcano, a groan that shakes the marble beneath us. Behind us, in the dining area, a collective gasp of fear rises from the crowd, and a woman's scream arcs above the lively jazz music.

The guards rush us along with such force that I'm having trouble staying on my feet without tripping. I'm at the back of the line and my guard is shoving me forward to keep up with Kyle, who's just ahead, and Roo, who's ahead of Kyle.

Far off down the hallway, Dad's guards stop in front of a white marble wall, and that's when it hits me. Of course. A prison cell, awaiting us. One of Dad's guards looks up at the same little device thingy on the ceiling that Patricia Chevalier looked up at (was it really less than a week ago?) when she brought us to visit Dad in the windowless marble room. The white marble wall begins to slide open, exactly as it did last time.

Just then something clicks in Roo, her old ferociousness snapping her out of her grief—she screams another spine-chilling scream and clamps her teeth into the wrist of her guard. It must be one of her best bites ever, because the guard lets out his own horrific howl and holds up his bleeding arm. Roo is squirming like crazy to escape from his good hand, and meanwhile Kyle is spitting in his own guard's eye and wriggling his strong, skinny shoulders back and forth, and I'm just standing there being amazed by how vicious Roo and Kyle are, so it's my guard who rushes up a couple steps to give their guards a hand, and it's only when Kyle glances back at me for a split second and urgently slides his eyes to the right that I realize I'm free, duh, plus there's a half-open golden door *right* there, and there's no time to think before I find myself slipping through that door and diving under a golden bed frame. Seconds later, the door slams behind me, and I know my guard is about to grab my ankles and pull me out from under the bed and drag me weeping across the marble floor of the hotel room.

But instead, I hear a woman's voice. With a British accent.

"Good God, Seth," she says. "What a nightmare!"

I watch her feet squeezing their way out of a pair of insanely yellow stilettos.

"Well, man, we're getting outta here now," Seth says. He sounds like a surfer dude.

"I'm furious, Seth!" the lady says, beginning to cry.

It's as though her words set off another rumbling deep in the volcano—you can hear it but also you can *feel* it.

"Utterly furious!" she screams above the noise of the volcano, her voice rising with panic.

"Keep it together, Kate," he says in his chilled-out way. "Where's the suitcases?"

"That nineteen-hour flight!" Kate shrieks at him. "And then they were *out* of the treatment! And now we're being *evacuated* because there's about to be a *natural disaster*! We might *die*, Seth! What do you think of that! I should never pay attention to anything that silly little starlet recommends."

"But she looked so great at Cannes. You can't deny that, Kate."

Now Kate is taking lots of quick in-out breaths and crying and moaning and going, "Oh oh oh, I'm having a panic attack, oh, oh, oh. My pills," she demands, "in the bathroom, in the pink case—"

Seth jogs across the marble floor. "Which pink case?" he calls out.

"Not the maroon case, not the rose case, the *pink* case, FAST!" she screams.

My whole body-and-brain feels like one huge beating heart, and I keep waiting for a hard, angry knock at the door. Out in the hallway there's the ruckus of evacuation, suitcases rolling on marble and doors slamming, a super-shrill woman's voice and the noise of people disagreeing about something, while I cling froglike to the floor beneath the bed—terribly, completely stuck. Alone. I've felt this way before, but only in nightmares.

Soon Kate and Seth leave, joining their noise to the hallway noise of rich people shrieking, of tuxedo shoes and high heels pounding marble. Then even those sounds start to fade, until eventually there's just silence. But it's a silence that feels slithery, like snakes.

And now I have no idea what to do.

Part of me wants to stay under this bed, protected by the golden dust ruffle, hoping no one will find me, hoping lava won't come pouring down the hallway. Besides, aren't there probably still guards roaming around out there? Aren't they all probably walkie-talkieing about a missing girl in a green dress? Isn't it best just to stay here?

Then there's the other part of me. The part that wants to run down the hallway to that sliding marble wall and figure out how to open it and get everyone out of there before the volcano erupts.

But it's so *peaceful* here, under this golden bed, and the marble feels so cool against my cheek, and I can pretend I'm safe, pretend I'm still little, playing hide-and-seek with Roo under Mom and Dad's bed.

And *right* then—like it's reading my mind—the volcano roars its loudest roar yet. I can feel it trembling against my stomach as I scoot myself out from under the bed.

I creep to the doorway and peek out. Most of the golden doors lining the hallway are thrown open, and beyond them I glimpse beds with messed-up comforters and closet doors flung open and trash cans overturned and vases of flowers knocked over and the general chaos left by people packing in a panic.

I take a breath and, quietly, step out into the hallway. The whole place seems deserted, though it's still bright with lights. I try to be completely silent as I move down the hallway. Tiptoeing past the open archways, I glance at the stage and see an abandoned tuba, the musicians' chairs cockeyed, and the dining area with desserts

256

half-eaten, champagne half-drunk, napkins scattered on the floor. In the distance, sparkling red flames shoot out of the top of the volcano, accompanied by swift bursts of smoke spiraling upward. And above all that, the night sky looks weird, orange, threatening.

At the end of the hallway, I run my hands over the marble wall. But it feels so solid, so cool and smooth and blank, that it's hard to believe it's a sliding door, even though I know it is. So: My little sister and my mom and my dad and the guy I love—too freaked out to pretend this isn't true—and his grandparents are there on the other side of this unmoving *wall*.

I press and push against the marble, trying to find, I don't know, a weak spot or something.

The hallways have been dead silent this whole time, so at first I think I'm imagining things when I notice a distant sound, the *tap-tap-tap-tap* of footsteps approaching. They're coming from the stairs we took when we were "escorted" out of the dining area. My heart speeds up and I flatten myself against the side of the hallway, remembering the chameleon Kyle showed me today and trying to pretend that even though I'm a human being in a green dress I can blend into a white marble wall.

The footsteps are crossing the lobby now. There's the harsh buzzing sound of static, like on a radio. "I SAID, GET THEM!" a woman's screeching voice blares out of the static. *"BRING THEM WITH YOU!"* Then her voice goes fuzzy again.

A man's voice replies to the static: "Lab A, right?" he says. "Pen 98?" And now he's approaching the mouth of this hallway, and I spot his bright orange tie as he speaks into the walkie-talkie.

I send the thought out as though it might actually serve as a shield: *Don't come down here, don't come down here, don't come down here.*

Then: a small miracle. Ken/Neth doesn't turn into this hallway, or even glance down it. He just dashes past, out of my sight. I've never seen him move so fast.

As his footsteps fade, I sink down to the floor and rest my head against the marble wall and let out a few of the tears that have built up behind my eyes.

And it's then, with my ear pressed against the marble, that I hear Roo.

I can't hear her words, but I can hear her voice, talking fast, its pitch moving up and down. I can tell that she's scared, that she's determined, that she's trying to figure out how to get them out of there. Then Dad's low, solemn voice. And Kyle, making some sort of suggestion. Roo again, insisting on something. Mom speaking with urgency. Dad replying. A rush of high-pitched words from Señora V, maybe some kind of chant or prayer. And back to Roo. I can even sense Señor V's gentle silence.

My whole life. My whole life is in that room. I can feel the two halves of my heart, twisting around in the left side of my chest—an actual physical pain.

I want to yell out to them but I know my voice would echo down these empty marble halls, and Ken/Neth would be back here in a second to toss me into the room along with them. Which at first doesn't sound that bad, but then it does—when it occurs to me that we'd all die, that there'd be no way for me to even try to save them.

Not that I'm doing much saving anyway.

Still, I stand up and stroke the wall. Jeez, is there even a *line* in the marble? Something, *any*thing?

"Roo!" I whisper into the marble. "Roo! Kyle! Mom! *Dad!*"

But of course they can't hear me. They carry on with their own conversation and I can tell that Roo's getting angry. I recognize *that* pitch of her voice, right before meltdown.

The volcano offers up this terrifically loud groan, a groan so loud I can feel it in my skull. It strikes me that any of these rumbles could be the final one.

And the reality slams me, along with the despair: The people I love are hopelessly trapped in a prison cell at the base of an erupting volcano.

I stand there with that fact for a second, and then my brain goes: Wait. Revision. At the base of an *almost*-erupting volcano.

And wait a sec. The words push their way into my brain: *ONCE THE LAST BIRD DIES, THE VOLCANO WILL BLOW.*

I have to admit: I'd totally forgotten about Miss Perfect. Like, until this very second, I haven't given her a thought. I've only been thinking about getting the humans out of here.

But: If the prophecy is true, all I need to do is make sure Miss Perfect doesn't die!

Which is a big *if.*

Not to mention I have no idea where Miss Perfect is right now. Or if she's even still alive.

But then I get it: Lab A. Pen 98.

Lab A, Pen 98!

When I stand in the lobby and strain my ears *hard,* I can hear the faraway sound of footsteps. I run after that sound faster than I thought I could run, down another long, white hallway, down a flight of stairs, and then another hallway, another flight of stairs, following the footsteps. From the outside you could never imagine how many hallways and staircases and doorways there are in this building. I mean, it doesn't look *that* huge, but here we go, another stairway, another hallway.

Finally, around one bend, I catch a glimpse of Ken/Neth, the black back of his tuxedo jacket. That's when I take a second-long break to slip out of my shoes so I can follow him silently. I pick them up and pull in my breath and pretend I'm not scared.

On the next staircase, Ken/Neth's footsteps pause, and, rounding the corner above him, I pause too, sucking my stomach in and pressing myself into the curve of the wall. It's like I can feel his eyes searching, can practically hear his nose sniffing for me. But then his footsteps continue onward.

It starts to feel like we're *miles* underground. There's this low grumbling as we descend, the murmur of the volcano, and it feels hotter here, as though with each step we're getting closer to the molten center where lava is brewing. I feel more and more claustrophobic, my heart freaking out, positive that on the next staircase Ken/Neth is going to turn at the wrong moment. Sometimes I think my body might just spin itself around and run up, up, up.

And then Ken/Neth stops.

Peeking out from behind the corner, I see that he's come to a dead end. I watch him stand there in front of the blank white marble wall. No stairways or hallways or doorways leading off in any direction. And I think, *Oh my gosh, is he lost?*

Then I feel stupid when the marble wall slides to the side. Duh. Of course. Another one of these.

As Ken/Neth steps in, I race barefoot down the hallway after him, overwhelmed by a strange double feeling—total desperation to get in there before the wall slides shut plus total terror at the fact that I'm about to follow an evil man into a sealed room. *Sealed like a coffin*—that's the phrase that jumps into my mind.

The wall is already three-quarters closed when I reach it, and as I squeeze through some kind of instinct kicks in, some kind of animal urgency, the blazing desire to avoid being sealed in, and without planning to, without even thinking about it, I twist around and stick my shoes into the crack between the sliding wall and the solid wall right after I pass between them. I only manage to get one shoe partway into the gap before the wall crumples its thin sole, but still the shoe is there, keeping the sliding wall not even a millimeter away from the other wall. I barely have time to think *That's so the kind of thing Roo would do* before my instinct, or my fear, sends me down onto my stomach. I abandon my other shoe there and crawl forward into the room, hoping against hope that Ken/Neth doesn't know I'm in here with him, that I didn't make too much noise, that only I heard the soft crunch of the shoe crumpling.

As I creep forward I look around in wonder. This isn't like any other part of La Lava. Yes, it's a huge white marble room, but it's filled with scientific equipment. It reminds me of the lab Dad used to take us to at his university. Microscopes and test tubes and sinks and long tables and high stools and whiteboards on the walls and hooks holding those white doctors' robes.

And cages. Rows and rows of empty cages. As though awaiting the day when there will be thousands of Lava-Throated Volcano trogons in this laboratory.

I'm there on my stomach wondering how I'm going to find Pen 98. I stare up at the cages but I don't see any numbers. And also, strangely, I don't hear footsteps anymore.

Staying low, I scan the room, looking for Ken/Neth's legs, when suddenly the silence is cracked by an impossible-to-describe sound. High-pitched, horrible, it makes your brain hurt and your eyes ache, forces your blood to run the wrong way in your veins, fills you with sickness.

Yet I move straight toward that sound, crawling beneath tables and between stools toward the fourth row of cages, because now I can see Ken/Neth's legs, sprinting away from the scream, galloping off toward the far corner of the lab. And I know that only Miss Perfect is wild enough to make a sound like that.

But as I approach the cage, as I stand up and see that its door is flung wide open, I realize it's not Miss Perfect who's making the sound.

It's a spectacular bird, the bird standing there at the front of the cage, screaming. I recognize it from Kyle's Polaroid—but that photograph was just a pale imitation of the creature before me now. And I understand in a flash of certainty that this is Dad's bird—the LTVT Dad surrendered to La Lava so they wouldn't harm us.

The bird's throat gleams like liquid gold, his body is such a pure true blue that it hurts my eyes, and his glittering wings are spread out across the door of the cage to protect Miss Perfect, who's lying limp and shrunken against the back of it.

So *this* is where they brought Miss Perfect when they shot her down at the gala.

And *this* must be her mate.

As if in response to the bird's scream, the volcano growls. A rumble from the core of the world joining a cry from what is probably the last living male of the species.

For a second I'm frozen, not sure what to do, stuck between the rumble and the scream. But then I think about what Roo would do if she were here, how happy she'd be to see Miss Perfect with her mate, how brave she'd feel.

"Mr. Beautiful," I murmur at the screaming bird. A name I know Roo would approve of. "Mr. Beautiful, Mr. Beautiful, Mr. Beautiful," I keep murmuring as I reach toward the cage. He claws my temple first, then slashes my cheek. I can feel hot, thick blood running down the sides of my face.

But I continue, reaching past him, through the small hole between his wing and his body, and he's so shocked I'm not running away that it takes him a second to gather himself enough to scratch at my eyebrow, a motion clearly intended for my eye. Somehow, though, I'm floating above pain right now, my mind focused on my hand moving into the cage, my fingers opening to gently seize Miss Perfect, expecting a protest from her and surprised when she comes easily.

As I pull her out of the cage past Mr. Beautiful, he lunges for my throat, but a millisecond before slicing me, he flaps his wings awkwardly and draws back.

Because Miss Perfect is nuzzling woozily into me, twisting her body to show me the place where the tranquilizer dart is still attached to her stomach. For the first time in my life the sight of a needle doesn't make me shiver. I just yank it out of her and toss it back into the cage. She shuts her eyes, and lies there weakly, and smiles up at me.

And then the craziest thing yet—Mr. Beautiful pushes off the cage, flaps his wings, and lands on my head. I barely notice his talons piercing my scalp.

Mr. Beautiful and I gaze down at Miss Perfect, watching in amazement as she begins to fill out before our eyes, her blood pumping strongly again, her feathers starting to shimmer, her muscles regaining their tension.

The miraculous silence is broken by footsteps behind me, and suddenly I'm back to where I was—how did I go even a minute without being terrified of Ken/Neth? I glance over my shoulder and see him there with a pair of enormous needles in his hands. A beak-shaped gash at his temple sends blood rolling down his cheek to his neck. He seems to grow taller and larger by the second, his face blank like the face of someone who's never smiled in his entire life.

As I start running, Mr. Beautiful lets out another earth-shattering scream, and Miss Perfect, now revived enough to stand up in my hand, joins him in the scream, a scream that rises from the depths of their bones. I know this scream is for Ken/Neth's benefit, but still I'm not sure I'll ever be able to hear again. I run between the rows of cages, their scream all around me and inside me, carrying me forward faster than I've ever been carried.

But the scream can't get me through the marble wall—I stop there, hoist Miss Perfect up onto my head to join Mr. Beautiful, and frantically try to wedge my fingers into the minuscule sliver created by my jammed shoe.

The wall makes whirring mechanical malfunctioning sounds but it's not budging, and Ken/Neth's footsteps are right behind me. I whirl around to face him with my weird crown of shrieking birds, and I look straight in his eyes, because if he's going to destroy me and my family and the birds I might as well show him some fury while I can.

And he's standing there with his needles, and he's about to lunge, and behind my back I'm still trying to shove my fingers into the sliding wall.

I only have a split second to wonder why Ken/Neth hasn't grabbed me yet when suddenly the wall gives—my shoe slips down, my fingers wedge in, the wall starts sliding open before immediately starting to slide shut again. I stick my leg backward into the gap, and the wall jams there, pressing hard on my calf.

"GO!" I scream at the birds. *"GO!"*

They're still shrieking, clawing and scratching and piercing my head as they launch themselves off it, squeezing through the narrow gap in the sliding wall, and there they go, and I crane my neck to glimpse them, heading up the hallway, up the stairway, upward, upward, their scream fading.

My knee is trapped and twisted by the wall and now that the birds and their shriek are gone I'm starting to feel pain again, the pressure of the wall becoming way too much to handle. I yank my leg out of it and it slides shut with an angry groan. I turn back to face Ken/Neth.

He's standing there, staring at me, his arms still raised at his sides, his hands clutching the needles. I stare back at him through the blood running down my face. I wonder what's going to happen next. Just me and Ken/Neth in this sealed room, and I've done exactly what he didn't want me to do, and now I know that he's the World's Greatest Liar, and now I know that all this time he's been spying on me and Mom and Roo for La Lava. He doesn't care about my family, or about birds that are almost extinct, or about being a good person. I don't even consider begging him for mercy.

All the courage is swiftly draining out of my muscles, and I can feel a tremor of dread moving upward from my legs to the rest of my body. I clench my jaw so Ken/Neth won't see my teeth chattering. It occurs to me that he's about to attack me with those needles, and I cross my arms over my chest, as if that would make any difference at all.

"You're brave, Madeline," Ken/Neth whispers, letting his hands fall limply down by his sides. His face looks solemn, maybe sincere, but his eyes won't meet mine. "And you come from a great family."

I blink at him in shock. Before I get the chance to absorb this— Is he *joking*? Is this just a cruel setup to lull me into calmness before he does whatever he's going to do to me?—a new sound comes marching down the hallway toward us, the *pow-pow-pow* of heels on marble. And red-hot panic races through my veins.

Patricia Chevalier! So he was just putting me off-guard before she showed up to torture me in some other way! She's probably already slaughtered Miss Perfect and Mr. Beautiful on one of the stairways. I shiver, picturing their blood dripping down the white marble steps.

I'm pulling away from the wall, preparing to face her, when I realize my dress is stuck in the sliding door! I look over at Ken/ Neth to see what he'll do with me now that I'm completely trapped, but he doesn't seem to notice. He's simply staring at my bloody hair. And I'm going, *Okay, so I guess he's just waiting to pass me off to Patricia Chevalier—the only person, frankly, who scares me more than Ken/ Neth himself.*

The footsteps pause on the other side of the wall. There's a heaving sound, a woman groaning, and the door slides slowly, slowly open. I scoot out of the way and shut my eyes. I'm not ready for this.

"Holy *Jesús,*" she murmurs, but it sounds more like a prayer than a curse.

My eyes pop open.

Whoa. Double whoa. *Quadruple* whoa!

Vivi! Vivi of the dark shining hair! Vivi of the grass-green dress! Her cheeks flushed, her eyes bright, her body jammed there in the doorway star-shaped, arms and legs spread wide to keep it open as it squeezes her. I can see her sculpted arm muscles straining against the pressure.

"Thank god for my personal trainer," she says, struggling into the room.

She straightens her dress as the wall slides shut behind her.

"*Dios mío,*" Vivi mutters as she takes in the laboratory, the cages, my bloody face, Ken/Neth's bloody temple, and the needles clenched in his hands. "It's all true, isn't it?"

Ken/Neth is still stuck in his frozen stare.

"Thank god I found you," Vivi says to me.

And the volcano rumbles, but softly.

Vivi turns to look straight at Ken/Neth. "Do you want to know what *hurts* my *heart* right now?" she demands. "Thinking about how much *money* I've given this place."

Then she shakes her shoulders, as though shaking it all off.

"Unless you want your name smeared across the front page of the *New York Times* tomorrow morning, you're going to come upstairs with me right now," she barks at Ken/Neth. "But first give me those needles."

I look up at her, amazed—she's treating Ken/Neth like he's not a threat to her or me or anyone else. And I look over at him, waiting for him to protest or yell or pull out a gun or something.

But, dazed, Ken/Neth steps toward Vivi and hands her the needles. She seems comfortable, maybe even happy, as though she's used to seizing all sorts of weapons from all sorts of men.

"So, where's your family?" she asks me, and then to Ken/Neth: "Why don't you open this godforsaken wall for us, buddy."

Vivi looks expectantly at him, and I try to imitate the look on her face as I stare at him. But Ken/Neth barely seems to notice us. He's gazing intensely down at the floor, as though the slabs of white marble might explain something important.

"I'm . . . sorry," he says, quieter than a whisper. "I . . . Somehow I . . ."

"The wall, buddy," Vivi says impatiently. "Open it."

"Oh yes, of course," Ken/Neth murmurs politely, stepping

forward and gazing upward at the face-recognition device on the ceiling.

As the wall slides open, he reaches down, picks up my crunched shoe and my noncrunched shoe, and hands them to me. I slip them on (the right shoe a bit uncomfortable, but better than nothing) and stare at Ken/Neth in wonder. What is *up* with him? Where's Mr. Evil, Mr. I-Won't-Help-You, Mr. I'm-Gonna-Chase-You-Down?

With Vivi on his left side and me on his right, Ken/Neth leads us through the sliding wall, down hallways, up staircases. And as we walk, Vivi talks.

"When I get a gut feeling about something I won't let it go," she tells us. I love her low, almost growly voice. These warm waves of relief are washing over me as I listen to her. Her words swirl around me—I hear some, others slip away on the warm waves. "See, ever since I got to La Lava I've been having these mystical dreams . . . too much to go into, old cultures and amulets and stuff like that . . . suffice it to say, I had this *feeling* I was needed here, this *gut* feeling . . . and then when I didn't spot the odd girl in the green dress as they were rounding everyone up for evacuation, I snuck away. . . . You should have seen that Patricia Chevalier, flying out of here in a white SUV all by herself, not stopping to help another soul, screeching in terror the whole way. . . . Well, let me tell you she doesn't know the first thing about terror, just wait till the world's best investigative reporters starting banging down her door. . . . I grew up in some pretty wild areas; I am *not* scared of volcanoes . . . so I started searching this whole place for whatever it was my gut was acting up about . . . knew I was on the right track when these two just *ridiculously* stunning screaming dream birds flew over me like bats out of hell on their way up and out . . . but the dead-end hallway . . . if it hadn't been for that little bit of green dress sticking through . . ."

I'm just floating along, drifting up staircases, feeling safer than I've felt in a long time, when Vivi suddenly stops.

"You!" Vivi shouts, turning to look at me head-on and pointing right at my heart. Startled, I seize up all over again. "*You* are something else, kiddo."

"You sure are," Ken/Neth murmurs in agreement. And here's what's crazy: He sounds like he means it.

CHAPTER 20

We don't have to force Ken/Neth to look up the second time either. He does it calmly, even *willingly*, raising his head to gaze at the face-recognition device until the wall slides open.

I can't describe the feeling I have as that white marble wall moves aside and the people I love appear in the dim room beyond.

They're standing in formation, ready to attack, Dad and Mom in front flanked by Roo on one side and Kyle on the other, Señor V and Señora V behind. So ready are they to rush whatever enemy is coming for them that they actually fall forward a few steps, too shocked to believe that it's me standing there, along with Vivi and Ken/Neth, his head hanging in what seems to be shame.

Roo is the first one who stops staring speechlessly.

"Mad!" she says. "You look *so freaky*!"

I'd totally forgotten about the blood drying on my face.

"Who *did* that to you?" Roo demands, scowling at Ken/Neth.

"Miss Perfect," I say, "and Mr. Beautiful, her mate. When I was helping them escape."

"Miss Perfect is ALIVE? And she *ESCAPED*? With her *MATE*?" Roo shrieks joyously.

With that they break formation and burst out of the shadowy room—Roo racing ahead of everyone else, and Kyle right behind her (Kyle!), followed by Mom and Dad and the Villaloboses. They all blink in the warm light of the hallway as they surround me.

"Well, yeah," I explain, "I got her and Mr. Beautiful from this cage, and then I held a sliding wall open with my foot, and they went flying out." It feels weird to describe it that way, as though I knew what I was doing all along. As though I wasn't just bumbling around.

Mom uses the edge of her ball gown to wipe the blood off my face. "My little monkey!" she whispers. "My mockingbird, my frog!" which is a lot more normal than *my beautiful, beautiful girls,* and I have to say it's a big relief. Kyle is staring at me all disbelievingly, and Dad puts his hands on my shoulders and calls me Madpie, and Señora V says something in Spanish that I can't understand but I think it's a compliment, and Señor V grins deeply and silently at me.

"I sent my chauffeur off with all the other evacuees," Vivi announces, "but my limo's out front, so let's get *outta* here."

But I'm distracted by Roo wrapping her arms around my waist and telling me how my guard was *so peeved* that I snuck away, but how Ken/Neth told him, "Oh, the kid in the green dress? Don't waste time looking for her—she's the wimpy one, she'd never try anything."

I look over at Ken/Neth, standing off to the side, and I'm seriously shocked to see that he's *smiling.* I'm pretty sure it's not a mean smile. I'm pretty sure it's an I-wish-I-had-what-you-have smile, an I've-done-bad-things-for-money-but-all-I-really-want-is-a-family-like-yours smile. And you know what? I want to feel other things toward Ken/Neth; I want to feel anger, I want to feel betrayed and tricked and *mad,* but right now all I feel is pity.

Ken/Neth senses me looking at him and steps toward me. I spring backward, clinging to Roo, suddenly frightened.

"Oh," Ken/Neth says sadly, as though I've wounded him. "Oh, I'm sorry. I'm sorry you jump away when I get close. But of course I understand."

Everyone goes silent and stares at Ken/Neth. The beak-gash on his forehead is dark with clotted blood. There's dried blood on the collar of his white shirt. His orange tie is cockeyed. He looks a little like a maniac.

Then he falls to the floor in front of Dad, his hands on Dad's feet, and I'm going, *Wait, is Ken/Neth* bowing *to Dad, worshipping Dad? Or is he trying to hurt him in some new way?*

But then I see that Ken/Neth is pulling something out of the breast pocket of his tuxedo, something black and plastic, and I see that he's lifting Dad's pant leg to reveal the green flashing light, and then he's bringing the plastic key up to the tracking device.

The tracking device falls off Dad's ankle, landing with a dull clunk on the marble.

"Let me just say," Ken/Neth mutters, slowly standing up and looking at each of us, though not at our faces, only at our feet. "Let me just say this one thing. Sometimes . . . a situation can spiral out of control. Sometimes you just . . . go along step by step, trying to do what makes the most sense at each turn. Someone approaches you, asks you to do something . . . offers you compensation that makes you feel like you're worth something. You tell yourself you've always been a person of good intention. You . . . somehow believe that's still true. You even start to feel like you're the best version of yourself when you're around the family you've been sent to keep an eye on. . . . Sometimes you're not sure if you're just an incredible actor or if you really do get a kick out of these kids, if you really do think their mother is a great lady. You convince yourself you're just doing what you have to do . . . and then suddenly you find yourself in a face-off with a bighearted twelve-year-old kid, and *bam,* there you are, the bad guy . . . even though you never meant to be."

For a moment no one speaks. I have absolutely no idea how to respond to Ken/Neth.

It's Roo, of course, who breaks the silence.

"What*ever,* Mr. Candy," she says, using his last name like it's an insult.

And then, almost as though nodding along with Roo, the volcano lets out a gentle grumble, like the sound of a giant whispering good night.

And I'm lucky enough to catch the sunbeam-bright glance that passes between Señor V and Señora V, the glance and the smile and the nod. I know it as though they've spoken it aloud: *The volcano bird has returned, and all is well in the realm of the volcano goddess.*

Roo skips down the hallway ahead of everyone else. She runs out the massive golden doors of the lobby, up to the white limo parked on the white pavement right in front of the golden entryway. She tugs hard on the door of the limo, which opens easily, springing her backward. Then she dives onto a row of velvety green seats. I follow her. Kyle's behind me, and then Señor V and Señora V, and finally Mom and Dad, hand in hand. We get ourselves all settled in, and I couldn't be happier to be here with these people.

I look back to check on Vivi, who's standing in the golden entryway with Ken/Neth.

"The *Washington Post,*" she's threatening him. "The *L.A. Times.* The *New York Post.* The AP. *Everyone.* And of course CNN, CBS—believe me, I don't have a single qualm about ruining your life. So you better not cause these good people any more trouble. I'll keep your name out of it if you *stay* out of it starting right this second, okay?" Then her voice deepens, and I start to get this feeling like she's doing a monologue from one of her movies, but from a movie that has yet to be made. "I will not stop until you and your people are out of here for good. Thanks to my active friend Volcán Pájaro de Lava, it may not be too hard to keep you cowards away. You tell that disingenuous little boss of yours, and whatever bosses there are above her, and whatever bosses there are above those bosses, that my eyes will be on you, on *all* of you, wherever you may be across the globe, and if you ever kill, or attempt to kill, one of these birds ever again, I will bring the wrath of the just world down upon your heads!"

Ken/Neth mutters something I can't hear, his shoulders hunched. Whatever it is that he says, it satisfies Vivi, who nods briskly and makes a twisted, bitter face before spitting on the golden threshold of La Lava. Then she strolls over to the limo, leaving Ken/Neth alone there in the huge doorway.

And when Ken/Neth lifts his arm to wave, it strikes me that he wishes he were here in the limo with us.

I'm still looking at Ken/Neth as Vivi hops into the driver's seat. She slides open the window dividing the back from the front.

"Dang," she says, twisting the key in the lock and fiddling with various controls, "how does this thing *work*?"

She twists the key even harder and suddenly the limo springs to life.

"BIN*GO*!" Vivi says, clutching the wheel.

I take one last look at Ken/Neth, who's standing there even now with his arm up in a wave.

As Vivi steers the limo down the pale silky pavement that leads out of La Lava, I glance at Kyle—we're sitting next to each other, his knee touching my knee, a point of warmth—wondering if he's wondering about me the way I'm wondering about him. His eyes meet mine. We give each other a small nod. I don't know how to describe the feeling that shoots through me when I nod at Kyle and he nods at me.

But Vivi interrupts that moment when she lets out a loud cowboy-style "Yippee!" We're passing through the enormous metal gate that used to guard La Lava. There's no guard standing watch anymore and the doors seem to be malfunctioning—they're stuck halfway open after the chaotic evacuation. La Lava is no longer separated from the rest of the world.

Roo echoes Vivi's happy shriek, and Señora V does too. An odd thing to hear emerging from behind an old lady's black lace veil, but that's just the kind of old lady Señora V is.

Outside La Lava, the darkness seems almost friendly as we glide through it. Vivi rolls the windows down, and it's only now, as the dangerous odor of the volcano gives way to the warm fragrance of flowers, that I realize how strongly the air smelled of sulfur all evening.

"Hey, you know what, Vivi?" Roo says. "You're *fantastalicious*!"

"Well," Vivi says, "I don't know about that, but I haven't had this much fun since Madonna and I went skinny-dipping in Cinque Terre. It's delicious to drive a limo, that's for sure! I can't believe I've never tried it before."

"Man," Roo sighs, "it's *awesome* not to be stuck in that room anymore." She barely pauses before perkily asking, "So, where does everyone think Miss Perfect and Mr. Beautiful are now?"

I'm proud that she's adopted my nickname for the male bird. I *knew* she'd like it.

"I bet they're already way past the sky-blue waterfall!" Roo says, answering her own question.

Across from me, Dad has his arm around Mom and is gazing at

her with this amazed look on his face, and Mom is gazing right back at him in the exact same way. Her face looks sharp and smart and full of thoughts—just the way it always used to, back before yogafication.

"Via," Dad says, and it feels nice to my ears to hear Dad call Mom the nickname he's always called her.

"Jimbo," she says, and there's that sound of tears in her throat, and I'm starting to blush a little now that Kyle is seeing my parents get all gushy and nicknamey with each other.

"I wasn't sure we'd make it, Via," Dad says quietly. "I can't believe we're all here. Ever since January—"

Then he stops, I guess because it's too hard to go on.

But Roo jumps across the limo into his lap and says, "You have to tell us everything! Tell us everything that happened. Because we were *confused*."

Dad looks exhausted. He sighs and slowly shakes his head as he hugs Roo.

"The early weeks here, back when I was under the impression that all La Lava wanted me to do was track and catalog the native bird species," he says tiredly, "those weeks were phenomenal. The best bird-watching I've ever done."

He pauses and looks around the limo at us.

"My wife and daughters," he continues, "can probably imagine how thrilling, how unspeakably thrilling, it was for me to spot a Lava Throat, to realize it was a Lazarus species. Easily one of the greatest moments of my life. After a couple of days, I managed to capture a bird for research purposes. I was just going to hang on to it long enough to measure it, put a tracking device on its ankle, make a few notes about its appearance, take some photos."

Dad pauses again, this time for long enough that I keep wanting to say, *Um, hello, Dad? Keep talking, please.*

"It was devastating," Dad says, his voice husky. "They tore the bird away from me. They threatened me, and then they killed it right before my eyes. I think they wanted to prove to me how ruthless they could be. Watching that Lazarus bird die . . ." He trails off.

Mom strokes his hand.

"And then," Dad says, his voice rising with rage, "to learn *why* they'd killed the bird, the most idiotic, superficial reason in the world."

"How did they even know they could make a skin treatment from the bird?" Mom asks. "It's not as though that's obvious."

Then suddenly Dad starts telling us *everything*, talking as fast as possible, like he can't wait until he's done speaking. What he found out was that La Lava itself had stumbled onto the miracle treatment— one of their hired scientists happened upon a dead LTVT deep in the jungle last fall. Everyone at La Lava had heard the local legends about the volcano bird's ability to restore youth, so going on a hunch, La Lava's biochemists created several treatments from different parts of the bird. It was just a lark, an experiment, but they decided to charge their wealthiest client—a rock star—an arm and a leg for this extra-special onetime treatment. They started with the bird's ground-up bones— and they were more shocked than the rock star when it worked, truly worked, unlike every other youth serum ever created. He looked fifteen years younger, his skin fresh and taut. Only the bird-bone substance had this effect; the substances made from other parts of the bird's body were useless. The rock star started spreading the word among his friends like gospel, and the reservations were rolling in like never before. Reservations from the wealthiest, most noteworthy people in the world, movie stars and rock stars and billionaires, and the management of La Lava realized it stood to make an astronomical amount of money if it could just get its hands on one LTVT every couple of months—many treatments' worth of the substance could be produced with a single skeleton. But of course the illicit source of the miracle substance had to be kept dead secret. That was when they sent their business consultant Ken Candy to get in touch with the Bird Guy. They needed Dad to capture LTVTs while simultaneously working to locate the elusive females and nests in the hope that they might breed the birds in captivity. As long as their attempts at synthesis and cloning were fruitless, they were forced to rely on the Bird Guy for their supply. But they quickly learned they couldn't buy Dad's compliance with money—they could only buy it with threats to *us*, to Mom and Roo and me. Dad could only hope they were bluffing about their plans to harm us. He could only hope they were lying about our house in Denver being under surveillance. Unsure whether their threats were idle or not, he had to give in to La Lava's demands.

"They *were* spying on us," Mom murmurs.

"I know," Dad says, shutting his eyes and rubbing his temples. "The girls told me."

"And there was Ken," Mom adds. "There was always Ken."

Dad just nods wearily at that.

"So . . . ," Roo says, hesitating a bit, "how many birds did you, you know . . . ?" I can tell she's trying to avoid using a word like *sacrifice*. She doesn't want to make Dad feel worse than he already does.

"I captured the bare minimum of LTVTs necessary, three total in six months," Dad says, his voice pained. "It was pure torture—with each bird I captured, I knew I might be capturing the last one on the face of the earth. I let the birds go as often as possible, knowing that the longer I waited, the more likely the bird would have the chance to reproduce. I only brought them in when La Lava was at the edge of desperation and full of threats."

"Oh, Jimbo," Mom says.

But Dad just keeps going, eager to get to the end of his story. In early July, he tells us, La Lava ran out of bird bone, and their attempts to produce the stuff artificially were going nowhere, and they were frantic to get more before the gala—it would be disastrous for them to have furious clients making a public fuss at the investors' event. They were dying to get the treatments up and running again, get over that hump, keep the ball rolling, bird or bust. They just *had* to make it through the gala with happy investors and happy clients. This was particularly important to them, Dad explained, because Vivi was there, a superstar who could be the new face of La Lava.

"Ha!" Vivi scoffs from the front of the limo.

They were willing to do anything at all, take any risk, to make sure they got a bird before the gala. Suddenly, though, Dad stopped spotting any LTVTs at all, and he started panicking and hating himself for being confident he'd find a bird whenever he needed one, and then we showed up, and he could no longer even hope we were safe. La Lava proved to him again and again how vulnerable we were, how easily they could harm us if they chose to—during a facial (those hands on my throat, Dad looking in at the window!), during yoga (I *knew* they were doing something to Mom!), during dinner at the Selva Café (when the electricity went out and Roo swore she saw Dad watching!).

It all clicks together and this very shaky feeling trembles through me. We were in even more danger than I ever realized.

Right then Kyle grabs my hand (man, I'd recognize his hand *anywhere*, the super-clamminess of his palm), and even though we're learning all these freaky things about what went down, even though I shouldn't have anything on my mind except how lucky we are, still I can't help thinking, *Jeez, this whole me-and-Kyle-holding-hands thing is seriously becoming a pattern.* The world's most awesome pattern.

His hand squeezes, saying hi to mine, and my heart does a few can-can kicks.

"I never," Dad says, pausing. "I never had any intention of cutting it so close. Can you believe that capturing a Lava-Throated Volcano trogon and turning it over to its murderers would fill me with joy? But I *was* overjoyed, to see you out there in the audience tonight, safe and well"—of course! *That's* why Dad looked so oddly happy and peaceful and calm up onstage!—"even though I was almost certain the bird I handed over to them today was the last male of the species."

"But Mad *saved* him! And he's *alive!*" Roo says, louder with each word. "And Miss Perfect is *alive* too! And they're back at their *nest* and the volcano *isn't* gonna *blow!*"

"And you kids," Dad says, his eyes widening with awe, "you found a female! With a *nest!* That's impossible, you know. *How* did you do it?"

Roo and Kyle and I look at each other, and then we look at Señora V, who smiles her veiled smile. How *did* we do it? There was Roo and Kyle being brave about the jungle, and there was me and Roo peeing, and there was me falling down the hillside, and there was Kyle and Roo recognizing the eggs, and there was Roo and Miss Perfect adoring each other right away. And there was Señora V with her magical drinks and green jungle uniforms and black-lace grins, and there was Señor V glowing knowingly beside her.

"Hey, wait a sec!" Roo yelps at Señora V. "You can take your veil off now! The birds are fine!"

And I'm going, *Wait, what?* That's *why Señora V has been wearing a veil all this time? Like, she was already in mourning for the LTVTs? How did I miss that one?*

Señor V reaches over and pulls her black veil up, almost like a weird version of a wedding ceremony, and then there's Señora V's face.

An old, old face, a delicate web of wrinkles. But with very young-looking eyes—as golden as Kyle's, or maybe even more golden! Something about the way she looks makes me feel frightened and comforted at the same time, as though she's both a witch and a godmother.

I think Mom may feel the same way I do, because she gasps, "Oh my *goodness*! Señora Villalobos!" But then she goes, "You're *beautiful*!"

Vivi twists around in the driver's seat to glance at Señora V. "*Dios mío*, beautiful lady," she says, "you are doing it with *grace*. Who needs twenty-one-year-old princesses anyway, right?"

Well, scratch that. I have no idea what they mean that Señora V is "beautiful." Extraordinary, yes. But beautiful, no.

Right then Vivi brings the limo to a jolting halt. I look out the window and realize that we're already in the parking lot of the Selva Lodge. And strangely enough, there are three old school buses lined up beside us.

"What's going on here?" I ask everyone. "Time for a field trip?" I add, the kind of dumb, giddy thing I wouldn't usually say.

"They seem to be evacuating the Selva Lodge," Kyle says. "Apparently they're still under the impression that we need to worry about the volcano."

"Grab your passports, folks!" Vivi shouts. "I'll be waiting for you right here."

As we clamber out of the limo, I smile to myself, thinking about the fact that if someone had told me a week ago that our hotel would soon be evacuated because of the volcano, I probably would have flown into a total panic. But here I am, strolling into the concrete courtyard, cool as a cucumber, even though men in khaki uniforms with large guns are standing among the half-dressed freaking-out tourists as they rush around and scream at their kids and try to zip overflowing suitcases. It feels like a nightmare carnival here, with all the people and lights and shouting but none of the fun. Yet the panic doesn't touch me. Señor V and Señora V are no longer worried about the volcano, so I'm not either.

I blink as we walk through the glaring courtyard. The light feels extra harsh after our soaring nighttime drive. It's probably a good thing our entrance is disguised by the chaos of the evacuation, because I have to say we look fairly alarming. My bloody face, Mom's bloody ball gown, a bunch of dressed-up, messed-up people.

Señor V goes over to the guy with the biggest gun, who at first ignores the small man in the rumpled white suit with the cockeyed bow tie until Señor V somehow proves that he and his wife own the Selva Lodge.

For a moment we stand there without speaking, just looking around at all these people who still believe the volcano's about to blow, until Mom claps her hands briskly. It makes me grin, because it's the kind of thing Yoga Mom never would have done.

"Ten minutes to blastoff," she proclaims. "Jimbo, get my stuff in room number five. I'll be helping the girls in number four."

Roo and I trail behind as Mom strides across the courtyard and flings open our door. She yanks our suitcase out from under the bunk and starts throwing stuff into it, tossing shorts and T-shirts and flip-flops at us.

"Put these on," she commands, "quick!"

"Jeez, Mom, *relax!*" Roo groans. But she turns around so I can unzip her party dress.

"Relax? Relax! I won't relax till that plane takes off and we're far away from anyone who wants to hurt us or ever wanted to hurt us," Mom announces, bursting into the bathroom to grab our toothbrushes—wow, I'm impressed she can remember toothbrushes at a time like this.

"You don't need to worry anymore," Roo says, as though she knows everything. Which, knowing Roo, maybe she does.

"Meet me in the courtyard as soon as you're all packed and changed." Mom shoves our still-damp two-pieces into the suitcase and hands me an armful of green fabric—our jungle uniforms. "Fold these up nicely, okay? I'm going to go make sure Dad got everything."

And that's when it hits me: We're leaving. We're leaving the Selva Lodge and the jungle and the volcano and Señor V and Señora V and Miss Perfect and Mr. Beautiful. And Kyle.

"I want to stay here! I don't want to leave! I *love* it here!" Roo says, once again beating me to the exact thing I wanted to say. Story of my life.

But I don't whine along with her, because I'm just that much older. Instead, I stand there hugging our jungle uniforms as though they're an actual person.

"We'll talk about your attitude later, young lady," non–Yoga Mom says. "I'll see you in the courtyard in five, okay?"

"Yeahyeahyeahyeah," Roo grumbles as Mom rushes off. And I place the jungle uniforms in the suitcase, wondering if we'll ever use them again.

We change out of our party dresses into normal clothes, and then Roo starts wiggling and waggling and bouncing around the room.

"Um, what are you *doing*?" I say, trying to give her a you-weirdo glare while also finding a place to pack our toothbrushes where the bristles won't get messed up.

"I have to pee *so bad*!" Roo yelps. "I haven't peed in like two weeks!"

"Then why don't you go to the bathroom?" I ask her.

"Brilliant!" Roo says, wiggling her way into the bathroom.

Roo. She cracks me up.

Right then I remember about my poetry notebook. Which is not under the pillow of my bunk bed. Because it's still in Kyle's room from that time all those hours ago when I wrote the letter to Vivi. And my heart feels like a bobbing red balloon of gladness and nervousness.

"Oh shoot!" I yell to Roo. "Got to go get my notebook from Kyle's room."

I slip out of the room before Roo can insist on coming with me. Things have quieted down in the courtyard, tourists lining up in the parking lot to board the school buses. I dash into the kitchen of the Selva Café, the screen door squeaking shut behind me. And then I'm running two steps at a time up the spiral staircase to Kyle's room, the cancan kicking in my chest all over again. I'm knocking on the door before I realize, Hey, he might not even be in here!

But he's there.

"Mad," he says as he opens the door, and when he says it I realize, Jeez, he hardly ever says my name. I get extra nervous.

"Kyle," I say back at him, and it's kind of awkward, and I realize I hardly ever say his name either.

We stand there.

"Um," I say. "Can I, kind of, come in?"

He steps aside to let me enter.

"I left my poetry notebook here," I say quickly, so he won't think I came because I have a crush on him. "Have you seen it?"

"Seen what?"

"My *poetry notebook*."

Then he says something in Spanish, and of course I have no idea what it is. Still, my face gets so hot that I can't look at him for a few seconds. I feel strange and funny and more strange and the unknown Spanish words hover above us. Kyle's face darkens with a blush (for the second time in one day!) and I realize he's embarrassed about whatever he said, and I feel weird because I want to tell him that he doesn't need to feel awkward because I didn't understand what he said anyway, but it's more awkward to tell someone they don't need to feel awkward.

And *that's* when I realize it: Kyle likes me! Suddenly it's obvious to me that when I look at him I'm looking at a reflection of the way I feel. He's blushing, like I am. He's nervous, like I am. He's awkward, like I am.

Wait, I just have to enjoy this for a second. . . . Yes, Kyle definitely likes me.

"I haven't seen your notebook," he says.

But I'm not thinking about the notebook anymore, because there's this question I have to ask him and I'm trying to get up the courage: *Why do you like me?*

I mean, now I know he likes me, but why? How? And when? I liked him (I'll admit it) from the very beginning. But I *know* he didn't like me back then. He didn't care about me any more than he cared about anyone else. So *when* did it happen? And *why*? What did I *do*? I just really want to ask him this before we never see each other again. (Then I think, *Hey, maybe we will see each other again. Colorado isn't so far from Ohio, is it?* Then I think, *Actually, it is pretty far, and we're just kids.*)

I try to ignore the tiny ache inside me and instead focus on the question: *Why, why, why do you like me?* But each time I open my mouth to ask it, I wimp out. Finally I'm opening my mouth one last time to really ask it and—get this—a bug flies in. Some kind of small fly or something, who knows what, but it goes down my windpipe and I'm choking and gagging and coughing, plus I'm getting redder and redder not only from choking but also from embarrassment. Kyle grins and thumps my back hard until the moment passes and the bug vanishes somewhere deep inside me. I take the bug as a sign that I should never ask Kyle that stupid question. Instead, I turn to him to say the notebook *has* to be here because this is where I wrote the letter to Vivi, and that's when it happens.

This has never happened to me before, obviously.

It's like suddenly his face is so close to mine that I can't even see him anymore, and our mouths are *so* close together, and then they're touching, and it's super awkward, since I don't know what to do, and my heart is making all this racket and moving around so much that I can't really feel anything else. Then he backs away and wipes his mouth and I realize I'm insanely happy and I realize the poetry notebook has been lying right there on the floor the whole time.

I have this blurry feeling as Kyle hands me the notebook, as I stumble down the spiral staircase, as I wander out into the courtyard and hazily wonder where everyone is, wonder if they'll be able to tell just from looking at my face what happened to me. I *feel* like it's written in golden cursive across my forehead, *M&K, M&K, M&K.*

"Where's Mad? I *told* her to be in the courtyard! Señora Villalobos, Señor Villalobos—are you two really sure you don't want to evacuate? *Mad-e-line!*" Mom's stressed-out voice cuts through the blurriness. Even though Mom is being kind of overreactiony right now, I don't mind it a bit because it's so much better than Spacey Smiley Yoga Lady. "Oh, Mad, thank goodness, there you are!" she exclaims, rushing toward me from the parking lot. "Come on out here, we're all waiting for you."

Obediently, I float out into the parking lot. The evacuation buses are all gone, and the tourists, and the men with guns. The volcano is still glowing away, but now it looks more pink than red. My family is getting settled into the limo, Vivi shouting jolly suggestions from the driver's seat about where Dad should put Mom's suitcase and our red rolly suitcase. Roo's already inside and buckled up. Señor V and Señora V stand by the open door of the limo, and I'm flabbergasted once again by Señora V's old/young face.

"Don't you worry, baby doll," Vivi says to Mom. It's weird to hear someone call your mom *baby doll.* "I'll have the *Post* on the phone in a few minutes here. And I already got through to my people at *Good Morning America*. Plus that international environmental group—what's it called again? *Ay, dios,* I'm spacing on the name right now. I can't believe this! I did a huge benefit for them. But now I'm thinking, hmm, would they be interested in creating some kind of bird sanctuary here? Those people go bananas for sanctuaries. . . . I should probably get in touch with those nice UN people, too. And Stephen Colbert! I love that man. He'll have a field day with this."

"That's great," Mom says, "but I'm not going to feel calm until my kids are on a plane."

"Oh, yeah, of course, sugarplum," Vivi says. "I read you, I read you. I've never been a mother myself but I can certainly imagine."

Right then Kyle appears behind his grandparents, but in the chaos of everyone saying goodbye to everyone, there's no special exchange between us. He just gives my shoulder the tiniest of pats and steps away. I don't allow myself to look back at him in longing as Mom and Dad and I climb into the limo and take our seats across from Roo, who has somehow managed to fall deep asleep amid all the goodbyes and whose sprawled body is taking up an entire row.

"Oh dear," Mom says, "let me wake Roo. I know she'll want to say goodbye."

"DO NOT WAKE HER," Señora V screeches, under her breath but with shocking violence, and I remember all over again how scared I was of her at first. "She must sleep. She has done so much. You must let her sleep a long, long time."

I'm sorry to be selfish here, but part of me is like, *Hey, what about me? Didn't I do something? Shouldn't I get to sleep a long, long time?*

I don't say anything, though. I just pretend it doesn't bug me. And then Señor V bends down—I can actually hear his spine creaking, a sound that for some reason reminds me of the volcano—and reaches into the limo and touches my cheek, and I close my eyes, and all of a sudden this very cool feeling washes over my face and even over my mind. A *green* feeling is the best way I can describe it—hazy sunny shady green jungle days—and when I open my eyes again I understand that I don't need to be jealous of Roo. Señor V steps back and carefully closes the door of the limo.

"*Adiós,*" Señora V sings, the screech vanished from her voice. "*Adiós, adiós. Vayan con la diosa.*"

I'd ask Roo what that means, *vayaconladiosa,* but of course she's still asleep.

I lean out the window, wanting Kyle to—what? I don't know—*something,* but he just stands there beside his grandparents as we pull away, and I can't tell whether his golden eyes are stuck on me or if they aren't.

We round the bend, and they're out of sight, and I have to blink away some tears.

"Oh, honey," Mom murmurs, glancing over at me. "You'll see him again someday if you want to."

If I want to! Jeez, adults really hardly understand anything at all.

"Leave her alone, Via," Dad says gently, and I look up at him and realize that he gets it. He reaches over and puts his hand on the back of my neck, just the way he used to, his warm hand rough from the scars of old expeditions, and it makes me feel very safe, Dad's hand there, and the way he doesn't say anything.

Up front Vivi is making calls on her smart phone and talking in a loud, serious voice, and with each phone call I feel that much farther away from the time when I believed the people I love most were going to die in a marble cell at La Lava.

We haven't been gliding down the road for long when I suddenly get slammed with drowsiness. I slump into the green velvet seat and rest my head on the window frame. And there's the volcano, getting farther and farther away with every second. It looks innocent, just a wisp of white smoke rising from it into the predawn sky. It's hard to believe it was rumbling and roaring all night. Already it feels like another version of myself, the Mad who ran down the hallways of La Lava listening to the volcano moan. The Mad who wasn't scared of screaming birds or a two-faced man.

Roo sleeps her weird, heavy sleep all the way to the airport. She sleeps while we unload ourselves and our luggage from the limo, while Vivi gives us double kisses (one on each cheek) and makes us swear to stay in touch, while Dad carries her though security, while we sit waiting for our flight, while the sun starts to come up as red and glowing as LTVT eggs, while the jungle takes on color as the day lightens, while Dad plunks her into the seat beside mine on the airplane.

I start to get worried the longer and deeper Roo sleeps. I put my face right up to her face and stare at her. I touch her cheek, which is creepily hot. Across the aisle, Mom and Dad fall asleep moments after buckling themselves in, Dad's mouth open and Mom's head lolling against his shoulder. I feel all warm seeing my parents together again, and I decide to let them be and not bother them.

I try not to panic about Roo. I try to shrug it off. I pull out my poetry notebook since, obviously, I didn't write a poem last night.

But I'm too distracted to write, worrying about Roo.

So I grab her limp hand and hang on to it. I look out the window, and then at Roo, and then out the window, and then at Roo.

Then, as the airplane rises, Roo squeezes my hand.

"Señor V and Señora V must be *so* happy right now," she says, as though we were in the middle of a conversation. She looks as lively and normal as ever.

Relief floods me, totally floods me, and I jump right in: "Don't you think they're probably feeling a little bummed that all their guests just got evacuated and tourists will be scared away now that there's an active volcano in their backyard?"

"Yeah, exactly!" Roo says. "This is gonna scare away all those La Lava tourists forever! The volcano did what she had to do."

I open my poetry notebook and stare at a blank page, wondering if a volcano can really be a "she."

"But it doesn't matter for the Selva Lodge," Roo explains. "Señor V and Señora V know the volcano's not gonna blow, at least not yet, and the kind of people who stay at the Selva Lodge aren't the kind of people who are scared of a sorta-active volcano."

She may actually be right about that.

Then she gives a cheerful little sigh. "I can't wait." She pretends she's just whispering to herself, but I know she wants me to ask her, *What can't you wait for?*, and so I do.

"For the next time we come here," she says.

"Who says we're coming back?" I ask calmly, as though I'm not suddenly filled with delight.

"Oh, we'll be back here, you bet," Roo informs me.

"What makes you so sure?"

Roo looks at me like I'm an idiot. "It's our *favorite* place, Mad."

I go back to staring at the blank page, trying to think about poetry rather than about Roo being so very positive we'll return to the Selva Lodge someday.

"Hey, sista," Roo whispers.

"Roo. I'm writing a poem." I hardly ever have to remind her to shut her trap when I'm trying to write.

"Sorry," she says, "but I'm just wondering if you want to know what Kyle said to you in the golf cart yesterday."

"What? When?" I say, faking innocence, though of course I know exactly what she's talking about.

"You *know* what I mean," Roo says, seeing right through me, as usual. "He said, 'You look like a tree frog in that dress.' Isn't that funny?"

And that's when the little ache in my heart grows and hurts with happiness. There's nothing in the whole universe I'd rather have Kyle say about me. I'm filled with longing but happiness. Here's how it goes: longing, happiness, longing, happiness, longing, happiness, longing, et cetera.

"That," Roo says, "is seriously the biggest smile I've ever seen on your face."

I blush and try to change the subject but I can't think of another subject right now. And then Roo lets out a small squeal of dismay.

"Oh *no*!" she says, staring down at her feet in their green flip-flops. "Oh no, no, no."

"What's *wrong*?" I say, panicking.

"Look!" she says, wiggling her toes.

"What?"

"No! Toe! Flowers!" she says.

Oh yeah. I look at her small, unflowery feet.

"Hmm," I say. "I guess your feet are finally just nice and clean and nonfungusy."

"No," Roo corrects. "It's because I used up all my magic."

She turns to look out the window.

"Oh well," she whispers. "It was worth it."

So here we are, Roo and I, side by side, while far below the jungle sparkles and hisses, and it seems possible, maybe even likely, that somewhere down there two shimmering birds are circling a nest where a beak is beginning to twitch inside an egg as bright as blood.

Author's Note

I remember being very upset when I first learned about extinction as a child. How awful that an entire species can vanish from the face of the earth! Scientists disagree on exactly how many species die out every year; whatever the true number, each extinction is deeply disturbing, because it can never be undone. Extinctions have always been a part of life on earth, but that only makes each remaining species more precious. Many biologists believe that present-day extinctions are often caused by human activities that destroy the habitats of our fellow species.

In the early 2000s, my dad (not an ornithologist but a great lover of nature) showed me an article about a recent sighting of the ivory-billed woodpecker, often called the Lord God Bird for its spectacular appearance. Declared extinct by the International Union for Conservation of Nature in the 1990s, it had supposedly been sighted in Arkansas, causing a flurry of excitement in the ornithological community and inspiring a great search effort throughout the southeastern United States. Unfortunately, no one has found any definitive proof that the Lord God Bird still exists.

Even so, this story stuck with me, a tiny bright spot amid the disturbing news about the earth's decreasing biodiversity. It seemed as magical to me as the sighting of a unicorn or a dragon. For years I knew I wanted to write a book about the thrilling possibility that a species believed extinct might in fact still survive.

There are some wonderful examples of these so-called Lazarus species. (Lazarus, in the Bible, was raised from the dead.) The Bermuda petrel, a bird believed extinct for 330 years, was found alive on some of Bermuda's small, remote islands. The Lord Howe Island stick insect, believed extinct since 1930, was rediscovered beneath a shrub on an isolated sea stack in the Pacific Ocean. The monito del monte, a marsupial believed extinct for eleven million years, was revealed in a thicket of Chilean bamboo. These are just a few examples from the intriguing list of thirteen Lazarus species on the Mother Nature Network website (mnn.com).

In *Here Where the Sunbeams Are Green,* my fascination with Lazarus species meets my love of Costa Rica, where I lived for two summers during high school and college, learning Spanish and volunteering. Coming from beautiful but dry Colorado, I found the landscape, the climate, and the variety of plant and animal life extraordinary. Tiny Costa Rica is home to an estimated 5 percent of the world's total species. Like Mad, at times I felt I was exploring a new planet.

The book takes place in an unspecified Central American country, but the setting is largely based on my visits to the rain forests of Costa Rica. The Lava-Throated Volcano trogon is a made-up bird, but there are a number of trogon species in Costa Rica (including the famous, and near-threatened, Resplendent Quetzal). More than eight hundred Costa Rican bird species have been identified, nineteen of which are considered endangered. The country also has seven endemic species (endemic species are those that only live within a very particular geographic region).

When developing the "villain" of the book, the fictional La Lava Resort and Spa, I had in mind the ways multinational corporations can take advantage of a country's natural resources. La Lava pretends to be protecting the environment when it is actually exploiting and harming the local ecosystem. That said, a place like La Lava, if run properly and ethically, can be an excellent way for a region to improve its economy in a sustainable fashion. Done right, ecotourism can help protect endangered species and the environment.

This book also draws on my experiences growing up with three siblings in the foothills west of Denver. My parents brought (dragged?) us on hikes and backcountry ski trips (or, as my younger sister, Alice, called them, "uphill skis") every weekend. During the summer we'd backpack and raft the canyons and rivers of Colorado and Utah. The wilderness always felt near at hand. TV time was limited, but we kids could read as many books as we wanted. Adventures, both physical and imaginative, were encouraged. Alice, upon whom the character of Roo is based, was my feisty sidekick. Or maybe I was her bookish sidekick.

Most importantly, this is a book about sisterhood, and about the things we do to keep our families together. It is a book about kids being brave, going on adventures, looking out for one another, and caring for a creature not because it can be *used* for something, but because its very existence is precious. These traits—bravery, adventurousness, compassion—serve us well as we venture forth to face the challenges of our increasingly complex world.

Acknowledgments

Here Where the Sunbeams Are Green passed through more than eight drafts on its way to becoming this book. My enormous gratitude goes to everyone who kept pushing the manuscript on. My agent, Faye Bender, gave me pivotal advice, editing and otherwise, at every turn. My editor at Delacorte Press, Krista Marino, helped the book become ever more fully itself; I stand in awe of her insights and her page-by-page precision. Lauren Flower encouraged me to actually *write* the middle-grade book I'd been thinking of writing, and shepherded it along once it finally existed.

Special thanks goes to those who sacrificed entire park walks, beach days, and lunch breaks to endless discussion of the plot: Sarah Brown, Jonas Oransky, Genevieve Randa, Maisie Tivnan, and my mother-in-law, Gail Thompson, a downright plot doctor. Big thanks to Kendyl Salcito, whose expertise in globalization-related eco-harm helped shape the author's note, and to Tess Wheelwright, generous reader and Spanish whiz.

As ever, I am grateful to the good people of the Brooklyn College MFA program, most especially Amelia Kahaney, who was always ready to talk shop; Jenny Offill, a splendid author and friend; and Ellen Tremper, who applied her eagle eye to the manuscript.

My father, Paul Phillips, gave me the idea for the Lava-Throat's youth serum, among many other contributions, not least the deep love of the natural world he instilled in his kids. My mother, Susan

Zimmermann, author of *Mosaic of Thought* and *Seven Keys to Comprehension,* has based her career on her commitment to helping children become passionate readers; she taught me to value literature for young people before I could even read. There are no words to express my gratitude for my husband, Adam Thompson—not only was he willing to read draft after draft and talk about this book for years on end, but every day he creates the simultaneous peace and energy in our home that makes it all possible. I thank my siblings Katherine and Mark Phillips for teaching me what it means to be a sister. Finally, I thank my sister Alice Light, a brilliant and big-hearted reader, and, moreover, my own true Roo.

About the Author

HELEN PHILLIPS grew up in the foothills west of Denver with her three siblings. When she was eleven, she lost her hair due to the autoimmune condition alopecia, which was pretty hard at the time, but now she thinks there are some major advantages to not having hair (no shampoo in the eyes, for one). Soon after she lost her hair, she (like Mad) made a New Year's resolution to write a poem a day, a practice she continued for more than eight years.

Helen graduated from Yale University and receieved a master of fine arts in fiction from Brooklyn College. She lives in Brooklyn with her husband, artist Adam Douglas Thompson, and their daughter. Visit her at helencphillips.com.